Alison Huntingford has a degree in humanities with literature, and has always enjoyed reading, especially, the great writers of the 19th century.

She is an only child of two only children and so has always felt a distinct lack of family. This has inspired her to research her family history and most of her writing is based on this. Her debut novel, *The Glass Bulldog*, was published in 2019, and was nominated for the Walter Scott Prize for historical fiction. This is her second full length novel, although, she has also written several short stories.

In her spare time, she enjoys spending time with her husband and their pets, listening to music, going to the cinema, and gardening.

Dedicated to Kate, Fred, and Joe (Grandad Pop) – may they rest in peace. With thanks as always to my dear husband, Nigel, for his patience and support.

Best wishes?
Alison Huntingford x

Alison Huntingford

A HA'PENNY WILL DO

AUSTIN MACAULEY PUBLISHERS™

LONDON • CAMBRIDGE • NEW YORK • SHARJAH

A CIP catalogue record for this title is available from the British Library.

ISBN 9781398408135 (Paperback)
ISBN 9781398408142 (ePub e-book)

www.austinmacauley.com

First Published 2022
Austin Macauley Publishers Ltd®
1 Canada Square
Canary Wharf
London
E14 5AA

Thanks is due to the following websites:

www.ancestry.co.uk
www.findmypast.co.uk
www.forces-war-records.co.uk
www.wikipedia.org
owlcation.com/humanities/Victorian-Maid-of-all-work-a-miserable-life
www.victorianlondon.org.uk
www.workhouses.org.uk
victorian-era.org
www.funeralwise.com/customs/irishwake
www.jack-the-ripper-tour.com
Plus, many more too numerous to list.

Foreword

Every family has its secrets, its mysteries, its half-truths. Ours is no exception.

When I was growing up, I was fascinated by tales of my grandad and his Irish mother. Her Irish origins seemed such a romantic and exciting notion that I was desperate to know more.

"She came from the poorest area of Cork," my mum told me, "and was a great beauty, so we believe. Her name was Kate. Unfortunately, she died when the children were quite young, and their father had to bring them up."

"Your grandad, Joe, was one of four brothers," she continued. "There was Ern, who was a hero in World War One; he married your gran's sister. Then there was Bill, the youngest, who used to do magic tricks on stage, and of course, Fred, who no one talks about."

"Why not?" I asked.

"Well, they say he went bad and disappeared off somewhere."

I was confused by what was meant by '*went bad*'. Had he been in prison, or worse? This intrigued me, but no one seemed to know the answers.

After extensive research, I have finally pieced together the truth of what happened to this family – a truth which is never plain, and rarely simple. The mists of time have parted briefly to reveal a glimpse of their lives. What I discovered was quite unexpected and surprising; including another brother who had never been mentioned before: Albert. Why has no one talked about him? I'll leave you to decide that for yourselves. I also found out what happened to Fred; but again, you'll have to read on to find out.

Therefore, I can now present the authentic stories of Kate, Fred and Joe, recreated through diaries, letters and my grandad's memories. The mysteries are solved, and the ghosts are appeased. I hope I've brought them justice at last.

Christmas is coming, the goose is getting fat.
Please put a penny in the old man's hat.
If you haven't got a penny, a ha'penny will do.
If you haven't got a ha'penny, God bless you!

Joe's Recollections, Introduction

I remember my mother as if it were yesterday, her dark curly hair piled up on top and a gentle Irish lilt to her voice. But I realise now that these are only my childhood memories of her, as she certainly wasn't like that towards the end. It's strange how time dims the things we don't want to remember. However, since you've asked, I'll try and tell it like it was, but my memory's failing a bit now, so bear with me.

Her name was Catherine (McCarthy by birth), but I only ever heard her called Kate, even by her mother, who would occasionally visit us. I know they both came over from Ireland, although I don't know exactly when. The family had lived in one of the most notorious slums in Cork – Barrack Street. It had a dreadful reputation for poverty, disease and filth, and yet my mother always spoke of it with the greatest affection.

"Joey," she would say, "I had a grand childhood, I'm sorry yours has had to be so hard."

She always called me by my middle name, Joe, (even though my first name is Andrew) and I still prefer to be called that. It reminds me of the good times with her and the feeling of being loved and wanted.

I hear the slum dwellings of Barrack Street have been cleared away now and new buildings put up, ones with running water, sanitation and electric lighting. My mother would have hated them and would have said they had no soul, not like the overcrowded, cramped hovels of the 'lanes'. She didn't live long enough to see her beloved street swept away; maybe that was a good thing. I don't know.

As to the rest of her family, I have very little information. I believe she had a brother somewhere, and some Irish cousins and aunts, but the details have vanished in the mists of time, just like the leprechauns and faery folk that she used to tell us about at bedtime.

It was my mother's very 'Irishness' that first attracted my father, William Duffield, to her, but it was also what most annoyed him when he was in one of his moods. On one occasion, I heard him shout at her, "There ain't no shamrocks here, woman! So, stop your Irish blarney."

My father was a dark, brooding kind of man, who usually only laughed at someone else's expense. He had a certain charisma, I guess, and a way of being able to talk himself out of a bad situation. Trouble was something that followed him around, especially when he'd been out drinking, which was often. Nevertheless, he was popular with the local crowd and recognised as something of a 'character'.

I've never been to Ireland, which is odd, I suppose, as my brother Ern lives over there now. After he married his second wife, Agnes, they moved out to be nearer to her family. Maybe the Irish connection was stronger for him as he was older than me and had more time with our mother. We still exchange Christmas cards and the like, but we've drifted apart a bit recently. I'm not sure why. Ern is quite a few years older than me, but we were close once. He even introduced me to my own dear wife, who was his sister-in-law. We had some great times then, the four of us together. I miss that. Maybe it's because Bet has passed on that it's all changed.

I'm closer to my youngest brother Bill than anyone else in the family. As for the others, I never see Albert these days and Fred has been gone a long time now.

Kate's Diary 1 January 1879 Cork, Ireland, aged 12

Athbhliain Faoi Mhaise Daoibh! Happy New Year!

Mam gave me this diary for Christmas because she knows I love writing. She's right – I really want to be a writer, though I know it's probably hopeless. That's why I'm going to make the most of this diary and write down all my memories and my innermost thoughts that I can't tell anyone else. I'm really going to try and keep it up, so here goes.

Last night we were all at home together, the four of us; me, Pat, Mam and Da. Of course, the O'Connells, who share the house with us, were around as well, but we kept ourselves to ourselves, as is usual on Year's End Night. Da said I could do the traditional fetching of the water from the well, as I'm old enough now. It has to be done before sunset and not taken out again until the next day. It's an old custom and I loved doing it. It felt like I was carrying on something special which has been passed down through the years. Mind you, Pat got to do the throwing of the bread at the door, this year. Da said as he's the oldest child and the only son, it was his right. I hope he did it proper like, so that we don't go hungry again this year. It's supposed to ward off famine and we certainly don't need another one of those. Pat had to recite this really long verse and he got a bit muddled in one place, I'm fair scared that we might end up starving, but Da just laughed and said not to worry meself about it. It's all very well, but the waters of the River Lee are really high today, and everyone knows that's a bad sign. Mam said it means that food will cost a lot more this year. There's not enough money to go round as it is, so I don't know what we'll do if it does. Mind, Pat's working now and I'm helping out, so I 'spect we'll be okay.

I love living here in Cork City. We may be poor but it's our home. Barrack Street is a great place, in spite of everything. Some people say it's a slum and should be cleared away, but I think it's grand. I'm proud to be a 'barracka'.

True, there is sewage running down middle of the street, and people get sick a lot of the time, but it's a real community. There're always children laughing and music playing, not like in those 'well to do' areas, such as Montenotte, where no one dares to laugh or speak a word. They're all too frightened of their own shadows. Live a little, I say!

Kate's Diary 5 January 1879

Today, I went back to my job at the South Presentation Convent School. I'm only doing a bit of charring and washing there, but if the truth be told, I hate it. The nuns just seem to want me to scrub those cold stone floors all the time. If I have to do any more, I think I'll go mad!

I used to hate going to school there. They were always so strict, and I often got in trouble when I spoke my mind. Mam says I need to 'keep a lid on it', but if I think something isn't right, then I feel the need to say so. Those nuns tried to tell me that the Holy Mother Mary was a virgin when she had Jesus, but Mam says women only get pregnant when men 'interfere' with them. When I argued about that, Sister Assumpta really lost her rag and sent me to the Mother Superior. She made me say fifty Hail Marys for penance.

I don't know why I took on the work there, really. I was dying to leave the place, but kind old Sister Bridget asked me to stay and clean for them. Mam said I should, even though I didn't want to, to help bring in some money for the family. Anyway, I like Sister B – she's one of the only ones there who seem half-human, and I know she was only trying to help us out.

Kate's Diary 2 February 1879

Yesterday was St Brigid's feast day to celebrate the coming of spring. It was a mighty craic! We went to Murphy's Bar in our street, where we danced, drank and sang all night. Da enjoys a pint or two and was singing along with the best of them; mind, he never gets nasty drunk, only ever good natured and fun. Some of the locals were playing the pipes and fiddles and everyone joined in, even Pat, who plays a bit of melodeon now and again. It doesn't matter how good or bad you are at the music, what matters is the taking part. Mam and I can't play nothing, but we danced and sang along till our feet ached and our throats were sore. It seemed like most of Barrack Street were there, though there were plenty of other bars with similar parties going on. What a night it was!

Kate's Diary 12 May 1879

Away from the city, everywhere is so green. Living in 'the lanes' of Central Cork, I tend to forget how beautiful Ireland is. Yesterday, Da gave me a rare treat and took me on his cart when he had to take a load over to Waterford. I got to go this time 'cos Pat was working and Da needed an extra pair of hands to help out. We took our time, enjoying the fine spring air and having a fair old laugh along the way. Da is always fun to be with.

We travelled along the wild Atlantic coast, up and down hills, the poor old horse taking the strain. The weather was grand, though there was a fierce wind by the sea. The sight of all that sparkling ocean fair took my breath away. The sun was glinting off the waves and it looked so inviting, though Da warned me of its dangers.

"There's more currents out there than you can shake a stick at," he told me, "just waiting to sweep you away in an instant. It's a wild patch of water, that one."

I asked Da what was over yonder.

"Beyont is the coast of England, Kate. Best left well alone."

It was a beautiful ride over to Waterford and back. The rolling hills were alive with the green of new spring growth, trees in leaf again after the long winter and flowers blooming. The track was strewn with blossom from the May trees, which rose up in a cloud as we passed by and settled back again behind us, as if we had never been there.

I felt I could have written a poem about it, right then and there. When we got home, I tried, but the moment had gone and the words I had in my mind have slipped away. It's so frustrating at times.

At midday, Da stopped the horse and cart for a rest. We left the horse munching hay in the shade and took our bread and cheese out onto the soft meadow grass. Da was in a talkative mood and told me stories of his youth, spent on a small farm in the local countryside.

"It's only when the Great Famine came and the crops failed that we had to move to the city," he told me. "There was no way to make a living, otherwise. Yer Uncle Frankie is still out there trying, but it's a real struggle. Ireland's a grand country, darlin', and no mistake, but a hard one to survive in."

Kate's Diary 5 July 1879

Today, I had a right set to with Mam. I didn't mean to, but she told me I can't go with my friend, Saoirse, to see her Da play in the Barracka Street band. Mam never minded when I did it before; but a couple of weeks back, something changed. There are a lot of temperance marching bands in Cork, but instead of getting on, they all seem to be rivals these days. There was a real carry on when the Fair Hill band accidentally met the Blackpool band at a crossroads, and it blew up into a rare old fight. There were stones flying and fists punching – not at all the kind of thing you'd expect from musicians. Talk about music bringing folks together – well, that's one way of doing it! Fair play to Mam – I can see where she's coming from, but it wasn't our band after all. Oh well, mebbee I should tell her I'm sorry.

Kate's Diary 22 August 1879

My, it's been a terrible bad summer this year. It's rained so much that water is coming through the roof and all our mattresses got wet the other day. I can hardly sleep at night 'cos it's so cold. Da has got an awful fierce cough that he can't get rid of and Mam is sneezing all the time. Over in County Mayo, however, they're having an even worse time; the potato crop has failed again, and the people are going hungry. It's not as bad as last time but folks are beginning to talk of famine. There's an air of panic and fear all around and Mam said food is getting really expensive. Last week, she went out to the grocers but could only afford some bread and cabbages. She told me she saw a man shouting at the poor shopkeeper because he couldn't pay his bill. Tempers are getting frayed and people are worried. I hope things get better soon.

Kate's Diary 1 November 1879

Da told us today that his brother Frank and wife Mairead are coming to stay with us. They were tenant farmers in Clonakilty until just recently, when they were turned out 'cos they couldn't pay their rent. There's been a lot of that going on in the last few months and a fair bit of angry grumbling about it, locally. Da reckons there'll be trouble soon enough, what with Charles Parnell and the Land League now trying to stand up for people's rights. I don't fairly understand it meself, but I reckon it's not right that folks should lose their homes.

Mind, I don't know how we're going to manage for space with me uncle and his family here as well. It's already mighty cramped as it is, what with sharing with the O'Connells, but I guess we must do our bit to help. I'm going to have to find extra space in my bedroom now for my cousins Bronagh and Colleen. Let's hope we will all get on.

Kate's Diary 28 November 1879

Today is the first time I've ever seen Da really angry. He's usually so calm, but today he fairly let rip at Pat.

"Patrick McCarthy," I heard him shout. "What do yer think yer doing? Going on a march! Don't you know it's asking for trouble? You coulda been arrested by the Garda and put in prison. It was a feckin' daft thing to do!"

Pat is a bit of a hothead anyway and shouted back that it was a march for 'Bread or Work' and that Da should be supporting him. He'd gone along with our Uncle Frank to protest at all the unfairness to the farmers and the rising unemployment. Only the other day, Pat was laid off from his job because there wasn't enough work, so I guess he was fair riled up about it.

Da calmed down a bit then and tried to explain to Pat that he was worried he'd get hurt or something.

"These protests can get out of hand," he explained. "They start off peaceable enough then it all changes. It only needs one person to raise a fist and all hell breaks loose."

Pat stormed off, effin' and blindin' under his breath as he went. I kept out the way but later I overheard our da talking to his brother Frank.

"I don't want my boy takin' part in things like this," he said, but then he saw me and took Frank off to another room, where I couldn't follow. I heard raised voices, and shortly after, Frank and Mairead gathered their family and their few possessions and left the house. I could see Mam was real upset about it.

"What did you have to do that for?" she demanded of Da. "They've got nowhere else to go."

"It wasn't me," Da replied. "They chose to go of their own free will. It's about time they got their own place, anyway."

Mam stomped around, banging pots and pans, having a right old sulk and Da went off outside. I could see he was upset, so I followed. He was messing around with the horse and cart, gathering up hay and moving it from place to place. I realised it was a feeble attempt to hide his feelings, so I went up to him and put my arms around him.

"It's all right, Da," I told him. "It'll all blow over soon enough."

"Oh, Kate," he said, "I don't mean badly by it. I understand how Pat and Frank feel, but it's so easy to get in trouble with these things."

"Surely you should fight for what is right?" I asked him, feeling confused.

"Fighting is never good, Kate," he told me, shaking his head.

"It always ends in violence and that never solved nothin'. Yes, you should make your feelings heard, but peaceful like, maybe by a letter or by talkin' to folks. Marching's all very well, but it can all too easily lead to problems. There've been riots over in County Mayo just last week."

I can't say I really know what he means, but I hugged him again to show I loved him anyway. This evening, Mam and Pat seem to have calmed down and the storm has subsided, thank goodness. I'm glad.

Kate's Diary 26 December 1879 St Stephen's day

I really meant to write this diary entry earlier, but I've had such a grand Christmas I haven't had a moment to spare! To start at the beginning with Christmas Eve, I always love that day. It has such a feeling of expectation and excitement to it. After we all finished work for the day, we gathered together to decorate the house and yard. Da had been out on the cart during the day with Pat and they'd fetched loads of greenery, which we put up everywhere we could think of. It looked real fine, so. We took particular care decorating the stable. It's an old Irish custom based on the nativity, because the Good Lord was born in a stable and all the animals were there, so we need to remember them. Our horse, Ned, looked at us in bemusement. I'm sure he wonders why we do it every year. Mam said she reckoned he understood, but I'm not so sure meself. Anyway, after we done the decorating, because I am the youngest child, I got to light the big candle and put it in the window. This is another tradition, which as Sister Bridget explained to me the other day, is to let the Holy Family know they're welcome in Irish homes. I think it's a lovely idea and when I looked out down the street, I could see the entire row of cottages with a light in every window. It was real magical.

We spent the rest of the evening getting ready for the next day, then later we all went to midnight mass. The O'Connells came with us and there was a big crowd all heading down the same way. It was a fair old sight; people laughing, talking, carrying lanterns. The night was very cold and clear, with all the stars sparkling above, just like it must have been when Jesus was born. Poor Da was still coughing real bad like and the cold air was making it worse, so I went up to him and wrapped my woollen shawl around his neck. Mam smiled at me fondly, and said, "You're a good girl, Kate." She and I don't always see eye to eye, she's a real sharp tongue on her and can be mighty fierce. The times when she speaks soft like that are few and far between, so I really notice it when she does. I know it's just her way though. She don't mean nothing by it.

After midnight mass, we all made our way home, where Mam and Mrs O'Connell set to and prepared the traditional Christmas Eve supper of saltling. This is a dish of white fish and potatoes in onion sauce, and I'm fair partial to it meself. We all gathered together to enjoy it; Aoife and Finbar O'Connell and their two children, plus Mam, Da, Pat and me. We made a toast to all who live in this house and wished each other a Merry Christmas, before finally falling into our beds, tired out.

Christmas day was grand, right enough. After we'd had our presents (which were mostly small homemade things this year), I was pleased to see Frank, Mairead and their family arrive to spend the day with us. I never heard when they made up their differences, but for sure, everyone seemed happy again. Mam cooked her special spiced beef, and we all had a rare old time. Frank and Da put away several jugs of ale, and Pat was allowed some as well, now that's he's sixteen. In the afternoon, we played games with the younger children, then in the evening we all had a singsong. Pat got out his melodeon, Uncle Frankie had brought his fiddle and Mairead had her bodhran. She tried to show me how to play it, but I got no sense of rhythm. She'll never make a musician outta me! Still, we had a great craic trying. We sang a mixture of Christmas carols and old Irish songs. I felt so happy I could burst. It was real deadly.

Today is St Stephen's day and the local boys have just been round, collecting money to 'bury the wren'. They were all dressed up, as usual, in masks and strange colourful clothing, making lots of noise and parading down the street. I'm glad they don't use no real wren anymore. That were cruel, but now they just use a model made of straw, stuck on a pole. The boys were all playing music and dancing and it was a real sight to see. One line of their rhyme stuck with me – 'Give us a penny to bury the wren; if you haven't got a penny a ha'penny will do, if you haven't got a ha'penny, God bless you!'.

Well, I hope we all have enough pennies in the new year. I can't believe nearly a whole year has gone by since I started this diary. Must try and keep it up again in 1880.

Kate's Diary 13 February 1880

My heart is broken, and I don't think I'll ever recover. Yesterday, we buried Da. It was a traditional Irish service. Mam said we couldn't afford much, so it was a plain box in the corner of the cemetery, where Father O'Sullivan said a few words for him, though we still observed all the usual customs. People came from far and wide to pay their respects.

Da has been driving his horse and cart as usual through all this recent bad weather and the cough he's had since last summer just got worse and worse. Mam told him to rest at home, but he said he needed to work or else we'd starve. We watched him just waste away. It was dreadful.

It's too late now – he's gone, and I don't know what we're going to do. May the Good Lord help us!

Kate's Diary 20 February 1880

Mam has just told me that we need to move to England. I can't believe it! How's that going to help? Pat and I won't know anyone. Apparently, we got relatives over yonder, but I never heard of 'em before. Mam says there are better opportunities there for us and that it's time I left the convent and went into service. Pat has been unemployed for a while, so I guess he'll be happy to move on. Mam reckons he'll find a job easy over there.

It's true that Barrack Street is run down and dirty, however, you have to see the good side of it. It may be rough and poor but it's our home and I don't want to leave. The people are warm and friendly here. Everyone helps out when there's a problem, like when Da was ill. We couldn't afford no doctor, but 'next door' came round with some medicine they had, and Mrs O'Flaherty, down the street, brought us a hot pie she'd baked. I know we don't have running water or nothing fancy like that but we're happy here. It's not fair! I got very angry with Mam when she told us, but I feel sorry now. She always says I overreact, but I can't help it.

Kate's Diary 10 March 1880

Today we sailed away from Ireland, our friends and family waving us off from the port of Queenstown. It was bustling with people, most leaving to look for a better life. Ireland is poor and starving, it seems; I don't think I ever truly realised it before. Maybe Mam is right after all.

Even so, I stood and watched with tears in my eyes, as the emerald green of the land got farther away. Mam said it was silly to cry but I couldn't help it. I could just make out the figure of my friend Saoirse still waving from the quayside, and I didn't take my eyes off her for a long time, until at last she faded from view. I don't think I will ever see her, or Ireland, again.

Kate's Diary 12 March 1880 Liverpool, England

The journey to Liverpool has taken two days and I've felt ill most of it. We have been crammed into the steerage quarters and herded like the beasts of the field. Mam struggled to get enough food and water for us. The sea has been really rough, and I've felt so sick most of the time that I couldn't eat anyway, but that's not the point. It's not fair that we paid our way and get treated this bad. I know we had the cheapest tickets 'cos that's all we could afford, but surely we're entitled to the basics?

We had to sell poor Ned to the people down the street in order to pay for our journey. I hope they look after him proper and give him enough hay each day. He's a good horse and he'll serve them well if they treat him right.

It smelled real bad down in steerage, of human sweat and excrement. Everyone was crowded together, men and women, with only straw mattresses to lie on. There was no privacy at all. One man approached me and made indecent suggestions, but luckily Pat came along and soon saw him off. He's had to stick real close to Mam and me for our protection.

Thank goodness, it hasn't been longer. I don't know how the poor folks manage who have to travel to America. It's so far! I hear a lot of them die on the way. At least the steamships are faster than the old sailing boats used to be.

Now we have finally reached Liverpool and have just got out of this hellhole. I still feel like I'm 'all at sea', though, and the ground seems to be moving. I am writing this in the waiting room, where we are sat now, hoping to find out how to get lodgings in this dreadful place. The noise of the docks is deafening and everywhere looks grey and dirty. I want to go home!

Kate's Diary 12 April 1880

I can't believe it's been a month today since we landed in Liverpool. The time has just gone by so fast. I thought Cork was busy and lively enough, but Liverpool is like a rampaging giant in comparison. In fact, I've actually grown to quite like it. There are so many Irishers here that it's almost like being at home, especially round St Anthony's, where we're lodging at the moment. Also, there's a river here called the Mersey, which reminds me of our own dear River Lee in Cork, though much dirtier.

Pat has got himself a job as a 'lumper' down at the docks already and Mam is trying to get me a position in 'service'. I'm fierce scared about this, though, 'cos I don't know nothing about what to do. What if I make a real bags of it? They'll think I'm an awful eejit and I'll probably get the push. Then what?

What worries me most is that Mam is planning to move to London, near a cousin of hers, as soon as she's got me settled, and Pat seems to have his life all sorted out. They don't seem bothered what happens to me. I feel like no one cares!

Kate's Diary 27 April 1880

Today Mam took me out to West Derby, in the north of Liverpool, to have an interview with the Ellis family to see if I'd be suitable as a 'maid of all work' for them. I'd hoped that, if I did have to go into service, it'd be in a big, grand house full of other servants and lots of finery, but it seems it's not to be. Mr Ellis is a middle-class butcher with his own business. He has a wife and five children: three young girls and two older boys. Mrs Ellis interviewed me, and she seems kindly enough. She said she would tell me what I needed to do, as I don't have no experience, like. She's even going to have a washerwoman come in on wash days, which will ease things a bit. Mind, it seems there's an awful lot of work to do each day.

Mrs Ellis was keen to get someone in quickly, so I start on Monday! I'll be living in their home, in the basement, and all my meals will be taken there. Sunday afternoons will be my time off, plus one day a month, so that's quite good. What's more, she's giving me an allowance of tea and sugar. My wages are £12 a year, which seems like riches to me, after Ireland. I ain't allowed no 'followers' though, so that means no visitors of any kind, mind, I don't know many folks round here, anyway, 'cept Mam and Pat, so it won't make no difference. Mam reckons this all seems pretty fair.

Truth to tell, though, I really want to be a writer, or to travel and see the world, but them things ain't for the likes of me. Mam says I must accept my lot for what it is, but it's hard.

Kate's Diary 28 May 1880

I'm sitting writing this in the spring sunshine of the local park, trying to make the most of my first day off. I'm so tired I could just fall asleep here, but I mustn't. It would be a waste of my own special day. I've worked nearly a whole month now and I feel exhausted. Every day, I get up at 5am and start work by 6. The list of things to do seems endless – lighting fires, sweeping floors, cleaning hearths and grates, washing dishes, cooking meals, dusting – oh, always dusting! The dusting is a task I can never hope to finish – chairs, tables, furniture, window frames and ledges, doors, shelves, ornaments, china, glasses – it never stops. Then there's the beds to change and make, and the children to see to. At least, the heavy laundry gets done once a week by the washerwoman. She is about the only person I ever see, apart from an occasional tradesman, or when opening the door to visitors. Bertha is a fat, jolly, red faced woman, who usually has a fair bit to say for herself. The language is ripe enough to make a young girl blush, but at least I get to hear some local news and gossip. I'd almost forgotten the sound of my own voice, except to say 'Yes Ma'am' to the mistress. At all times, a servant must be invisible to the family, except when called for. It's like I don't exist. I feel so lonely most of the time. The children are nice enough and one of the lads, Master George, looks about the same age as me. Sometimes, he smiles at me, but I'm not allowed to smile back. I just have to turn my face aside. The rules of the house are clearly written down and displayed in the kitchen for me to see, so there can be no mistaking. It's a real shame, he looks nice.

The other son, Master John, is older and helps his father in the butchery. I've not seen much of him. The two younger girls, Frances and Emma, are sweet enough, but the older one, Hannah, is a cheeky little madam. She's about 12, I reckon, and she thinks she can order me around, just like her Mam. I find it hard not to answer back; it's not in my nature to be so submissive, but I'm having to change.

The worst loneliness comes when I finally retire to my basement at the end of each day. There's no one to share any thoughts with or laugh with. I miss my family so much – Da, with his ready laugh and big loving hugs, Pat (even though he's a bit rough and ready, and always teasing his little sis), and Mam, in spite of her sharp tongue and fierce temper. I know she means well.

I can never replace my Da. I know that – no one else can fill that empty space. It's hard to believe he's gone forever. Yet, I have a job to remember his face sometimes and that saddens me.

My room here is basic, with just a simple wooden bed and chair, a small dresser and a wash basin, but at least it's not damp. I thank the Lord for the mercies he grants me. Even so, I keep thinking back to my bedroom in Barrack Street, which, although I shared it with my cousins, was still home. I had my own precious bits and pieces: childhood toys, mementoes and pictures. There's nothing personal allowed here, not even something on the wall. I had to give Mam my things for safekeeping, and I pray one day I will be reunited with them. She promised to keep them for me.

Anyway, today I am going to walk in the park and take tea in a local tearoom, just as if I were a real lady!

Kate's Diary 30 July 1880 Midnight

Today, it's my usual monthly day off and I took it into me head to go and visit Pat. I've not seen him since I started here. Last week, I had a letter from Mam in London, giving me her new address and telling me Pat was settling in well. She also gave me his address, so I thought I should go and see him. He works down the docks, I know, so I thought I'd go and find him there first of all. I took a tram into town, and after some shopping, I got over to the docks at lunch time. In my innocence, I never realised what it might be like. The area is vast. Since then, I have found out that the docks stretch for six miles along the Eastern bank of the Mersey, but at least I knew Pat was working on the New Northern docks, so I had an idea where to look. I wandered around, amongst all the strange machinery and the goods piled up like mountains, trying to find him, asking here and there. Many of the men were Irish, like meself, but they were a rough lot.

"Come 'ere, darlin'!" shouted one. "I'll help you find what yer looking for!"

They all laughed in an unpleasant manner and I felt frightened. Another called out, "How much do you charge, darling?" but I hurried off. Some followed after me, calling and jeering, and I suddenly realised I was the only female in the area. I was beginning to panic a bit, so I quickened my pace, and to my relief, saw Pat in the distance. I called out to him desperately, and he turned, surprised to see me.

"Kate! What on earth you doing here? This ain't no place for a girl. You shouldn't a come."

I felt tears come to my eyes as I went to hug him, but he shrugged me off.

"Not here, Kate. What do you want?"

I told him that I just wanted to see him again, that I felt lonely and lost and that I needed my family, but to my surprise, he looked embarrassed and irritable.

"We can't talk here," he said. "Come and see me tonight, after six, at my lodgings. I'm working now."

"I know," I said, "but I thought you'd be pleased to see me."

"Come and see me this evening," he repeated, but more kindly this time. "We'll have a bite of supper together. How will that be, eh?"

So, I left and went off round town. There are some fine museums in Liverpool and a reading room which I spent some time in, but the afternoon passed slowly, until the time when I could visit Pat. All the time, I kept thinking about his reaction to me and I felt disappointed, but I told meself it was just because he was at work.

Just after 6pm, I knocked on the door of his lodgings. A young woman, with sandy hair and a gentle face, opened it and showed me in. Pat told me her name was Jenny and that she was the landlady's daughter. They seem close. Pat and I had supper together, but the conversation was stilted and awkward. He didn't want to talk about the past at all. It's clear he's moved on and don't think about the family now.

I had to leave at 8 o clock, in order to get the last tram back. As I left, he said, "Don't come again, Kate, unless you let me know first. It ain't always convenient, like."

I went to kiss him goodbye, but he turned away, saying, "Cheers then. See yer."

Now I'm 'home' and about to go to bed, but I feel even worse for having seen him. Something's changed. Pat's become cold and unfeeling, and he weren't interested in me.

It's like he's trying to forget all about his old life. Mebbee that's his way of coping, but I can't understand it, meself.

Kate's Diary 26 December 1880 Midnight

What a different Christmas it has been this year, compared with last. I never dreamed so much could change in a year. As a 'maid of all work', I had to be here on Christmas Day to get the dinner and everything for the family. There was no time off for me this year, apart from a short while today. On Christmas Eve, I was expected to go to church with the family, but it weren't nothing like ours at home. It's different to the Catholic faith, not so grand and no confessionals. I'd a liked to confess all my bad thoughts about how much I hate being a servant, and about what I'd like to do to 'darling' little Hannah if I got the chance. I coulda done with having my sins absolved, but they don't do that here. Does that mean everyone still carries all their sin around with them, I wonder?

Anyway, it was all very solemn and serious to be sure. We walked to the church, with me several paces behind, as is befitting to a person of my 'status'. It's awful. At times, I feel worth less than an animal. I really don't think it's fair; I'm just as good as them!

Master George smiled at me again as I sat down in the pew behind them, but his mam was looking, so I didn't dare smile back. The service was boring; the hymns and the sermons seemed to go on forever and I nearly fell asleep at one point.

There was no hot supper of saltling this year when we got home. Instead, I had to make everyone warm milky drinks (ughh!) and then we all went to bed. I don't have a window in my basement to put a lighted candle in, but I left one burning on the kitchen window ledge, just to keep the tradition up.

Yesterday was Christmas Day and I had to cook a turkey. I'd never even seen one before and I didn't know what to do with it. Mistress gave me some instructions, but I got real flummoxed what with all the plucking and preparing. I tried my best, but mistress complained it was a bit tough and Hannah said the gravy was lumpy. Cooking's never really been my thing, so they'll have to put up with it!

During the day, the whole family celebrated together, playing games, opening parcels and having a very gay time. They've even got one of them fancy Christmas trees everyone's talking about. I was left alone in the kitchen to eat my solitary meal and consider my situation. I have to admit my tears fell when I remembered the way things used to be.

Halfway through the afternoon, however, Master George came in to ask me to fetch them all some tea and cake.

"Yes, sir," I murmured politely.

Then to my surprise, he said, "I wanted to wish you a Merry Christmas, Kate."

"Thank 'ee, sir," I replied.

"What are you doing tomorrow?" he continued. "You have a day off, don't you? Will you see your family?"

"I hope so, sir," I told him.

In fact, a couple of weeks ago I had a letter which cheered me up, no end. It was from Mam, saying she was coming up to see Pat and that I was invited there for Boxing Day lunch. I was fierce looking forward to seeing them both again as I'd missed them so much. The only trouble was the trams weren't running and it was a four-mile walk into town. Still, I figured

34

I could manage it, as long as it weren't snowing. We had some last week, but it's eased again now, thank goodness.

"Master John has some errands in town tomorrow," Master George said, "and Papa has said that if you would like a lift in, on the horse and cart, you can have one, but you'll have to find your own way back."

"Really, sir? Oh, that's very kind. Please thank the master for me." I was fair delighted. Later, the mistress also came out to the kitchen, with a present for me – a very pretty sewing basket which I thanked her for, profusely.

"Merry Christmas, Kate," was all she said, then she went back to their cosy parlour. For a very short while, I felt I had been visible as a human being again, but this moment vanished as quickly as it came.

This morning, I joined Master John outside with the horse and cart at 9am. Then there was another surprise – Master George joined us, saying he needed some fresh air. I sat on the back of the cart while we rode into town. The colour and markings on the horse reminded me strongly of our Ned, and for some reason, this made me feel fair emotional, but I tried not to show it. Master John was taciturn and silent nearly the whole way, but Master George kept chatting and asking me questions. I answered politely but couldn't engage in conversation, proper like. I knew it wasn't allowed. About all I could say was 'Yes, sir' and 'No, sir', but it was nice that someone was recognising that I existed. About three quarters of the way there, however, Master John spoke sternly to his brother.

"Don't keep talking to the servant, George. It's not right and proper."

George responded with, "Oh don't be such a snob, John. She's just a person like ourselves, you know, and it is Christmas, after all."

"Mama will be very displeased if she finds out, so just stop it now," John ordered. "You could even get her dismissed if you're not careful."

George turned and looked at me.

"I'm sorry, Kate," he muttered, then fell silent for the rest of the journey.

I had lunch with Mam and Pat, which was jolly enough in its way, but I feel they've got new lives now and don't consider me much anymore. I was desperate to see them, but it isn't the same. Mam is in London, living with her cousin, Gracie, and she told us lots of tales of what she'd seen and done recently, which both entertained and surprised us. Apparently, Da has a younger sister, Louisa, living there as well, though I ain't never met her. London sounds right deadly. I'd love to go there one day.

Pat is obviously in love with Jenny and spent the whole time talking about her. He is working hard at the docks to get some money together for the future. I can't say I blame him. He's become quite Liverpudlian now and is fast losing his connection to Ireland. I asked him to play his melodeon after dinner, but he just laughed, and said, "Don't be silly, Kate, that's all in the past now. I got rid of that old thing, months ago."

He's even starting to lose his accent, mind, I think we all are. I hardly get to use my voice these days, so it's not surprising really.

On the other hand, all I do is eat, sleep and breathe this house and this family. I'm a 'non-person', a 'nobody' who just exists to serve. I tried to tell Mam how I feel, but she said I should consider meself lucky to have a good job. Pat said he wished he was earning as much as me and they both thought I was making a fuss about nothing. They should come and try it. See how they like it!

I can't stay here forever, I know that, but I can't see a way out. If I were of a better class, I could have been a governess, maybe. I know it's not possible to make a living from writing. I've written some short stories and I'm working on a novel, but what's the use? Who will ever read them?

After a long walk home in the rain, I'm tired now and feeling depressed. I'm going to bed.

Kate's Diary 29 June 1881

It seems I only get time to write this diary now on my monthly day off. Life is just so busy all the time – work, work, work, non-stop.

It's been so hot here in the last week or two and I've been feeling real poorly at times. The uniform I have to wear is so heavy: petticoats, high necked dresses, aprons, caps – I've been feeling stifled. At home, I would have stripped down to a simple cotton frock, but here I don't dare. A servant must always be properly dressed. There is no time for me to relax and just be meself. Even on Sunday afternoons and on my one day off a month, I must be back on duty again by 9 o'clock in the evening. My life is not my own anymore.

Anyway, last Tuesday it was 'specially hot and I was almost fainting from the heat. The mistress had gone into town for the day and when the children came home from school, I got them their usual afternoon snack, but I was feeling real giddy. I saw Master George watching me, but I tried to pretend he wasn't there. That little madam, Hannah, was demanding a cup of tea, in spite of the weather, so I had to go out in the hot kitchen to make it. It had been wash day that morning and the room was swamped with steam from the laundry and heat from cooking. As I returned to the parlour, I could feel meself going hot and cold all over. Coloured stars swam before my eyes and I nearly dropped the tray. In fact, I would have done but Master George was up on his feet in an instant, steadying me, saving the tray from disaster and sitting me down in the nearest chair.

"Hannah," he ordered firmly, "take care of the tea for everyone and pour Kate one as well."

"I can't pour for a servant!" Hannah replied indignantly.

"Can't you see she's not well?" demanded Master George. "You do as you're told!"

He bade me rest in the chair and bustled about opening windows, fanning me and fetching tea. I was quite overcome for a while and unable to speak, except to murmur my thanks.

"I'm so sorry, sir," I said, as soon as I could speak, and I tried to get up.

"No. You stay there and rest a while," Master George replied firmly.

"It's just the heat, sir," I explained. "I'll be better directly."

"She can't stay here," protested Hannah, "I'll tell Mama, and she won't like it."

So Master George escorted me back through the kitchen, out into the garden. Once there, he seated me down outside the back door to cool off and recover. I was embarrassed but grateful.

"Thank you so much for your trouble, sir," I said. "I'm sorry to be a nuisance."

To my surprise, he sat down on the seat next to me.

"Kate, you're no trouble. It's only natural in this heat." He paused. "Tell me about yourself. Where do you come from?"

I blushed. "I don't think I can tell you that, sir," I stammered. "It's against the rules to talk to the ladies and gentlemen of the household about meself."

"But I've asked you," he persisted. "That's different, surely?"

I looked at him then and noticed for the first time his gentle face, some fine, wavy fair hair and twinkling blue eyes. In spite of meself, I smiled.

"Well, I s'pose it is, sir, yes."

"Don't keep calling me sir!" he exclaimed. "My name's George."

"I daren't call 'ee that, sir. Madam wouldn't like it."

"Well, Master George then," he told me, "if you insist. Our family are nothing special, you know. Father's been lucky in business, that's all. Until a couple of years ago, we were just ordinary folk, and to be honest, I preferred it. Now, tell me about your life. You're from Ireland, aren't you? I can tell from your accent."

I have to admit I couldn't resist the chance to talk to a real human being about my beloved country and my life so far. Of course, I'm ashamed to say I talked freely, and we only stopped when Hannah came into the kitchen looking for him. I felt quite well again by then and hurried back to my duties. Master George left, promising to talk again.

Since then, however, everyone else has been there all the time and we've not been able to even exchange a smile. But now, I think about him often, and in my dreams, I sometimes see his face. What does all this mean? I wish I knew.

Kate's Diary 29 September 1881

Today is my day off again but the weather is wet and I didn't know what to do with meself, so I've spent it in Picton reading room, catching up on letters and reading the latest novel by Mrs Oliphaunt. She seems to write such a lot. I wish I could be like her!

(Letters written today: Mam, Saoirse, Pat. Must post them later).

Over the last month or two, I've bumped into Master George a few times on his own and he's always made an effort to talk to me. We've managed to exchange a few words here and there. I don't feel quite so lonely now, which is great, but I feel guilty because I know it's not allowed. We can only talk in secret when there's no one else around, but in a way, that's quite exciting. It's like doing something naughty behind the Mother Superior's back. But to be sure, I know he and I got no future, even as friends. I ain't in his class and never will be.

Kate's Diary 29 December 1881

Another Christmas spent working! Not even a visit to see Pat and Mam this year – they're both 'busy' (whatever that means). If only I had more chances to talk to Master George. I know he likes me. I have to admit, I've started to find excuses to go the same way as him, just so I can 'bump' into him. Silly, I know, but I can't help it. I wish things were different.

I've decided I'm not going to write this diary again until I've got something worthwhile to put in it. There doesn't seem much point. All my time for writing has gone for now. Words come into my head but by the time I get to my own room at the end of each day, they've gone again, or I'm so tired I just fall asleep. I guess I must just try and accept my lot.

Kate's Diary 8 May 1882

What an awful week it's been! A couple of days ago, two British politicians were stabbed to death in Phoenix Park in Dublin, and now everyone seems real riled up against us Irish. It's not fair! It wasn't the whole country, just a few individuals causing trouble. It's a real shame about the victims, mind; they'd barely been there five minutes. Phoenix Park is fierce lovely as well, all those beautiful flowers and the Glen Pond. Me and Pat went there once when Da had to take his cart to Dublin, and it was great; we walked for ages. We were only children then, but I remember it well. It don't need no crime to make it famous.

Trouble is now everyone's saying the Irish should never be given 'home rule', cos we don't deserve it. 'T ain't right that we should be dictated to by other people, but we can't do nothing about it. Charles Parnell came out and condemned the murders, but folks are still in an uproar, all the same. It ain't done no good to the cause.

What's more that nasty little madam, Hannah, had a go about the Irish right there in front of me.

"Mama," she said, all coy like, "don't you think it's terrible what happened in Ireland this week? They must be

41

savages over there." She looked right at me as she said this, being real provocative. I tried not to meet her eyes.

"Aren't you worried about having an Irish maid, Mama?" she continued. "She might take it into her head to murder us all in our beds one night!"

I didn't dare speak, as, if I had, I'd a lost my job, to be sure. Her mam told her not to be so silly and they moved off upstairs, Hannah laughing as she went. I'd certainly like to murder *her* in her bed if I got the chance. The spiteful little trollop!

Kate's Diary 27 January 1883

My sixteenth birthday, not that you'd know it. Another day, the same as all the rest. When will things ever change? Where will I be this time next year?

Kate's Diary 16 June 1883

I was out in the kitchen garden today, gathering flowers for mistress's drawing room, when I heard a faint sound behind me. I turned and was surprised to see Master George, his face red and flustered. Without a word, he suddenly moved forward, took me by the hand and led me behind the wall, where no one could see us from the house. Then he leant me against the wall and kissed me on the cheek, then the lips, passionately.

"Dearest Kate," he whispered afterwards, "I'm sorry. I can't help myself. I think I love you."

"Master George!" I exclaimed, but I knew I had kissed him back just as passionately. I wanted him so much at that moment. My whole body was tingling. His face was so close to me and I couldn't resist touching it gently and then kissing him again. I have no experience of men, and where this could have led to, I dread to think, but I managed to pull meself together. Mam always says that girls get into trouble if they go too far, so I pulled away a bit, saying, "Please, sir. We mustn't!"

"Don't you want me, Kate?" he asked anxiously.

I gazed into his eyes and could not deny it.

"More than anything," I told him, "but I can't. We mustn't. I'm just a servant and you're my mistress's son. I really can't. 'Sides, I don't want to end up as one of them 'fallen women'. They'll send me to the workhouse!"

"Oh Kate," he murmured, but moved further away. "I don't want to dishonour you, but I can hardly stand to see you so near, every day, and yet not be able to touch you or even speak to you. You're so beautiful."

We sat down then, in the garden, both gloomy and thinking our own sad thoughts. Tears ran down my face, as they are doing even now, as I write this. I know I love him too. Surprisingly, I never realised what this strange, painful feeling was before. I feel both wildly happy and desperately sad at the same time.

After a while we parted, George again declaring that he loves me and wants to be with me.

"Please," he begged, "let's try and spend time together when we can. I promise I'll restrain myself and behave honourably. I just need to be with you, Kate."

I reassured him that this was what I wanted as well, but repeated that if his mother found out, we'd be in real trouble. Nevertheless, I have agreed to meet him in the garden whenever I can. I'm hoping this isn't a mistake.

Kate's Diary 29 July 1883, 4am

I can't sleep, so I need to write this down to try and clear it from my head. All I can think of is George's dear face, his lips, his eyes, his soft, fair hair. His image obsesses me and yet fills me with joy. I can't think straight anymore. My chores are done mechanically, and I don't know where I am with them. Hannah has started to criticise my work and I can't say I blame her. Yesterday, I forgot to clean one of the grates. My head's in such a whirl.

This afternoon, mistress had gone into town, and George and I were out in the garden again. We've met many times lately but managed to control ourselves. Today, however, the sun was hot, the grasses lush and the flowers heady with scent. We sat down together but before I knew where I was, we were laying in the grass kissing and cuddling. His hand was on my breast and it felt so right, though to be sure, I know it's a mortal sin. I closed my eyes and just enjoyed the sensations. He was so close and so real. I was overwhelmed by desire, but to my relief, (and I must admit, some disappointment), George stopped suddenly.

"We mustn't go too far, Kate," he said, sitting up hastily, brushing grass off himself. I felt so unfulfilled, but I knew he was right. I pulled meself to my feet and tried to straighten my clothes. A golden dust of pollen was on his fair hair, making it shimmer in the heat. I was dazzled by his beauty and moved closer to him again.

"No Kate," he said. "This won't do," though I could see he was struggling with his own feelings.

"I'm going to talk to my mother about this. Maybe she'll let us start courting. It's not being able to see you properly that's making me so desperate. I'm sorry."

"George," I tried to tell him. "Your mother will never allow it. You know that, surely? Please wait for a while. She'll think we're too young, anyway."

But he won't listen, and he swears he will speak to her about it very soon. Now, I'm tired out with worry about what might happen if he does, but with a faint, unreasonable hope that, just maybe, something good will come of it. We'll have to wait and see.

Kate's Diary 16 August 1883

Finally, I'm on the train from Liverpool to London and now I've got time to reflect on everything that's happened in the last couple of weeks. I suppose I always knew that it would never work out with me and George. It was just a beautiful dream, but I never realised quite how bad it would all turn out. Now I've lost everything – home, job, wages, true love; even my family seems unsure of me.

It was only a couple of days later that I got called up to see the mistress of the house. Mrs Ellis was furious; calling me a slut and a temptress, saying I was trying to seduce her son and lead him astray. George was there, red-faced and silent throughout. I felt sorry for him but annoyed as well. I could see that he couldn't stand up to his mam, which fair disappointed me. I tried to explain to madam how I loved George and didn't mean any harm, but she wouldn't listen.

"Get out of this house immediately!" she shouted at me, "and don't think you'll be getting any references. You're nothing but a cheap, immoral harlot. I should have known an Irish peasant girl would be like that. I was a fool to take you on."

"But I've worked hard, Ma'am," I protested, "and I've always done everything you asked. I deserve a reference, at least."

"Don't you dare talk back to me!" she cried. "Get out before I call the constable."

I collected my things and fled in tears. I can still see George's face looking after me in shame, as I left the room. I don't think I'll ever forget him. He's a gentle, sensitive soul but no match for his family's rigid ideas of class and status. My heart still cries out for him and I know we could have been happy together. In my dreams, I still feel his touch and the warmth of his kiss, but when I wake, I know that it will never be, and I cry all over again.

My first instinct was to go and find Pat. He's the only person I know in Liverpool and he is my brother, after all. The day was cloudy and damp, in spite of the time of year, and the walk into town was a long one. The greyness of the day matched my emotions. I felt so sad, yet angry at the injustice of it all as well. My mind was in turmoil and tears poured down my face. I must have looked a right state by the time I got to Pat's lodgings.

It was still quite early in the day, me having been summoned and dismissed all in the space of half an hour that morning. No one was at home and I couldn't think what to do. I sat down, in utter misery, on the doorstep, contemplating my future. My head ached with crying and my eyes were sore. Looking towards the River Mersey, which seems as wide and deep as an ocean at that point, I briefly wondered whether I'd be better ending it all. But I'm not stupid enough to do that and 'sides, I have too much survival instinct. Maybe it's the

Irish spirit – who knows? I gave meself a good old shake, so to speak, and pulled meself together.

Pat's lady friend, Jenny, came home, luckily, at midday for her lunch and was shocked to find me there. Seeing a friendly face reduced me to tears again and destroyed all my brave thoughts, but after a cup of tea and a kindly hug, I felt a fair bit better.

I told her all my troubles and she was sympathetic.

"It's all very well for them fancy folks," she said, "with their high and mighty morals. Just look at how their own offspring behave! Ain't no good putting all the blame on you – it takes two you know. He should be right 'shamed of himself, that lad."

"But he loves me," I said feebly.

"They all say that," she replied, "but when it comes to the crunch, they don't want to know. Just be thankful you ain't '*in trouble*', if you know what I mean! Now sit you there and wait for us to come home. Pat and I'll be back at sixish and we'll talk proper then."

I was grateful for her kindness and rested for the afternoon (I believe I even fell asleep for a while; I was so tired). Pat's reaction, however, was somewhat different.

"What you doing here?" he demanded. "Gone and lost yer job, have you? Well don't expect me to be able to help, money don't grow on trees, you know! You can stay a few days, but you'll have to move on. We can't afford to feed you."

"I never expected you to," I told him stiffly. "I just came to you because you're all I have. I didn't know where else to go."

We argued late into the evening about what I should do. Pat said I should go to the workhouse and ask to be taken in, but Jenny begged him to reconsider. I'd rather die than go the workhouse, and I told him so, in no uncertain terms. I feel real hurt by his attitude. I never thought he'd be like this. I said I wanted to go and find our mam, but I had no money to get to London.

Eventually, we settled it that I would write to Mam, asking for her help to get to London, and meanwhile, they'd put me up for a few days. So that's what I did and here I am on my way. Mam sent the money for my fare but was clear that I can't stay long with her either. She's arranging for me to go to a home for girls, run by an association for 'befriending young servants'. She says they train and support you to get a placement in a decent household, so that's a good thing, I suppose. I hope I won't be all on my own like last time.

Pat and I have really fallen out over this, which is a pity. He thinks I brought it all on meself. Mebbee I did, but I couldn't help it. Was it such a sin to fall in love?

Last week, I did a bit of laundry work to help pay my way, which pacified Pat a bit. Jenny's a real nice girl and I hope he treats her well. He's getting to be quite hard-hearted these days, not the affectionate brother I used to know. I guess people change. I know that if Da were still alive, things would have been so much different.

Anyway, now I must look to the future. I wonder what London will be like. Here's to better times!

Joe's Recollections, London, 1903

What is my earliest memory, you ask? Well, I suppose it is the birth of my younger brother, Bill, (though it is hazy now). I was only two and a half and couldn't think why Mum wasn't able to play games or run after me like she normally did. For several months, she just didn't seem herself. Then one day, the household was thrown into chaos. Strange women I'd never seen before appeared and started rushing around with towels and hot water. It was all very mysterious. I'd had no supper that evening as everyone seemed to have forgotten about me, so I sat on the floor and howled until my older brother, Fred, who was nearly 10 years old by then, scooped me up, deposited me in a chair and proceeded to shovel some food into me.

"You've got to be good now, Joey," he said. "There's going to be an addition to the family."

I didn't know what he meant, but the next day I was taken into my parents' bedroom to meet the new arrival. Mum lay in bed, looking pale and weak but smiling. She held a strange bundle in her arms, which, when I peered curiously at it, moved and gurgled.

"This is your new brother, William," Mum said. "He's so sweet, isn't he? He'll be your special friend, Joe."

His tiny face was red and wrinkled, but I loved him immediately. Nevertheless, I have to admit I was jealous at first. How dare another baby come along and take all of Mum's time and attention? Wasn't *I* supposed to be the one she sang to sleep with Irish lullabies each night? Wasn't *I* the one who was allowed to climb into bed with her after another bad dream? However, I soon learned that there was still plenty of Mum's love to go round, and I found a special place in my heart for my new sibling. Bill and I have always been close, and we still are. Albert had never been much of a friend to me, and Ern and Fred were too old to really relate to.

Father seemed disinterested in the addition to the family and had gone off to work, but then this was nothing new. As I was to find out, he had little interest in any of us children, except Albert, who adored him and followed him around like a devoted dog. Mum's own mother was there that day; an ancient crone, as I remember, with blackened teeth and wrinkled face, quite terrifying to a toddler. I heard her calling my mother 'Kate', which I found very strange, because to me she was always 'Mum'.

Another distant foggy memory from around that time is moving house. Suddenly, we were all bundled up, loaded into carts and taken to a new residence (in Lambeth, I think). For some reason, I have an image in my head of 'camping out' at one point, but perhaps I just made that up. After all, memory is the greatest trickster.

Our new home was barely more than a shack from what I remember; a cold, damp basement which was falling apart. There always seemed to be noise and shouting going on somewhere in the tenement block it was part of, and the locals were a rough lot. Bill was born there, and I vaguely recall Mum saying that she didn't think it was fit for a new-born baby, but I may have just imagined this. All the older boys shared a bedroom, and Billy and I had a curtained off area of my parents' room. The privy was outside, I believe, and was shared by several other families in the block.

This was the first of several moves that I remember, during my younger years, though interspersed by my time at Hanwell School. These moves often happened without much warning, and sometimes even at night, which seemed strange to me, I must admit. Not only that, but the dwellings seemed to get progressively shabbier each time we relocated.

Despite the harsh conditions of our various homes, Mum worked hard to keep them clean. There were always vases of wildflowers around, a dresser full of the best china, a shelf of books, and an air of respectability, in spite of the neighbourhood. Many of our homes were in tenement blocks, with countless other families all struggling to eke out an existence. Even so, until Mum finally passed away, we somehow managed to rise above the poverty and pretend that we had a more genteel existence than we actually did.

Kate's Diary 29 August 1883 London, England

Today, I have moved into the Dudley Stuart Home for Befriending Young Servants. My time with Mam in London was brief and bitter. She clearly didn't want me around; I'm not sure why.

I arrived in London on a damp, misty afternoon, the fog swirling around the horses and the crowds in the street. The roads were awash with horse dung and mud. I thought Liverpool was busy, but it weren't nothing compared to this. There were so many people I couldn't take it all in.

Mam came and met me off the stagecoach and things seemed to go so well to start with. My eyes were dazzled by all the grand buildings and the fine dressed ladies, but our part of London was somewhat different. A general griminess and soot descended upon me as we entered the more working-class areas, weighing me down and making me feel oppressed. The sheer poverty and misery here is enough to drive anyone into the arms of the dreaded drink, and it certainly has. Many a poor wretch lies slumped in doorways, blotting out the pain of their existence with yet another bottle of the cheapest liquor. Mam has put on weight, I noticed, and when she kissed me hello, there was a strong smell of alcohol. She's been lodging with Cousin Gracie in Mile End and was keen to point out that there wasn't enough room for me as well.

"Life's real difficult here, Kate," she told me, "and we're only just getting by. It's a shame that you wasted that wonderful opportunity you had. You shouldna got involved with that lad – it was only ever going to lead to trouble."

Gracie chipped in as well, "We ain't got enough money to feed you as well, dearie. Sorry, but that's the way of it."

"That's the honest truth," Mam said. "We don't have nothing spare. As it is, I'm gonna have to pay five shillings a week for you in that home!"

"I understand," I told her stiffly. "Just let me have the things you were looking after for me and I'll be moving on."

"Things? What things?" Mam asked, puzzled.

"Mam – you said you'd look after my bits and pieces – my souvenirs and pictures – all the things in that box I gave you."

"Sorry, Kate," she mumbled. "They had to go. Ain't no room here for extra stuff. They weren't worth nothing, anyhow."

"They were worth a lot to me!" I cried and rushed out of the room. It fair hurt me to think that they were gone forever. There were a couple of my favourite old childhood toys, a drawing of Da, a poem and some other writings I'd done, a string of beads Saoirse had given me and so on. Little things that meant a lot. And now they're gone. I'll never forgive her for that.

52

So today, I've moved in here and am looking forward to a brighter future. There are about twenty girls here and we're all sleeping in a big, long dormitory. There's another girl next to me who has just started here as well. She's called Elsie and seems a real livewire. I hope she'll be a friend.

Elsie tells me she comes from somewhere called Devon, far over to the west of the country. It sounds a bit like dear old Ireland – green, wet and with lots of hills.

"The sea mist comes down sometimes," she said, "and you can't see a hand in front of you, but it's clean and pure, not like this filthy smog here. There bain't no soot in Devon, leastwise not yet. Mind, it's changing fast."

"I used to live on a farm," she added, "but we couldn't make it pay anymore. I came here to make me fortune!" She laughed. "Well, I can try, anyway. Mebbee I'll marry some rich gentleman!"

We giggled and chatted half the evening. It's so good to have someone my own age to talk to. Elsie's a right laugh. Nothing bothers her.

Kate's Diary 14 September 1883

I can't believe I've been here two weeks already! The lady superintendent, Mrs Thompson, is fierce strict but at least we're getting some training. I never been much of a one for cooking, but now I'm learning fast. We're also being taught all about the different roles in a grand house. As for the home itself – well, the beds are hard but clean, and the food basic but plentiful. We don't get to go outside though, well, not official like! Last night, Elsie managed to find a key for the outside door and 'er and I sneaked a peek outside. We ran down the lane that goes down past the home and found ourselves out by some houses. We saw an alehouse nearby, all lit up and cosy looking, and Elsie wanted to go there, but I talked her out of it.

"It ain't proper," I told her. "We might get molested by some man or other."

"Sounds like fun!" declared Elsie, but she knew I was right, really. We can't take the risk, so we crept back in before anyone missed us.

Kate's Diary 30 September 1883

We've spent all week learning how to polish silverware and my hands feel red raw. I'm right fed up with it all, but I guess I'm learning useful stuff.

Anyway, last night Elsie and I got out again and this time we made it down to the local music hall. I ain't never seen anything like it before. There were bright lights, strange folks, coloured costumes and wigs, singing, dancing and crowds of people in the audience. We managed to get in on the cheap as Elsie was flirting with the doorman, and we stayed for half an hour. But then some gentlemen started looking at us and gesturing to us to come over. I got real nervous and wanted to go back, but Elsie wanted to stay. Eventually, I managed to persuade her to come away, but she was fair put out.

"It's all right for you, Kate," she told me on the way home. "You're a real looker. You'll soon get yerself a man to marry, but I'm not like you, maid. I have to make the best of the chances I get."

We had a few words unfortunately, and I told her I didn't want to go out there again. She went off in a bit of a sulk, but

I know I'm just being sensible. It's just too easy to get 'in trouble', and then you can be ruined for life.

Kate's Diary 3 October 1883

Thankfully, me and Elsie have made up again now. I didn't want to fall out with her; she's the only friend I got. She's been a bit cool for a couple of days, but today she was laughing with me about something the superintendent had been saying. I told Elsie I was real sorry if I'd spoilt her fun the other night, but she told me not to worry about it.

"Seriously," she said, "I know I get carried away sometimes and if I'm not careful it'll lead to trouble." She lowered her voice and looked sad. "Truth to tell, Kate, I'm worried I'll be left on the shelf. I'm not much of a catch, like, and if I don't marry, I don't know what I'll do. I'm scared I'll end up a lonely old maid."

I told her not to be so silly and reassured her as best I could. It's true she's a bit on the plump side, with a mass of unruly fair hair which won't stay put, but everyone loves her because of her lively nature. She's always such fun to be with, whereas I guess people probably think I'm distant or boring, just because I'm quiet. I know men seem to notice me, but I'm not sure I want that kind of attention. I'd rather just have some friends.

Kate's Diary 29 November 1883

Three months have come and gone since I came here and it's with a sinking feeling that I know I have to leave very soon. Though I've disliked the discipline and some of the tasks I've had to learn, still I've had a really useful time here.

Not only that, but I've made the best friend I could ever have in Elsie, and I'm sad to think that I may never see her again. These last few weeks have been such fun and we've gotten really close. There ain't much we don't know about each other now. Since the music hall incident, we've stuck to having more innocent fun indoors, drinking cocoa and sharing our dreams. We've played games, sung songs, sewed dresses, styled our hair; we've talked and talked. But tomorrow it will all end – Elsie is off to be a kitchen maid in Chelsea and I've got a place as a parlour maid in Bloomsbury. The chances of us seeing each other again are slim to non-existent, and my heart feels full of emotion at the loss. I can hardly keep from crying as I write this.

Yet, I'm excited as well, at the thought of going to work in a big house with other servants. I'm so glad I won't be a lonely old 'maid of all work' again. Maybe I will make friends with the others or even find someone to love. The house is in Bedford Square and I'll be working for one of the university professors and his family. I'm really pleased to be in that area because the British Museum is there. I've heard it's wonderful; packed with rare treasures from around the world, which I could never hope to see any other way. Bloomsbury, they say, is full of writers and academics. Maybe I'll get a chance to mix with some – you never know – and improve my own writing. Well, I can dream, can't I?

Kate's Diary 30 November 1883

Today I said a tearful farewell to dear Elsie. We promised to keep in touch, but those kind of promises are rarely kept. All too often, good friends drift apart, not meaning to, just because day to day life gets in the way. We said we'd write but it probably won't happen. We'll see. Elsie told me not to be so daft when she saw I was upset, and laughed it off, but I know she's feeling it too, really. When she hugged me goodbye, I thought her eyes looked suspiciously moist. I'm fair choked up just thinking about it.

Kate's Diary 7 December 1883 Bloomsbury

I've been here a week now and I'm beginning to make sense of it all. I feel I must make a list of all the staff here, because it's so confusing otherwise.

HOUSEKEEPER	Mrs Stanley	Seems like a real monster!
BUTLER	Mr Chapman	Very serious and stern, never smiles.
COOK	Martha	Older, quite a good laugh
CHAMBER MAID	Mary	Very quiet
LADY'S MAID		Molly, but she's known as Jane. (Madam insists she has to be called Jane for some reason. Feckin' daft!)
KITCHEN MAID	Lizzie	

SCULLERY MAID	Young Sarah (she's only 13)	
STEWARD	Charles (Rather snooty)	
MASTER'S VALET	John	
FOOTMAN	Alfie (Though the Master always calls him James).	He doesn't care though, he's a real card!
COACHMAN	Tom	
GARDENER	Henry (Bit of a flirt, but all right, really)	

Plus 'up above':

HEAD NURSE   Nanny Smith

GOVERNESS   Miss Seaton

(These two don't mix with the rest of us!)

Most of 'em seem friendly enough and have made me feel welcome. I eat my meals in the servants' hall with the rest, and we get to chatting and joking. We rarely see the master and mistress. About the only time I've ever spoke to the mistress was when I came here for interview and then it was only briefly. I remember she asked me where I came from and I told her Ireland, but she wasn't really interested. She seems a mighty fine, but proud, lady, who certainly don't know what it's like to do an honest day's work.

It's a very grand house, three floors, plus the basement and attic. The outside is decorated with all kind of lavish stone trimmings as is the fashion for townhouses, and the whole thing faces out onto a beautiful garden, in the middle of the square. Only the residents of the houses are allowed into the garden, mind, and that don't include us servants, sadly. I'd have liked to walk there, but it is kept locked. Folks tell me there is a garden up the road that *is* open to us, so maybe I'll try that one. Don't seem fair though when I live here as well.

The house itself is furnished in all the latest styles, with fancy curtains, carpets and even that new-fangled 'wallpaper' on the walls. I ain't never seen the like of it before. The Ellis's home was never as splendid as this. Here, we have the latest gas lighting everywhere and there are even some sparkling chandeliers hanging in some of the main rooms, as if the house is wearing its own diamond necklace. They are beautiful but take a lot of cleaning and must not be seen to be dirty under any circumstances. There are so many ornaments and pictures around the house that the job of dusting them all seems to take forever.

There's a back entrance into the basement of the house for the servants. We have to be concealed as much as possible. My job as parlour maid is to clean all the dining and reception rooms, light fires, wash curtains, dust china, clean windows etc but I mustn't be seen doing it. I also get to serve the family afternoon tea, but I'm not supposed to speak to or look at them. It's like us servants aren't really there.

Well, it's a good living and I got all me food and lodgings, so it ain't too bad. I'm sharing a room in the attic with Lizzie, the kitchen maid. She's a bit of a lively one – red hair and a temper to match, but she seems good hearted. I know Henry the gardener's been setting his cap at her, but she don't feel nothing for him, she told me.

"I'm aiming higher, me!" she said. "Fancy meself with a valet or something."

Trouble is, our valet John's too old for her, as he's been here for years, so she'll have to look elsewhere. It's a fair craic to see all the ins and outs of the relationships here. Tom obviously likes Mary but they're both too shy to say anything. Then there's rumours Miss Seaton has her eye on Charles, but I never seen them together, so I couldn't say. Personally, I like Alfie – he makes me laugh – but he ain't likely to get serious with no one anytime soon. He has two or three girls on the go already, I hear.

It's fun to be working with other people. I think I'm going to like it here.

Kate's Diary 27 December 1883

It's been the first decent Christmas I've had for a while, to be sure! After we'd done all the work for the day, we had a rare old party in the servant's hall, with music, dancing and presents from the mistress. We worked all through the holiday, of course. After all, it's our job to give the household the best Christmas we can. But we had a right laugh. Even Mrs Stanley let her hair down a bit and told us some funny stories about her earlier life.

"I once saw a naked young man coming out the master's bedroom, in the first place I worked, (long ago now), and him married and all! Of course, I had to pretend not to notice a thing. Master knew I'd seen, though, and gave me a silver necklace to keep quiet!"

What's more, I saw Lizzie kiss Henry under the mistletoe, even though she flatly denied it afterwards. Sometimes I wish I had a young man chasing me. I'm nearly seventeen now and feel it may be time. I still think about dear sweet George occasionally and pine for what might have been.

Kate's Diary 30 January 1884

I can hardly believe what I saw today. It's my day off, so I went to the British Museum which was amazing. So many fabulous things. It was deadly!

I was fierce nervous walking in through the grand columns of the South Entrance, but it was all so exciting that I soon forgot my nerves. First, I visited the Egyptian rooms, where I saw strange looking mummies. I've heard about them before but never expected to see them. They're all wrapped up in bandages and surrounded by gold and jewels. I s'pose the Egyptians considered death more like us Irish do – as an adventure in another world, not as the end. Not only that, but I saw the great Rosetta Stone, one of the first pieces of writing, which meant that people could work out what all those hiro... (can't remember the word – funny symbols for letters) anyway, what they all mean.

Then I went to look at all the classical sculptures. There were ancient Greek ones that came off the Parthenon, and massive Assyrian stone figures. I was so impressed by the great sculptures of the winged bulls, which they had either side of the gates to the city. Just imagine entering a place walking past them! What an entrance. It would put the fear of God into any enemy, I reckon.

I saw some strange exotic things in the African rooms – brightly coloured shields, spears, boats and pictures of some very small black people. Some people say they're all savages but I'm not so sure. When you look at what they have created, it's really quite beautiful and clever.

I didn't see much stuff from Ireland, which fair disappointed me, I must admit, but I guess they're more interested in things from abroad, that we wouldn't otherwise see. The oriental art is so lovely – how could we compete with that?

I felt quite overwhelmed with all the sights by the end of the day and stopped to take tea in a nearby tearoom. All that walking up and down steps was quite exhausting. One thing I noticed whilst I was there was a sign saying, 'Reading Room this way'. I would have liked to have gone this time, but I was just plain tired out, so will have to do it another day. I heard a lady saying that all the writers and poets go there regularly to discuss their work and get inspiration. I think that's great and I may even try and get an opinion on my own poems, if I feel brave enough.

The whole visit has inspired me to write something this evening – a poem about the passage of time. I don't know if it's any good, but I like it and that's the main thing.

Kate's Diary 25 February 1884

I can't believe it! Several railway stations were targeted today by people the newspapers are calling 'terrorists'. A bomb went off at Victoria and several others were found, but thankfully destroyed. They reckon it's the Irish Americans to blame, but I don't know. It's true the Irish are still fighting for home rule, and they are getting desperate, but surely, they wouldn't do this? At least no one was injured, thank goodness.

Kate's Diary 28 March 1884

Today I did something I'd been looking forward to for ages. I went along to the Reading Room of the British Museum. I was so excited, and I even took some of me poems in case I got the chance to talk to someone about them. The sign said, 'All Welcome', so I went in and was almost overwhelmed by the wonderful building. It's circular, just like the Picton Room in Liverpool, with stacks of books all around the inside and a magnificent domed roof. I spent the first few minutes just gazing up at it all in awe. However, after about five minutes, a man in a uniform came up to me, and asked, "Are you looking for your master?"

"My master?" I said, rather confused. "No, should I be? I came to join in with the reading and the writing."

The man frowned. "Do you have a ticket?"

"No," I told him. "I didn't know you needed one, sorry. How do I get one?"

At that moment, a very finely dressed lady passed by and overheard us.

"Oh," she laughed. "A servant girl writing – how quaint!"

Another voice joined in, "No doubt she ponders the big questions while she's doing the dusting!"

They all laughed, derisively.

"You can't come in here without a ticket," the uniformed man repeated. "I'm sorry but you'll have to leave."

"Well, how do I get one?" I asked, as politely as I could manage, though I was beginning to get annoyed.

"You need to apply in writing, but there are certain restrictions, you know. We don't just take anyone. We like our clientele to be respectable."

"I am respectable!" I retorted. "Just because I'm a working girl that doesn't make me any less respectable than those jumped-up fancy people over there!" I was real angry now. My face was flushed with temper and embarrassment.

The lady who'd been laughing at me turned to the doorman, looking shocked and said, "Really, Jones, we can't have scenes like this in here. Get rid of her!"

"Yes, Your Ladyship," he murmured and took my arm to lead me out.

"You let go of me!" I cried. "I can find my own way out. I wouldn't stay here with this bunch of snobs anyway. I'll go where I'm more welcome. Picton Reading Room was never like this. It's true you had to be dressed proper, but anyone could go there, not just hoity-toity folks like this lot."

Feeling humiliated and annoyed, I stormed out. I shan't go back there again. So much for 'All Welcome'. But I have to say, I've cried over it this evening. I wanted so much to be a part of it all and now it's ruined. I don't even feel like visiting the museum again.

Kate's Diary 6 April 1884

So happy! Got a letter from Elsie at last. I wrote to her at Christmas but didn't hear nothing and thought she'd forgotten me, but no! Thank goodness. She was just really busy. She fair made me die with her tales of what is going on in her household. Her master is an 'artist' and there's all kinds of strange folk who visit, at all hours. Elsie's also found out that he's got another woman ('sides his wife!) tucked away somewhere. She's one of his artist models and poses nude for him, Elsie says. To think of it! Whatever next?

Elsie told me her master has asked her to model for him as well, but she turned him down flat. She's started walking out with the footman, James, and he wouldn't like it, she says. We're going to try and meet up sometime if our days off coincide. I'll write her tonight and let her know my times and see what we can sort out.

Kate's Diary 3 May 1884

More bombings in London, this time aimed at the police. How shocking. The Fenians have now claimed responsibility and people are getting fair alarmed about it. Lizzie teased me yesterday, saying, "Go on, Kate – admit it! We all know you like a few explosions now and then. Fancy having a go at the coppers, though, really!"

I laughed it off, but I have to admit I don't like that kind of banter. It's not in my nature to hurt no one, as she well knows. Dangerous talk like that won't help my position here either. If she can think it, even in fun, so could others.

Kate's Diary 19 June 1884

Even though I'm always busy here, my mind has been wandering lately to thoughts of Mam and Pat. I haven't heard from them in such a long time. At Christmas, I sent 'em both a card but I ain't heard nothing back. Anyway, Sunday being a half day, I took it into me head to pay Mam a visit. We didn't part on the best of terms, but she did pay for me to go to the MABYS home and I wouldn't be here now if it weren't for that.

I was a bit nervous going into their area, as it ain't as respectable as I'm used to these days. Living in a fine place like Bloomsbury, I tend to forget that there are slums in the east end of London just as poor and rotten as the ones of Barrack Street in Cork. At least we had a camaraderie there, which don't seem apparent round here. People cared about each other.

I knocked on the door of Mam's lodging house at about 2 o'clock, expecting her and Gracie to be back from church by then. To my surprise, a young girl of about 13 or 14 opened it.

"Yeah?" she said. "What do you want?"

Her hair had been blonde once, but it was dirty and straggly. The clothes she wore were barely more than rags.

"I'm looking for me mam," I said, "Mrs McCarthy, or her cousin Gracie MacGuire."

"Don't know who you mean," the girl replied sullenly. "There ain't nobody here called that."

I was confused. I knew I was in the right place; after all, I had stayed there for a while.

"Are you sure?" I stammered. "They were here, not long ago."

"Hang on, wait here," she said, and disappeared inside the house. I heard her calling out, "Ma! There's a woman asking about some folks who used to live 'ere."

An older woman appeared, just as rough looking as her daughter.

"Yes?" she asked, suspiciously. "Who are you? What you after?"

I told her that I was looking for me mam, Mrs McCarthy.

"I dunno," the woman said. "We ain't been here long. The previous tenant died."

"Died!" I exclaimed. "How? Why?"

"All I know is this place was vacant, so they let it to us. Try the landlady. She lives in that tenement over the way there. Mrs Kelly's her name."

The door shut firmly on me and it was clear I'd get no more information from there. My mind was reeling – surely not? My mam – dead! Or maybe she meant Gracie? I suddenly felt very guilty that I hadn't been in touch before. Perhaps I should've gone to see her at Christmas. I raced over the road and banged loudly on the front door. A large, elderly lady appeared, shuffling along slowly.

"All right, all right! Keep it down – you'll wake the dead with that racket!"

"Sorry. I just need to know what happened to your tenants from over the road – Mrs McCarthy and Miss MacGuire. Someone said they were dead!"

"And who might you be?" she asked, gruffly.

"Mrs McCarthy's my mam and I ain't seen her in ages and now I'm real worried that I'll never see her again!" I began to cry in fear and panic.

"Heh. Hold on there, dearie. Come on in." She led me into a dark, grimy front parlour.

"Sorry, dearie, thought you might be the tax man or something. Well, your mam – Mrs McCarthy, is it? She's fine as far as I know, though that other lady, Gracie, she's up with the angels, if you know what I mean. She died of the pox –

67

nasty it was – but yer mam's okay. Mind, she left without paying the last week's rent, which didn't please me none, I can tell you. An old woman like me depends on things like that."

She looked at me closely and I could tell what she was thinking.

"I was going to let the coppers know, but they ain't too interested in debtors. There's so many of 'em these days. Now, if you could just see your way clear to settle it, well then I could just forget all about it."

I ignored the last remark for a minute or two.

"Do you know where she went?" I asked.

"If I did, I'd be after the rent now, wouldn't I?" she reasoned.

"Well, yes, I guess so, but have you any idea at all? Does she work?"

"Takes in a bit of washing now and then, dearie, but mostly spends her time drinking, far as I can tell. You'll probably find her round one of the local alehouses."

"Mam's not like that!" I protested, but I knew that wasn't quite true.

After looking at the landlady's rent book, I had to agree that Mam did indeed owe her some money, and I reluctantly settled up.

I spent some time circulating around the nearest hostelries, asking for information, but it soon became clear, I wasn't welcome there. As I was enquiring in yet another alehouse, I heard a harsh voice call to me, and a woman came out of the shadows in the corner. The bright coloured clothes and overdone make up betrayed her occupation. Her hair hung in dirty ringlets.

"'Ere Missus – what you think you're doing? You trying to poach me customers?"

"No, of course not," I began, "I'm just here to…"

"Yeah, yeah! We know, madam," said another woman I hadn't noticed before. "This here's our pitch, so clear off!"

She moved closer threateningly, and I could see that next to the cheap bangles on her arm, there were some nasty scars.

"I've got my pride!" I declared, "And I'm not after your jobs, so you needn't worry!"

"Oh so, you're Miss Hoity Toity now, are yer? Bit of high-class stuff! Get outta here before we spoil your pretty looks!"

I was angry, but I'm no fool, so I left the area hastily.

It seems that no one knows Mam here. At least I know she's okay, but I have lost all contact with her now. I can't think why she didn't let me know she'd moved; after all, she knows where I'm working. Maybe I'll write to Pat and ask him if he knows anything.

Joe's Recollections, 1905

I never knew for sure how my mother broke her arm. I was only four years old and too young to realise what was going on. She told me she fell, and I believed her, though as I got older, I suspected what the truth might be.

It had been a noisy evening the day before. I lay in bed, hearing shouting and crying next door, but not understanding what it meant. When I heard crashing noises, I buried my head in my pillow, in order to block them out, and cuddled up tighter to my little brother, Bill, who now shared the same bed. Thankfully, he was fast asleep. The older boys were in the other room, so I don't know what they thought about it, but they seemed oddly quiet the next day. Fred's eyes looked red, as if he'd been crying, and Ern was very pale, but Albert seemed the same as ever. There were smashed plates all over the floor, which Fred was attempting to clear up. Father seemed subdued and told us that Mum had had an accident and was at the hospital but would be back soon. When we asked questions, however, Father just thundered at us, "Shut up and eat yer breakfast!"

Sure enough, she reappeared later that day, with a black eye and her arm in plaster. She looked so fragile, like a delicate flower whose stem I might break if I went too close. My tears fell when I saw her but when she tried to comfort me, I was scared and ran off, screaming, into the other room. I've always regretted doing this, but I was only four and couldn't come to terms with it all.

It was only the next day, I think, that the men came calling. Having recovered from my recent shock, I was running around playing whilst Mum was cleaning the house as best as she could with one good arm. In our bedroom, Bill was crying, demanding to be fed yet again.

Suddenly, there was a terrifyingly loud knocking on the front door and men shouting, "Open up!"

I ran and hid as Mum opened the door. I didn't understand what was going on but there were a lot of raised voices and I heard Mum protesting about something. Some men pushed past her into the flat and proceeded to remove some of the furniture and take down the curtains. Mum started to plead with them, but they took no notice. As they went out with the final pieces, I heard one of them say, harshly, "Should pay yer bills, lady, then this wouldn't happen!"

Mum sank down onto the last remaining kitchen chair, her head in her hands. I went over to her but didn't know what to do. I was confused.

"Why have they taken away our sofa, Mum?" I remember asking.

She tried hard to smile and told me it was just being cleaned. I only half believed her. Even at that young age, I knew something wasn't right.

When Father came home from work that evening, he went mad at her.

"Why did you let them in, you stupid woman?" he cried at her. "Don't you know what you've done?"

There was a stony silence whilst we all had supper, then Father sent us to our rooms, briskly dismissing us with, "I need to speak to your mother alone. Go to bed."

Fred, who was nearly 12 by then, tried to protest, but after a swift slap to the side of his face, he soon retreated sulkily.

I huddled in bed, scared, hearing the argument raging in the kitchen. My father snarled and snapped at our Mum like a wild dog. She in return, whimpered like a lost pup. I couldn't hear what they were saying, and I wouldn't have understood it anyway at that age, but I knew something awful was going on. My tears fell on my pillow and I felt my world was coming to an end.

Kate's Diary 16 August 1884 Bloomsbury

What a grand day I've had! Caught up with Elsie at last. Been trying to arrange something for ages but our days off were always different.

Met up with her in Kensington Gardens, as it's about halfway between Chelsea and Bloomsbury, and after a cup of tea, we went to see the Albert Memorial. It's so sad to think of poor Victoria losing her husband so young. I weren't born at the time, but I was taught all about it at the convent. Seems Albert was a good man, who tried to improve things for everyone, even the poor. I'd a liked to have seen the Great Exhibition that he organised. They say it was mighty.

His memorial is very grand with fine carvings of the things he was involved in, like agriculture and the arts, all around it, and bronze angels at the top. I don't know if he was an angel himself, mind; not sure anyone is, really. We're all just a little bit flawed, I reckon.

Kensington Gardens is so beautiful. Today's been very warm, so we sat by the Serpentine, enjoying the view and cooling off. The ducks were busy preening themselves and the sunlight was glinting off the water. Everything was at peace. The summer flowers are still colourful at the moment, but soon enough, they'll have burned themselves out, just like a young girl's beauty. That's why we don't have long in which to find a husband.

Me and Elsie talked and talked. What a laugh we had. Then she told me she had some special news, "I'm getting married to James. He's a decent man and I love him."

Her eyes were shining with happiness and I felt quite envious, but I'm very pleased for her. She's a lovely person, so full of life and humour, who deserves to be happy. We hugged and talked about her plans for the future. She promises to invite me to the wedding, but it'll depend on whether I can get the day off. I hate being so tied down but it's a good job, so I mustn't complain.

When we parted I felt really sad. The only trouble with meeting up with someone you really want to see is the leaving of them again. It's so hard.

I'm tired now after all the excitement and the walking. Must get to bed – up early again tomorrow.

Kate's Diary 1 September 1884

Sent Pat a letter back in June, but no answer yet. I wish he'd write.

Kate's Diary 12 October 1884

Had a real set to with that old tyrant, Mrs Stanley, today. Just because she's the housekeeper she thinks she runs the place! I went to ask if I could have a day off in December 'cos it's Elsie's wedding, but she was real mean about it.

"Surely you know we can't run the household around you, miss?" she said, glaring at me.

"I wouldn't ask, ma'am, but it's special for my friend's wedding."

"We all have special things on, my girl, but we have to work. You're very lucky to have this job. How long have you been here now – a year?"

"Yes, ma'am."

"I'll have to ask Her Ladyship, but I don't think she'll take kindly to it. It means everyone else will start asking for this, that and the other."

"I won't tell no one," I pleaded, "please!"

"You've no right to ask," she continued. "You're only a parlour maid after all. Who do you think will do your work when you're not here?"

"Mary normally covers me on when I'm on me day off, like I do her. It wouldn't be no different."

"Don't be impertinent! You're a jumped-up little madam to be asking this, and it doesn't bode well."

"I'm sorry, I didn't mean nothing. I was just hoping..."

"Well, don't hope! It won't do you any good."

She considered for a minute and softened slightly.

"Well, I'll ask Her Ladyship and see what she says."

Of course, Her Ladyship turned my request down, which Mrs Stanley had great pleasure in telling me later.

"I told you she'd say no," she said, almost gleefully. "Now don't be so foolish again."

I wanted to shout at her, but I held me tongue. I don't want to get dismissed. It's so hard to get another job if they don't give you a reference. So, all I said was 'Yes, ma'am', and I went back to me work, but I'm fair upset and I couldn't stop me tears falling as I cleaned the grate.

Lizzie's just asked what's wrong and I told her how sad I am.

"That's really unkind of 'em," Lizzie said. "I don't blame you for being upset. Tell 'em you're going anyway!"

"I daren't," I told her, and it's true. I can't risk losing everything. I'll just have to get over it.

Kate's Diary 10 December 1884

Elsie got married today and I couldn't be there. I felt awful about it all day. As I cleaned the windows, I pictured her walking up the aisle and making her vows. Then when I was taking in the afternoon tea, I knew she'd be celebrating with her new husband by then. Looking at Her Ladyship, sitting there so serene with the tea I just served her, I wondered why she felt the need to be so hard-hearted. What would it have cost her to be more understanding?

I feel so sad I've missed everything. Nothing can make up for it. I wrote and told Elsie how sorry I am, and she told me not to worry. She understands, but still, I am so miserable. Lizzie said I looked like a wet weekend and she's right. The usual banter of the servant's hall was too much for me to face this evening, so I came up here to be alone, but all I want to do is cry.

Kate's Diary 2 January 1885

What an awful day! After serving the afternoon tea, I went back below stairs to find the place in an uproar. Mary, the chamber maid, had come running in, her face covered in blood and in a state of near hysteria. It was her day off today and she'd been waiting for a train at Gower Street station, when there was another explosion. Broken glass flew everywhere, causing cuts to anyone nearby.

Everyone was gathered near her, comforting and trying to help. Tom sat next to her, his arm around her, dabbing gently at the cuts on her face with his handkerchief.

"What's happened?" I asked.

"Another bomb," replied Lizzie. "Poor Mary was caught in it. They say it's the Fenians again."

"How dreadful."

Tom suddenly noticed me there and his face changed from concern to anger. His words came tumbling out, all in a rush.

"You're Irish, aren't you? Tell me this – how could your people do something like this? Mary didn't deserve it, she

75

never hurt them. She's just an innocent victim. How is that fair? What gives your lot the right? You should all be ashamed!"

I felt his words stinging me, as fierce as wasps in the summertime, and I turned and fled.

I kept meself apart from 'em all for a while. At supper time, when I went into the servant's hall, the conversation was stilted and difficult. Mary has now recovered a bit, thank goodness, but no one knew what to say to me. As I left the table, Tom followed me out and said awkwardly, "Kate, I'm sorry. I was just upset about Mary. I didn't mean it."

"I understand," I told him, and I do. I know how he must feel. He was right; we should all be ashamed. I'm beginning to feel embarrassed to be Irish.

Kate's Diary 25 January 1885

What a day yesterday! I can only just think straight now. I still feel in a state of shock and I've had a headache all day.

It was my usual day off, so being a Saturday, I decided to make the most of it and see some more of London. The weather was bright, in spite of the time of year, and the day was crisp, blue and sunny, though not at all warm. I've always wanted to see some of the historic landmarks, so I decided to head for the Tower of London. What could be more historic than that, after all?

The entrance fee was about as much as I could afford, but I had a great time looking round. My imagination ran riot, hearing all the stories of kings and queens through the ages. In my mind's eye I could visualise the gruesome executions at Traitors' Gate and it made me fair shudder to see where it took place.

Just as I was making a final circuit around the grounds, there was a tremendous noise such as I never heard before. At the same moment, there was a blinding flash of light, which came from somewhere inside the tower, and a huge blast of air which hit us all and knocked me flat. I lay on the chilly grass, too stunned to move. My ears were buzzing with a noise which seemed to be inside my head and my eyes hurt. I sat up gingerly and heard people screaming, but the sound was muffled and distorted. Smoke was pouring from the building and police were rushing around. *Another bomb!* It suddenly occurred to me and I felt sick at the thought of it. A few moments later, I heard a second explosion go off in the distance, followed by another shortly after.

I tried to pick meself up, but I could hardly stand, I felt so dizzy and weak. I staggered over to a nearby bench and slumped onto it, thankfully. There was a state of chaotic panic all around me. A policeman came up and asked, I think, whether I was all right. His words seemed fuzzy and distant. I nodded, too dazed to say a word.

Slowly, I examined my hands and face and tried to see if I was injured, but it seemed not. However, my mind was numb with shock and would not function no matter how I tried. The hubbub died down gradually, and the sun revived me a little, enough to move to the much-needed sanctuary of a nearby tearoom. I ordered tea but found my hands shaking so much as I lifted my cup that it nearly spilt.

Not long after that, I made my way back here. As I walked in, Alfie exclaimed, "Jesus, Kate! You look like a ghost! What happened?" (Apparently, I was so covered in dust that I was white from head to foot)

I still couldn't bring meself to do more than mutter, "A bomb, I think."

I have a vague memory of Lizzie guiding me firmly upstairs, where she put me to bed, but I slept only fitfully, amidst dreams of terrible light and noise.

Today, we hear that yesterday has been nicknamed 'Dynamite Saturday'. The other places that were attacked were London Bridge and the House of Commons, but thankfully no one was killed. Sadly, the Fenians have claimed responsibility again and public opinion of the Irish has sunk to an all-time low. The newspapers are really coming out against us and whipping up unrest. This worries me.

I still feel ill. My hearing seems mostly better, though still a bit fuzzy, but my head is splitting, and when I bend down, the room spins. Hope I feel better tomorrow.

I pray that there are no more bombs now. It's making things real bad for us innocent Irish civilians.

Kate's Diary 27 January 1885
My 18th Birthday

I had hoped for a better day than this. I can't believe what's just happened. Mrs Stanley came to me this morning and asked me to step into her housekeeper's room for a few minutes. This worried me immediately, as it's not somewhere we're normally invited.

"Sit down, Kate," she said. "I need to talk to you."

"What's wrong?" I asked anxiously.

"It's difficult," Mrs Stanley told me, and she sounded less sure of herself than normal.

"I've been talking to the mistress just now, and to be straight with you, she has asked me to dismiss you."

"What? Why? I've worked hard. I ain't done nothing wrong!"

"I know, I know," she continued, "but the mistress is afeared because – well I hate to say it – because you're Irish. I mean there's been all these bombs lately and she thinks it's dangerous to have you around."

"But that's not right!" I flared up. "It's not my fault!"

"Look, Kate. I've pleaded your case and told her you're a good girl and no trouble, but she's quite fixed on it."

"Well, if that's the case, I'll collect me things and go," I told her indignantly, standing up.

"No, listen, as I say I pleaded for you and I got a bit of a concession, but I don't know if you'll like it." She eyed me nervously.

"The only suggestion I could come up with was for you to be working somewhere where you wouldn't come into contact with the family," she paused, "like the scullery. The mistress agreed that you could stay if I put you down there and moved Sarah up to parlour maid. Of course, it's less money, but it's still a job, and maybe in time, you could move up again, once the mistress forgets all about it. It's up to you to decide."

I stared at her, trying to take it all in. The scullery maid is a lonely, uncomfortable job, the lowest of the household. Always wet, always cold and alone; not even allowed to eat in the servant's hall with the rest. Still, at least I'd still see Lizzie and Martha the cook. Was it better to have a worse job rather than no job at all? I wasn't sure. My pride was hurt, and I was close to tears.

"I *am* sorry," Mrs Stanley said. "I did my best to help. Let me know your decision this afternoon."

I've thought it over all day but had to accept in the end. I ain't got much choice. Maybe things will work out better in time. What a great birthday this is!

Kate's Diary 13 April 1885

Oh woe! I'm fed up with being wet and cold. From half past six in the morning to half past nine at night, all I do is boil, wash, scrub, scour and heave water around! Water rules my life, as much as the sea does a sailor. My hands and arms are red raw and the only way I keep me feet dry is by standing on a wooden platform. The minute a utensil is used by Lizzie or Martha, it has to be washed, dried and returned for further use; it's a never-ending cycle.

Not only that, but I also have to clean the kitchen, all the servant's rooms, the offices *and* scrub the front steps of the house, just to show how respectable we are. We have to keep up appearances at all times. They may be very fine steps but I'm beginning to hate them!

My greatest sadness is not being able to eat with the rest of the staff. I have to serve them their food and then have my meals alone. I miss the gossip and the jokes we used to share. I know they all feel embarrassed about my change of circumstances. The talk stops when I come in the room, and people seem awkward in front of me. Poor Sarah blushes crimson whenever she sees me, but I don't blame her, or any of 'em, for this. It ain't their fault.

Lizzie does her best, as kitchen maid, to keep me company, and she lifts my spirits a good deal, so it's not all bad. Martha is a real character as well and we do have a laugh at times. She swears and cusses as she cooks and can't stand Mrs Stanley!

"She's a sour old bitch, that one," she told me, "all down to 'er being crossed in love!"

"Really? Do tell!"

"Well, I heard it from my friend Mabel, who is cook in the house where our Mrs S used to work as lady's maid years ago. Apparently, the missus was all set to marry the head steward there and had trusted him with her life savings, but he ran off with the chamber maid instead, and took all her money with him! It was after that that she left and came here to be a housekeeper."

"Isn't she married, though? I mean, she's *Mrs* Stanley."

"No, dear. They always call 'em *Mrs*, but it don't mean anything. She's an old spinster, that one, never married and not likely to be!"

I feel a bit sorry for her now, especially remembering that she tried to help me out when the mistress wanted to fire me. Mrs S ain't a bad old stick, really.

My back is aching now, and my hair is a bedraggled mess. I feel tired and wretched. Sometimes, I wonder if I will ever escape from this drudgery. Am I destined to be here forever? Is this my fate? Surely there is more to my life than this.

Kate's Diary 8 February 1886

What is the world coming to? It seems to get worse and worse these days.

Today, Lizzie came running in from her afternoon off, out of breath and somewhat excited. "'Ere, what do you think?" she cried, "There's a riot going on in the centre. Seems there's a huge crowd been at some meeting in Trafalgar Square, and they've run amok!"

We were all agog and keen to find out more. From what Lizzie told us, there were thousands of angry unemployed people, who, having been stirred up to a frenzy by some political speeches, decided to wreak havoc on the upper classes. They rampaged through Pall Mall, St James' Street, down to Piccadilly and beyond, smashing and looting everything in their path – shops, houses, carriages – you name it! There was an air of shock in our servant's hall, which increased still further when Martha shared some more gossip later (I don't know how she gets it all, but she never fails!).

"Well, I don't know!" she told us. "The master has just come in, in a foul mood, so I've heard. He was in his gentleman's club, Brooks's in St James Street, when it had all the windows smashed by the rabble. Would you believe it? He's threatening to string 'em up if he gets hold of 'em. Mind, he's all talk, anyway. Wouldn't lift a finger to do anything himself – he'd get a bobby to do it for 'im! I'm not surprised the mob wanted to get revenge on these 'ere gentry folks. They all treat us like dirt, don't they?"

Well, I've thought about it a bit and have to admit there's some truth in what she says. I don't hold with violence, mind, but I can understand how desperate people become when they're starving and penniless. The master and mistress certainly don't care about us, even though we work hard for them every day. If the master got a bit of a 'wake-up call' today, well, he probably deserves it.

Kate's Diary 15 March 1886

I'm devastated! Lizzie is leaving here and is going to marry Henry. I certainly never saw that coming! The amount of times she told me that she can't stand him and yet all this time she was secretly seeing him. I can't believe it. I feel in a state of shock. I know I should be happy for her, and I am in a way, but I also feel betrayed. Why didn't she feel she could share this with me? I thought we were friends.

I don't know where this leaves me now, in my job, either. Maybe I will be able to move up to kitchen maid instead. It's not much better, but at least I wouldn't be quite so cold and wet all the time. I do hope so. I'll talk to Mrs Stanley about it tomorrow.

I suppose I mustn't be too hard on Lizzie. If I had the chance to get out of here, I'd do the same. All I want to do is run away, but I've got nowhere else to go. I wish I could just escape and be free.

I really *do* hope that she'll be happy because she's a nice person and deserves to be, but I know that I'll miss her so much.

Kate's Diary 17 March 1886

Just had a long heart to heart with Lizzie and I feel better about everything now. She tells me she didn't mean to keep anything a secret, but she felt embarrassed. There was a sudden change in their relationship the other day, and she says she realised then that there was another side to Henry that she'd never noticed before. He's always hidden his true feelings behind a load of jokes and cheeky remarks, but really, he's quite serious about her. She also tells me that she feels ready to settle down now and have a family, and that this is the best offer she thinks she is going to get. Our choices are very limited, after all. We rarely meet anyone except the other staff, and personally I can't think of anyone here who'd be right for me. Tom has finally started courting Mary and they seem happy enough. Alfie still has at least three girlfriends, all of dubious backgrounds. All the rest of the men here are far too old for me. Maybe someone new will come along and join the staff – that's my best chance.

I've spoken to Mrs Stanley and she's agreed that I can move up to take Lizzie's place as kitchen maid. Perhaps things are looking up.

Kate's Diary 21 May 1886

Today, Lizzie married Henry and most of us were there to watch and wish them well. She looked so beautiful all in white satin, with a tight fitted bodice and a big bustle at the back. Right fashionable it was, though truth to tell, her dress had been made over from her older sister's. Lizzie's red hair looked so lovely under the white lace veil and I felt just a tiny bit jealous. If only *my* day would come and then I could get out of here as well. I dream of being married to a decent man and starting a family.

We've now got a new girl starting as scullery maid and I've moved up to take Lizzie's place. Flossie is very young, about 12, we think, though she isn't sure herself, having spent all her life in the workhouse until now. She is so thin and fragile looking – I hope she's got enough strength for the job. I'm going to try and help her where I can; she's very sweet and I feel real sorry for her. She calls me Miss Katie and we're going to share a bedroom, but I don't think I'll be able to talk about 'women's stuff' to her like I could Lizzie. Makes me feel quite motherly, she does, dear little thing.

Kate's Diary 5 July 1886

I'm fair delighted! Mam wrote at last, saying how much she misses me and asking me to visit. I've finally got her new address – wonder why she didn't let me know before. It's been well over two years since I heard from her and I thought I'd never see her again. Pat hasn't replied to my letters either.

This evening I was talking to Flossie about it all and I noticed she looked real wistful.

"What's it like to have a ma?" she asked. "I never had one."

"You must have done," I told her, "else you wouldn't be here!"

"Well, leastwise I never seen her," she said.

"Do you know what happened? Did she die or something?"

"I dunno," Flossie replied sadly. "Maybe she just didn't care about me. The matron always said that I was no good and that's why I wasn't wanted."

"That's nonsense!" I told her firmly. "What a horrible thing for her to say. I'm sure your mother would have loved you very much if she'd known you. You're a good girl and any mother would be proud of you."

This reduced the poor child to tears, so we hugged, and I dried Flossie's eyes.

"What's it like in the workhouse?" I asked her.

"It's awful. We get treated like dirt," she replied. "Oh, Miss Katie, I still have such nightmares about it! All the time they're ordering you around. They try and school you, but it ain't a lot of help really. I can only just about read. And if you break their rules, they're allowed to beat you. But the worst thing is the lice…" she shuddered. "They make you feel so unclean."

"But they feed and clothe you, don't they?"

"Oh yes, but the food is so basic; gruel, bread and stewed meat, which don't taste of nothin'. As for the clothes – you have to wear the workhouse uniform every day and it's grey and hard. It ain't soft or warm. No, it's a real blessing to come here to work. Seems like luxury! Before, I shared a dormitory with twenty other girls, now there's just you and me."

There's one thing I'm sure of, I ain't never going to the workhouse if I can help it. May the Good Lord preserve me! I realise now I am really lucky to have had a mam and da who loved me and brought me up. I will write to Mam tomorrow and arrange to see her soon.

Kate's Diary 10 August 1886

Visited Mam today at her lodgings in the Old Nichol near Shoreditch. I was shocked to see how poor and rough her home was, not much more than a shack really. I remember that our place in Barrack Street was not up to much, if truth be told, but it was better than this. I s'pose I'm used to better now, living in Bloomsbury as I do. I may only be a servant and my own room is bare and plain, but the house and surroundings are so rich and luxurious they make up for it.

The area I live in is wealthy and high class with genteel residents, so unlike the harsh realities of the poor hereabouts.

Mam greeted me warmly but seemed to have deteriorated in herself. She offered me tea with rum in it, but I declined the added extra and took it just with milk instead. We sat in a dirty, dimly lit room, oil cloth hangings keeping out the worst of the draughts from the broken windows. She told me that Gracie had died suddenly from cholera and that she felt that she had to get away for the sake of her own health.

"Why didn't you let me know?" I asked her. "I was very worried about you."

"I'm sorry, to be sure," she told me, "but Kate, darling, I'd lost your address and didn't know what to do."

"You've found it again now, then?" I said puzzled.

"Pat gave it to me," she answered. "He's married to Jenny now and she's 'with child' already."

Married? Why didn't he invite me to the wedding? We were close when we were growing up. What has happened to us? I feel so hurt.

Mam made some feeble excuses for him when I asked her this.

"They didn't tell no one," she said. "It was all very quick."

After chatting a while, Mam mentioned that Pat used to send her money, but that now he is married and going to be a father, this has stopped.

"I've tried to do some work," she said, "but I'm not as strong as I used to be. I'm an old lady now. I do a bit of washing here and there, but it`s hard standing up all day. My legs can't take it no more." She got a bit tearful. "There's so little money coming in and I'm frightened I'll end up in the workhouse one of these days."

She looked at me and I realised she was hoping for me to help her out. Guilt tugged at my heart and my purse strings, so of course I had to offer.

"You're such a good girl, Kate. You'll look after your old mam, won't you?" She grinned through blackened teeth, and when she kissed me goodbye, the smell from her breath was unpleasantly overpowering.

I was pleased to catch up with Mam again but part of me wonders if she would have bothered to contact me if it hadn't been for the fact that she needed money (I am going to send her regular payments now). She was pathetically grateful, but I'd rather have had her interest, than her thanks. She barely asked what I'd been doing or how I was. Maybe I'm just seeing it wrongly. I'm sure she cares, she's just desperate. If I can help her in any way, then of course I will. I owe it to her.

Kate's Diary 22 June 1887

My, what a grand time it's been! The queen finally came out of mourning to celebrate her Golden Jubilee with a spectacular parade through London. Although it was a Tuesday and we were all working hard in the household, the mistress did allow us all a short time off to go and watch, which was real good of her.

The streets were all brightly decorated with flowers, union jacks and patriotic symbols and I have never seen London look so gay. There were street parties, and all sorts of fun laid on for the children. The procession itself was splendid; the queen's carriage glistened in the sun and was accompanied by some very fine-looking soldiers, all on horseback. Someone said they were all princes from distant lands, but I don't know if that's true.

In the evening, the master and mistress went out to a ball with some wealthy friends, so we had time in the servants' hall to have a mighty party. Mrs Stanley pulled out some dusty old bottles from the depths of the wine cellar.

"Been there for ages," she said. "They'll never miss 'em! Let's make a toast to Her Majesty."

We partied until late, when the master and mistress came home, then returned to our duties as if nothing had happened. I don't think they guessed what we'd been up to; certainly, nothing's been said.

It felt a bit strange, though, celebrating with the rest. After all, there've been protests in Ireland recently, about the unfairness of British rule over our homeland. Mind, I have to admit I enjoyed myself! Does that make me a traitor to my country? I hope not. I got nothing against the queen personally; I don't think it's her fault. I just wish these politicians would get their act together and sort it all out.

At the moment, they've got their hands full with some problems over here. The other day, I came past Trafalgar Square and was shocked to see loads of makeshift tents there, like some strange canvas city. Apparently, many poor people have started sleeping there because they have nowhere else to go. The weather is hot and dry at the moment, it's true, but it can't be right for folks to be living outdoors. I can only imagine how desperate they must be.

Kate's Diary 7 September 1887

I was scrubbing those damned steps again this morning when a shadow fell across me, blotting out the sun and I shivered. For a moment, I had a faint portent of doom but when I looked up, I saw something which fair changed my mind. A man stood there smiling down at me – a tall muscular man with thick dark hair the colour of night, and a short well-trimmed beard. His eyes were twinkling as he looked at me.

"Can I help you, sir?" I asked nervously.

"Well, my fair maid, I'm sure you can." He indicated a large box which he had with him and I realised he was a tradesman. I s'pose I could have guessed it really from the clothes he wore, as he weren't dressed like no gentleman, but he weren't in rags neither. *A working person then*, I thought, *like meself*. He smiled broadly.

"I have a delivery for the master of the house. Could you show me where to leave it?"

"I'll fetch the butler, sir," I told him and took him in the front door. "I'm only the kitchen maid."

"And a very charming one too, I must say," he said. "From Ireland, I guess?"

I was so pleased he recognised my accent that I glowed with pride.

"Yes, sir, from Cork, but I'm surprised you noticed it. I've been in England a few years now. I didn't think it showed anymore."

"You can't miss it," he told me, "and it's lovely to hear. Personally, I feel the Irish have had a rough time of it lately."

"Too true, sir, but I mustn't talk about it now. Mr Chapman – this gentleman's got a delivery for the master."

I went back to my duties, feeling flushed with excitement, hoping I might see him again as he left, but to my disappointment I didn't.

However, this afternoon, Mary came rushing downstairs, clutching a bunch of flowers and looking excited.

"Kate! Kate!" she called. "You done got an admirer. Some gent left these for you!"

I blushed and took them from her. There was a note: 'To the lovely Irish maiden of the front steps. Meet me tomorrow afternoon by the statue in Russell Square Gardens, if you can. I'll be waiting. Signed – an admirer.'

Tomorrow is Sunday, so I get a half day off, but I'm not sure whether I should go. He could be a rogue or a villain or something. My mind's in turmoil. What should I do?

Kate's Diary 8 September 1887

It's been a mild autumn so far this year with some nice sunny days like yesterday. But typical – this morning I woke up to grey storm clouds gathering, laden with rain. I felt so disappointed, thinking I couldn't possibly meet anyone in the gardens if it was wet. Common sense kept telling me I shouldn't go anyway; maybe this was a sign, I thought. But every time I looked at the flowers he'd sent me, I knew I had to find out about the mysterious stranger.

We went to church in the pouring rain and I felt really depressed. He surely wouldn't be there in this weather. However, by the time the family luncheon was finally over, and I was free to leave, the rain had just about stopped, though the sky was still dark and threatening.

Hurriedly, I changed and tidied meself and sped off to Russell Square. My mind was in a whirl, half nervous, half excited. For a brief moment, I worried that he would have got tired of waiting and left, but as I approached the statue, I saw him standing there.

He smiled, and without a moment's hesitation, took my hand and kissed it, saying, "My fair Irish maiden. I knew you'd come."

His self-confidence annoyed me a bit and I said stiffly, "I can't see how you'd know when I didn't even know meself. You're very sure of yourself, aren't you?"

"Not at all," he replied. "I just know we were meant to be together. It's fate. I didn't mean to offend you. Come and walk with me a while."

"But I don't even know your name, sir," I said.

He smiled again. "You're quite right. Let me introduce myself. My name's William Duffield, and I'm a printer by trade. I live in Clerkenwell near my work. The trouble is I fear I've fallen in love with you at first sight!"

"Sir – I mean Mr Duffield! Really!" I was getting flustered, but also, I have to admit, feeling flattered.

"You can call me Will," he told me, "and what's your name?"

"Kate McCarthy," I answered, "and I'm originally from Cork in Ireland, as you've guessed, but I live in London now. I was in Liverpool for a while before this."

I don't know how it happened, but he persuaded me to walk around the gardens with him. He is so charming and funny. I haven't laughed so much in ages. The rain came on again, so we took shelter in a nearby tearoom, and I told him all about my childhood in Ireland. He listened intently, holding my hand at times when I got a bit emotional. When I mentioned that I used to enjoy hearing the Irish music, he laughed out loud.

"Well, what a coincidence. I love music myself – in fact I play the fiddle a bit, and people have said it's a joy to hear. We must go out to a dance together."

Its night-time now and I feel I've been swept away on the tide to an unknown destination. Will makes me feel so alive, but nervous as well. I've never met anyone like him before. Of course, I've agreed to meet him again, but I really don't know if I should.

Kate's Diary 13 September 1887

Due to meet Will tomorrow but I've made up my mind not to see him anymore. Something about him scares me. I feel like a small insect being drawn into a spider's web. I'm going to tell him I can't continue with this.

Kate's Diary 14 September 1887

Went out to the music hall this evening with Will. I promised meself I'd tell him I wouldn't go, but when I started to, he looked so disappointed that I couldn't face going through with it.

"My lovely Kate," he said, "you must come now. You can't disappoint me like this. What can it hurt to just relax and have a good time? You deserve it."

I softened and relented. What's more, I really enjoyed the show and the supper afterwards, so much so that I let him kiss me goodnight, though only on the hand.

Will is attentive and witty, but I feel there's a hidden depth to him and it makes me uncomfortable. I can't quite put my finger on it, but I'll have to see what happens.

Kate's Diary 25 September 1887

Today, we had a grand day out. It was my day off, so we went on a tour of London, taking a horse drawn omnibus to see some of the famous landmarks. Will knows such a lot and kept me amused all day. We saw the Houses of Parliament and Big Ben, then walked by the river, taking in all the sights and sounds. Sad to say though, the Thames is brown with 'who knows what', and the smell is enough to make you hold your 'kerchief to your nose, not like our own dear River Lee in Cork.

Later, we went and looked at Buckingham Palace where the queen lives, God bless her. Will paid for us to have a slap-up luncheon at a smart hotel nearby and I even had a glass of wine, which made me feel quite giddy.

I wanted to go to the Victoria and Albert Museum as well, but as Will pointed out, there wasn't enough time to see everything properly, so we took another omnibus to see St Pauls Cathedral instead. We have talked all day and I even felt brave enough to tell him about my writing. To my relief, he didn't laugh at me but was very encouraging.

"I'd love to read some of it," he said, "and maybe I could play you some of the tunes I've written." He's so talented – to be able to play and write music – what a wonderful thing.

When we parted, I let him hold me in his arms for a moment and kiss my cheek. I still feel nervous when he's so close, but it's exciting as well. My reaction is always to pull away from him. I'm not sure why, but I guess I'm just inexperienced in the ways of love.

Kate's Diary 6 October 1887

That was a strange afternoon to be sure. Will escorted me to see his mother and sister over in Lambeth. I did meself up real nice for the occasion, but by the time we had walked there, my best dress was spattered with mud, and worse, from the road. On the way, Will talked enthusiastically about how much his mother would like me, but I was met by a stern matriarch, all in grey. Her massive skirts billowed out around her ample figure, but I sensed no kindness beneath that large bosom. Her face was hard and forbidding and she certainly didn't make me feel welcome. Will introduced me saying, "This is the woman I've lost my heart to, Mother. She's from Ireland. I know you'll like her."

She glared at me.

"Can't stand the Irish!" she said. "They're always trouble."

I would have protested but I was trying to be polite for Will's sake, and anyway just as I opened my mouth to speak, Will whisked me away to show me the garden. Not that there was much to see, but once we were outside, he pressed my hand, and said confidentially, "Take no notice of her. She doesn't mean anything by it."

He tried to kiss me on the cheek, but I moved away.

"Kate, darling, don't you know how I feel about you?" he asked.

I didn't know what to say, but fortunately never got the chance, because then he brought me back into the living room and made me sit down with Mrs Duffield whilst he fetched his sister to meet me. Conversation was awkward and I felt embarrassed.

"What do you do?" his mother asked sharply.

"I work as a kitchen maid in a house in Bloomsbury," I replied. "It's a very respectable family and a good position."

"Kitchen maid – huh!" she snorted. "Not much more than a skivvy then. Don't you want to aim higher than that?"

"Yes of course," I said indignantly, "but it's not that easy."

I was saved from further questions by Will's sister, Amelia, entering the room. She is older than him, about 30, I think, and a spinster. She seems sweet – a quiet, mouse-like woman, very much in the shadows of her mother. We all talked a little, polite small talk about the weather etc. Then Will suddenly brought out his fiddle and decided to play. The atmosphere lightened immediately, like the sunrise of a new dawn, and for a half hour or more was most delightful. Will played us tunes which his sister and I sang along to, whilst his mother listened. Then he played a beautiful Irish air, which I remember my da loved and it made me feel real emotional. For a moment, I suddenly felt very close to Will and after the tune finished, I moved over to him and smiling deep into his eyes, thanked him profusely. He was obviously pleased to have my approval and took both my hands in his, smiling.

"Anything for you, my fair Kate. You mean the world to me."

But it was just after this moment of genuine affection that everything changed, like a cold wind sweeping through on a sunny day. His younger brother James arrived, and it was obvious from his mother's reaction that he was her favourite.

"James, my son," she cooed, "come and kiss your old mother. I've missed you so much."

"It was only last Wednesday that I saw you, Mother," he said smiling, but he kissed her and fussed over her, nonetheless. There was nothing wrong in that, I thought, but then I saw Will's face had turned as black as thunder.

"William," ordered his mother. "Get James a cup of tea. Can't you see he's thirsty?"

Will looked annoyed but went off to do as he was asked. It's clear that there's no arguing with the old lady. She's a force to be reckoned with.

"This is Kate, Will's new fancy woman," his mother told James.

"Excuse me, ma'am," I said haughtily, "but I'm a decent girl, not some floozy!"

In answer to that, she just waved her hand dismissively.

"Of course, of course. It was just a figure of speech. No need to get on your high horse! William, haven't you got that tea yet?"

Will didn't hear what she said to me, but by the looks of things, he was already upset about something. He placed the cup and saucer down with a clatter, then muttered, "We must be going now, Mother." He picked up his fiddle, hastily said goodbye and left the house, dragging me along by the hand as he went.

"Will," I protested, "what's wrong? Have I done something to annoy you? Why have we left?"

"Just leave it!" he growled, and his voice sounded harsh and strained. He said no more on the way back, striding along, barely noticing me. I struggled to keep up, my long skirts trailing in the filth, and eventually lost patience.

"For God's sake, Will, slow down. What's going on?"

He stopped and glared at me, no love in his eyes now.

"Can't you see it – the way it is with her? Of course, *he* can't do anything wrong! Are you blind?"

"Do you mean your mother and James?" I asked.

"Of course!" he snapped, and his handsome features were contorted with rage. "I can't believe you didn't notice it!"

"Well, I did see something," I began hesitantly, "but I…"

"Oh, just forget it!" he declared. "You wouldn't understand."

He stormed off up the road again and I followed at a distance, dejectedly.

However, when we reached Bedford Square, he turned and smiled as if nothing had happened.

"So, I'll see you next Sunday then?" he asked.

"I'm not sure," I said, "maybe you don't want to."

"Of course I do, you idiot! 2 o'clock at the statue, same as usual. See you then."

He kissed my hand and walked off rapidly, leaving me totally confused. I really don't know what to think now. If only I could talk to another woman about it – Mam? No, I don't think so. She ain't never been much help to me. Elsie? Maybe – she's married now and might be able to give me some advice. Lizzie? She's a woman of the world – perhaps. I need to talk to someone, that's for sure. Think I'll write to Elsie.

Kate's Diary 13 October 1887

Met Will at the square again and he seemed just the same as ever. Maybe I imagined it all. In the evening, we went dancing and it was great fun. He was the perfect companion again and I feel that I am falling in love with him. Up till now, I haven't been too sure. How do you know when it's real? It's different to the feeling I had for George, but I was very young then. When I see Elsie, in a couple of weeks' time, I'll talk to her about it.

Kate's Diary 20 October 1887

Today I wanted to go to the zoological gardens in Regent's Park because I've never been there, and I've always wanted to. Will seemed just as enthusiastic as meself and we headed off towards them, gaily. It was a bright enough afternoon, but as we walked, Will kept saying that it looked like rain.

"Don't think it will be much fun if it's wet," he remarked. "You might catch a chill or something and I'd never forgive myself."

"I'll be fine," I reassured him, "but you're kind to worry about me."

We carried on, but a bit further on, Will suddenly suggested, "Let's go in here for a rest," and led me into a small tearoom. It was a pleasant idea so I didn't object, but by the time we'd had tea and cake, the afternoon was wearing on and Will suggested that we go to a strange place called Madame Tussaud's instead. I didn't like it much. It was full of waxworks of famous people and they gave me the creeps a fair bit. They looked almost alive, yet they weren't.

"You won't be able to see the animals now, anyway," he said. "It's too late. They'll all be inside."

I had to agree that this was possible, but I was disappointed all the same.

"Never mind," he said, as we left the waxworks. "I'll take you to the zoo next week."

That's when I had to tell him that I've arranged to visit Elsie next Sunday and can't see him. His reaction surprised me.

"Why? What for? I thought you and I were going out. Surely friends are not so important." His face was clouded with irritation.

"We can go out one evening instead," I explained. "I just want to see my friend again. I haven't seen her in ages."

"So, it doesn't matter if it's a bit longer, then," he said.

"Yes, it *does* matter," I told him. "It's all arranged and I'm not cancelling it."

He sounded angry now.

"I don't think you care about me at all. You never show me any affection and now you're going off without me. How can you treat me like this? It's not right!"

"Don't be ridiculous," I replied. "I do care about you, Will, but there's no reason why I shouldn't see my friends as well."

He usually took my arm as we walked, but now, he stomped off ahead, sulkily.

"Will," I pleaded, "surely you can understand."

I tried to explain but he just didn't want to listen. We parted at Bedford Square without setting another date and now I feel awful. I've obviously upset him, and I didn't mean to. Surely, it's not so bad to see our own friends as well? Still, I know I'll miss him something terrible if I don't see him again.

Kate's Diary 27 October 1887

Saw Elsie today, which was wonderful. She reckons I need to talk to Will about his family and try to get him to open up to me.

"He's obviously got a few problems with his mother," she suggested. "Maybe you can help."

The only trouble is that I don't know if I will get the opportunity now. I told Elsie about our disagreement and she frowned.

"He needs to accept that you have your own life as well," she said, "otherwise you'll never be happy. Be careful."

We had a grand old time chatting and laughing before I had to head back. I just wish I hadn't upset Will. I hope he'll be okay.

Kate's Diary 2 November 1887

Waited in Russell Square today as usual, but Will didn't show. I stayed there an hour and got more and more depressed as the afternoon went on. As the grimy fog rolled in and the sky grew dark and murky, I decided to give up. It ain't safe to hang around when it's like that. By the time I got back here, I was in tears. Flossie noticed and tried to comfort me, but she's so young she don't really understand. I think I've lost him forever.

Kate's Diary 6 November 1887

Oh joy! Today I received a huge bunch of flowers from Will and a note which asks me to meet him next Saturday evening to go to a concert at the new Queens Hall in Mile End

Road. He says he'll pick me up here and we'll go for supper first. I feel so happy again! He ended his note with:

'I miss you and love you, my darling. Don't let me down. All my love, Will.'

Of course, I won't let him down. I can't wait!

Kate's Diary 9 November 1887

Been to a wonderful musical concert with Will tonight. It was like nothing had ever been wrong between us. He never mentioned our argument. He probably just wants to forget it, so I didn't bring it up either.

The music was wonderful. It was so vibrant I felt I could almost touch the notes. They floated like magic in the air. I've never seen an orchestra before, so I was amazed by how good they were. Mind, Will said he reckoned he was as good as the violin players there and could have done just as well. Mebbee he's right. I know he's talented.

On the way out, I saw an exhibition of chrysanthemums advertised for next weekend and I begged Will to take me. He didn't seem keen, but I didn't give up and persuaded him to get us two tickets.

"They're only two pence," I said, "I'll pay if you like. Those flowers are real exotic and beautiful, so I've heard. It'll be grand."

Quite often, I seem to get side-tracked by him from the things I want to do, but this time I insisted, and he gave in. I'm sure he'll enjoy it when he gets there.

Kate's Diary 16 November 1887

Met up with Will today, expecting to go to the chrysanthemum show with him, but as often seems to happen, things didn't go to plan. He embraced me as normal when I arrived but then said how he was feeling real ill.

"You poor thing," I said. "What's wrong?"

"Oh, I feel so sick and dizzy," he told me. "I wasn't sure I could even make it here to meet you, but I didn't want to leave you standing here, waiting for me. I'm so sorry but I really don't think I can make it to the show today. It's so far. Why don't we just stay here for a while instead?"

I was concerned for him.

"I don't think that's a good idea in this weather, Will," I told him. "My da stayed out in the cold when he wasn't well and now, he's gone forever. I think you should go home and go to bed."

Will agreed I was probably right but said how sorry he was to disappoint me. He's so good to be always thinking of me.

"Please, can you see me home?" he asked. "I'm not sure how far I can walk."

We made slow progress back to his lodgings, which I'd never been to before. I did feel proper sorry for him; he looked so miserable.

"Can you come in and sit with me a while?" he said. "I'd feel better with some company."

I understood but couldn't risk my good reputation by going into a single man's lodgings without a chaperone.

"I can't, Will, I'm sorry," I told him. "It's not proper. People will talk."

"Let them!" he declared. "Who cares?"

103

"Well, I do," I explained tactfully, "and I'm sure you wouldn't want me to be compromised."

"No, no, of course not," he agreed. "I wasn't thinking, sorry."

We agreed to meet next week, so I headed off, but not home – no. I still went to the chrysanthemum show, although I did feel a bit guilty going without poor Will, but I'm sure he wouldn't have wanted me to miss it.

It was glorious; brightly coloured blossoms everywhere you looked, like a treasure trove of jewels. I had a great time and even bought meself a small bunch of bright yellow chrysanthemums to put in my bedroom. When I got back, however, Martha the cook saw me with them and exclaimed, "Yellow chrysanthemums – oh that's not good! They stand for *'lost love'*, they do."

She's right superstitious like that, but I tried not to take any notice. I wasn't about to throw away such beautiful flowers just because of some stupid belief. So now I'm lying in bed, watching the candlelight flickering around the yellow blooms, making them glow even more brightly. The only trouble is I keep thinking of what Martha said and hoping against hope that they won't turn out to be a bad omen. Oh well, time to blow the candle out and let things be.

Kate's Diary 20 November 1887

Wanted to go along to watch the protest in Trafalgar Square today but after last week's riots, Will told me I mustn't go. I feel I should because I'm Irish and it's my duty to support my countrymen, but Will was very firm.

"Don't be stupid, Kate! There'll be trouble again. Just look at what happened last week. You're not to go. Forget about it!"

It's true that there was lots of trouble last Sunday. Crowds of people tried to demonstrate in the square, mostly to prove that they had the right to do just that if they wanted to. There has been a ban on meetings there lately, since all the unemployed started camping out there in the summer. There's just not enough work to go around at the moment, and people are being made homeless. It's a dreadful shame.

The protest wasn't only about the Irish issue, but that was a part of it. They wanted the release of that MP who's in prison at the moment (can't remember his name), but the police moved in and were brutal by all accounts. Many people were badly injured, and loads were arrested.

I feel I should show solidarity, but I guess Will is right. I don't want no more problems at work either; I can't afford to lose me job, otherwise I'll be camping out too!

Kate's Diary 21 December 1887

I've had a grand time with Will these last few weeks. He's taken me out dancing and over to his married sister Mary's house, where he played his fiddle again. The music always brings me closer to him. It's like he's opening up his soul. I just wish I knew how I really feel. He was asking me last night.

"My dearest Kate," he said. "You know how much I love you. Please tell me that it's the same for you. You never say."

I found it so hard to know how to respond, so I tried to change the subject. It's awful because I want to be honest with him, but I don't yet know what my true emotions are. I know he loves me; he's always telling me so and it's obvious he means it, but I don't know if I feel the same. There are times when I am really fond of him, but at other times his sudden mood changes scare me. It's like I'm being swamped by a giant wave. His kisses are passionate but somehow, they don't seem right and I always pull away. When I was with George, I was almost overwhelmed by passion but it's not that way with Will. He's always fun to be around and so charming, but I can't fully commit meself to him yet. I don't want to just use him for entertainment; that wouldn't be fair and it's not my nature. Maybe my fling with George was nothing more than youthful desire and this is a more mature love. I don't know.

If *only* I could find out more about his inner demons. It's clear he has problems with some of his family. I keep meaning to try and talk to him about this, but it never seems to be the right moment. It's awkward to know how to start the conversation. If I could get to the bottom of it all, maybe I could understand him better and love him more. I must try.

Kate's Diary 28 January 1888

All day I've been trying to make sense of what happened last night. It being my birthday, Will asked me over to his sister Mary's house for a celebration. Normally she's there with her two children and sometimes her husband John as well, but when we got there, I was surprised to find they were all going out.

"I thought we were all going to be eating together," I said, confused.

"No dear," Mary replied, smiling. "Will wants you all to himself tonight as it's a special day. Make yourselves at home. We'll be back later; we're just taking the children to visit John's mother."

I was a bit worried about this as it meant that I wouldn't be chaperoned, but Will has never compromised me, so I let it go. Besides, they would probably be back quite soon.

Will bustled around getting us a meal, which Mary had kindly prepared in advance. It was quite delightful and felt just like we were a real couple. Will poured me a glass of wine to go with the meal and proposed a toast, "To you, my darling Kate, of 'full age' at last."

Glass after glass followed, and I was getting quite tipsy, in spite of my feeble attempts to prevent it.

"Please no, Will," I told him. "It's going to my head. I've had enough."

"Oh, go on, Kate, it's your birthday! Relax," he said persuasively.

The meal finished and we sat by the fire, where I was disturbed to find Will cuddling up very close to me.

"Will," I protested, "I think maybe we should…"

"Should what?" he replied. "Kate, you're 21 now and a full adult. Surely we deserve to be close."

He stroked my hair, and I began to feel uncomfortable.

"Close?" I said, "Well yes, but Will I'm not sure that I want to, well you know…" My voice trailed off. I was embarrassed and nervous.

His hand came up to rest on my bosom and his mouth came down hard on mine. His kiss tasted strongly of wine and I tried to pull away.

"No, Will, please! I don't want to."

He turned on me, looking annoyed.

"Why not, Kate? Are you just teasing me? Don't you know how much I want you? All this time you've only been leading me on and using me, is that it?"

"No, Will," I pleaded, "I'm very fond of you, really I am. I'm just not sure that I want to commit to something more at the moment."

Will was quite obviously drunk by then and didn't want to listen.

"Fond?" he sneered. "Sounds like the pet dog!"

My own head was whirling, partly from the drink and partly from the awkward situation I seemed to have got meself in. I tried to stand up to get away, but Will grabbed my arm and kept me there.

"Come on, Kate," he muttered drunkenly, his voice slurred, "don't be a tease."

He pushed me backwards on the couch and attempted to kiss me again, but I found some inner strength and wriggled out of his grasp.

"Leave me alone!" I cried. "I don't like this. Look, Will. I'm sorry but I can't see you again. This isn't working out."

I grabbed my cloak and headed for the door, a little unsteadily. Outside, it was cold and dark and I wasn't sure how best to get home, but I didn't care. I just needed to get away. I heard his voice behind me, calling, "Kate – come back! Don't be a fool. I love you. I didn't mean to upset you."

The frosty air slapped me in the face as I ran out into the night, tears streaming down. My memory of getting home is vague, but I distantly recall hailing a hansom cab. It cost a lot but was safer than trying to make it through the streets alone at that time of night. London can be a dangerous place, especially for a solitary woman.

In spite of the large quantity of wine I had drunk, sleep failed to come to me, and I rose this morning even more tired than when I went to bed.

Young Flossie saw my tear-stained face and tried to console me.

"It'll be all right, Miss Katie," she told me. "Don't worry."

But I've thought it over all day, and I know it's not going to be all right. It's over between me and Will. I suppose I *have* led him on, but I really *wanted* to love him. I'm just not sure that I can.

Kate's Diary 30 January 1888

Oh Will – why did you have to be like that? I feel so awful now. Today, I stood in the kitchen, tears pouring down like rain as I chopped the vegetables. Martha suddenly noticed and remarked, "Here Kate, take it easy! We don't need no more salt on those carrots! What's up, lass?"

Sadly, I told her the gist of it, expecting sympathy, but to my surprise she said, "Well that's men for you, dearie. Too much to drink and they all try it on. Can't expect nothing else, really. No need to take it too serious like."

"But I'm not that sort of girl," I protested, "and besides, I'm not sure if he's 'the one', if you know what I mean."

"It's never easy to be sure," she told me. "Just have to find out as you go along. No one's perfect, as they say. Can't keep waiting for no knight on a white charger to ride up. They don't exist!"

"Still," I said uncertainly, "surely I should feel more?"

"You gotta make the best of the chances you get," she said. "Don't waste 'em, my dear. You'll regret it."

This set me to thinking and I was overjoyed therefore when some flowers arrived later from Will, with a note which read:

Dear Kate

I love you. Let's try and put all this behind us. Meet me on Sunday at the usual place.

All my love, Will xx

Then I thought, *he hasn't even bothered to say he's sorry*, and I got so angry I flung the flowers into the nearest bin. Ten minutes later, however, I rescued them from their terrible fate and set them in a vase in my room. I can't bear to see flowers just wither and die. It seems so unfair to pick them and just leave them.

I've been through so many emotions today – heartache, anger, indignation, guilt – you name it, but I mustn't weaken. On Sunday, he'll be waiting there for nothing. I won't be going to meet him, but oh, how it tears my heart apart to think of it.

Kate's Diary 7 February 1888

All day I've been in torment, trying to be sensible and not see Will again. It was a cold, wet afternoon and the thought of him standing there forlornly in the pouring rain made me feel so bad that I nearly gave in. But now it's evening and I know the moment has come and gone. It's just as well really, but all the same…

Well, my chance of love with him has gone now. I know he'll never forgive me for letting him down, and I'm still angry with him for the way he behaved, so I guess we've reached the end. Oh misery!

Kate's Diary 3 March 1888

I'm determined not to give way to this creeping melancholy that is threatening to engulf me at the moment. So today being my day off, I went to the zoo just like I wanted to do before. It felt like I was defying Will in some way, which temporarily made me feel better.

It was a fine place, filled with exotic beasts I never seen the like of before, but somehow, I didn't enjoy it so much on my own. I've no one to talk to about it all and share things with. I thought I would feel free without Will, but I don't – I just feel lonely and miserable. I was stupid, throwing away what we had. Why couldn't things have been different? I miss him so much and every day it gets worse not better. Perhaps I really did love him after all.

Kate's Diary 19 April 1888

All change here at Bedford Square! What a surprise. Today, Mary and Tom announced they are leaving to get married and open a little grocers shop over in Camberwell, and last week, John the valet told us that he was going to have to 'retire', as he is too frail to carry on working. He is going to live with his sister in Brighton, as he says the sea air will do him good. He's been struggling to cope lately, so it was half expected. The master has offered to give John a long service payment as well, so that'll help him out.

The biggest surprise is that Mrs Stanley's leaving. She fell out with the mistress over something the other day, and yesterday she told us that she's found another job in a very grand house in Westminster. Says it's a step up for her and she's real glad to be leaving here. I was shocked how frank she was with us.

"I've had enough of the mistress's penny-pinching ways," she told us, "always scrimping and saving when they got plenty of money. Wouldn't be so bad, but she always expects the best quality of everything, but don't want to pay for it. Tight fisted, that's what it is, and I told her so!" She paused. "Well, I'll be sorry to leave all of you. You've been good workers and I'll miss you. If ever any of you want a reference, I'll be only too happy." Her voice sounded a bit choked up and she turned and left the room abruptly.

We all stared in shock.

"Well," said Sarah, the parlour maid, "that's a bit of an upset. Wonder who we'll get in place of her."

Martha, the cook, chipped in, "Well, I already heard some gossip from my friend Mabel that there's a real old dragon who's coming in, called Mrs Harper. She used to work in Hanover Square before this and everyone there hated her. Makes Mrs S look like a saint by comparison!"

Everyone groaned and went back to their work feeling depressed. Mrs Stanley is a fierce old thing, but always stands up for us when needed. You don't mess her around, that's for sure, but we all respect her. Why do things have to change? I was so happy here.

Kate's Diary 14 May 1888

Glad to have a day off today. The new housekeeper, Mrs Harper, is horrible. She shouts at everyone and we can't do nothing right. The whole house is different now and I don't seem to know where I am anymore. At least Mrs Stanley made me up to chamber maid before she left, as Mary was leaving. It's a fair sight better, though I don't get to hear so much gossip from Martha. I feel so lonely these days.

I still miss Will dreadfully, so I thought I'd go out and visit the Victoria and Albert Museum today to keep meself occupied. My route took me past Russell Square Gardens again and brought back painful but treasured memories of my time with Will. To my utter astonishment, just as I got past the entrance, who should I see but the man himself, walking slowly down the road with a woman on his arm. As we got closer, he realised it was me and his face lit up. I felt meself blush and would have hurried away but he seemed keen to say hello. The woman hanging on his arm looked quite rough and common, though I don't mean to be a snob (It ain't for me to judge). Her dress was a dirty dark red satin, torn in places, with heavy frills and flounces, a tight bodice and a cleavage far more on show than is proper. Her hair was in untidy ringlets and her face heavily made up.

"Kate," said Will awkwardly. "How are you? It's good to see you again."

I noticed at once that he was as handsome as ever; his dark hair and brooding eyes seeming to add a charisma I hadn't seen before. He smiled at me and I felt my heart melt. Had I really turned this man away? I must have been mad.

"I'm fine," I replied hesitantly, then blurted out accidentally, "I've missed you!"

"Sorry," I stammered, when I realised what I'd said, "I didn't mean – well you know…" my voice trailed off.

"It's okay," said Will. "I've missed you too."

"'Ere!" interrupted the woman by his side. "Who's this then? You going to introduce us or what?"

"Sorry, yes, Hettie this is Kate, an old friend. Kate – Hettie. She works down the market."

"How do you do?" I said politely and held out my hand, but she laughed.

"Oh my, we're a grand one, ain't we? How do you do, dearie! Come on Will, are we going to the park now?"

"Yes," he replied but I could see his heart wasn't in it.

"Are you still in the same house, Kate? Maybe I could call?" he asked me.

"Yes, I am, that would be nice."

We moved off and I could hardly control my emotions. I feel so mixed up – happy that he wants to see me again but distraught at the thought that he has another woman. I realise now that I must have loved him all along but didn't know it. I am so jealous of Hettie. Why has he taken up with such a cheap, down at heel sort? He can do better than that. Maybe it is only for one thing. Why should I care anyway? Oh, but I do care! My hopes keep rising like green shoots in the spring, against all reason – hopes that he will call and maybe we can start again. If only.

Kate's Diary 31 May 1888

Two weeks have come and gone and still no contact from Will. I feel more and more desperate as each day goes by and my mind is not on my job. Mrs Harper disciplined me yesterday for not dusting one of the shelves in the master's bedroom.

"Any more slacking, miss," she thundered, "and you'll be out on your ear! And don't think you'll be getting a reference either! Can't understand why Mrs Stanley let you have this job – you don't deserve it."

She was fierce horrible to me, but she's right really. I was daydreaming and missed the shelf completely. All I could do was to beg her forgiveness and promise to do better in future. It ain't like me normally. What has happened?

Kate's Diary 14 June 1888

That's it! I've had it with Will. It's been a month since I saw him, and he still hasn't called. If he comes 'round now I shall tell him to go away. He was obviously just teasing me. And yet, when he smiled…no, no, he didn't mean it! It was all a lie. I don't care anyway. I must be strong.

Kate's Diary 21 June 1888

What a day! Today I got back from church to find Will outside the house, waiting for me.

"Kate," he called. "Hurry up and get ready. We're going out."

The mistress looked at me disapprovingly but Sunday afternoons are my free time and so I ignored her. My heart was pounding as I collected my things from the bedroom. Half excited, half annoyed – I could hardly think straight. Flossie saw me leaving, and said, "It's that man again isn't it? That one who made you cry. Be careful, Miss Katie."

"I will," I reassured her calmly, but inside I was in turmoil. My stomach was fair doing somersaults and my breath came fast. I rushed downstairs to meet Will.

It's been a real fine day today and Will suggested we walk in the park again. My reaction was cool (at least I like to think so) but I supposed it could do no harm to listen to what he had to say.

"Dear Kate," he began, "I've wanted to see you so much."

"I can't see that," I replied coldly, "otherwise you'd've visited a deal earlier."

"Kate, please," he pleaded, "I couldn't give Hettie up just like that, it wouldn't have been fair. 'Sides, she was not that easy to give up, if you know what I mean. She was rather clingy."

"Well, you shouldn't take up with that sort of woman," I told him stiffly. "She's no good."

"I know that now, Kate, but I was so lonely without you, and a man needs feminine company, you know."

"Oh yes?" I said, "for one thing, I suppose, like you tried it on with me!"

"No!" he cried, "Kate darling, I was drunk and overcome with passion for you, my love. I'm sorry. I never meant for that to happen. If you give me another chance, I'll never do that again. I promise."

I considered his words and felt my heart melting. Maybe it was true. I know we'd both had a lot to drink that night. *Perhaps I should forgive him*, I thought. We sat down on a park bench under the lime trees. The scent of the new mown grass was heady, and insects buzzed around us, busy with their work. It was such a beautiful day; it was hard to stay cross with him.

Will took my silence for a good sign and held my hand gently.

"Kate," he murmured. "You're all I want, believe me."

I hesitated and knew suddenly that I wanted him too, but that I needed to know more about him.

"Will," I said seriously, "you asked me before if I loved you, and I wasn't sure, but now I feel that I do."

"That's wonderful!" he exclaimed.

"However," I continued, "I need to know more about you Will, to be able to understand you and love you properly. If we're to start again, then I want you to tell me about your family, especially your mother."

His face changed. A shadow of pain and anger fell across it.

"That's none of your business!" he snapped, rather surprising me by his reaction.

I stayed calm.

"I'm afraid it is, Will. If you want me to love you fully then you need to open up. I can't love what I don't understand."

He stood up and walked away a little, and I didn't attempt to follow. A few minutes went by, then he returned to the seat.

"My mother hates me," he began, "and loves my younger brother James above all else! Is that what you want to hear?" His tone was angry and sarcastic now.

"Will, please, just calm down and tell me about it."

His head drooped and he was suddenly overcome with emotion.

"Oh, Kate. I was so close to my father. I idolised him, I suppose. Mother has always loved James best. The rest of us don't get a look in. When my father passed away, I tried to

117

get closer to Mother, but she turned me away. Amelia feels the same. Nothing we do is good enough for her. She's evil!"

He broke down into huge, gasping sobs and I held him gently, trying my best to soothe and comfort him. Having seen his vulnerability, at last I felt ready to give him my heart. When his distress subsided, I told him.

"Will, I'm so glad you've shared this with me. I now feel that I understand you and can truly love you."

"Can you really, Kate?" he asked, his eyes shining. "You know I love you more than anyone in the world. Can we start again?"

So, we have and I'm so happy. At last I know that I love him, and I think we have a future. I hope so.

Kate's Diary 2 September 1888

Not seen much of Martha lately, so it was grand to catch up today when the mistress had a big dinner party and we all had to help out in the kitchen.

There was much talk below stairs of the dreadful killing of a young woman recently in the Whitechapel area, one dark foggy night.

"People say there's a madman on the loose, prowling on women, so you look out my dears," Martha warned us all. "Take care which gents you're seeing now. You never know who or what they might turn out to be!"

Then Martha turned her attentions on me.

"'Ere Kate – what you been up to, lately?" she asked in her usual forthright manner. "Rumour has it that you're seeing that young man again."

I blushed. I usually try to keep things to meself, but there ain't no getting away from Martha. She always likes to know everything, though she's a kind soul.

"Yes, we've made a new start," I admitted. "It seems to be going well."

"So, you forgave him then?" she said. "Good on yer! Makes sense, really. There's none of 'em any better than any other. Might as well catch 'im while you can!"

"Martha, really!" I protested. "I'm not out to catch him."

"Oh, come off it, dearie. We all need a man to provide for us in the long run. Stands to reason. I wouldn't be working here if my Stan was still alive. I'd be able to have me own house."

She looked a bit dreamy eyed for a minute.

"Wouldn't have to work for 'Madam' there and put up with that old battle-axe, Harper. If you get the chance to get outta here girlie, you take it! Best thing you can do."

Work intervened at that moment and thankfully the subject changed. Still, there's much sense in what she says and certainly something to think about.

Later, I found meself daydreaming as I set the table, imagining my own front room laid for dinner; but it don't do no good to get too carried away. Probably only lead to disappointment.

Kate's Diary 9 Sept 1888

I've been having a grand time with Will these last few months. It's been a real craic. We've been to shows, museums, dances and even visited each other's families, which hasn't gone too badly on the whole. Today, however, was rather disturbing and I can't get it out of my mind.

We were over at his mother's house, and as usual, she was getting him to do all the chores whilst he was there. Amelia was out at the shops, so I volunteered to make the afternoon tea, whilst Will got some more logs in for the fire. As I bustled around the kitchen, Amelia came in the back door.

"Hello, Kate," she said, "how are you? I can make the tea now I'm here, if you like."

"No, it's all right. Have a rest," I told her. "You always seem to be working so hard."

"Well, Mother can be demanding, it's true," she replied, "but she's had a hard life."

"I expect you miss your father a lot, don't you?" I said, innocently. "Will told me how much you all looked up to him."

"Looked up to him? Well, Will might have done, but not me. Father was an unpleasant drunk!" She flushed with embarrassment at her sudden outspokenness.

"Really?" I said, confused, "but I thought…"

"Look, Kate, be careful," she told me. "I know Will's my brother, but, well…" She paused, reluctant to continue but obviously wanting to share something with me.

"Well, what?" I asked. "Please tell me."

"It's just that Will's not quite what he seems," she said. "Take care."

"I don't understand," I said, but got no more out of her. She hurriedly gathered up the tea and took it into the living room, making further conversation impossible. Just then Will came back in with the firewood as well.

Since then, I've tried to dismiss this from my mind, but it lingers there still, like a fungus growing in the dark. What did she mean? Why did she feel the need to warn me? I wondered whether I should mention this to Will but decided against it. I'm sure it will only upset him.

Kate's Diary 15 September 1888

It's no good. My mind refuses to let go of the words Amelia said to me the other day. They just go round and round my head. Even at night, they haunt my dreams. I have to speak to Will.

Kate's Diary 30 Sept 1888

Feeling much happier now. I know now that I was just being stupid and panicking. It even crossed my mind that Will might be the 'Whitechapel Murderer', but it was just my paranoia and the general air of suspicion that seems to be everywhere at the moment.

Managed to speak to Will today. The chance came because he was in a really low mood already because of an argument he'd had with his mother earlier. He was bitter and angry but at least he opened up about it instead of brooding to himself. I really feel that I can help him through this, in time. Seems it's all down to being compared with James again.

"If only Mother would recognise what *I* do for her, instead of just him. He's hardly ever there, but he gets all the praise. It was all different when Father was alive."

I comforted and soothed him with kisses, talking it through bit by bit, until he became calmer. Then I decided to broach the subject of my own tormenting thoughts.

"When I saw Amelia last time," I began, "we talked a bit about your father."

"What did she say?" he demanded; his eyes instantly hostile. "Why did you have to talk to her about that?"

"Will, please. I was only making conversation. I just told her that I understood how much she must miss him."

"What did she say?" he repeated, but more calmly this time.

I chose my words carefully, not wanting to get her in trouble.

"Oh, she told me he was quite a character and that life's not the same without him," I answered tactfully (I suppose I was lying a bit, but it was almost the truth).

"Oh," said Will, "well yes. That's certainly true. I'm glad she said that. We don't always see eye to eye over some things."

"She did mention he could be a bit difficult at times," I added.

"Difficult? Well yes, I suppose he had his moments, but he was a fine man; strong, powerful, never one to suffer fools gladly. I could never hope to live up to him."

"You don't need to, Will," I reassured him. "It's true that strength is attractive but so is kindness and gentleness. There's nothing wrong with being vulnerable. You're wonderful just the way you are. I wouldn't want you to be any different."

Our emotions overspilled like a flooding river and he held me tightly in his arms, kissing me again and again. There were tears in his eyes and I felt so close to him at that moment. All my fears faded away.

After a few moments, he said, "You do me so much good, Kate. You make me calmer and happier. I'm always flying off the handle, I know, but I don't mean anything by it. I love you, Kate, and I'd never hurt you. You're the best thing that's ever happened to me."

I responded, saying, "I feel the same, Will. You've changed my life for the better."

Then suddenly, he said, "Why don't we get married, Kate, make it permanent?"

I hesitated. I love him dearly, but Amelia's warning still sounded faintly in my head.

"It's all a bit soon, Will," I explained. "Let's not rush into anything."

He looked disappointed, so I added, "I love you very much, my dearest. I just need more time. After all, we've only been together again a short while."

He looked relieved and smiled. "So, you'll think about it?" he asked.

"Of course," I said and relaxed into his arms again. It feels so good to have him hold me and I can't imagine life without him. And yet, something made me reluctant to accept his proposal this afternoon. I'm not sure why. Was it just what Amelia said, or something else? Maybe time will bring me the answer.

Kate's Diary 3 October 1888

Dreadful news about all these murders in Whitechapel. I'm always careful to make sure Will escorts me home now, after we've been out on the town. Can't be too careful with 'The Ripper' around. Makes me fair shudder to think of what he did to those poor women. At least I was with Will at the time it happened, so any lingering doubts can be put to rest, thank goodness.

Kate's Diary 10 October 1888

That awful woman Mrs Harper has gone and sacked dear Flossie! It's dreadful. The poor young girl's been doing her best, but the old cow says she's no good at her job and dismissed her without even a reference. What's more, she's sent her back to the workhouse!

I saw Flossie this evening as she packed up her things before she left. She was crying fit to burst and was in a right state, almost hysterical. I felt so helpless. I did my best to comfort her and promised to come and visit, but it was a sad occasion. I'll miss her. There's hardly any of my friends left here now. It feels like I'm being abandoned. I just wish I could leave.

This whole place seems to be falling apart. Last week, Alfie walked out, telling Mrs H she could stuff her job. He ain't worried, he's got something else already, but poor Flossie – I just wish I could help her. There must be something I can do.

Kate's Diary 21 October 1888

Been feeling real awful about poor Flossie so decided to take some action. After making a few enquiries, I went to see her at the workhouse today. The supervisor there – a grim looking matron, all in grey – was reluctant to let me in, but I insisted. Flossie fell on me with squeals of delight when she saw me, and I was soon able to make her happier still. I've arranged for her to go to one of the nearby MABYS ('Association for Befriending Young Servants') homes, just like Mam did for me, and I've paid the fees upfront, so she'll get lodgings, training and a decent work placement in the future. They were a real help to me, so I hope things will work out for her too. When I left the workhouse this afternoon, Flossie came with me and I took her straight to the home. She was so grateful but she don't need to be. She's a good girl and I wish her well.

On the way there, we chatted, and she asked me if I'd accepted Will's proposal yet.

"Not yet," I told her, "maybe soon."

"Aren't you sure about him, then?" Flossie asked, concerned.

"Oh yes, of course I am," I said. "I love him."

"Then why not accept him, Miss Katie?"

"I can't say exactly," I told her. "It's just such a big step. I'm a bit nervous."

Flossie squeezed my hand.

"I hope he makes you very happy, Miss Katie. You're such a good person. You deserve it."

My mind has been swimming with thoughts of marriage all week and I even caught meself looking in a shop window at wedding dresses. Maybe the time has come to take the plunge?

Kate's Diary 31 October 1888

It feels like the world shifted on its axis today. Things have changed dramatically and my life, I know, will never be the same again.

When I met Will today, it was immediately obvious that something was wrong. His face was flushed with rage and he was breathing heavily.

"What's happened, Will?" I asked him in alarm. "You look dreadful."

He could hardly speak. "Come with me," he stammered, "I need to show you something."

As we walked, I managed to get out of him some of the details of what had happened. Apparently when he went to see his mother, she had a long list of chores for him to do as usual. When he told her he couldn't stay long because he was meeting me, she went mad at him.

"How dare you be so selfish? Don't you realise I'm just a helpless old woman? You don't know what it's like to be old and frail. You're just like your father – a lazy good for nothing! He was never there when I needed him. You're just the same, you don't care about me at all. The only one you think about is that fancy woman of yours. At least James cares!"

From what I gather, Will lost his temper completely and vented his full fury on her. He admitted to me that he had thrown things around in his frustration and broken a much-treasured vase. There was a storm of abuse on both sides, I believe, and then he left the house, vowing never to return.

"What hurts the most," he told me, "is the way she insulted Father. He always did everything around the house for her and yet all she can do is criticise him. It's not fair. He can't defend himself now."

We had reached Will's lodgings and went in. Normally, I wouldn't have, but he insisted that he wanted me to see something.

"It ain't respectable, Will," I told him. "I really shouldn't."

"Just for a moment, Kate, please!" he begged, so I gave in.

Once inside, he made me sit on the couch whilst he fetched out some photographs of his father. Looking through them, I could see that he had been a commanding presence, tall, dark and forceful.

As we talked, Will's anger ebbed away like the waves at low tide. It was replaced by a desperate sadness, however. His tears fell and he laid his head on my shoulder. Gently, I held him, stroking his hair, trying to ease his pain. We nestled closer. All I wanted was to make him happy again. I kissed him tenderly and he responded eagerly, needing the physical contact.

Our kisses became more passionate and I was aware of his hands moving about, touching my breasts and awakening strange, new feelings I had never experienced before. My body began to tingle with pleasure, and, against my better judgement, I let him explore further. My own inexperienced hands fumbled in response until he led them into deeper, more hidden areas. He started to undo the buttons on my bodice and (to my shame) I helped him. All I could think of was the delicious sensations coursing through me, like a tidal wave, which I didn't want to stop. And stop, they certainly didn't. I'm shocked to think of what we did. I never intended it, but it felt so right. I just wanted to heal his heartache.

After the pleasure beforehand, the act itself was almost disappointing. It was fast and rough, leaving me sore and bleeding. Mam had already warned me that this is what happens when you first lie with a man, so I wasn't worried, but it hurt nonetheless. Will was loving and gentle afterwards.

"My darling Kate," he said. "That was wonderful. Now please say you'll marry me."

I felt that I had to agree now, which made him very happy. I can't see that I've got much choice, after all I could be 'with child' already. Will's been pressuring me for an answer these last few weeks and I had practically made up my mind in any case, so I might as well.

I know I should be really happy, but I feel in a state of shock. My life has changed forever and there's no going back. What's done can't be undone, to be sure. I guess I just need time to adjust.

Kate's Diary 1 December 1888

Last night, I dreamt I was standing on a high cliff on the lovely Emerald Coast, between Cork and Waterford. I was so happy to be home again. The land was green and the sky a vivid blue, but then I looked down at the sea and saw that it was dark and raging. The water seemed to boil with fury, foam dancing upon the waves. I leaned over to get a better view and could see sharp rocks just below the surface. Something seemed to urge me forwards and suddenly I was falling towards it, screaming but making no sound. Then I woke up, thank the Lord, before I hit either the rocks or the angry sea. My heart was racing so fast and I was sweating; it seemed so real. What does it mean, I wonder?

Today was my last working day here and tomorrow morning I am to marry Will. I am so happy, but nervous as well. That's probably what sparked that awful dream, I expect

128

(To be sure, I don't want no more like that!). My things are packed, and my wedding dress is hanging up ready. Flossie is going to be my flower girl and dear Elsie and Lizzie will both be there, as well as most of our families. I'm glad Will has sort of made it up with his Mam now. We don't need no trouble at the start of our married life.

'Married life' – that sounds strange! Will I ever get used to being called 'Mrs Duffield'? I've heard tell that, once you become a wife, you don't get much say in anything anymore. Well, that's what they say, but I won't believe it. Will is a good man who will respect me and look after me, I know. He'd never order me around or treat me badly. He loves me far too much. Oh, I can't wait for tomorrow!

Joe's Recollections, March 1905

The day we entered the workhouse will stay imprinted on my memory forever. It was only the day after the men had taken away our furniture that Mum told us all to pack as we were moving home. We'd done that before, for some reason or other, so it didn't particularly worry us. We dutifully got our things together and followed Mum outside to a waiting horse and cart.

"Where's the new house, Mum?" asked Ern enthusiastically. "Will we have to change schools as well? Can I have my own room this time?"

"I don't know," muttered our mother. "Wait and see."

After a while, we turned a corner and caught sight of a large, graceful looking building, complete with towers and spires, which made Fred suddenly exclaim, "I recognise that place, Mum. Isn't that the hospital that Ern and I were in when we were little?"

"Yes," agreed Ern, "and I went to it again when I had influenza that time, didn't I?"

Mum nodded. "Yes, that's St Saviour's Infirmary," she replied.

I thought maybe that's where we were going but the horse and cart plodded on, until it pulled up alongside a much larger and gloomier looking building. It was grey and imposing, with an air of misery hanging over it.

"Mum!" exclaimed Ern. "That's Newington Workhouse. Why have we stopped here?"

"We're just going to stay here for a while," she explained, but the words sounded as if they were choked out of her. "Just while my arm's bad and I can't work." (She'd been taking in washing and doing cleaning jobs lately)

"Is Father going to come here with us?" asked Albert.

"No dear, he's working, hoping to pay off all the er…well, the bills, so that we can get a new house all together very soon."

Albert started to cry and wail loudly. "I want my Dad. Where is he? Why have you taken us away from him?"

Meanwhile, Fred, who was the oldest, also exclaimed loudly. "This isn't fair! Why should we be here? I don't want to live here!"

I didn't really understand what the place was, but it all seemed very scary and so, affected by everyone else, I started to cry as well. Bill, who was only a toddler, was blissfully unaware and cuddled in tighter to our mother. So it was that our poor mother entered the workhouse with a group of crying, protesting and angry young children.

Firstly, we were all taken to see the Relieving Officer, who interviewed my mother at length, bombarding her with personal questions about our financial circumstances and her marriage. The paperwork took hours. Meanwhile, we children waited in a cold, bare room, wondering if we would ever see her again. Mum was in tears at the end of it, and told me, many years later, that they'd made her feel worth less than nothing.

Once reunited, we were all taken into a receiving ward, where a doctor checked us over, then we were all stripped, bathed and had our hair cut very short. Our own clothes were taken away and we were given a workhouse uniform to wear. The material was stiff and uncomfortable and rubbed my skin in places. I'd worn my favourite brown jacket that day, and even though it had holes in both elbows, I cried when it was taken away. Mum tried to reassure me that I'd get it back when we left, and in the event, I did, but by then I'd grown, and it no longer fitted me.

We spent the first night there all together, huddled into just two beds between us. Worse was to come the next day, however, when we learnt the awful truth that we were all going to be split up in different sections. Fred, Ern and Albert, being over 7 years old, would be going to one area, whilst I would stay in the children's area with some access to our mother, and little Bill would stay with Mum in the babies' room. I now believe this was the cause of our sibling relationships disintegrating, as I hardly saw anything of my brothers in the next few years. Mum was allowed to see me daily at first and I got to see Bill as well. These evenings were precious times. Mum would sing us beautiful Irish folk songs and tell stories of mighty Irish warriors, long since passed into eternity. Her tales of Cuchulain still haunt me even now.

The daily routine consisted of rising at 6am, followed by exercise, prayers, breakfast, history, maths, reading and writing, more prayers and bed. There were breaks for dinner and supper, but little time for play.

However, two weeks later, horror of horrors, we found out that we were all being transferred to Hanwell District School. This was also run by Newington, the aim being to provide education away from the harsh conditions of the workhouse. The last evening before we were due to move, we were gathered together as a family again. However, even in that short time much damage had been done. Albert was sulky and sullen, Fred and Ern angry and I was just confused. I felt so lost and lonely every day; only seeing Mum and Bill in the evenings and never seeing the others. Albert was equally isolated, our two older brothers being in a different section to him. What's more, he blamed our mother for taking him away from the father he adored. Mum looked tired and strained. In spite of the broken arm, she was still expected to work to earn her keep. She tried her best to be positive, explaining to us that we'd all be home again soon and that we would benefit by being at a good school in the meantime. Her words sounded hollow even to me. Our last evening was marred by arguments and tears from all of us, except Bill. Father had promised to visit but had not appeared. Thinking back now, I realise our Mum must have been devastated by his abandonment of us all, but she never said a word.

Early the next morning, we were forcibly removed. I screamed and screamed as they pulled me away from her and took us off to another strange, unfriendly looking building. Here, I was separated from my brothers yet again and did not see more than a brief glimpse of them for almost three years.

As I was in the infant's section, I was occasionally permitted to visit Mum and my baby brother at the weekend, but it wasn't often enough for me. Bill stayed with our Mum until he too became old enough to attend school, when he followed the rest of us.

The proposed 'short stay' whilst Mum's arm healed, lengthened unexpectedly when she became ill with her first episode of tuberculosis towards the end of the third month. She was admitted to the workhouse infirmary for several months, and by the time she came out, she was so frail she could barely stand, let alone care for us, so she stayed on in the workhouse. Unfortunately, recurrent bouts of ill health continued to afflict her for the next year or so, and she struggled to regain her health.

At school, I learnt history, geography and science as well as English and maths. The older boys also learnt some useful work skills. However, there were many diseases, such as the eye disorder opthalmia (which thankfully I avoided) and ringworm (which unfortunately I didn't). My head was shaved completely and treated with iodine, in order to get rid of this unpleasant infection. This led me to suffer much teasing from the other boys, until fate intervened, and they too went down with it.

Discipline was overwhelmingly strict, minor offences being punished every Friday morning in the gymnasium. I particularly remember one occasion, when my poor friend Robbie was laid face down on a desk and subjected to several brutal strokes of the cane, after which he fainted and had to be carried away to the infirmary. I somehow managed to avoid these punishments, which was a miracle in itself, as often pupils were punished just on hearsay without any proof. The unfairness of this didn't occur to me at the time, even though I was now in the older boys' section. It was just the way it was.

When Bill started infants' school in 1907, Mum was finally able to move back home with Father. He'd got another house now and had paid off his creditors for the time being, but he didn't seem to want, or maybe couldn't afford, to keep us kids, so we struggled on at the school. Sometimes, our mum would come and discharge us and take us home for the weekend, which was glorious, though Father was never very welcoming. We would briefly enjoy a wonderful time of freedom and fun, but then on Monday morning we would all be back there once again.

One weekend, I remember Mum took us all to Southend for the day and we got to go on the pier, which was wonderful. I'd never seen the seaside before, and it was an experience I never forgot. So much sea and sand! Father came as well that time, but was sullen and withdrawn, as if he'd been dragged there against his will.

We ran along the pier, enjoying all the amusements on offer and trying every ride available. At one point, I looked back and saw Mum leaning on the rail, looking out to sea.

"Mum, look at me!" I called and she turned, smiling. She looked so beautiful then, tall and slim with her long dark hair blowing freely in the breeze, and I felt my heart swell with love for her. It was a perfect moment, an image forever captured in my memory.

I have to admit it always seemed strange when we brothers were back together again. I hardly knew any of them anymore. We had become strangers. Despite the efforts that

Mum made to make us feel like a family, school became the norm and home the oddity.

As a child, I always wondered why Mum didn't come and take us home for good. She had now recovered her health and was working again; couldn't she see that we weren't happy at Hanwell? I know Albert felt that it was all her fault that we had to stay there. He blamed her for her illness, and kept saying that she didn't care about us, but I don't think that was true. It was obvious how much she loved us. Still, each time we were taken back to the school I kept hoping that this would be the last.

"Mum," I asked her once. "Why can't we come home?"

She flushed bright red. "You will do very soon, Joe, I promise. We're just getting things sorted out at home."

I thought I saw tears in her eyes, but in spite of this, the promises kept getting broken. Even now, I can't really understand it.

I'm sorry, I can't talk about this anymore now. We'll have to carry on another day.

Kate's Diary 10 December 1888 Broadwall

At last, I've got time to write this journal again. This week has been a whirlwind, but I want to try and capture it on paper before these bright shining memories fade and dim with the passing of time. I know that even a day or two can make you look back at things differently, and details get so quickly forgotten, so here goes.

Our wedding day was surprisingly dry and bright, in spite of the time of year, though it was chilly, and I shivered in my flimsy lace dress. When I saw Will at the church, he looked so handsome I thought my heart would burst. He was real emotional, which was so sweet, and he got fair choked up as he said his vows. '*Love, honour and cherish*', he promised – it sounded so lovely. I responded with '*Love, honour and obey*'. I wonder why it has to be different wording for women. Obviously, I'll obey my husband anyway as he's the man I love, but I do think it makes me sound a bit like a servant.

Of course, it was Church of England, not a Catholic church, which was a shame. I'd a liked a traditional Irish service with confession and all but it weren't to be. A wedding between a Catholic and a Protestant is only legal if it's a Protestant service, over here. Mam was there, of course, and she remarked how it weren't her idea of a wedding, but what do she know? She still acted as a witness anyway, despite her grumbling, and even brought my Aunt Louisa along, who I'd never met before (she seems a kindly soul, and she looked after Mam all day, which I was glad about, as she's not as strong as she used to be). I dare say our service was a deal shorter than an Irish one, which was good really. All that standing around fair tires you out.

Sadly, Pat and Jenny couldn't make it. They've got two young children now and can't travel so far. Pat sent me a brief note apologising. I understand of course but it made me feel real sad for a while. Will told me to forget about it.

"Family don't matter much," he said. "It's you and me that count."

I expect he's right, but all the same…

After the ceremony, there was a photographer, who wanted to take one of them fancy portraits of the newlyweds! I've never had me picture taken before, and I was quite nervous but actually it was easy. We went to his studio, which was next to the church, and then had to stand really still for ages. Will started getting annoyed because it was taking so long and at one point he threatened to walk out, but I pleaded with him not to.

"Please, Will, this is such a special day. We want to be able to remember it, don't we?"

He grumbled and muttered under his breath but put up with it, just to please me.

The wedding breakfast was grand (Everyone has been so good, chipping in to help provide such a fine spread). We chatted to all our friends and family, and then a band played some tunes so we could dance. The only trouble is it all went on a bit too long and we had a train to catch. Will's mam had given us the money to take a 'wedding tour' (bit of a grand name that for a few days in Southend, but still!). Anyway, Elsie's husband James offered to drive us to the railway station in his horse and cart, so we could just sit back and enjoy the ride. It felt fair grand to be taken like royalty along the roads to the station. James had done up the cart with white ribbons and flowers, and lots of people turned to wave to us, wishing us well. But when we got there, disaster struck. James dropped us off and we made for the platform, unaware that we were already too late. The train had left ten minutes earlier! Will went mad then, swearing and shouting abuse about poor James.

"It's all his fault! Why did he have to drive so slowly? The idiot! He's ruined everything."

I know Will was only upset because he didn't want me to be disappointed, but I wish he'd been a bit calmer all the same. While he was storming up and down the platform, I went and found a railway official who was able to reassure me that another train to Southend was expected in just over an hour. Encouraged, I returned to Will with the information.

"Where have you been?" he demanded. "What's going on?"

"Calm down, my darling," I said. "I was just finding out about the next train. It won't be very long, it's due at 4 o'clock. We can get on that one, so that's good news."

"Over an hour to wait!" he exclaimed bitterly. "I don't call that good news. That stupid numbskull, James – he's so slow. Why did you have to ask him to take us? Are you mad?"

"There's no need to be like that, Will," I said stiffly. "I only asked him because you suggested it. It seemed like a good idea."

"Well, it wasn't!" he cried and stomped up the platform towards the waiting room. I followed slowly. *What a great start to married life, this is*, I thought.

"Well come on!" he said. "We might as well wait in here – a whole hour – really, I ask you!"

For the next hour and until we were safely on the train, I heard little else except his angry complaints. I sat there quietly, feeling desperately sad that the day was ruined. Once the train started moving, Will sighed and said, "Finally!" It was then that I decided that I must speak my mind, but I tried to stay calm.

"Look, Will," I said, "I know this is a disappointment, but it's happened and that's all there is to it. This is our wedding day, please don't ruin it."

With that I felt myself welling up with tears, all the hurt and distress spilled out and I couldn't stop it.

Will saw me crying and immediately became contrite.

"My darling, I'm so sorry! I didn't mean to upset you. I was just so disappointed for your sake. I know it's not your fault. I promise I won't say another word about it. Let's just enjoy ourselves now."

We kissed amidst the tears and made up. The rest of the journey was pleasant and, thankfully, uneventful. I hope we don't have too many of those kind of scenes in future. It's so hard to deal with. Will's moods seem to sweep through him like a wildfire, destroying everything in its path. Reason and common sense just disappear.

That night, we made love in a boarding house in Southend. I'd hoped for a hotel, but this was the best we could afford. It was basic but clean, and the landlady had a saucy sense of humour.

"Oh, newlyweds!" she chortled. "Watch those bedsprings, won't you, me dearies!" And she went off, laughing at her own remarks.

We went out to eat first, and also drank a great deal, it must be admitted. By the time we got back to the house, we were rather unsteady on our feet. Our love making, consequently, was clumsy and inept, but at least it wasn't our first time. There'll be plenty more chances to get it right, I'm sure. We awoke late in the morning rather hungover and sore and staggered down to breakfast. After some nourishment, we felt strong enough to face the sea air of Southend and set out to explore the town. The pier is only partly open at the moment, as they are busy building a very grand new one made of iron. They say it's going to be the longest one in Britain once it's finished. We walked out as far as we could and took in all the entertainments on offer. It was strange to be standing over the waves looking down and it reminded me, just for a moment, of my dream the other night.

Southend is a fun place to be, full of stalls, fairground rides, music halls, theatres etc. There was so much to do there that the three days we had just disappeared like a puff of smoke. Every night, we were out drinking and dancing. It was a mighty craic, just like Ireland, but with the seaside thrown in as well. We had a fine time.

Will went back to work on Thursday and I was left in our new home to 'keep house'.

We've got a tiny, terraced house in Southwark, which Will says will be handy for the printing firm he works at. I might have to take in some washing to make ends meet, as he only earns about a pound a week and our rent is 6 shillings. Then we've got to eat of course and pay the bills, but I shall try hard to make the money stretch. We had to do this in Ireland all the time, so it ain't new to me. Anyway, I don't mind doing some work as well. It helps me to feel useful. If we have any little ones, of course, I may not be able to do so much, but we'll have to see how it goes.

It's so wonderful to have our own place. Mind, there's only one bedroom, a small parlour and a basic kitchen with a privy out the back, but I shall clean everywhere until it shines so bright that folks will stop and stare with admiration. It will be my pride and joy.

When Will came home at night, I had supper ready for him and he was real impressed.

"My darling little wife," he said smiling. "What a wonderful girl you are; everything a man could want."

The future looks bright to me. I keep dreaming of a house filled with children's laughter and us, the happy couple, loving and living to a ripe old age. I can't see why that shouldn't happen, so here's to us!

Kate's Diary 20 December 1888

Oh, I'm so looking forward to Christmas this year; spending it with Will in our own home. It will be grand. I'm fierce determined to do a real traditional Irish Christmas with saltling and candles and spiced beef, just like Mam used to do. Will is sure to enjoy it. He's always saying that's one of the things he loves most about me – my Irishness. The only thing I'm a bit nervous about is that both mams are coming over on Boxing Day for lunch. Not sure how they'll get on; they didn't mix much at the wedding. Oh well, fingers crossed!

Kate's Diary 2 January 1889

So that's Christmas over then. Didn't exactly go as well as I hoped; still, it could have been worse. By the time Will came home from work on Christmas Eve, I'd made the house look fierce beautiful. There were candles everywhere, casting their lovely flickering light and making enormous shadows from everyday objects. I'd put greenery around as well and Will was real impressed.

"Candles!" he exclaimed. "How romantic! Just the thing for a quiet night in with the two of us alone."

His arm went round my waist and he held me fondly. I felt warm and happy inside but then I had to break the news to him about going to midnight mass.

"What?" he said, "Church again? But we only went on Sunday last. Surely we don't need to spoil Christmas Eve by going to church."

"But that's what Christmas is all about, Will," I explained, "and it means a lot to me."

"But darling," he persisted, smiling suggestively, "I'm sure there are better things we could do here."

I tried to keep things light and playful.

"There'll still be plenty of time for 'other things' later," I smiled, "and I'll cook you a lovely hot supper as well."

"Oh, all right then," he said, reluctantly giving in.

It was a beautiful service, despite it being C of E and not Catholic. The church echoed with song and glowed with candlelight. As we walked home, Will took my arm protectively and I was proud to be by his side.

Supper, unfortunately, was a disaster. I served up the saltling proudly, but Will poked at it gingerly with his fork and sniffed.

"What on earth's that?" he asked.

I explained. "It's a traditional Irish dish – saltling. You like fish, Will, so I'm sure you'll enjoy it."

"The fish I eat ain't anything like this," he grumbled and pushed it around on his plate. "It's in some kind of sauce or something."

"Just try a bit," I coaxed. But as soon as he did, he spat it out in disgust.

"It's awful!" he exclaimed. "I'm not eating that!"

My eyes filled with tears suddenly, though I tried to hold them back.

"I'm sorry, Will. Really I am. I thought you'd like it."

"Well, I don't!" he snapped, but then he noticed my face.

"Oh, Kate darling, I don't mean to be horrible. It's just not my thing. Hey, let's not quarrel about it. Let's just forget it and have something else instead."

Sadly, I threw away the remains of the unwanted supper and fetched bread and cheese. After a glass of ale, Will became amorous again and we retired to our marriage bed. I shan't serve up saltling in the future, to be sure. I didn't realise it would upset him so much.

Christmas Day was quiet and peaceful, though my spiced beef was disappointing. I found it dry and tough and said so to Will with many apologies, but he was very kind about it, telling me how much he liked it. Dear man! I know he was only saying it to please me really. Just wait till I see that butcher again! He sold me a right piece of rubbish. Must have seen me coming. Still, it was my fault as well. It could've been cooked better, to be sure.

On Boxing Day both mothers came around, but it was like a frost had suddenly descended. The atmosphere of the room was like ice. Will was very nervous, as he desperately wanted his mam to approve of everything, and I was worried about how they'd get on with each other. However, they barely spoke to each other all day. My mam tried hard to be jolly, but it all fell flat with the sour faced old hag that is Mrs Duffield! I managed to persuade Will to play his fiddle after lunch and we sang some carols but there weren't no chance of any Irish tunes. My mam suggested it but that was immediately put down by Will's mother.

"We don't want that kind of stuff, now," she said. "It's not right for the occasion."

So that was that. Will, of course, had to go along with his mother, and I didn't want to upset anyone, so I just kept quiet.

It's not fair – it's our home. We should be able to do what we want! I was relieved when it was all over, and they went home.

Well, it's the New Year now and I'm sure it will be a grand one for us. I feel like a real married lady at last and am hopeful that we will have a family (if the Good Lord wills it) and live happily ever after. Here's to 1889!

Kate's Diary 28 January 1889

My, what a fine birthday I had yesterday! When I think back to last year – well, it's probably best to forget about that, it's all in the past now. Will and I are so happy together and that's all that matters. Yesterday, he came home with a present for me; a lovely necklace, which looks like real jewels (though, of course, we couldn't afford that). It is all in beautiful shades of green and Will said he hoped it will remind me of happy times in my dear old Ireland. It does, of course, but my life is here now, with him.

Then he told me to put my best dress on and get ready to go out to supper.

"We're going to the Holborn Restaurant and Casino," he told me, and I was real excited. I've heard about it, of course, it being one of the few that allows ladies in as well (I can't see why ladies shouldn't be admitted everywhere. What difference does it make?).

We had dinner in the Grand Salon, with the orchestra playing music as we ate. I felt like a real toff! We ate huge plates of grilled steak, which I could hardly manage, not being used to such food. The dining room was so ornate and impressive that I could scarcely take my eyes off the gilded walls and ceiling. It was a vision of gold and white, which fair took my breath away.

Afterwards, we took to the dance floor with all the rest. The surface is solid marble, though with all the crush of people you could hardly see it. Still, even with such a large crowd, the whole place is very quiet and decent; there's no rowdy or noisy behaviour here. Proper order and decorum is kept by the attendants (all dressed in fine evening clothes!) and presided over by the Master of Ceremonies. Of course, I know Will would never take me anywhere that wasn't respectable anyway.

I am a bit worried that we may have spent too much on the evening, but Will has reassured me that he's been saving up and putting a bit aside for the occasion.

"You deserve it, my darling," he told me. "You know I'd do anything for your happiness."

That's so sweet of him. He's real wonderful to me!

Kate's Diary 23 February 1889

Feeling fair tired out today! Went out again last night with Will to the 'Bull in The Pound' tavern, which is nearby. We seem to have been there a lot recently, but it's a grand evening out to be sure. The customers ain't exactly like the gentry of the 'Holborn' but they are decent enough. Sometimes, Will plays a bit of fiddle with some of his friends, and then there's always games of 'pitch and toss' to be had. Mind, I ain't sure this is too respectable like, as it involves throwing money at the wall and the closest one wins. A lot of people bet on it and this makes me nervous. Sometimes things get very heated. Not only that, but it looks an awful lot like gambling, which is illegal for us working folks. Still, as Will says, it's only a few pennies and can't hurt no one.

I am a bit anxious about the amount of money we're spending at the moment, but when I said so to Will the other day, he just laughed and told me not to worry.

"Don't you concern yourself, my little darling," he said. "We're okay with the pennies. You know I keep a close eye on it all."

I guess he knows what he's doing, after all, he's a man and it's his job to deal with all the bills. Everyone says women don't have a clue when it comes to this sort of thing. I just wish I had a bit of extra money so that I could carry on helping to support Mam, but now I'm married it's not mine to do what I like with, so I've had to stop giving her anything. She says she understands; after all, married women don't have any money or property of their own; but I feel bad all the same. I did ask Will about it, but he said he didn't think it was a good idea.

"If we do it now, my darling," he explained, "we'll always have to do it and then what will happen when we have children, eh?"

I suppose he's right, and I'm just not thinking it through properly.

Kate's Diary 5 March 1889

I can't believe it – I'm pregnant! It seems so soon, and yet I'm delighted all the same. The last couple of weeks, I've been feeling real sick in the mornings and my 'monthlies' have stopped, so today I spoke to a doctor and it's confirmed. Should be due about September, he reckons. I do feel a bit scared about the responsibility of bringing up a child, but excited to think of the new life growing inside of me. I told Will and he was overjoyed. He wanted to take me out to the pub to celebrate but I told him I'm not sure that's good for the baby. He got a bit huffy then, but I explained we have to look after its health. He agreed but then went off on his own later to see his mates and tell them all about it. I was left alone to ponder the future. Will it be a boy or a girl, dark or fair, tall or short? Only time will tell.

Kate's Diary 25 May 1889

Will wanted to take me out dancing this evening but I really didn't feel up to it. My belly is swollen now and uncomfortable and I wouldn't be able to enjoy it. Will said I was being a killjoy and that I should go along just to listen to the music, but I had to refuse. These places are full of smoke and crowded with people. I'm sure I would feel ill in that atmosphere and it might be dangerous for the baby. Also, it ain't considered decent for pregnant women to be showing themselves in public. I tried to explain to Will, but he didn't really understand. I know he's only thinking of my happiness, but I've got to take care of myself at the moment. I've another one to think of as well. Will sulked for a while then suddenly decided to go there on his own. Now I feel lonely and abandoned, but I'm probably just being silly. After all, as Will pointed out, why should he miss out, just because I can't go?

Kate's Diary 6 June 1889

Today Will surprised me by coming home and telling me that we are going to move house.

"I've been thinking, Kate," he explained. "When the baby comes, we're going to need to save every penny we can, so I've decided we need to move to somewhere cheaper."

"But I love this house," I said, feeling disappointed, "and I thought we were managing okay."

"We won't be able to get by once we've got a child as well," he told me. "So, I've taken a lease on a place in St James' Street in Clerkenwell. It's a flat above a shop, so it'll be real handy for you. You can get all the things you need right on your doorstep. I might even try and get a job nearby as well. There are lots of printing firms in that area."

So that's that. We're moving. I don't seem to have a say in it (I suppose women never do). Still, Will's right about the money; we'll certainly need extra for the baby. I just hope it's a nice place.

Kate's Diary 1 July 1889 6 St James Street

I'm exhausted. Today we moved into St James' Street and I've been up and down stairs all day, taking our belongings in. Will won't be back until the evening, so I've had to do most of it myself. The carter moved our stuff over to the street and then dumped it on the pavement. Luckily, I was able to pay him and a friend to take the big furniture upstairs, otherwise I'd never have coped. But there were still all the clothes, crockery, utensils etc to take up and put away. Not only that, but the flat was disgustingly filthy, so I spent the best part of the day cleaning. There were flies buzzing around, cobwebs hanging down and mildew on the walls. I did the best I could but there are still patches of grey mould in areas I can't reach.

The flat is smaller than our old house, but it does have a tiny box room that the baby can sleep in, so that's good. I paid special attention to washing that down.

The shop below is a hardware store, so won't be much use for food shopping, but we're right in the middle of all the other shops, so it isn't far to go. I said hello to the shopkeeper, Mr Tucker, but he was surly and rude.

"Just make sure you keep up yer rent!" he growled, as I went upstairs for about the fortieth time. Charming!

I must say I'm a bit worried about the water here. When I pumped some out just now, it looked brown and tasted sour. Hopefully it'll clear once it's been used a bit.

Kate's Diary 21 August 1889

This afternoon I must lie down because I feel so tired out. My back aches and I feel so heavy that I can hardly move. The child keeps kicking and it's grand to feel it moving, but this heatwave is getting to me. Just a short rest, that's all I need. Got to be up by six.

Kate's Diary 22 August 1889

I feel so guilty! When I rested yesterday afternoon, I overslept. Will came home and there was no supper ready for him. He was furious and I don't blame him.

"Where's my dinner?" he demanded. "I've been working hard all day. What have you been doing? Lazing around?"

I couldn't help it; I promptly dissolved into tears, begging his forgiveness. Luckily, he was very understanding and forgave me. I rushed around and got him some food, which soothed him, and later, he was kind and loving towards me.

He even told me to go to bed early and brought me up a cup of tea.

"My little darling," he said, "soon to be a mother. We must look after you, mustn't we?"

He kissed me on the forehead and left me to rest. I can't wait for all this to be over now.

Kate's Diary 11 September 1889

I can't believe it's been a week since I gave birth to our son, George Henry Duffield. What an experience! The first week has been a blur, and I've only just surfaced enough to write this. I can't explain the feelings I have. There was so much pain, which I could hardly bear. Mam was there, of course, and the midwife too, but Will had to go to work as usual. It started in the early hours of September 4th with the most dreadful stomach cramps, and my waters breaking. The midwife had told me what to expect so I knew what was happening. Will rushed around getting people in, but then he had to go off. I wish he'd been able to stay; I needed him so much. The labour was long, and I believe I shouted and screamed a great deal, but when they lifted my new baby into my arms, it was the most incredible moment of my life. Something so pure and lovely filled my whole being, like the sun coming up on a new day, or water pouring into the desert. I can only marvel at the miracle of new life that we have created. Will was quite emotional when he came home and saw his son for the first time. He brought me flowers and told me again and again how much he loved me. It's so good to have a loving man by my side. I don't know what I'd do without him.

As for my beautiful baby, all I can do is hold him and gaze at him in wonder. I named him George in memory of the gentle soul I loved and lost. I hope this precious one will turn out to be as special. *What will he do in life?* I ask myself. *What will he become?* One thing I know, he will be much loved by his parents, dear little angel.

Kate's Diary 28 January 1890

Will's been on at me for weeks, ever since I gave birth to George, to go out for an evening with him again.

"You can get someone to look after him for a while," he suggested. "It'd do you good to have a break."

Recently, he's been out to the tavern each Saturday night without me and I've been fierce lonely, but I still feel nervous about leaving my baby. I've hardly left him for a moment since September, and when I do, I just feel worried all the time.

Yesterday being my birthday, however, Will was particularly persuasive.

"What about your mum?" he said. "She would love to look after him for an evening, I'm sure, and then you and I could have an evening out to celebrate. Come on, Kate, you deserve it. It's your birthday."

Reluctantly, I gave in this time and asked Mam to babysit. She was only too happy and turned up promptly, but I felt uneasy.

"You won't leave him alone, will you?" I asked her anxiously.

"Of course not," she reassured me, "now go and have a good time."

To be sure, we had a fine time out at the music hall watching the show, and in spite of myself, I relaxed and enjoyed it.

However, when we got back, I found Mam fast asleep in a chair, a half empty bottle down by her side. Baby George was crying loudly in his cot, so I rushed in to see him. Fortunately, he was fine, but badly needed feeding and changing. When I'd done what was necessary, I felt I had to speak to Mam about it.

"Mam, surely you could have looked after him better than that!" (I was angry of course and it all spilled over). "Anything could have happened. I trusted you!"

"Give it a rest, Kate," said Will. "He's all right."

"No thanks to Mam!" I declared.

Mam rose unsteadily to her feet and when she spoke her speech was slurred.

"I ain't gonna stay here for your insults, madam! Find yerself someone else to look after 'im next time." With that, she walked out.

"Mam!" I called after her. "I'm sorry. It's just that he's everything to me."

But she'd gone, and my apology went unheard.

"Well, that's clever!" Will said. "Now who we going to get to babysit? You needn't think I'm staying in every week, just 'cause of you!"

He stalked off and I was left to sit sadly on my own. Trust me to speak without thinking, it always gets me into trouble. At that moment, baby George chuckled happily in his cot and I felt a wave of pure love come over me. I dread anything happening to him. It's silly really but he's just so precious to me. The trouble is that I'm not sure whether Will feels the same. Maybe it's not the same for men, I don't know. I *do* know I made a fool of myself yesterday and I need to sort it out. Better go and see Mam tomorrow.

Kate's Diary 25 March 1890

My mind is in a whirl. I am so angry and hurt. I just don't know what to think. Yesterday I ran into Rosie, who we used to see a lot when we lived in Broadwall. We exchanged pleasantries and the usual gossip, and she admired little George, which made me feel very proud. Then she asked after Will.

"How's yer old man these days? Is he enjoying his new job? No more arguments, I hope!" she laughed.

I was confused. "What do you mean?"

"Oh, my hubby Len told me all about that 'set to' he had with the boss before he left. A right old punch up by all accounts! When your Will stormed out, we all thought he might come back and apologise, but no, I guess he moved on. Probably just as well."

I made out I knew everything 'cos I'd a looked stupid otherwise, but it's the first I've heard about it. So that's why Will changed jobs suddenly, and presumably that's why he thought we needed to move house. Why did he lie to me? Surely, he could have explained instead of making an excuse. I would've understood. I know he's got a filthy temper at times, but to get to the stage of fighting – well, really – what a thing to do.

What should I say to Will? How can I approach him about this? Probably I ought to try and pretend I don't know, but I'm not sure I can. I wish I'd never found out.

Kate's Diary 26 March 1890

Another sleepless night, turning everything over in my mind. Will noticed yesterday that I wasn't quite myself. I was quieter than usual at dinner because I couldn't think of what to say.

"Cheer up, Kate," he said. "Why not bring the baby and come out to the pub tonight?"

"Oh Will, really! I can't do that," I replied. "It's not right."

"You're just no fun anymore, since the baby arrived," he declared. "Well, I'll go on me own then."

I must talk to Will about all this, but I need to stay calm. I think it's the best way.

Kate's Diary 28 March 1890

Well, it all came out at dinner time yesterday evening.

"I saw Rosie a couple of days ago," I casually remarked, "and she asked after you."

"Rosie?" he said, "Who's that?"

"You know, Will. Len's wife. Len, who used to work with you at Johnson's."

"Oh yes," he said, looking a bit nervous, "I remember. What did she have to say?"

I passed on a few bits of news then carefully broached the difficult subject.

"Will, I'm not sure how to say this, but I understand you left Johnson's under somewhat unfortunate circumstances."

He flared up immediately.

"That's not true!" he cried defensively. "What's she been saying?"

"Look," I said calmly, "I'm not criticising you, Will. I want to understand that's all. Please just be honest with me. I'm not here to blame you; I love you; you should know that."

He quietened down then and told me what had happened. There was a nasty squabble about hours worked and wages paid apparently, and he lost his cool and walked out.

"I just wish you'd told me earlier," I said. "You don't need to hide things from me, I'm on your side. I suppose that's why we moved, is it?"

"No, no, that was for the baby," he insisted. "Nothing to do with that."

"Well, if there's anything else, please talk to me," I told him. "I'm your wife, after all. If you can't talk to me, who can you talk to?"

Will was visibly moved by my demonstration of solidarity and we embraced at length.

"I love you, my darling Kate," he told me. "I'm sorry. I was just embarrassed about it. I'll never hide things again, I promise. No more lies."

A flood of emotional and romantic intensity swept us away at that point and I spent the rest of the evening in his arms. Afterwards, as I lay in bed, I thanked the Good Lord for the decent, loving man who is by my side and prayed that this will never end.

Kate's Diary 28 June 1890

I don't know what to do! George won't stop crying all the time. Last night, I was awake the whole time, looking after him. He's had diarrhoea a lot and this morning he was sick. I told Will the other day that we must get a doctor, but he said to wait a little.

"Babies always get these things," he said, "you're just panicking."

Yesterday, I came into the bedroom to find Will standing there, holding George out in front of him. At first, I thought that it was nice that he was helping to care for his son, but then I saw Will's face and it frightened me. There was a look of murderous rage on it, as if he would have killed him if he could (I hope I am only imagining this). I'm sure Will loves him and would never hurt him, but he looked so angry.

"Do something with him, Kate!" he demanded. "Stop him making that infernal noise all the time."

"He's ill," I told him. "He needs medicine."

"Well get it then! Anything – just sort it out!"

He thrust the baby at me; I took him and rocked him gently till at last he fell asleep. Dare I tell Will that I think I'm pregnant again? Maybe now is not the time.

Kate's Diary 15 July 1890

My world feels like it has come to an end. George died yesterday. My little darling has gone forever. That awful sickness and diarrhoea exhausted him so much that he became weaker and weaker. The doctor did his best and I tried everything, but to no avail. All our efforts were in vain.

I can't help thinking that this is all my fault for naming him after my first doomed love. Maybe he was doomed as well, from the start.

Since his death, I've cried many bitter tears; my throat feels raw and my eyes are so sore I can hardly see. Will told me today that I need to get a grip.

"There's a new baby on the way," he said. "You need to focus on that one now. This is just bad luck, can't be helped."

He means it kindly, I guess, but another baby coming won't replace the one that's lost. I still think the water in this place is to blame. I try and boil everything, but I know there's something wrong with it. I hate it here!

Kate's Diary 18 November 1890

I can feel this child moving and kicking inside of me, but I am frightened that I won't be able to love it, when it finally arrives. It can never replace George, but I know it's not this child's fault that he died. He, or she, deserves to be loved, and if George were still here then I know I'd be happy to think he was getting a brother or sister.

Read in the news today about Charles Parnell and the O'Shea divorce. He's done so much for Ireland and I always follow any story about him. I must say that it's quite shocking to think of him living 'in sin' for so long, having children with the lady as well! But I do feel sorry to think of those poor mites being taken away from their mother and put with the man she used to be married to, who they don't even know. It can't be right. Children should be with their parents, even if they're not married legal like.

I do hope this won't affect the Irish Home Rule bill. It's been looking promising lately. Parnell's always trying to further the cause; he's a good man.

Kate's Diary 11 January 1891

Welcome to the world, my little one! William James Duffield Junior, born 10th January 1891. It's strange, I wasn't sure what I'd feel until I saw him and then I loved him immediately. He has tiny tufts of dark hair on top of his head, the same colour as his father's, and a quiet, serious disposition. He rarely cries but lies there contentedly smiling to himself, like he knows some secret the rest of us are not privilege to. A mysterious stranger that I hope I will get to know in time. Here's to him!

Kate's Diary 7 March 1891

What a week it's been. I hardly know whether I'm coming or going. There's been barely a minute to spare, so that's why I'm finally writing this now. Last Wednesday (or was it Thursday?), I was up early cleaning the house, whilst baby William slept peacefully in his cot. All of a sudden, there was a loud knocking on the front door, enough to wake the dead. It sent chills down my spine. Who would come calling without warning? I never get any visitors normally. Turned out it was an urgent messenger sent to me by Mam, who had fallen and broken her ankle. I took the baby and went rushing off to the infirmary to see her. Things have been pretty cool between us lately, since the 'babysitting' incident last year, even though I tried to apologise. Now, however, she was desperate to see me and so needy. She couldn't afford to stay at the hospital and can't manage on her own at the moment, so I've brought her back here and managed to get her into the one room flat next door, just temporary like. For once, that miserable so-and-so Mr Tucker was willing to help (probably

158

'cos of the extra money) and rented the place to me for three months only. I had to pawn my green necklace in order to pay for it; hopefully, I'll be able to get it back again very soon (I daren't tell Will). It nearly broke my heart because it means such a lot to me, but I had no choice.

When I told Will about Mam that evening, he wasn't impressed.

"So, you'll be running around after her now, then?" he said.

"Well, I'll have to, I'm afraid, Will." I replied. "She can't do much for herself at the moment with only one good leg. It'll only be for a while, I promise. The doctor says it should heal in about three months."

"Well, make sure you look after the rest of us as well," he reminded me. "You've got a home and family of your own, you know."

He means it kindly, I'm sure, and is only thinking of me, but I have to do this. She's my mam, after all.

The week has been a nightmare, though, I have to admit. Mam has been ringing the bell I gave her every five minutes! I've had to take her to the privy, get her dressed and undressed, clean her room, fetch her meals, medication and sometimes, even ale. It just goes on and on, and what's more she doesn't seem to appreciate it. I've had to take baby William with me a lot of the time, as he's too young to be left alone. He's barely two months old and I'm still breastfeeding him. Mam doesn't seem interested in my life or my problems; she just keeps demanding more and more of my time. It's endless.

Will has grumbled constantly about it and hasn't exactly helped out at home either.

"Not a man's job to do that kind of thing," he told me, when I asked him to help with the dishes. I know it isn't, but I'm so worn out. How can I carry on like this? I don't know.

Tonight, Will has gone to the pub again, complaining bitterly about my lack of attention to him. I can see his point, but I'm doing my best. What else can I do?

Kate's Diary 25th March 1891

What a bad day! Mam has been so demanding. I know she can't do much with her ankle in plaster, but I've been in and out constantly, fetching her this and that. In between, I've been looking after the baby and he's been real fractious today. I think he may be running a temperature, which worries me. Will has gone to the pub again, even though it's not the weekend, says he needs a break from us all, we're driving him mad. I can't blame him, but I wish he would be more understanding. He also needs to stop spending so much money on drink, otherwise I think the bills might not get paid. I feel exhausted.

Kate's Diary 26 March 1891

Will was very pleased with himself when he came home late last night. Strangely, he had a lot of money on him, more than when he went out. I think he's been gambling; I know he's done it before. When I asked him about it this morning, he told me to mind my own business.

"I could do with a bit of that money, Will," I said. "The stove door's nearly hanging off."

"Well, fix it!" he said. "You're a woman, surely you know about these things. Why should you need money for that?"

With that, he went off to work and left me to try my best with the darn thing. Disaster struck, however, when I tried to clean and repair it. The whole door came off, falling onto the hard tiles below, and shattering into pieces. I was very upset, as I knew it wasn't usable now, which meant we couldn't do much cooking or heating, and I felt so guilty.

Sorrowfully, I confessed my mishap to Mam, but she didn't seem to think it was worth worrying about.

"These things happen," she said. "Can't be helped."

"I don't know what Will will say," I told her. "I think he'll be cross."

"Not if he's a decent man," she replied. "Your da never let rip about things like that. Anyway, did you get the things I wanted from the shop?"

It was clear I wasn't going to get much help from that direction, so I steeled myself for what was likely to come. Unfortunately, Will's reaction was even worse than I expected. He was absolutely furious and didn't think twice about showing it. He grabbed me by both arms roughly and shook me hard.

"You stupid woman! Why didn't you leave it alone? You've wrecked it now!"

"Will, please," I pleaded, "I'm sorry, I was trying to fix it like you said. I couldn't help it."

He pushed me away from him in disgust.

"You're useless, aren't you? Contemptible! Where's my dinner?"

I'd only been able to make some stew as the stove was so damaged. As Will ate, I enquired nervously what we could do to fix it.

"I suppose you'll have to have some money," he said begrudgingly and flung a handful of coins at me. "See if Mr Tucker downstairs knows anyone. Really – you've just wasted loads of money that we can't spare. If we end up in debtor's prison, it'll be all your fault!"

"But Will," I tried, "it was already broken."

"You had to go and finish it off, though, didn't you?" he exclaimed bitterly. "I think you just saw I had some money for a change and wanted to get at it."

"No, no, really," I implored. "It was an accident, forgive me, please."

My tears fell freely, and Will softened at last. He patted me kindly on the shoulder.

"Come on, old girl, we'll get by. Let's just get it fixed and forget about it, eh? Of course, I'll forgive you, just be more careful in future."

I feel so bad that I've cost us all this money. It's all my fault, I know. Thank goodness Will has been good enough to overlook it this time.

Kate's Diary 5th April 1891

What a relief! Aunt Louisa has turned up today and has agreed to help out with looking after Mam. I hardly know her, but she is da's younger sister and is very like him in a lot of ways. She's a tall, upright lady, calm, with a certain strength of character about her. She speaks her mind, but not in a bad way. I found her open and refreshingly honest. When Mam started moaning about the pain again and asking for a drink, she put her firmly in her place.

"You're not having that, Shona," she said, "so don't think you are. To be sure, you need to clear your head of that stuff and no mistake."

Mam always argues with me if I try that with her and then takes no notice, but she was as meek as a new-born lamb with Louisa and did just as she was told. Aunty Lou is working herself but has promised to come and help out whenever she can, at least twice a week, to give me a rest and time to see to my own home and family. What an angel she is!

Kate's Diary 1 May 1891

Had a grand time today, chatting to Mam and Aunty Lou (Mind, I should've been home working on the housework really – better not tell Will!). It's funny how different Mam is when Louisa is around. They were both reminiscing at length about the old days in Ireland and it was so good to hear all the stories. Louisa is such a character, full of funny anecdotes and not afraid to call a spade, a spade! Today, she told us all about what she got up to with her brothers, Uncle Frankie and dear old da, when they were children growing upon the farm together. It fair made me die. Mam seemed quite young again as well, remembering all the happy times.

It seems Louisa moved to England to follow her sweetheart, but he soon tired of her and abandoned her for another. Poor thing! It's made her tough and resilient though and she says she don't have no regrets.

"That's life," she told us, "what doesn't kill you, cures you!" Then she looked keenly at me.

"You okay, Kate? Sometimes I think you look a bit down in the dumps."

I couldn't tell her how Will can be cruel and harsh at times, so I just said I was fine, but I'd love to have the chance to talk to her alone someday. She seems like someone who would understand.

Mam's getting a lot better now and hopefully will be able to move out and take care of herself shortly. The lease on her room runs out at the end of May and I ain't got no money to extend it, so can't help any more (If Will finds out I pawned the necklace, he'll go spare, I must try and get it back before he finds out).

Louisa has promised to find Mam somewhere to live, and privately she told me that she would keep an eye on her from now on. Mam has had to stop drinking since the accident and that's improved her health no end. Aunty Lou said she'd try and make sure she doesn't slip back again (I wish someone would do the same for Will. I'm sure he drinks far too much). I'm real grateful to Louisa. Don't think I could have managed this without her. Hope she keeps in touch. Will says he don't like her, she's an 'interfering old witch', but that's not true. I think she's just too outspoken for his liking.

Kate's Diary 10 June 1891

I been worrying meself silly about my necklace recently. It's the one decent thing I own, and I miss it dreadfully. Will would be so upset if he knew what I'd done, I know, so yesterday I came up with a plan to try and raise some money meself, in order to get it back. What with having baby William to look after, I can't go out to work, but I suddenly thought that maybe Mr Tucker would be glad of some help. I mean, he ain't married and he must need some washing or cleaning done, or perhaps I could help out in the shop. Once Will's gone to work tomorrow, I'm going to pop down and ask him.

Kate's Diary 11 June 1891

I can't believe it! How could Mr Tucker be like that? That's just so low!

I went down to see him midmorning, leaving baby William asleep in his cot upstairs. As always, Mr Tucker was his usual grumpy self.

"Yes? What do you want?"

I explained that I was looking to do some work to raise some money and he looked thoughtful.

"I can do anything," I said, "I'm very hardworking."

"You know you're behind with the rent again, don't you?" he grumbled.

This surprised me. "No, I didn't, surely Will paid you last week?"

"Huh!" he snorted. "Haven't had anything since about three weeks ago! You need to talk to your old man."

"Yes, I will," I promised, "I'm sorry, Mr Tucker. He probably just forgot."

"Well, I don't know about that, but anyway, come into the stock room at the back. I've an idea of something you might be able to do. Jim – look after the counter, will you?"

Pleased at the prospect of possible work, I went with him willingly. We entered the small back room and he shut the door behind us. It is barely more than a large cupboard really, lined with shelves crammed with hardware goods of all kinds.

"What can I do for you?" I asked eagerly.

He edged closer.

"You're an attractive woman, Mrs Duffield, or can I call you Kate? It's a shame to waste all those charms, when you could be doing something with them. Now if you were disposed to offer me some, shall I say, 'comfort' and 'companionship', I could easily put some extra money your way."

"Mr Tucker, really!" I exclaimed. "I ain't that kind of girl!"

His hand rested on my shoulder now and I felt uncomfortable. I backed away and found myself hemmed in by bottles of glue, jars of nails and shiny hand tools.

"It'd just be between us," he said persuasively. "No need for your husband to know. I'd be very generous if you 'co-operated', so to speak. I'm only human, after all." He grinned unpleasantly at me.

"No, I'm sorry, I couldn't do that," I said firmly and tried to move towards the door, but he blocked the way, looking annoyed now.

"What's wrong with me, then?" he demanded. "You too proud, is that it? Well, you won't be if you're turned out on the street, will you? I could you know, if I wanted to. You ain't paid yer rent after all!"

"We'll pay it!" I declared. "Now let me go, Mr Tucker. I love my husband and I won't betray him. Besides, I'm no whore!"

"Please yerself," he said and moved aside reluctantly. "Pay up or else!"

Now I'm upstairs again and I feel shaken to the core. How naïve I was! I feel embarrassed at my own stupidity and horrified at his threat to make us homeless. What's more, I'm no nearer to getting my necklace back. What can I do?

Kate's Diary 1 July 1891

How dreadful! We heard today that Pat's wife Jenny has died in childbirth, leaving him with three young children to bring up. I really liked Jenny; she was kind to me when I met with hard times in Liverpool. A truly good-hearted soul, who'd do anything for anyone. No wonder Pat loved her. He must be in an awful state.

Anyway, Mam is going to move up there permanent like, to look after and bring up the children so that he can still work. That's a good thing, though I feel like I'm being abandoned by her again. I don't think she would do that for me and Will, even after all I've done for her recently. Still, I mustn't be selfish. Pat needs her desperately. I wish I was free to help, but here I am with Will and baby William, struggling to keep going in all this heat. Louisa is going to accompany Mam up to Liverpool, so I won't see her for a while either, which is a real shame. Hope she comes back soon.

Kate's Diary 20 July 1891

What a relief! Today, I had a visit from Louisa, just back from Liverpool. Mam is all settled in with Pat now and things are going well, apparently. I was pleased to see Louisa and we chatted pleasantly for a while, then she surprised me by saying, "Look Kate, please don't take this the wrong way, but, well, your Mam, Pat and I; we realise you had to pay the rent for your Mam whilst she wasn't well and we'd like to repay you."

"No," I protested. "There's no need. I was happy to do it for her."

"We know that," replied Louisa, "but there's no reason why your Mam shouldn't pay her way." She looked closely at me. "I know it must have been hard to get the money together."

"Well, yes," I admitted, "that's true, but I–"

"No buts," she said firmly. "Here you are. We all chipped in and we want you to have it."

I have to say I was delighted and no sooner had Louisa gone than I hurried over to get my necklace back. At first, I was real worried because the man thought he might have sold it, but to my relief, he found it at last and I was able to reclaim it. I am so happy now. Thank goodness! Let's hope I never have to part with it again.

Kate's Diary 8 September 1891

No, no, no! Baby William has gone, taken by the same sickness as dear little George. When will this ever end? It must be this house, I'm sure. He was so ill, poor darling and nothing helped. Doctor Palmer had little interest in the case, as he knew we couldn't pay our bills; but even so, I thought he would try and save an innocent child. What is wrong with this world?

Kate's Diary 13 September 1891

All I've done all week is cry until my head hurts and my eyes are sore. I don't feel I shall ever recover from this grief. Will doesn't seem to understand and has been very blunt with me, telling me to pull myself together. Today, I tried hard to work around the house and had started to make the supper, when I suddenly caught sight of a stray baby's bootie on the floor. This set me off again and I retired with it clutched in my hand to the bed, where I sobbed and even screamed at times. I was so exhausted I fell asleep and was woken by Will coming home. He came marching into the bedroom and shook me awake roughly.

"Kate, what you doing, girl? For God's sake, get a grip!"

He grabbed my arm and dragged me forcibly to my feet, wrenching my shoulder badly in the process (It still aches now). Then he tugged my head up and back by the hair and made me look at him. I know I must have looked a right state, my face covered in tears, eyes puffy and hair bedraggled.

"Come on, Kate!" he said firmly. "This ain't no good. Look at you! Go on like this and you'll end up in an institution."

I blubbed out my woes to him, but he wasn't really listening.

"It happens, Kate. Babies die every day. I know it's sad, but life has to go on."

More kindly, he added, "Look, you said you wanted some dress material the other day."

(It's true. I did. My day dress is so patched up it's more 'patches' than 'dress', but he told me we couldn't afford it)

"Why don't you get yourself some stuff and make something pretty to wear? It'll make you feel better. Look, here's some money. Now come on, let's get some food and try and forget all about it."

I can't understand how Will can dismiss all this loss so easily. I suppose he's right and I must try and move on, but it's hard. He's just thinking of my wellbeing I know, but I wish he'd be a bit gentler.

Kate's Diary 9 October 1891

Read about Charles Parnell's death in the newspaper today. This made me feel quite melancholy, but when I talked to Will, he just said, "Why are you so sad about it? You don't know him. He's nothing to you."

"But he's worked hard for Ireland," I said, "and it's such a miserable end – pneumonia – after all his efforts."

"Well, he shouldn't have stayed out in the rain, then," said Will. "Plain daft, I call it. Anyway, he's an adulterer, isn't he? Serves him right!"

I couldn't answer that, but it don't seem fair. Parnell was much more than just that.

Kate's Diary 17 October 1891

I had to do something to try and shake off this terrible depression that I have had since baby William died, so today I have enrolled at Morley College for Working Men and Women. They do creative writing classes, which is what I've always wanted to do. It's only a few hours a week so won't interfere with any of my work at home. I'm happy again for the first time in weeks and can't wait to tell Will. He's always telling me I must cheer up so I'm sure he'll be pleased.

Kate's Diary 18 October 1891

I feel so shocked and hurt, I don't know what to think any more. Proudly, I told Will all about the course I'd signed up for, but to my astonishment, he went mad, swearing and shouting at me.

"You're just deserting me, aren't you?" he cried. "Trying to be independent – well don't start that. I won't have it! You're here to look after me and don't you forget it."

"But Will," I tried to explain, "please understand. Can't you see I need to do this to stop me dwelling on sad things? It won't stop me looking after you."

"Oh no?" he jeered. "Well, you didn't do a very good job when we had your mother next door, did you? No wonder the baby died. It was through your sheer neglect. That's you all over!"

This really got to me and I exploded with rage.

"Will! How could you? That's not fair. I did my best. No one could have done more. I didn't notice you doing much to help!"

To my utter surprise, I suddenly felt a sharp stinging pain as Will slapped me hard across the face.

"Stop your cheek, woman!" he shouted. "You're here to do as you're told; love, honour and obey, remember!"

No one has ever hit me before and I felt stunned to the core. I fled to the bedroom and flung myself down on the bed, crying wildly. *To think he could be like this – my loving husband!*

Moments later, he followed, contrite now, kneeling beside the bed.

"Darling Kate, I'm so sorry. Forgive me. I didn't mean it. You know I love you." He stroked my hair and tried to dry my eyes with his kerchief. "I was just so worried about losing you. You'll meet all kinds of people there and you won't want me anymore. Please don't go. I need you."

I suppose I've forgiven him now, although the memory still hurts. Of course, he's persuaded me not to go to the college, which is really disappointing, but I don't want him to be upset again. He has his rights as a husband, it's true, and I must abide by what he says.

Kate's Diary 16 April 1892

Last night, Will went to the pub and came home in an awful state. I didn't go because I've been feeling real sick with this new pregnancy. He didn't get back till nearly midnight and I was beginning to get worried. He staggered in, half falling over, and it was clear he was very drunk.

"Will, are you okay?" I asked. "You're later than usual. Is everything all right?"

"None of your business, woman!" he slurred and lurched into the doorway.

"Those bastards!" he suddenly exclaimed. "How dare they? They took everything!"

I was confused. What had happened? Trying to find out, however, only made him angrier and he suddenly let fly at the house, knocking saucepans to the floor nd deliberately throwing and smashing crockery. He was quite uncontrollable, rampaging through the kitchen and living room like a monster. I've never seen anything like it before and I cowered in the bedroom, scared he would turn on me next. A trail of destruction was left behind him, until he suddenly passed out in a drunken stupor on the couch. I tiptoed out the bedroom when it all went quiet; covered him up with a blanket and left him to sleep it off. What sparked all that off, I don't know, but it was quite terrifying for a time.

This morning, he slept late and only groaned at me when I tried to wake him, so I left well alone. I wonder what is going on.

Kate's Diary 30 April 1892

Today, I caused a huge argument with Will by asking him whether he had paid the rent. Mr Tucker, the horrible man, snarled at me yesterday as I came up the stairs, that we needed to *'pay it or else'*. Though, he added with a leer, *some other arrangement could still be made, if I were 'sensible'.* I shudder at the thought of it. Seems like it's been that way for months now; us struggling to pay and him trying to get more than just money!

Anyway, when Will came home, I felt I had to speak to him about the rent, but that was a mistake. It was like letting off a stick of dynamite. He turned on me like a wild animal.

"How dare you ask me about money?" he cried. "You got no right."

"I was just telling you what he said," I explained. "Please be reasonable, Will."

With that, he exploded at me in rage, like a tempest. His words overflowed like an angry river bursting its banks. I don't think he knew what he was saying. All self-control was gone.

"Me, reasonable? What a cheek! Women have no reason whatsoever in these things. I'm the head of the household and you're just the hopeless waste of space that I have to live with! It's nothing to do with you. How dare you question me?"

Without warning, he let fly at me, his fist striking my cheek hard, like a thunderbolt. This time, I knew he had drawn blood and I sank onto the nearest chair, covering my face with my hands. Thankfully then he stormed off and returned much later, exceedingly drunk. Meanwhile, I cried and cried. I can't understand why he was so angry; it seems such an overreaction. What did I do wrong?

Kate's Diary 1 May 1892

Tonight, Will came home early, and to my surprise, did not go out to the pub as usual. At supper time, he was unusually quiet. He looked across the table at me as we finished eating and said in a low voice, "Did I do that to you, Kate?"

My cheek has a nasty cut, is bruised and very sore, so I could not tell a lie.

"I'm afraid so," I murmured, "but it's okay." The last thing I wanted was to annoy him again.

Will pushed his plate aside.

"I'm sorry, Kate. I have so many problems at the moment and that was just the final straw. I didn't mean to take it out on you."

Choosing my words carefully, I asked, "Can I help?"

Will hesitated and looked embarrassed.

"I need to talk to you, Kate, but please don't criticise because I know I'll probably lose control again if you do."

"Okay," I told him. "I'm listening."

It frightened me as to what he might say. *Did he have another woman? Was he in trouble with the law?*

He looked shamefaced and muttered, "I'm not sure where to start, but I've got myself in a mess, Kate. We need to move house again." He paused but I said nothing.

"Well, it's like this – I'm in debt and there's some bad men after me. I been down the pub a bit too often, I admit, but I needed to relax, especially with your mum here and all, but then I got to betting on the 'pitch and toss' and that was okay at first. Then my mate Sid said he had a dead cert on the horses, and it was great. I made a killing. That's what paid for the stove repair."

I flushed, remembering my unfortunate mishap, but remained silent.

"Of course, I had another go, didn't I, and this time it didn't work out so well and I lost quite a lot. Unfortunately, this was our rent money."

I repressed a gasp. So that's what's been going on.

"I had to borrow money, then," he continued, "to pay off the rent and then it got worse and worse. I'm sorry, Kate, but I used the money that was put aside for the bills to pay the interest on the loan and it's just gone on and on. Now, the loan has got so big I got no chance of paying it and the rent's gone again. My wages are already spent by the time I get them. If I don't meet the repayment on the loan by Monday, I'm likely to end up in the infirmary. They're a nasty bunch, these sharks! All we can do is move, quickly. I've found a room for us over in Woodwhistle Street and we need to get out of here tomorrow night. If we leave quietly, very late, no one will know." He stopped and look at me. "Well?"

"Whatever you think," I said tactfully. "I don't like it here, anyway. What about our furniture, though?"

"I'm sorry, Kate, but we can only take what we can carry. I have arranged to borrow Sid's horse and cart for the evening to take a few of the larger things but we'll have to leave it

175

round the corner so that Tucker doesn't get wind of it. We'll wait till everyone's asleep and then go."

So that's it. We're off tomorrow night. Can't say I'm sorry to be leaving this place, but it's a shame about our bed and the dresser. What can I say to Will about it? Nothing really. He begged my forgiveness, and I gave it freely. We all make mistakes and at least he's been honest with me at last. He promises he will change his ways from now on. Let's hope this will be a fresh start.

Joe's Recollections, 1909

It was when we came out of the workhouse again that the rows between Father and the older boys started. Father was always ready to deal out a slap or a punch, whenever he felt anyone deserved it, and I guess Fred and Ern were old enough then to understand what was going on. Like any son, they longed to protect their mother. Fred, being the oldest, seemed to feel a real responsibility for her and clashed with our father frequently.

You're asking me why no one ever talks about Albert? Well, he always seemed the odd one out. From an early age, he was always our father's favourite, and the only one to side with him in an argument. I don't remember our father ever hitting him, like he did the rest of us. Albert was also someone who could never be trusted to keep a secret; he'd always sneak off and tell Father.

One day after I got home from school, my mother asked me to go and fetch some plates from the dresser, in the other room. I must have been about nine years old at the time. It wasn't long after we left the workhouse school, I know. Fred and Ern were working as labourers at the printers, and the rest of us were at a local school. Things were looking up.

I was keen to help now that we were all at home again. The trouble was I couldn't reach the top of the dresser, being quite small for my age. In my eagerness, I didn't hesitate but got a chair and stood on it to achieve my goal. It never occurred to me that it was one of those that Father's mother had given him, as an heirloom, so to speak. As I reached up and got the items my mother wanted, I heard an ominous cracking sound. I leapt off quickly, but the damage was done. A large split had appeared across the seat. I examined it in horror. Could it be fixed? I hoped so. Just then Albert came into the room to find me peering at it.

"Oh ho," he cried. "What you done? You're gonna catch it now!" He surveyed the damage. "You've fair wrecked that. Father'll go mad."

"Please, Albert," I begged him. "Don't tell him. I'll try and get it fixed."

He laughed. "You'll be lucky! Anyway, why shouldn't I tell? You gonna make it worth my while?"

"You can have my toy car," I offered. "It's my best one. It's all I got."

I wished I didn't have to part with it as I had so few toys and this was my favourite, but I had to buy Albert's silence somehow. Albert laughed again, but took the offered bribe, more to deprive me of it than because he actually wanted it.

"We'll see," he said. "I bet he finds out anyway."

I hid the broken chair as best I could and returned to my mother, a bit sheepishly. She noticed something was wrong, but I denied everything and pretended I was okay. I wasn't –

I was terrified. I could only imagine what Father would say. I was cold with fear and could think of nothing else.

That evening passed peacefully enough, and the mishap was still undisclosed, but I tossed and turned in bed that night, tormented by guilt and fear. By the next morning, I was almost hoping it would be discovered, in order to stop this awful feeling of dread.

The following evening, I got my wish, unfortunately. Father came in from work asking my mother to put round extra chairs for some of his mates, who were coming round for drinks later.

"Where's my mother's other chair?" he enquired. "I can only find three." He searched around and, with a bit of help from Albert, soon found it.

"What on earth? It's broken! How did this happen? Kate," he called, "do you know?" He sounded genuinely upset and I thought I saw tears in his eyes. This made me feel awful.

Albert then piped up in an ingratiating tone, "Joseph broke it, Father. I saw him."

I glared at Albert, regretting that I'd wasted my toy car on him. Father turned on me, grabbing me by the collar.

"Is this true?" he demanded, exploding with rage. "Don't you know these chairs mean a lot to me? My mother gave them to me."

"I'm sorry!" I cried in self-defence. "It was an accident. I didn't mean to."

Father then went into one of his rages, shouting abuse at me and threatening me with a good beating.

"You hopeless little good-for-nothing! If you were working for me, I'd have you fired. You're useless, careless, a hooligan! You belong in the workhouse. I wish I'd never got you back home again. You don't deserve it."

With that, he picked up a large stick and advanced towards me. I was shaking from head to foot and, to my shame, I began to cry. I was only nine and I knew I couldn't stand up to him. At that moment, however, our mother came in from the kitchen to find out what all the noise was about.

"Whatever's going on?" she asked. "Will, put that down. What do you think you're doing? Please stop!"

He turned on her, all self-control gone.

"Leave it, woman! This ain't no concern of yours."

"He's my son. You leave *him* alone. If you want to beat him, you'll have to go through me first. What's he supposed to have done, anyhow?"

"See this!" my father cried, pointing to the damaged chair. "The little vandal's breaking up the furniture now."

"I'm sorry," I pleaded. "I didn't mean to, Mum, really! I was just standing on it to fetch the plates you wanted."

"Will," my mother said in a reasonable voice, "can't you see? Joe was a bit careless, I admit, but accidents happen. He didn't mean it."

Our father moved towards her, threateningly. To my horror, he grabbed her by the arm and shook her roughly.

"Defend him, would you?"

Then he struck her hard against the face and she crumpled into the nearest chair.

"Leave her alone," I begged. "It's not her fault."

I'll always remember his face as he turned towards me. It was as black as thunder. I backed away in panic. What would have happened next, I hate to think, but just then Fred and Ern arrived back from work. Instantly, they knew something was

179

going on and they sprang to our defence. Fred was tall and strong and Ern, though younger, was wiry with good muscles. They placed themselves between us all and demanded to know what was going on. Mum was crying silently, with a large bruise on her face and a split lip. I was in a complete state of nervous terror and could hardly speak. Albert, meanwhile, stood there grinning stupidly.

Father knew he couldn't take us all on and stormed out of the house, banging the door behind him. He returned much later in a state of utter drunkenness, shouting and crying intermittently. From my bed, I heard my mother soothing and calming him. I could never understand why she bothered, but in the morning the tempest had passed, and the incident was never mentioned again.

Kate's Diary 4 May 1892 Woodwhistle Street

Here we are in what can best be described as a hovel! One room for everything; cooking, eating, washing, sleeping; and a shared privy out the back. The courtyard is running with raw sewage – it's disgusting, not that any of the other tenants seem to care. Maybe they've just got used to it. It's a tenement house, the rookeries they call 'em, and I never seen such poverty and woe as this. To think we'd end up here! Still, at least it's a roof, of a sort, over our heads.

There are holes in the floorboards, where you can easily twist an ankle if you're not careful, and the plaster is falling off the wall in patches. Thankfully, we are on the ground floor, so if the roof leaks (which it probably does), it won't affect us, only the poor wretches above. And at least we're not in the basement. I hear that's where all the sewage finds its way down to, eventually. If I'm completely honest, I know it ain't much different to 'the lanes' in Cork, really. Barrack Street was overcrowded, and looking back, I admit it was filthy and broken down, but as a child it never worried me. The fact there were at least two families in every house just seemed like fun at the time. Oh, what childhood innocence! But there was certainly a closeness of spirit there, with people pulling together and helping out, not like this pitiful collection of isolated human misery.

We are sleeping on a straw mattress on the floor, and in my condition (more than four months gone now), it ain't the most comfortable, but we have to make the best of it. Will has been kind to me this week and I hope it will continue. If we can be strong together, then I know we will be all right.

The night we left was mighty fearful, creeping out at midnight with our belongings, trying not to make a sound. Once we heard a noise from Mr Tucker's flat and we froze for ages, terrified of discovery. We managed about three trips back and forth to the cart round the corner before we had to resign ourselves to taking no more. As I shut the door for the last time, leaving our bed and most of our chairs behind, I could hardly keep from crying. Today, my limbs ache with all the exertions and I feel quite faint and weak. Will told me to rest whilst he goes out to look for work nearby (He daren't go back to his usual job because the loan sharks will find him there). I have already arranged with the people in the big house round the corner to do some ironing for them, at least until my confinement is due, so that is something coming in. The only water pump here is out in the yard, so doing laundry is out of the question; but ironing is quite calming in a way, smoothing down the sheets with the flat iron heated on the stove. Mind it's a hot and steamy job and I end up with my hair sticking to my forehead with perspiration. I must look a proper sight!

Thank goodness I don't have to see Mr Tucker again; his attentions were getting unbearable. The only trouble is, none of my family or friends know where I am now. I must write to them, if I get time.

Kate's Diary 10 June 1892

Wrote to Pat today, telling him our new address but I asked him not to tell anyone else. Truth to tell, I'm fierce ashamed of where we live now, in this broken-down slum. 'Course, I didn't tell him that; I only said we were likely to be moving on again shortly, so just to use it in emergencies only. I wish it were true – that we would be moving on from here, but I can't see it yet. Our poor little baby will be born here, no doubt, amongst the filth and the squalor. What chance does he, or she, have? I can only pray for them.

Kate's Diary 9 October 1892

Alfred James Duffield, born October 7th, safe and well, in spite of this accursed place. At least Will is working again now and the bills appear to be getting paid. Alfie is perfect – all fair hair and blue smiling eyes, but I feel scared to let myself love him too much. If I do, I know my heart will be broken again if something happens to him; and then my mind will follow. Third time lucky, they say, and I pray it's true, but I will try and keep my distance for a while, in order to preserve my soul.

Kate's Diary 3 December 1892

It's no good. I can't keep my distance from Alfie and it's not fair on him if I do. I admit it – I love him just as much as the others! Oh Lord, please don't take him from me.

Kate's Diary 7 March 1893

Little Alfie continues to do well, thank goodness. He's six months old today; surely life will be kind to him now. Just think, another baby on the way as well – a brother or sister for him; how wonderful. Due in October, so they'll be about a year apart. I can only imagine the fun they'll have together growing up. Still, it`s early days yet, mustn't get too excited.

Kate's Diary 11 April 1893

Today I bumped into Aunt Louisa for the first time in ages. She had been concerned that she hadn't heard from me.

"Are you all right, Kate?" she asked anxiously. "I went by your old place, but I heard you'd moved. That shopkeeper – Mr Tucker, is it? – He was less than polite about your manner of leaving! Told me you did a moonlight flit!" She laughed mischievously. "Can't say I blame you. He's a right ogre. I expect you had your reasons. Where are you living now?"

Feeling real embarrassed, I was rather vague, "Oh, over in another part of Clerkenwell; it suits Will's workplace better. Mr Tucker was making advances towards me all the time, so we thought it was best to get out."

At least this was partly the truth. I've always hated lying.

"The swine!" Louisa said. "Men of his kind think they can do what they like. I'll give him a piece of my mind if I see him!"

"No!" I exclaimed; a bit worried. "Please don't say anything. I'd rather just forget about it."

"Well, of course," she replied, "whatever you want. Look, why don't you pop in for tea sometime? You know where I am, don't you – 1a Compton Street? My half days are Wednesday and Saturday."

"I'll try," I promised, but didn't commit myself to anything. After all, Will doesn't much approve of her and I don't want to upset him again.

Kate's Diary 30 June 1893

I don't know what we're going to do. Yesterday, we had a letter from the authorities, informing us that they are doing 'slum clearance' and that everyone here has got to move out by the end of August. I wouldn't mind but they ain't given us anywhere else to go, just 'clear out' – that's all they said. These improvement programmes are all very well, but what about us? What are we supposed to do? Where can we live? Will and I have been getting by recently but there's not a lot of money spare, and certainly nothing to pay a deposit on a better place. We sat down in the evening together, our heads bowed down by all the worry. Already got one child and another on the way – what can we do?

Will was thoughtful and serious all evening. At one point, I saw him looking at my green necklace and fingering it lovingly.

"It's beautiful," I said, standing by his side, "the nicest thing I ever owned."

I put my arms round his neck and kissed him.

"You're beautiful too," he said, "with or without it," and he kissed me back.

I felt really close to him then and in spite of our problems (or maybe because of them), we found a comfort in the closeness of lovemaking, but this morning I am worried all over again.

Kate's Diary 7 July 1893

A week's gone by and we're no nearer to finding a place to live. It feels like time will run out on us if we're not careful, though I know two months is ages, really. Will's been out hunting around but everywhere is too expensive. What with the slum clearances, all the cheaper places are disappearing or being snapped up straight away.

Kate's Diary 12 July 1893

Alfie seems out of sorts and I'm sure he has a temperature. There's nothing I can put my finger on exactly, but I feel he's sickening for something. Talked to Will about getting him to a doctor, but we ain't got the money, he says, and I know he's right. Perhaps I am panicking unnecessarily.

Kate's Diary 15 July 1893

Alfie very poorly with diarrhoea. Please let him be all right! Have called the doctor – hang the expense!

Kate's Diary 10 August 1893 Woodwhistle St/Compton St

I can hardly begin to describe what has been happening in the last few weeks. It's such a blur of pain and regret. It must have been the 16th July, I think, when Will came home in a furious temper. He stormed into our solitary room and I knew I was in for it. Just seeing the murderous look on his face was enough to make me shrink away.

"Will, what's wrong?" I asked.

"Wrong?" he exclaimed. "Wrong? You tell me, you little hussy! What have you been doing? I take that damned necklace of yours to sell and the man in the shop tells me it's already been pawned once before, by my *dear* wife!" His voice was angry and sarcastic, but I was more concerned about the necklace than anything else, so I foolishly questioned him.

"Sell it! Tell me you haven't, Will, please!"

"Yes, of course I did. It's worth a lot of money. You didn't think it was a cheap bit of glass, did you? It was the real thing!"

"But I loved it," I said. "How could you do that?"

"Loved it?" he sneered. "Oh yes, so much that you pawned it, didn't you? So, what did you do with the money and how did you get it back? Are you seeing another man, eh?"

With that, he pushed me back against the wall and gripped my arm harshly.

"No, Will, there's no one else. I had to pawn it to pay for Mam's rent when she wasn't well. Then she repaid me later and I got it back. I love it. I never wanted to do that, but I had to. I'm sorry!"

"A likely story!" he said and struck me viciously across the face. "You're a dirty whore who doesn't value the things her husband gives her. Bitch!"

His face was contorted with rage and I struggled to get free, but he twisted my arm behind my back, and I couldn't move.

"How can you say that?" I retorted. "You've sold the one possession that I really loved!"

"Love – you don't know the meaning of the word!" he cried, and with that, vented the full force of his fury on me. The beating I got was savage and I can hardly bear to remember it. Helplessly, I tried to protect my unborn child from his punches and kicks but can only hope that it will be okay. At one point, I passed out briefly, only to come to and find myself alone. Will had gone off somewhere and I didn't hesitate for a moment. Tears streaming down my bruised face, I grabbed Alfie from his cot, plus a few essentials, and fled from the house, not even stopping to close the door. I had no idea where I was going; I just ran down the road, holding tight to my dear child. It might have been hours later, I really don't know, but somehow, I found myself outside Louisa's house, banging on her door for all I was worth. When she saw me, she was horrified and dragged me inside.

"Kate, my dear one! What's happened? You look awful!"

Between hysterical sobs, I told her my story and fortunately she made us both welcome. She is a good kind soul and that's what makes everything worse now.

"You must stay here," she insisted, "away from that brute. You must never go back to him. He isn't worth it. No one deserves such treatment!"

The next few days were a haven of peace as Will didn't know where I was; however, dear little Alfie continued to sicken as every day went by. On 26th July, I sat with him, willing him to live but knowing it was the end. It ended in a series of terrible convulsions brought on by dehydration. It was dreadful to watch and I still have nightmares about it now. He has passed, my little darling, and all I could do for days afterwards was scream and cry. Louisa held me and comforted me, and if it wasn't for her, I would certainly have lost my mind. Thank goodness she was there.

I swore I'd never go back to Will, but two days ago, he came round to Louisa's. She tried to refuse him entry, but he pushed her aside, roughly.

"I want to see my wife and child," he insisted.

I stood up. "Your child is dead," I told him in a flat cold voice.

He gasped and I was surprised to see him visibly upset.

"Another one? What happened?" He turned on Louisa then.

"This is all your fault! He was okay when I last saw him."

She pulled herself up straight and tall. "You're not to speak to me like that, especially in my own home! Get out! You're a wife beater and a bully."

He glared at her but didn't answer. Instead, he turned his attentions to me and changed his manner suddenly.

"Kate, darling – are you all right? I'm so sorry! It will never happen again, I promise. Let me hold you and tell you how much I love you."

"Get out," repeated Louisa.

"Yes," I said, but feeling a bit unsure of myself. "I don't want to see you. Go away."

Will looked deflated but didn't give up that easily.

"Let me visit again," he said, "when you've had a chance to think. I'm sure we can work this out. After all, you're carrying my child."

He left, but that struck a note with me. Whilst we had that connection, how could I leave him? The child would need a father and I couldn't manage on my own. My inclination was to have nothing more to do with him, but that wasn't going to be possible.

Louisa, however, was adamant that I mustn't listen to him and that I must only think of myself.

"He won't change, you know," she said, "and he'll end up killing you or something. Don't do it, Kate. Don't go back to him."

But turning it over in my mind, I knew I had no choice really.

Will came back a couple of days later and I was willing to listen. Louisa glared at him but reluctantly left us alone for a while to talk.

"Kate, my darling," he entreated, "I miss you. You know how much I love you. I was just so hurt by what you did."

"You hurt me too," I said, "by selling my necklace; let alone what you did to me! That was unspeakable."

His eyes have always had the power to soften me and he turned his full charm on me now. I was aware of it but powerless to resist.

"Darling one – I swear I'll never hurt you again and if you come back to me, I'll be better, I promise. I'll work hard and we'll have a lovely home. I'll even buy you a new necklace!"

"I don't want a new one," I said stiffly. "It was the old one I loved."

189

"I've found a flat in St James Street," he continued, ignoring my last remark, "it's got a sleeping area, a kitchen and even a tiny parlour, though it's upstairs again, above another shop. The deposit's all paid and there's still enough money left over to get some new furniture. We could have a good life again, just like we used to. I love you, you know that, don't you? I always will."

He moved close to me and took my hand gently, raising it to his lips.

"Please Kate. It'll be different this time. Give me another chance."

At that moment, Louisa returned.

"Don't do it, Kate," she said. "Be strong. Tell him to get lost."

"I can't, Louisa," I replied reluctantly. "There's the child to think of; besides, it's only fair to give Will this opportunity to prove he can change."

"Do that and you can forget about any more support from me!" she declared. "You're a fool and I don't hold with fools. Surely you can't mean it, Kate!"

Will let fly at her then.

"Leave my wife alone, madam! She's a right to make up her own mind. She don't need you putting ideas in her head!" He paused. "Come on Kate, let's go home."

I looked at them both – Louisa, angry and ashamed of me – Will, loving and persuasive – and I had to make my decision. I knew it was the wrong choice at the time, but it was the only thing I could do. Of course, I've come back to Will, and we're trying to make a life together again. It will never be easy, but whilst we have any children, even unborn ones, then it has to be this way. Louisa will never speak to me again; I've let her down too badly, but Will is delighted and has been very kind and gentle these past few days. Let's hope it continues.

Kate's Diary 20 October 1893 8 St James Street

Lying here in bed writing this after the birth of another son – Frederick Dennis. Will has said that I must rest, as it was a long and arduous labour. Little Freddy is in his cot sleeping peacefully and I feel all at peace myself. Our new surroundings are so much better than before, and I really feel there is hope this time. Ironically, we are only just over the road from where we lived before, but I hear Mr Tucker's moved away, thank goodness. The bank foreclosed on him and he lost the shop. Serves him right, I guess, though it's not a nice thing to happen to anyone.

The new flat is clean and well kept, with no dirty water or holes in the floor, thank goodness. The landlady is Mrs Lewis, a widow, who has a little draper's shop on the ground floor, all very neat and tidy. Mind, there are a lot of stairs as we are up on the third floor, and in the last few weeks of my confinement that's been mighty hard. But Will has been much kinder and more understanding this time. I know he is trying his best to be a good husband, and these have been a happy couple of months since we moved in. He's hardly been to the pub at all and has been working hard to keep the bills paid. I can't say I've really forgiven him for the beating he gave me last July, but I hope he has learnt his lesson. Must try and forget the past and move on. His temper has certainly been better lately, thank the lord.

Saw Louisa in the market the other day but she looked me straight in the face, then turned away. It's a shame, I like her, but she doesn't understand the position I'm in. After all, she's never been married or had any children.

I read in the newspapers that the Irish Home Rule bill's been defeated again – got through the 'Commons' this time but was turned down by those snooty old Lords. Typical! Ireland will never be free, I think.

Kate's Diary 2 February 1894

What a dreadful evening I had last night! I still feel myself shaking with fear. I'd hoped that this would never happen again, but Will has been getting more and more moody and bad tempered lately, snapping at me whenever he sees fit. Only the other day, he smashed a glass in anger at supper time, and then there was that incident at Christmas – but it's best not to dwell on that. Since then, he's been out drinking a few times, which don't help.

I have to get the washing done for Mrs Bennett today, but I must write this down first. It's my only solace – my writing – and it's a chance to clear my head. There's no one I can talk to about this, since Louisa left. I feel so alone.

And yet, when I look down at my precious baby Freddy, sleeping peacefully in his cot, I have so much love for him that it hurts. I pray the Good Lord won't take him away from me, like the others. I couldn't bear any more. I feel I shall go mad.

It all started last night after supper when I asked Will if he had paid the grocer's bill. I always have to check because otherwise these things get forgotten, I find, and then we get in trouble about it. We don't need people chasing us for money again like last time. Anyway, yesterday I saw the grocer's boy and he passed a message on from his master to remind us about it, so I had to ask.

"Pay the bill?" he said. "I haven't had it. How can I pay it?"

"But you must have done," I replied, "I gave it to you two weeks ago."

"You did not!" he exclaimed. "I've never had it. You're lying. *You've* got it somewhere!"

Well, of course my memory is prone to be a bit unreliable at the moment, what with a young baby and all, but I was sure I remembered giving it to him when it arrived. After all, he hates me getting involved with those kinds of things, and he has told me time and again to leave it all to him. I protested that I didn't have it, but he wouldn't listen.

"You must have lost it," he accused. "Well, it's your job to find it, not mine. I want it found, *now!*"

So, I searched the flat high and low, panic in my breast and fear in my heart, but to no avail. The more I looked, the less I could see any more. Will stood over me, arms folded, hurling abuse at intervals.

"You good for nothing piece of horse dung!" he flung at me, "You're rubbish, aren't you? Useless! We'll all go to jail for this and it will be your fault!"

With that, he grabbed me and pinned me up against the wall, his hands at my throat. For a moment, I really thought he was going to kill me.

"Please, Will," I gasped, "I'm sorry, I didn't mean to lose it. Give me more time, I'll find it. I know I will."

His face was as black as thunder and he shook me vigorously, but at least his hands had moved away from my throat to my arms. The back of my head banged against the wall, and my shoulders were bruised by his forcefulness, then he flung me away from him angrily and I ended up sprawling on the floor. In tears, I pleaded with him, "Don't hurt me, Will. You promised, remember! I'll look again. I'm sorry, honestly."

In the back of my mind, I was sure I'd given the bill to him, but I wasn't about to argue the case. It doesn't pay to try and prove anything against him, he only gets even angrier.

"You're pathetic!" he shouted and swiped me across the face with the back of his hand. My cheek stung like mad, but fortunately wasn't cut this time. I struggled to my feet and continued to search frantically, my heart pounding. In the other room, little Freddy started crying to be fed and I took the chance to escape and do just that. Holding Freddy close to me on my breast felt warm and reassuring. Salt tears poured down on him as he fed but he didn't notice. Such innocence and beauty – how I wish it would last forever. He's the only reason that I stay here. The moment calmed me, and I felt a bit stronger again.

Will followed after me, glaring silently as I fed his son. I settled Freddy down again in his cot and decided to look again nearby. Will's coat was hanging on the back of the door, and for some reason, I felt compelled to search it.

"Leave that alone, woman!" he snarled. "You got no right going in there."

This time I wasn't going to be put off and I quickly slipped my hand in the pocket before he could stop me. Guess what I found? The grocer's bill, *and* several other ones that didn't appear to have been paid.

"What's this then?" I demanded. "You had it all the time! And what about these – have *they* been paid? You said things would change, but it don't seem like it to me!"

I was angry and upset, feeling real put out that I'd been wrongly accused.

Will snatched them from me.

"You put them there yourself," he cried, "just to make a fool of me!"

"Will, you know that's not true. You should apologise. I didn't lose it after all."

His fury at my reproach overwhelmed him and he shoved me violently backwards.

"Shut up, you bitch!" he shouted. "Don't talk to me like that!"

I fell against the side of the wooden bedstead and felt the bruises start to form immediately. Stunned by the fall, I did not attempt to get up; luckily, he stormed out of the room, and the incident was finally over.

Later, he cried in my arms in bed, saying how he didn't mean to break his promise and that it's only because he's having a bad time at work. Of course, I told him I understood, but I don't really.

Kate's Diary 1 July 1894

What a grand day we had yesterday! It being a Saturday, I managed to persuade Will to take us out to see the opening of the new bridge – Tower Bridge it's called – and we had a fine time. Being nearly 4 months pregnant now, I got Will to push the pram with Freddy in it, though he grumbled that 'it's not man's work!'. Still, I told him, that in my condition it might put too much strain on the forthcoming baby and he reluctantly agreed. I took his arm and we walked slowly down to the Thames, where all the excitement was happening. Freddy stirred and chuckled happily to himself in his pram. He seems such a healthy, sturdy little chap and is 9 months old now, so I am optimistic for the future.

Bands were playing, flags were flying, and a huge crowd had gathered. Up and down the Thames, there were boats of all kinds, brightly decorated for the occasion. The sun shone on the whole scene, making everything colourful and gay. Even Will was impressed by the arrival of the Prince of Wales in his stately carriage to formally open the bridge.

It's strange that it's called Tower Bridge. There's one called that in my beloved Cork, though it ain't nothing like this. Cork's is a simple stone bridge over the dear old Blarney River, where a couple of carts could pass. But this one is huge, tall towers either side of the river with a walkway high above our heads for pedestrians brave enough to venture up there; and a roadway lower down, which, (I can hardly believe it!), opens up in the middle when boats need to pass. It's mighty clever to be sure!

The prince made a speech and cut the ribbon, declaring the bridge open, though we were too far away to hear his actual words, but we could see what was happening. Afterwards, Will was feeling in a rare indulgent mood and he took us to a lovely tearoom for tea and cake. It was almost like the old days and I felt truly happy for a change. It's a shame it can't be like this more often.

Kate's Diary 18 October 1894

Fred's first birthday today! I never thought we'd make it but perhaps the worst is over now. If only Will was a bit more interested in him. He's been moody again lately and I can tell something is troubling him. I'm trying to make sure the rent gets paid out of the bit of money I get from doing washing for folks. Mrs Lewis is a nice lady, and I wouldn't want to let her down. We often chat when I'm passing through the shop, and she has been tactful enough not to mention the shouting that she must overhear at times.

Had a letter from Mam today, telling me all the news from Liverpool and sending good wishes to little Freddy. It was great to hear from her again. I miss them both and wish they weren't so far away.

Kate's Diary 29 October 1894

For the last few days, Will has been laden down with one of his dark moods, like a storm cloud on the horizon. I've tried to steer clear whenever possible but last night I found out what it's all about.

He came back from work, looking even more thunderously unhappy than usual, but I said nothing and fetched his dinner to the table. No sooner had we started eating, however, but there was a knock at the door. I would have gone but Will jumped up and opened it, like he was expecting it. I saw it was a friend of his, so I wasn't worried, though oddly, Will went outside and shut the door behind him. I heard the distant murmur of their voices but did not attempt to listen. I've been told often enough to 'mind yer own business!'.

After some -time, Will returned to the supper table. He took a mouthful but then spat it out in disgust.

"Cold!" he exclaimed. "How dare you expect me to eat this?"

With that, he flung it across the room at the nearest wall. The plate shattered on impact and its contents ran messily down onto the floor.

"Oh Will, really!" I said. "What a mess!" I stood up to go and clean it, but he grabbed my arm.

"Leave it!" he snapped. "I need to talk to you."

I sat down, wondering what was to come.

"We've got to move," he muttered.

"What? Why? Are we in debt again?" I said. "Surely not?"

"No," he replied, "and stop asking about things that don't concern you!" Then he added sullenly, "It's them men I borrowed money from before – they know I'm around here again. That was Sid coming to warn me that they have found out my address."

"Can't you just pay them off?" I asked.

"No!" he cried. "Don't be stupid. It's far too much, what with all the interest they charge. Don't you think I'd have done it if I could?"

"So where will we go?" I said.

"Well," he replied, "with the new baby on the way, I figure we need a bit more room. There's a flat going fairly cheap over in Red Lion Street and it's even got a separate bedroom."

"Why's it so cheap?" I asked suspiciously.

"I know the landlord. It's next door to a pub and it's a bit noisy round there; but just think of the space we'll have."

I considered it for a few moments (not that I have much say in it), but it seemed to make sense. An extra room would be useful, it's true. So here we go, off again as quickly as possible. At least we're not running off in the middle of the night this time. I shall have time to settle up and say goodbye to Mrs Lewis properly, thank goodness. In the meantime, Will told me not to open the door to anyone.

Joe's Recollections, 1910

I have never been sure whether Mum was mixed up with the suffragettes or not. Certainly, Father believed she was, and regularly accused her of it. His paranoia overwhelmed his reason at times, convincing him that she was plotting against him, or planning a revolution. This was all nonsense, of course.

I remember one argument I overheard. It all started simply enough.

"What have you been doing today?" he asked her.

"Oh, just running some errands," she replied, "and I took the laundry back to Mrs Dixon's house."

"I hope you didn't go near that march that was going on," Father said, his face beginning to darken.

"No, of course not," she answered. "I wouldn't do that."

"Oh really? That's not what I heard!" he declared. "Mrs Jones told me she saw you the other day, in amongst the crowds. You're lying again, aren't you?"

"No," Mum pleaded, "really, I'm not. I may have gone that way when I had to collect some washing but that doesn't mean I was involved."

"You better not be," he threatened. "We all know those women are just low down, dirty whores, looking for a fight. They can't get husbands like any decent woman, because they're all dried up ugly old shrews!"

"That's not fair!" Mum flared up. "Really, Will – you're going too far!"

"See!" he cried, "You *are* involved. You just want to destroy me, don't you? Just because I'm a man! Well, I tell you one thing, woman – try any more of it and you'll be sorry!"

He had her by the arm now and was glaring into her face.

"You need to know your place, and that's to look after me. It's your duty – love, honour and obey – remember!"

Fred came in at that moment, and exclaimed, "What's going on?"

Father released Mum's arm.

"Just remember what I said," he muttered and moved away.

I didn't really understand what it was all about at the time. The newspapers were very negative about the suffragettes, painting them as dreadful harridans who would stop at nothing to destabilise the nation. Father was always lecturing us boys about how dangerous and wrong it all was, and I suppose I believed it to a certain extent. Poor Mum was the only female in the household and had no support from anyone else.

Later, I learnt to think for myself, especially during the war years, and I realised how narrow minded and mistaken those attitudes were. As for Mum, well, I know she had sympathies with the cause, but I really don't think she ever took part in anything. I'm sure she would have been too scared to take the risk.

Kate's Diary 10 December 1894 Red Lion Street

Ernest Charles Duffield was born yesterday 9th December in Red Lion Street. All went well, though I feel absolutely exhausted. What with trying to get the new flat straightened out in time for his arrival, it's been a busy time for the last month. The flat was very dirty and dusty, and I had to scrub everywhere thoroughly to make it fit for a new baby and a young child. Fred is toddling around quite a bit now and is liable to pick up anything he finds, so it needs to be safe and clean. But I'm pleased with it now though, it looks fine.

The flat is spacious and our furniture fits in well. We're up on the third floor but we've got our own 'upstairs', where the bedroom is. Apart from that, we've got a kitchen/living room, where we also wash, and we have the use of a shared privy, but it's not outside this time, so that's a bit of luxury. What's more, there are only three families in this block, so it ain't too bad really.

There seems to be more pubs in this street than I've ever seen in one place before. The area is certainly noisy, even rowdy at times, but the rent is reasonable and I'm thankful for that. Mr Ings, our landlord, owns the pub next door as well and seems a fair man. Will seems quite friendly with him and I gather that's why we got it at a good price. Let's hope we're settled for a while now.

Kate's Diary 9 December 1895

Can it really be a year since I last wrote in this diary? It seems so, and yet I can't think why I haven't. I suppose I've been busy working and looking after the boys and time has just slipped past, like sand through an hourglass.

It's been a calmer, more settled year and for once I haven't been pregnant, which has allowed me to recover and get strong. It is Ern's first birthday today and Freddy is over two years old now and into everything! He's a healthy, energetic little boy, thank goodness, and Ern seems to be following in his footsteps. We had a little party to celebrate today with games and cake, though Ern is a bit too young to fully appreciate it.

Will has been working hard lately, though the numerous pubs in this area certainly draw him in at times. Red Lion Street is lively but at least half respectable, so that's a relief. Can't say I really approve of the folks Will mixes with, but who am I to have any say? He always tells me I have no rights, and I guess that's true. It's just the way it is for women these days.

Kate's Diary 19 January 1896

It occurred to me today, as I was doing the ironing (don't know why but thoughts always come into my head at that time!), that lately Will hasn't been as 'amorous' as he used to be. I know we've got two young children sleeping in our room but that wouldn't stop him if he felt inclined, to be sure. He's a man of strong appetites and is never one to worry about others if he wants something. Not that it concerns me particularly, it gives me some peace and means that I'm not constantly pregnant, but it's odd all the same. His temper has lessened a bit as well, which is good, but it almost feels as though he has lost interest in us. He rarely chats much at supper and mostly ignores the children, except if they annoy him. He often stays out late (at the pub, I imagine), and I know there's a variety of 'loose' women available there. Maybe he has turned to them, I don't know. As long as he doesn't treat us too badly, then we should be grateful, I suppose.

Kate's Diary 1 September 1896

When I went in to get Fred out of bed this morning, he complained loudly.

"Mum, my throat hurts!" He coughed and moaned in pain as this hurt him even more. Ern lay quietly in his cot, but I noticed that his breath was rasping. Neither of them seemed to want much breakfast and I am worried about them. They've been quiet and moody all day. Hope it's just a cold coming on.

Kate's Diary 2 September 1896

Getting real anxious about the children today. Both are coughing loudly, and their throats are so sore they can't eat and can barely drink. When I looked at Fred's throat, it seemed to be covered in some kind of thick grey substance. I don't know what that is, but it can't be good. They're both running a high temperature as well and their glands appear swollen. Spoke to Will about it but he said I was just making a fuss about nothing again.

"Face it, Kate – kids are always picking up illnesses. Happens all the time! I wish you'd stop panicking so much. There's nothing to worry about."

Please let him be right this time.

Kate's Diary 4 September 1896

Fred and Ern both in hospital with diphtheria! Apparently, it's going round like wildfire. In spite of Will's protests, I called the doctor in today and I'm glad I did. They're both really ill now, feverish and struggling to breathe. My poor little darlings. I can hardly believe that this has happened after getting them through the first year or so. I'm going to visit them every day. It's so awful to think of them there away from home. Fred cried with anxiety when I had to leave them, and Ern is frightened of all the doctors and nurses. I tried to explain to him that they were there to help him get better but he's a bit too young to understand.

The house feels so empty without them, though Will seems oddly happier. He was quite jolly this evening, until I got upset about the boys and then he told me to 'grow up'.

"You always make too much fuss about it," he said. "They'll be okay, and in the meantime, it's nice to have the house to ourselves."

"Will!" I said, shocked. "They're very ill. I thought you'd be concerned about them."

"Of course, of course," he muttered, "but give it a rest, will you, Kate?"

He's gone to the pub again now, leaving me alone, desperate and sad, praying that my two beloved boys will survive.

Kate's Diary 11 September 1896

Both boys unconscious when I visited today. Hardly able to breathe. The doctor called me aside and told me that if we don't do something drastic, it's likely they will die. Then he gave me a faint hope.

"There's a new anti-toxin out," he said. "We're trying to get hold of some, as we've got so many cases here. It might work. I've heard great things about it."

"Oh please," I begged in tears, "if there's anything at all – please help them!"

"We'll try," he promised.

Oh, I only hope it arrives in time. How I wish I could describe in words what my sons mean to me, but I could never capture the love I feel for them on paper. My darling ones.

Kate's Diary 28 September 1896

Saw Fred and Ern today, conscious for the first time in two weeks. It was so good to see, though they're still very ill. The anti-toxin is working slowly, thank the Lord. Wanted to tell Will the news but he's hardly been in, just ate his supper silently and left. I don't know where he's gone.

Kate's Diary 16 October 1896

Slow steady progress, thank goodness. Fred tried to eat something today, which is a start.

"Mummy," he croaked, "I want to come home. When can I?"

"Soon, darling," I told him, "just eat up and get strong again."

But they're both so weak, they can't even stand up, so it's going to be a while longer yet. Told Will how things are going but he don't seem interested. I'm alone again this evening. Feel so tired after visiting the hospital every day, plus trying to keep everything else going – think I'm going to bed early.

Kate's Diary 20 October 1896

Yesterday, an odd thing happened. After supper, Will went out as usual, 'to go to the pub', he said. Going upstairs to turn down the bed for the night, I noticed from the bedroom window that he was out in the street below, obviously talking to someone. In the gaslight below, I could see it was a woman there with him and although I couldn't hear the words, it was clear that there was an argument going on. Opening the window wide, I was able to hear raised voices. Will was gesturing and attempting to get her to take notice of him, but she seemed unprepared to listen. It appeared to be getting more heated and I saw him take her arm roughly, but she slapped him hard across the face, then pushed him away. She flounced off and he started to follow her. Then he stopped, turned and headed back towards our house. I hurried downstairs as I didn't want him to know I'd been spying on him. When he came in, I was sat calmly in my chair, my sewing in my lap, pretending I knew nothing about it.

"Kate!" he declared. "Put that down!" He paused and looked at me. "Have you seen the children today?"

I nodded and was about to give him the latest news when he raised his hand to stop me, and came forward, gazing at me.

"You're still a beautiful woman, Kate. Come here," he coaxed.

With a sinking feeling, I knew what he wanted and reluctantly put my sewing aside. He pulled me down onto the hard, wooden floor, and his passion was urgent and demanding. I used to enjoy our lovemaking, but these days there's little love in it, only his fierce lust which must be satisfied. He takes everything but gives nothing in return. It is useless to resist, so I surrendered myself to his need. Strange, it's the first time in a while. I thought he'd lost interest in me completely – it seems not.

Kate's Diary 15 November 1896

What a wonderful day we had yesterday. Since Will resumed 'marital relations' with me, he has been more amenable and affectionate. I was keen to visit the children in hospital again and for once Will was persuaded to come with me. On the way, we went quite near Trafalgar Square and just outside the Metropole Hotel, we saw lots of those strange new motor carriages – 'cars', they call them – all lined up at the start of a drive to Brighton. There must have been at least thirty of them and they looked so fine and colourful. It was a 'rally' apparently, to mark the fact that the law has changed and that no one has to go ahead of them with a flag anymore. Mind, that sounds quite frightening to me; imagine those things running around with no warning. People will get hurt! But it was exciting to watch, even though it was raining and cold. Will seemed fascinated.

"Them's the future, you know, Kate," he remarked.

"Surely it's just a passing fad – a whim?"

"No, I don't think so," he said. "Horses are on their way out. These are quicker and cleaner."

I thought briefly of dear old Ned, our horse in Ireland, and wondered what happened to him in the end. I guess he's long gone by now.

The 'cars' moved off, making a tremendous noise. Crowds waved and cheered, and the scene was certainly a merry one. It raised my spirits on the way to the hospital.

When we got there, there was yet more cause for happiness. Fred and Ern were both out of bed, sitting in chairs! The doctor told us they'll be able to go home very soon now and have recovered well. Fantastic news! I can hardly wait.

Afterwards, Will took me out to a tearoom in the park, and in spite of the grey, rain filled clouds, we also went for a short stroll.

"I do love you, you know Kate," he told me when we stopped to shelter under a tree for a moment. This made me very happy, but something made me ask,

"And the boys as well, of course?"

"Oh yes, of course," he said, "but you're the one I need the most."

We kissed and it was the final seal on a perfect day.

Kate's Diary 5 December 1896

Fred and Ern are both home at last! Today we had a joint 'welcome home/birthday party' for them both. We missed Fred's birthday because he was so ill at the time, and Ern's is only next week. He'll be two years old!

Had a wonderful time playing games and having treats. Will refused to join in but at least he was kind and fatherly for a change. Haven't told him yet about the forthcoming baby. I hope it's a girl this time.

Kate's Diary 4 January 1897

A strange thing happened last night. Just after supper, there was a knock on the door and when I opened it a young woman stood there, in much the same 'delicate' condition as myself, about three months pregnant, I would say. She looked vaguely familiar, though I couldn't quite place her. She wasn't wearing a hat like decent folk; her hair hung down loose, long, and nearly as dark as my own.

"Can I see Will?" she asked, scowling at me.

"Yes, of course," I said and disappeared to fetch him. Will saw her, groaned slightly then went to speak to her outside. A few minutes later, he returned and told me, "I have to go out, Kate. I'll be back later."

From the window I watched as the two of them made their way down the street. At one point, the woman tried to take his arm, but he shook her off. I wonder what is going on. Will made an excuse when I asked him about it later, then got moody and told me to 'keep out of his affairs'.

Kate's Diary 16 January 1897

Will's been shouting in the street at that woman again, but he won't tell me what it's all about. I'm sure it was her who called again last week as well. When I asked Will, he just swiped me across the face with the back of his hand and told me to 'Shut yer mouth!' I shan't ask again. Don't want him to hurt me whilst I'm 'with child'.

Kate's Diary 7 February 1897

Will's been quite shifty and, I would say, secretive this last week, so I was pleased when he started to chat pleasantly to me after supper, instead of going out.

"I've got some exciting news, Kate," he told me enthusiastically. "I've managed to find a better job with more money over in Southwark, and I've put our name down for one of those new flats in the Stanhope Buildings."

"Really?" I said, surprised. "But they're brand new. Are you sure we can afford it?"

"Of course," he said, "and with the new baby coming, we'll need the extra space. There's an extra bedroom that the children will be able to sleep in, which will make life easier for everyone. You and I will be able to have a private life again, eh?" and he winked at me, grinning.

"Well, that's wonderful, if you're sure," I said. "It'll be better to be away from all these pubs, what with the boys getting older. It's so noisy around here."

The evening was spent making happy plans. It's the first move we've had that I'm really looking forward to. Maybe things are looking up.

Kate's Diary 17 June 1897 210 Stanhope Buildings

It's been a week now since Albert Thomas was born and I've only just managed to find my strength again. It was a long and painful birth; Albert's a large baby; I tore quite badly and bled a lot. Today is the first day I've felt like myself again.

Will's sister Amelia has been very kind, looking after Fred, Ern and Will whilst I haven't been able to. Last time I gave birth, Fred went over to stay with sister-in-law Mary and her family for a few days, but he's older now and there's Ern as well, so it was better to keep them here. About all I've managed to do is to look after little Albert and that's been an effort. But today, Amelia has gone home and we're on our own again.

Will is delighted about the new arrival, as Albert was born on his father's birthday – June 11th. He keeps saying how Albert is 'special' and is sure to be 'a wonder' in the future (I love all my children so they're all special to me). I have to admit I'd have liked a girl this time, but it seems it's not to be.

This afternoon, Will has gone over with Amelia and taken Albert to visit his mother. That's the first time he's ever wanted to show any of the babies off; must be something different this time. Not that the old battle-axe will be interested anyway!

It's just so nice to relax for a change. Fred and Ern are playing happily downstairs and for once all is peaceful. I do like living in the Stanhope Building, even though it's a huge block of flats and we're up on the second floor, number 210. Everything is so bright, shiny and new – no damp, no dirt, no holes in the floor. All we had to do was move in. There's a kitchen, a tiny parlour, two bedrooms and a privy just down the corridor, which only a few families share. Seems like luxury. There's even a green area out the front of the building, where the children will be able to play when they're older. It's grand! Mind, the rent is 4 shillings and 6 a week, so we'll have to be careful. As soon as I feel better again, I'll take on some more laundry jobs to help out.

Today, I feel quite exhausted as I'm only just getting over the birth, but I had to take the children out to join in the Diamond Jubilee celebrations. Fred kept on at me about it and I could hardly refuse.

"Please, Mum," he said, "I want to see all the soldiers in the parade."

"Your mother's not well," Will snapped at him, but I roused myself in spite of my weakness. Freddy's my darling child and I didn't want to disappoint him.

It's been a bank holiday today and the weather has been bright and sunny, so there were street parties everywhere. The whole of London seems to be draped in banners, flags and bunting. It's like the dear old city has its party clothes on! I persuaded Will to help me take the children down to see the procession, partly by telling him it would be good for baby Albert. I know he didn't want to really, but he gave in, thankfully. I don't think I could have managed on my own.

There was a massive procession of brightly dressed soldiers, fine horses and gorgeous carriages. Fred and Ern were very impressed.

"I'm going to be a soldier when I grow up, Mum," Freddy said enthusiastically. "They look so fine."

I smiled at the child's innocence.

"There's a lot more to being a soldier than just that, my darling," I said. "They have to go off and defend their queen and country."

"I could do that!" Freddy told me. "I'm very strong!"

"I'm sure you are, my darling. Well, maybe one day."

We couldn't see the queen as she was shut away in her closed carriage; everyone says she is quite frail now. Imagine

– 60 years on the throne – amazing! Just wish she'd think about letting poor Ireland go free. The whole occasion seemed designed to show off the empire, and I wondered how many other countries ruled by Britain would like their freedom as well.

After the procession, I took Fred and Ern to our nearest street party and asked Will to take Albert home. When we got back later, I found him snoring in a drunken haze, with Albert fast asleep in his arms. They were giving away free tobacco and ale, apparently, so I couldn't really say anything.

This evening, they are lighting beacons all over England, and fireworks are going off around the city. The sky is alive with flowers of fire and crackling silver fountains. What a dazzling occasion!

Kate's Diary 20 January 1898

Freddy, who is usually so bright and cheerful, came running up to me this afternoon, looking very worried and a bit tearful.

"Mummy, Ern won't play with me. He says he don't feel well. His head's all hot and sticky."

This made me rather anxious, so I went to see for myself. Sure enough, poor little Ern was flushed with fever and burning like fire. I put him straight to bed and called the doctor. I knew Will would object 'cause of the expense but I don't care anymore. The children have to come first.

"Influenza, Mrs Duffield," he told me. "Very nasty, it can be. Make sure the other children don't come near him. I'll give you some medicine and call again tomorrow."

"What's wrong with Ern?" asked Fred, after he'd gone. "Can I go in and see him?"

"No darling, I'm sorry. You have to keep away," I said, and he burst into tears.

He loves Ern so much, I know, and it was pitiful to see him so upset. I did my best to comfort him, but I don't feel too confident about it all myself.

When Will came home, I told him the news. His immediate reaction surprised me.

"What? That's infectious, ain't it? Albert must be taken out of the house. I'll ask my mother to look after him for a few days."

"That's a good idea," I replied, "and Freddy can go as well."

"He'll be too much for her at her age," Will said, frowning. "He never does anything he's told. She'll be worn out by him."

"I'm sure he'll be good if she tells him to behave," I said.

Will snorted but reluctantly agreed. However, when I told Freddy, my dear little angel became a five-year-old demon.

"I don't want to go, Mummy!" he shouted. "I'm not leaving. You can't make me!"

A full-scale childhood tantrum ensued, until Will came into the room, and to my alarm, dealt him a swift cuff to the ear.

"Shut up, you little monster!"

"Will, really!" I exclaimed. "There's no need for that!"

"You need to discipline him properly, Kate. He's getting wilful and difficult."

Fred stared at him in shock, his screams suddenly silenced. Tears fell down his cheeks and I felt such pity for him. Bending down, I gathered him into my arms and tried to explain things to him.

"Freddy, what your father means is that you have to be a good boy, for all our sakes, Ern's too."

I dried his tears with my 'kerchief and calmed him down. My eyes met Will's over his head, and I glared at him in rage. I know children have to be chastised at times, but does he have to be so rough? I dare not say anything else, but he knows what I think.

Reluctantly Freddy trudged out with his father and baby Albert to his grandmother's house. His words of parting were heart wrenching, "Mummy, don't leave me there, will you?"

"Of course not, dear, you'll soon be home again," I reassured him, but my heart aches with the pain of separation.

Kate's Diary 22 February 1898

I feel like I'm drowning beneath a wave of anxiety and chaos. These last few weeks I haven't known whether I'm coming or going. A month ago today, the doctor took one look at Ern and promptly sent him to the infirmary. The influenza was so serious that he developed pneumonia, my poor darling. They say he will pull through now, but it was touch and go for a while.

What with visiting the hospital most days, seeing Freddy and Albert over at their grandmother's, plus looking after Will's needs, I've barely had a minute to spare. Exhaustion is threatening to overwhelm me like a tidal wave, but I mustn't let it. Needless to say, Will hasn't been a lot of help. He still expects a clean house and his dinner on the table, but at least he has visited Albert a few times.

Today, I collected Freddy again and we had an emotional reunion. He wants to visit Ern in hospital, and I've said I'll take him next week if things continue to progress well. Thank the Lord, Ern's over the worst now, though I don't think he'll be home for a while yet. Still very weak and breathless, but conscious and eating, thank goodness.

When Will came home this evening and saw Freddy again, he appeared to be annoyed.

"What's he doing back here so soon?" he said, "and why ain't Albert home as well?"

"I just can't cope with a baby as well at the moment," I told him, "what with visiting the hospital so often."

"Huh! Not much of a mother then, are you?" he retorted.

Freddy gazed at him nervously and clung to my side. I think he's frightened of him now, since Will smacked him. Hopefully that will wear off with time. It won't happen again, I'm sure; it was just on the spur of the moment. I know Will wouldn't want to hurt a child.

Kate's Diary 16 April 1898

I'm so glad to have Ern home again. He seems quite well now and is enjoying running around with Fred again. Baby Albert seems to be thriving, and for once, Will is showing an interest. It's a relief because he hasn't seemed to care much about any of them before this. Fred started school this week but doesn't like it much. It's true that the discipline is harsh, but he's lucky to get free schooling after all. I remember going to the convent school in Cork – all those nuns, they were mighty fierce!

Kate's Diary 29 July 1898

A terrible day! Now that it is the school holidays, I have Fred at home every day and he's been keen to let off steam after being stuck in a classroom for the last few weeks. He has so much energy and doesn't know how to control it, but he's only five after all. Today being Sunday, we were all at home this afternoon after a particularly long (and truth to tell, rather boring) sermon in church this morning. Will was dozing after lunch and the children were playing in the street. The other day, Fred saw the trains at the station and has been mad keen on them ever since. This afternoon, he and Ern were dashing around happily, pretending to be trains, outside. Unfortunately, a sudden heavy downpour of rain sent them running for shelter indoors. I was upstairs changing Albert and smiled to myself when I heard the two of them come in – so noisy! You could hardly miss them. The sounds of tramping feet and shrieks of excitement carried a long way. Suddenly, I heard a crash, followed by an ominous silence. This worried me and I hurriedly put Albert in his cot so that I could go and investigate. By the time I arrived on the scene, Ern was crying loudly, having fallen and grazed his knee, and Fred was cowering under his father's wrath. Will had been woken up by the two children crashing into the room, sending things flying in all directions, and he wasn't best pleased.

"Frederick!" he shouted. "How dare you behave like this? Come here!"

Freddy approached him warily.

"Sorry, Father," he muttered. "We were being steam trains. It's our new game."

"You stupid, ignorant little boy!" his father cried. "Look at your brother – don't you know he's been ill? Now you've hurt him."

"No, Father," Ern piped up. "I'm all right. It's just my knee."

But still the tears rolled down his cheeks. I cuddled him in close to me.

"There, there, Ern, my darling. No harm done. Mum'll put something on it to make it better. You two need to be more careful next time."

"Sorry, Mum," said Fred, but Will wasn't so easily appeased.

"You will be, son! It's time I took you in hand. Come here."

To my surprise, Will grabbed his arm and dragged him off into the front room. Fred was protesting loudly.

"Let go, Father. You're hurting my arm."

"Will, what are you doing?" I asked, alarmed, following with Ern by my side.

"Teaching him a lesson," he replied, and to my horror, took off his leather belt and started to beat him. I was shocked. I know Will has knocked me around at times, but to strike a child – well really!

"Stop!" I cried, "Will, please!"

"He needs to learn how to behave," he growled. "As his father, I have every right to discipline him, so leave it, woman! He can think himself lucky I'm not using the buckle end!"

He administered two more strokes; Fred screaming in pain with every blow, but I couldn't bear it anymore and had to intervene. I placed myself in-between and tried to wrench the belt away. Will turned on me, eyes blazing.

"Oh, so it's like that is it?"

The next thing I knew, the belt lashed viciously sideways at me several times and was followed by a hard shove, which sent me flying across the room, but at least it stopped him hitting our child anymore. Then Will turned and left the room, leaving all three of us there in tears.

I comforted Fred and Ern and tried to ease their pain. Ern recovered quickly from the graze but was frightened by what he'd seen. He clung to me for ages afterwards, his eyes wide with fear. Fred was withdrawn and sullen and avoided him for the rest of the day. I can't blame him. What a thing to do!

I tried to talk to Will about it later, but he rather forcefully told me to '*keep quiet or else!*'. There ain't no reasoning with him on this, that's for sure. I just have to make certain that I protect my children as much as possible in future. It doesn't matter about me; I'd die for them if I had to. They're my life.

Kate's Diary 14 February 1899 Valentine's Day.

Sometimes I ask myself whether I still love Will. We've been married over ten years now, but it's a hard question to answer. He is often brutal and unkind to both me and the children, he drinks far too much, and I wouldn't be surprised if there were one or two women in the background. Freddy keeps away from him whenever possible, I've noticed. Normally he's such a happy, cheeky little boy, but he's very quiet when his father is around.

Yet, at times, Will can be charming and funny, and he knows how to have a good time. There's no denying he's intelligent and quite handsome in a rough sort of way, but his moods are unpredictable and dangerous. I just don't know what to feel anymore.

Kate's Diary 21 October 1899

"Mummy, where are all the soldiers going?" Ern asked me today. "Is it another parade?"

I had to smile.

"No darling, they're off to the war." I told him.

"What's that?" asked Fred, who was there as well.

"War is when one country fights another," I explained.

"Why?" asked Fred.

That's a good question, I thought to myself.

"Well, sometimes a country is upset because another one has tried to take something away from it or has hurt some people. Then they fight until one of them wins."

"Do they make them say sorry?" asked Ern innocently.

"They try to, dear," I replied.

"So, they're stealing then?" asked Fred.

"Yes, usually," I said.

"It's wrong to steal!" declared Fred. "They should call a policeman!"

"I want to be a soldier," said Ern suddenly.

"Yes, me too," said Fred. "I'd stop them stealing from each other."

"I'm sure you would, darling, but it's not an easy job and sometimes people get hurt."

"Why do people hurt each other, Mummy?" asked Ern.

"I don't know, dear. It's silly isn't it?"

With that I changed the subject – too many awkward questions! It's amazing how children see things so differently, and perhaps more clearly, than adults at times.

Let's hope this war doesn't go on too long. I can't quite decide which side I'm on – the British, who say they are protecting the citizens, or the Boer, who just want their land back.

Kate's Diary 1 January 1900

Happy New Year! The dawn of a new century – what will it bring, I wonder? Will seems unimpressed by the event, but I am full of hope and anticipation at the thought of a new start.

Kate's Diary 18 April 1900

I look back at my last diary entry and realise that the excitement of a new century has soon faded. A certain gloom and foreboding has appeared to settle over the whole nation. Many soldiers have died in the war in South Africa, so the newspapers say, though thankfully the siege of Ladysmith was relieved recently. Not only that, but the 'flu' is rife. People sicken and die in just a few days. I try hard to keep the children safe, using these new soaps to wash and clean everything. Albert is nearly three now and toddling around, putting his fingers everywhere. He objects loudly to me washing his hands all the time, but it must help stop this deadly disease, surely. We were lucky to save Ern last time; we certainly don't want to go through that again.

Yesterday, Will came home from work and told me he'd been made up to foreman because the other man had died from the flu. He was really pleased and I'm glad for him, but sorry that it has to be because of someone else's misfortune. We argued a bit, of course. I was stupid enough to say that he shouldn't be so happy about it.

"Happy? Why shouldn't I be?" he cried. "I'm the best worker there and I deserve to be promoted."

"I'm sure you do, dear," I said, "but even so–"

"Even so, what?" he interrupted. "Anyway, with you pregnant again, we need the extra money. I'm going to find us a bigger flat, we'll need the space."

"But I don't want to move again, Will. It's nice here and it'll be too expensive."

"I told you," he said angrily, "I'll be earning more now. Not that you care, obviously. You'd rather see us struggle just so as not to hurt someone's feelings!"

The children retreated hastily as he went storming off. Unfortunately, Ern got in the way accidentally and received a rough shove out of the way from his father. Just a normal day, I guess.

It's true we will need extra room when this baby arrives. It's due September and I'm looking forward to it. Don't think Albert will take it well, though, he's used to being the 'special' one of the family.

Today, I had such a surprise when I was out returning the laundry to my lady in Hanover Square. A tall, well dressed young woman came up, calling me.

"Miss Katie!"

I could scarcely believe my eyes – Flossie! She looks so elegant and well to do now that I hardly recognised her. She was excited to see me, but I felt drab and old compared to her. Apparently, she did well in 'service' and ended up marrying the valet. He's now gone into business and is doing very nicely. I'm real pleased for her, she's as sweet as ever and deserves to be happy, but it was such a shock.

"Dear Miss Katie," she said warmly. "What would I have done without you? You saved me from the workhouse; I can never thank you enough."

She pressed me to tell her all about Will and the children and I did my best to be positive, but truth to tell, it was hard. Will doesn't improve in temper, in spite of his constant promises to do better. How many times have I forgiven him, only for it to happen again? Perhaps this new job will help.

Joe's Recollections, 1912

I often wondered what my mother saw in my father. I mean; she was attractive, intelligent, hardworking, and at one time, not afraid to speak her mind. She had no need to take up with a rogue like him. She could have done so much better. One day, whilst I was sat with her in one of her frequent bouts of illness, trying to ease her pain, we got to talking and I summoned up the courage to ask her. I was only 12 at the time and I didn't really understand about love, so I couldn't think why she married him. She lay there, propped up in bed, a deathly shade of white, coughing intermittently but trying to explain. I remember her saying, "Joe, you have to understand, I'd been in service for many years and I was desperately lonely and bored. I didn't know anyone except my mam when I came to London and the circle I moved in was so limited. Even though I worked in a big house then, the only people I usually saw were other servants. Your father called at the house as a tradesman, with an order of printing for my master's business, and he just seemed so much more interesting and exciting than the rest."

"Was there never anyone else?" I asked, and I remember she looked sad and wistful.

"Yes," she answered slowly, "once, but it wasn't to be. Just a hopeless dream." She sighed and her eyes were misty.

"Your father offered me a way out, away from domestic service and loneliness. He offered me a world of music and dancing, and he knew all sorts of interesting people. I used to love it when he played his fiddle. It was grand, but he refuses to do it now, says there's no point, no one listens."

She sighed again, then continued, "There was a spark between us, which was exciting. I knew he was damaged and dangerous but that was part of the attraction. I don't expect you to understand, Joe, you're not old enough yet, but sometimes there's a need for a certain amount of danger. He was vulnerable as well and he needed me; I thought I could 'fix' him, but I was wrong."

I didn't quite know what she meant but I listened anyway. My father – vulnerable? All I'd ever seen of him was brutality and drunkenness. My mother started coughing again and this time more blood came up. I sponged her down, helped get her comfortable again and was about to leave the room to let her rest, when she suddenly spoke again, "Don't be too hard on him, Joe. He loves us all really."

I patted her hand reassuringly. "Of course, he does," I told her, though I didn't believe it for one moment.

Kate's Diary 18 September 1900 189 Stanhope Buildings

Andrew Joseph born 6 o'clock this morning, bless him. I feel well and happy and just need to rest a while. Mind, I prefer the name Joseph to Andrew (Will insisted on that one) and I shall call him that whenever I can.

At least we haven't moved far – just down one floor to a bigger flat. It's not so clean and new as the other one was, but it's okay. Unfortunately, the last tenants were evicted when the husband died. So sad – the woman and her children out on the streets. I never met them, but I feel for them all the same.

Kate's Diary 23 January 1901

The queen is dead. It seems like everyone has been expecting it for ages and yet it is still a shock. The end of an era, a change in the world – what will happen next, I wonder? They say that Prince Bertie will be crowned, but opinion has it that he's a waster and a scoundrel, though it's true that he's popular with the public.

This morning, every window is shrouded in black. It's raining hard and it seems as if the sky itself is in mourning. Everywhere you go, people are gathered in small groups (some singing the national anthem), and the church bells are sounding sorrowfully across the city.

Ern came home from school today, asking, "Why is everyone crying, Mummy?"

I tried to explain but he only just about knows who the queen is.

"Is that the lady who lives in that big house in the park?" he said.

"Yes," I told him. "She's died and gone to Heaven."

"Where's Heaven?" piped up Albert (he's at the stage of asking lots of questions now and it drives me mad at times).

"Heaven's where all the good people go," said Fred, "but you won't be going there, you're too naughty!"

"Fred!" I exclaimed. "That's not a nice thing to say. Apologise now."

Albert started screaming – yet another outburst – and pushed Fred hard. They started a tussle, which I had to stop before it got out of hand. Really – I have to say they're both getting quite difficult. Albert is so jealous of baby Joe and hates not being the youngest anymore. He's always throwing tantrums these days, and Fred reacts badly to him. Dear Ern, ever the peacemaker, tries his best to calm them down but it's a hard job.

It's a shame that Albert is being so temperamental at the moment. Joey is such a sweet baby, all chuckles and smiles. Mind, Will still spoils Albert and never tells him off like he does the others, so of course he's bound to feel he's 'special'.

Kate's Diary 2 February 1901

Took the children to watch the funeral procession today. Don't know why, but I felt they needed to see it. It was impressive – all the military trappings – guns, horses, carriages, etc, proceeding through the city streets in silence. There were crowds everywhere but hardly a sound. I suppose everyone felt they loved her. As for myself – well, I think she did well to last so long, but she could have done more to free poor Ireland. What would it have hurt her?

"Why have they got white horses, Mum?" asked Fred. "Isn't everything supposed to be black at a funeral?"

He's eight now and beginning to understand these things. One of his school friends died last year of the flu, so he knows about death; they've discussed it in class.

"I heard she didn't want it to be all black," I said, "and she's dressed in her wedding dress as well, they say."

"Why, Mummy?" asked Ern.

"I suppose she loved her husband very much," I replied, "and wanted to show that her wedding was the happiest day of her life."

"Will you do the same, Mummy?" he asked.

"What an odd question!" I said, feeling rather unnerved. "Let's not think about that now!"

The innocent question surprised me and made me think. Was my wedding day my happiest moment? Well no, not really, if I'm honest. Looking back, I realise it was just the start of many arguments that were to come.

Needless to say, Will didn't come with us today, even though it was a Saturday. I asked him to look after the baby, but he said he was going to the pub, so I had to take Joe in the pram. Quite a handful – three young children plus baby, but I managed to get Ern to hold Albert's hand to stop him running off and getting lost. There was one nasty moment when a group of people suddenly pushed in front and Fred was separated from the rest of us, but we were soon reunited, thank goodness.

Kate's Diary 3 April 1902

Will didn't go to work today. At about 6 o' clock this morning, just as I was staggering around, my eyes still full of sleep, making his breakfast, there was a loud desperate knocking on the front door. I came to fully then, with a start. Why would anyone call at that time of day? Something must be wrong.

My sister-in-law Amelia stood there, her face pale and her eyes full of tears.

"Will!" she cried. "Please come. I think Mother's dead!"

At that point, she broke down, so I led her in and sat her in a chair. Will's face was white with shock and I truly felt for him.

"What's happened?" he managed. "Are you sure?"

Amelia related how she'd found her this morning, cold and still as stone. She hadn't called the doctor yet, but she was sure she was dead.

Will roused himself.

"I'll come," he said and collected a few things together.

"Will, let me come with you," I said. "I could help."

"No, my dear Kate," he said gently, and to my surprise, stroked my cheek softly. "Thank you, but who will take care of the children? They need you here."

"But I want to be there for you," I told him, "to comfort you. You shouldn't have to go through it alone."

"I know," he said, "but I don't want you tangled up in all this. It'll be messy and unpleasant. I'll be back as soon as I can."

He kissed me on the cheek, dragged the almost insensible Amelia to her feet and went out. It's 5 o'clock now and I'm still waiting to hear how things are. I hope he's okay. It such a wrench to lose a parent, I know, and it must be worse when you didn't get on with them. There's so much regret.

Kate's Diary 4 April 1902

Finally got Will to sleep. He came home very late last night in a terrible state, alternately ranting and crying. His mother died of an apoplectic seizure, the doctor said. Nothing anyone could have done. Of course, Will had such a love/hate relationship with her that he doesn't know what he feels. There's so much anger inside him, but grief too. He's always wished she would love him more, but it's all too late now. He cried in my arms for hours, until he wore himself out and eventually slept. Our dear children are bewildered by it all and are keeping out the way; probably just as well. I wouldn't trust Will in this mood.

Kate's Diary 8 April 1902

The funeral today. All of Will's family were there, with their children, and I had to take ours along, as there was no one I could leave them with. The graveside was muddy and wet underfoot, but thankfully the weather stayed dry. Will leaned heavily on my arm most of the day and I was glad to be able to give my support to him. This week has been difficult – Will has drank a lot and cried a lot. I hope the funeral will allow him to accept his loss now and move on.

Afterwards, we went back to his brother James' house for the wake, but there was an uneasy atmosphere. Disagreements over the sharing out of the household property, such as it is, have sprung up already and Will was in a furious temper by the time we got home. He's gone out drinking again this evening. It doesn't bode well.

Kate's Diary 12 April 1902

I'm sitting here in the ruins of what was our kitchen this morning; the children still lying, afraid, in their beds. Will had a terrible argument with James, Amelia and Mary yesterday over what to do with all their mother's things. I'm not sure what all the ins and outs were; all I know is that when Will came home, he was like a demon. He'd been drinking, that was clear, and not just ale, but rum too, I'd guess. He swept into the house like a whirlwind, shouting, smashing, throwing things. My feeble attempts to stop him breaking up our home only enraged him even more, so I retreated with the children to cower in the bedroom, leaving him to wreak his fury on our flat. What is it that possesses him at these times, I don't know, but there is no reasoning with him. It's like there is a dark devil on his shoulders. If I got in the way, I think he'd probably kill me.

At last, he is sleeping it off, stretched out on what is left of the sofa. I doubt he'll remember much when he finally comes round. Let's hope it's out of his system now.

Kate's Diary 17 April 1902

Had a heart to heart with Will last night and persuaded him to go back to work. It's been two weeks now and there's no money coming in, apart from a bit from my laundry work. All our tiny reserves of food and savings have evaporated, and we can't manage much longer without his wages. Not only that, but they won't keep his job open forever. Stands to reason. There're too many other people wanting work.

It's not been an easy time these last few days. Even trying to look after the children and do the laundry has had to take a back seat to comforting Will. He is so needy, yet so angry. But this morning he got up and went to work, so that's a good thing and a step forward.

Kate's Diary 18 April 1902

Oh dear! What a disaster! Will has lost his post of foreman at the printers. He came home in a foul mood yesterday and for once I can understand. The boss said he needed someone there all the time, so he gave the job to another man. You can't really blame him – I mean work has to go on after all, but it's a shame and will really affect Will's wages. Of course, I went and put my foot in it when Will came home yelling about it, by saying foolishly, "That's a real pity, Will, but you weren't there, so I guess they had to look elsewhere, unfortunately. It's not fair, I know, but these bosses can do what they like."

"It's all your fault!" he cried.

"Mine?" I said. "How can that be?"

"You kept me away. I'd have gone back if it wasn't for you. '*Take your time*', you said. Now look what's happened!"

"That's not true!" I declared. "I know I said you needed time to get over it, but I been trying to get you back to work for the last few days."

I got a black eye for my impertinence, and it's still throbbing this morning. Lucky, it weren't worse, I suppose. Not sure how we'll manage now; the rent on this place is seven shillings a week and what Will earns now will barely cover it. At least he's working, that's something. I'll just have to try and increase the work I do, in order to keep us fed. There's no other way.

Kate's Diary 31 May 1902

The war is over at last! Today, a spontaneous display of national celebration prompted Londoners to take to the streets in their thousands. As far as the eye could see, there were people singing, waving flags, cheering. It was a fantastic atmosphere.

Will is still grumpy and miserable, so refused to show any interest, but I felt the children deserved to be part of it, so we joined in with the crowds. They all came home with free balloons and tiny flags on sticks and were very happy.

"Look, Father," said Ern enthusiastically. "Look what I've got!"

He waved his flag vigorously under Will's nose, but it was like a red rag to a bull. Will grabbed it angrily and snapped it in half.

"We've no cause to celebrate anything here, my lad, so get out of my sight before I make you sorry!"

Ern fled, crying, from the room. Fred followed, calling after him, "It's all right, Ernie. You can have mine!"

"Will!" I exclaimed. "That was a mean thing to do! He's only a child and it meant a lot to him. How could you?"

My lip is still swollen now from the blow he gave me, but I left the room to find my dear boys. Ern was still in tears, though Fred had kindly given him his flag. Albert always refuses to share anything, so he took himself out of the way. I brought Joe along into the boys' room and we all played a few games and ate some cakes, which we had been given. Much can be soothed with cake, I find, if you're a child, and the tears soon subsided. If only an adult's pain could be eased as easily.

Kate's Diary 13 July 1902

Lord help poor Ireland! Arthur Balfour has been elected prime minister and everyone knows he's dead against Irish Home Rule. Mighty slim chance of him helping us, to be sure.

I been thinking a lot about the old country recently. There's a wonderful exhibition on in Cork at the moment, and the newspapers are all full of it. It fair makes my heart ache to see it again.

The other day, on my way home from delivering laundry to Mrs Gordon, I noticed a sign outside a local hall, advertising *'moving pictures of Cork'*. I had to go in and see for meself. I ain't never seen anything like it before. It almost felt like I was there again! Real images of people and places moving on a huge screen – it made me feel so homesick.

When I got home, I didn't dare tell Will what I'd been doing, 'cause he'd have said I was wasting time, but I did say I was thinking of Cork again and how I'd love to see the exhibition. He laughed cruelly.

"How do you think that's going to happen, then?" he said.

"I know," I said sadly, "it won't. We can't afford it, I understand. But one day, I'd love to go back and visit."

"Better get that idea out of your head right now!" he declared. "I wouldn't go there if you paid me, and you ain't going neither!"

It weren't worth bothering to argue. I know I'll never go there again. Ireland is lost to me but will always be in my heart.

Kate's Diary 9 August 1902

It's been a cool, damp summer this year, which has reminded me again of my Emerald Isle, with its rain and mist. I remember how the green seemed to drip from the trees, it was so lush and moist. Here, in this busy city, there is a little greenery in the parks and squares, but it is usually covered in a layer of dust and soot. The unseasonable showers have penetrated that this year, though, and washed the stains away for a fresher, cleaner look.

What a time it's turning out to be. Yet another national event today – the slightly delayed coronation of Prince (now King) Edward and his wife. We all watched the procession in awe at the sheer numbers of carriages, soldiers, horses, guns, etc. Still, it seemed to me that I'd seen it all before. Maybe these military parades are the only way England knows how to celebrate/mourn/commemorate.

The day was a grey one, but the crowds were out in force and everyone had a good time. Even Will joined us for a while and was jollier than he's been in a long time. Perhaps he's getting over things at last. Afterwards, we all went to a street party and partook of all the treats on offer. These days, food at home has been getting fairly basic, to say the least, due to the bills which are piling up. We had to have just bread and dripping for tea the other day. I think we may have to think about moving to somewhere cheaper in the future. It tried suggesting it to Will the other day, but he snapped, "You don't know nothing about it, woman, so keep yer trap shut!"

I wish he'd speak more kindly to me at times. Still, today he has been happy and quite charming again, making jokes with the children and holding my arm like he used to. A rare glimpse of gentler times, but very welcome, nonetheless.

Kate's Diary 10 September 1902

Oh, Mam! Why did you have to go and write me you were moving back to London? I was fair delighted until I told Will and then everything changed.

"Your mother?" he growled, "Visiting? That's just you being selfish, rubbing it in that you still got a mother and I haven't! How do you think that'll make me feel?"

"It's not meant that way, Will," I explained. "I ain't seen her in ages and I sorely miss her. I do understand how you feel, but I can't help it. 'Sides she won't be around much, I don't suppose."

"She better not be!" he snarled.

I can't tell you all this, Mam, 'cos Da was a very different sort of man, and as far as I saw, always kind and caring. You wouldn't understand. I'm proper fearful that Will may try and stop me seeing you, though I don't know why. It ain't doing any harm. He just likes to control me, I know.

Kate's Diary 5 October 1902

Mam came for tea this afternoon and we had a grand reunion. Even *she* got a bit emotional, which is unlike her really. We caught up on all the news about Pat and the family; his children are grown up now and he's courting a local

widow. I hope he'll be happy. Mam hasn't changed much –
still likes a drink and a laugh, though she's not so mobile these
days. Says her dancing days are over, but there's plenty of life
in her still and she's always up for a party. When she asked
me how things were, I had to admit times are hard. She
sympathises, I know, but ain't in any position to help. She's
on the breadline herself.

Will knew she was coming, but rather forcefully
suggested that she visit whilst he was at work and be gone by
the time he gets home. Really, I was quite happy to comply –
they don't get on too well anyway, so it's best that way.

Couldn't offer Mam much in the way of refreshments,
mind, just a cup of tea. Can't afford extras like cake at the
moment. Last week, the grocer threatened to stop supplying
us if we didn't pay the bill, but I managed to make an
agreement with him to pay bit by bit. Will weren't happy but
we don't want to end up in trouble again. Money is very tight
these days. I just hope we can survive.

Kate's Diary 17 October 1902

Apparently, violence broke out yesterday in the House of
Commons because Balfour refused to discuss the 'Irish issue'.
How can he do that? It ain't right. Mam and I couldn't talk of
nothing else when we met today. Ireland is still our homeland
and as important to us as ever.

Kate's Diary 20 October 1902

Will came home from the pub in a really good mood last
night. He's been there a lot recently, but I was pleased to see

him back early for a change. He was whistling cheerfully, and when he saw me, he came up and kissed me for a change.

"Are the children in bed?" he asked. I nodded.

"Good," he said, smiling playfully. "I've had a bit of luck tonight, my darlin'. Must have been that darn shamrock you're always talking about!"

He put his hand in his pocket, pulled out a wad of notes and coins, and tossed them onto the table.

"Will!" I said surprised. "Where did all that come from?"

He put his arm round my waist and pulled me to him.

"Well darlin', I put some money on a fight, and it came good. Lady Luck smiled on me."

"A fight!" I exclaimed. "What do you mean?"

"Oh, it's all right; not me," he reassured me. "You know – a bare knuckle fight – it's a common sport these days."

"And you mean you bet on these?" I said, horrified.

"Well of course, darlin', and look what it's got us. This'll help out, won't it?"

I had to agree, in spite of my disapproval.

"Well, that's grand, Will, but maybe you shouldn't be gambling. You could lose."

"Oh, don't worry, my little darlin'," he said airily, "it's quite safe. You can trust me. I know what I'm doing. Now come here and help me celebrate!"

This morning, I feel tired out after the sweet memories we made last night, but it felt good to be loved and wanted again.

Kate's Diary 4 December 1902

Oh dear, what have I done? I seem to have invited Mam for Christmas! I didn't mean to – it just sort of happened. I

237

been seeing her quite often when Will's not around, 'cos he says he thinks it's better that way. Tells me it'll upset him too much otherwise.

Anyway, Mam's always saying how she wants to see the rest of the children. She usually only sees little Joey 'cos they're all at school, so I couldn't resist asking her to come for Christmas lunch. I mean with the extra bit of money that Will's been winning lately, we can afford to feed one extra, just for the day. Mam was so pleased – I can't disappoint her now, but Will is going to be furious, I just know it. He's always trying to keep her away, but it ain't fair; she's got a right to see her grandchildren. Maybe when I tell him I'm expecting again, it'll distract him.

Kate's Diary 23 December 1902

All week I've been trying to work out how to break the news to Will that Mam's coming to us for Christmas lunch. I'm fierce worried about it and I don't know what to do. All I can think is that he's been in such a good mood these last couple of months; what with his lucky streak; that maybe he'll be kind and understanding, but it's a slim chance I know.

It worries me, I must say; that he keeps betting the rent money on these fights. If something goes wrong and he loses it all – well, I dread to think. It's been grand having the extra money and I've managed to settle all the bills up to date, but Will's been spending a lot as well, so it doesn't last long. Of course, there's another baby on the way as well now, though I ain't told him yet. Once he knows about that, I'm sure he'll see sense and be more careful.

Kate's Diary 28 December 1902

I can hardly bear to think back about the Christmas we've just had. The memories are so painful and difficult. The only good thing is that the children seemed oblivious to our troubles. If only things had turned out differently.

I suppose it's all my fault for not telling Will about Mam earlier. On Christmas Eve, I tried to drop it casually into the conversation that she would be coming for lunch the next day.

"What?" he exclaimed. "Not really? Kate – you're joking!"

"No, I had to ask her, Will. She's all on her own and she's hardly seen us recently."

"What about that other trollop – what's her name – Louisa? She can go to her, surely?"

"I can't see what's wrong with her coming here," I said stiffly. "She's my Mam and I want to see her."

"Oh, yes!" he cried. "You would, wouldn't you? Anything to hurt me! You know how it will make me feel, not having my own mother anymore, but you just don't care, do you?"

"That's not true," I replied.

Just then Fred came in.

"Mum, are you all right?" he asked, looking worried (he's nine now and understands an awful lot).

"Yes, dear. Your father and I are just sorting out what we're doing tomorrow. It's a surprise, so you go off and play with your brothers. It's cold outside, but dry, so wrap up warm and have a run around."

"Do I have to play with Albert?" he whined. "He always spoils things."

"Yes, you do," I told him firmly, "now off you go."

The argument resumed the minute he was out of the room.

"You don't care about my feelings, do you?" Will said. "Anyway, she won't enjoy herself here. All these children will be too noisy for her. You're not being fair to her, either. It's just typical of you!"

"But she wants to come," I answered. "She's hasn't seen any of the children in ages, so it's important."

"It won't help her to get so tired out by them all," Will continued, more persuasively now. "She's getting on a bit and will find it hard going."

"It's true, she is quite frail now," I admitted, "but all the more reason to have a nice Christmas lunch cooked for her."

"I think you need to tell her not to come," he persisted. "It won't be good for her, nor me neither. I shall be upset all day – do you want that?"

"Of course not," I said, "but I'm not cancelling at this short notice. It's not fair!"

I was adamant and stood my ground, though as things turned out, maybe I shouldn't have. Will grabbed me by the hair and pulled me roughly towards him.

"I'm warning you," he said. "It's going to be a disaster. Just wait and see!"

He released me with a shove and stormed off.

The next day dawned bright, frosty and cold. The children were all very excited, especially as I'd had enough money to buy them each a present this year, for a change. Mam turned up promptly at eleven, but Will was sulking and refused to do more than say hello to her. She spent some time talking to the children at first and things seemed to be going well. Then disaster struck when they went off to play and she tried to make conversation with Will.

"How are you, Will? I was so sorry to hear about your poor mam. Was she ill for long?"

He glowered at her.

"Don't talk about her!" he exclaimed. "You got no right."

"Will!" I protested, "Mam was only asking."

"Shut up!" he cried. "You don't understand. If you did, you wouldn't have invited her."

"Well, really!" Mam declared. "If I'm not wanted here, I'll go." She stood up, in a huff.

"Please," I said, "both of you, let's calm down. There's no need for all this." I paused. "Listen, I've got some good news – I'm 'with child' again. It's due in June next year."

"Again?" said Will angrily. "Do you never stop?"

"That's grand news, Kate, dear," said Mam sitting down. "We should make a toast to the child."

"What for?" exclaimed Will. "It's just another mouth to feed!"

Mam glared at him.

"It's your child," she said, "and you're just as much responsible as Kate, so grow up and act like a man, not a spoilt baby!"

Will flared up immediately. "Get out!" he cried, "and don't come back here ever again! We don't want you in our home."

"Will, really," I begged, "please…"

"Shut yer mouth!" he said. "You're my wife and you'll do as I say."

Mam stared at us both. "Kate," she said, "what's going on here? Your da never spoke to me like that. You shouldn't have to put up with it."

"Get out, you old witch!" Will shouted. He was on his feet now and very threatening. He took hold of her arm and pulled her towards the door. "Clear off!"

"Kate!" she cried. "Are you going to let him treat me like this? He's trying to throw me out. Do something!"

My words were feeble and faint. "Please Will – no – you can't."

He turned and punched me viciously in the face. I felt a tooth break and I fell back into a chair, covering my eyes with my hands. When I came to myself again, Mam had gone, and Will was scowling at me.

"Get the dinner!" he ordered. "We're hungry."

Just then the children all came running in and I had to pretend that everything was okay. I bustled around in the kitchen, fetching plates and dishes. Tears ran down and the blood dripped from my broken tooth. It was a miserable meal, which I could hardly eat. Will told me later that I must never see Mam again, but I won't promise that. She's my kin and I love her. I just hope she still loves me.

Kate's Diary 12 February 1903

Things have not been going well lately. Will's winning streak has vanished like a thief in the night and money is getting awful short. Since Christmas, his moods have been terrible again and he blames it all on me and Mam. Says we put a jinx on him (wish I could sometimes!)

Today the rent collector came to see me, demanding to be paid. I scraped together every penny I could find, but it still wasn't quite enough. He says I can pay the rest next week, so that's something, but it'll have to be bread and jam for tea again for a few days.

Kate's Diary 14 March 1903

A couple of days ago, Ern came running in to see me, when he got back from school.

"Mum, that man's asking to see you again."

"Man?" I said confused. "Which man?"

"That grumpy one who collects the money," Ern replied. He meant Mr Mitchell, the landlord's agent – a cold hearted, officious little man with grey hair, a clipboard and no sense of humour.

"Okay, darling. Mum will see to it. Don't worry."

Truth to tell, I been trying to avoid him of late. We're a few weeks behind with the rent now and I just don't have the money. My bit of money from the laundry just about feeds us, but as my confinement gets closer, there's less I can do. Finally, yesterday, I came to a decision to try and stop Will spending all his wages. It was payday, and he was in a good mood at dinner. The children were making a lot of noise but for once he didn't react. Using the rumpus as cover, I went to his coat and took out enough money for one weeks rent, then hid it in a china jug in the kitchen. However, I dreaded what might happen as a result.

Later, when the children had gone to bed, Will announced, as usual, that he was going out. He put on his coat, and unfortunately put his hand in his pocket.

"My wages!" he gasped. "Where's it all gone? There's only a few bob left."

I weren't about to lie, so I bravely replied, "I took out enough to cover this week's rent, Will. Mr Mitchells been chasing us again."

"You did what?" he thundered. "How dare you? Where is it? Give it to me!"

I was shaking as I answered.

"No Will. You mustn't take it every time. We can't afford for you to keep losing it."

He advanced on me threateningly.

"Give it to me now or I'll tear this place apart!"

Backing away, I whimpered, "No."

With that, he started to pull things out. The pots and pans went flying, then the cupboards were opened and turned out. Plates went crashing to the floor. Then to my dismay, he found the china jug I'd put the money in and hurled it to the ground. It shattered, and notes and coins flew everywhere. We both made a dash for the money, struggling and wrestling to get to it. We ended up in a tussle on the floor. Just then Albert came in, rubbing his eyes sleepily and saying crossly, "Mum, Dad, you're making so much noise, I can't sleep."

We stopped, embarrassed and shame faced. Will looked up at him and unexpectedly laughed.

"Albie," he said. "It's okay. Mum and I are just playing a game. We're sorry. We'll be quiet now, promise. Go back to bed."

Albert withdrew and we sat there, feeling foolish. Will stood up and looked down at me. He still had a handful of cash, but he grinned wryly and tossed it at me.

"Here, take it, pay the stupid man. See if I care!"

He went out then, leaving me to find all the money and clear up the mess. Having added it all up, I find I can just about pay the rent this week, thank goodness.

Kate's Diary 6 April 1903

I was standing at the sink, up to my elbows in hot soapy water, doing Mrs Andrew's laundry yesterday, when Will unexpectedly arrived home. My surprise was hard to conceal, as it was only 2 o'clock. Little Joe was playing by my feet and Will nearly fell over him as he came in. He cursed and staggered a little, and I could tell he'd been drinking.

"Will, what are you doing home at this time? What's wrong?"

"Kate," he said, his voice slurred, "those bastards – they let me go. I've lost my job!"

I stared at him in horror. That's all we need. We're only just getting by as it is.

"They said I was rude to a customer when I delivered their order," he continued. "It's not true. They were just looking to pick a fight, telling me I was late and that the work weren't done right. I told 'em where they could go! Trouble is, they complained and I got fired."

He hung his head in shame suddenly.

"Sorry, Kate. I couldn't help it. It just weren't fair and I wasn't about to put up with it."

I sighed. There wasn't any point in dwelling on it, whatever the rights and wrongs.

"Don't worry," I told him. "It'll be all right. You'll soon find something else."

"I ain't got no reference, though," he said bitterly, "and that ain't gonna help. Oh, Kate, what can we do?"

I didn't know how to reply. We're already over a month behind with the rent and there's little enough food in the house. All I could offer him was some feeble words of comfort, but I worry for the future. What will become of us if he can't find another job? I hate to think.

Kate's Diary 10 June 1903 Lambeth

At last, we have a roof over our heads again, though it's not much of one, to be honest. It must have been two weeks ago that Mr Mitchell served us with notice to pay the rent due or get out by the end of the week. Three months' rent! That's what we owe. I don't know how we'll ever pay that off.

All that week, we tried desperately to get the money. We sold what we could, and Will managed to do some odd jobs around, which brought in a bit. I'm so large with child now, I can hardly do anything, but I tried.

"Please, Will," I said. "Go to your family and see if they can help. James is on a good wage, maybe he could lend us something."

"I will *not* go to him!" he declared firmly. "I'd rather be dead in a ditch!"

"Well, what about your sister Mary then?" I asked, but Will has his pride and flatly refused. I can't say I blame him, really. Amelia would have helped, I'm sure, but she's moved to Southend now. As for Mam – well, we can't expect anything from there after the way Will treated her; besides, she ain't got nothing herself.

Luckily, one of the jobs that Will did last week has led to an offer of employment; just as a labourer with the lowest of wages, but better than nothing. Unfortunately, they didn't need him straightaway, so it couldn't solve the immediate crisis. Nevertheless, we hoped that if we told Mr Mitchell about it, he would relent. The money we managed to pull together barely covered one week's rent, but we thought it might help. Just in case, however, I started to pack.

Saturday morning came and with it, Mr Mitchell, with his clipboard and an assortment of heavy looking men around him.

"So, Mr Duffield, do you have the three months' rent owing?"

To give Will his due, he stayed calm, at least initially, explaining that he would be starting work again shortly and offering him what we had in the meantime as a down payment.

Mr Mitchell snorted derisively.

"So, basically, you don't have the money then? This doesn't even cover one week – do you think I'm an idiot?"

He paused and pulled himself up to his full height, puffed up with self-importance, as he made an announcement, "The Stanhope Buildings Committee requires all rent to be paid regularly on time, and therefore, by the power vested in me, I am evicting you. These gentlemen will assist you in removing your property."

"But, sir," I begged, "please – our children – we have nowhere to go."

His face was implacable and cold.

"That's not my problem. You should have thought of that. There's a cart outside for you to load your things onto, at your own cost, of course."

He looked at the pitiful amount of cash that we had given him and said begrudgingly, "You might as well take this; at least it'll pay for the cart. It won't help with much else. We'll be in touch through the courts for the debt. Don't think you'll be getting away with it. Men – do your duty. Get them out!"

The removal of ourselves and our children was brisk and forceful. In no time at all, we found ourselves standing out on the pavement, surrounded by our furniture and belongings. One man laughed as he tossed the last box down on the ground, hearing breaking noises from within. Will had had enough by then and grabbed him by the collar.

"Laugh at us, would you?" he cried, shaking the man. "Think it's funny, do you? Just wait till you're in the same position one day!"

"Will, leave him," I pleaded. "We don't want no more trouble."

"I guess not," Will agreed and pushed him away.

The children stood there, looking bewildered as we hauled our possessions onto the cart. The carter was reluctant to help and just ignored us, holding his horse. Where could we go? I didn't know.

"We'll have to try Mary," said Will. "If we can stay there for a few days, then I can get us a new place when I start work."

We directed the carter to her house in Lambeth, climbed up on top of the rickety pile and headed off.

It was afternoon when we got there, and the children were all complaining they were hungry.

"It's all right," I told them, "when we get inside, we'll have something to eat."

We stopped outside and Will went to the door, but there was no answer.

"Out!" he said. "Surely not. Where have they gone?"

"Perhaps their neighbour will know," I suggested, so Will went next door and asked.

"All gone away for the weekend to Southend. Said they were going to visit her sister. Why, what do you wanna know for? You ain't a burglar, are you?"

"I'm her brother," explained Will, "and we need somewhere to stay for a few days. Can you help at all?"

"You got to be joking!" the woman said. "I let you in and you'll probably cut all our throats for all I know! Now clear off!"

"But the children," I implored her, "please…"

The door shut firmly in our faces and we stood there forlornly, not knowing what to do.

"'Ere," said the carter, "You gonna unload this lot or not? I got other jobs to go to, you know!"

"We'll have to go to James," I said.

"Yes," Will acknowledged, "I suppose so. Carter – can you take us over to Islington, please."

"Not flipping likely!" he retorted. "Leastways not on this money. It's north of the river and it'll take ages. You get some more money, then I'll think about it. Otherwise, I'm unloading it all 'ere and now on the pavement!"

We were broken and desperate.

"Please, sir," I begged, "Is there nothing you can do? These children will be out on the street tonight."

The man glanced at the children and his eye rested on little Joey, happily toddling about, and he softened slightly.

"Well, look, as you're in the family way and you got all these kids, I'll tell you what I'll do. There's a park quite near here, that's got one of them pavilions in it with seats for gentlefolks. I'll drop you there and you can camp out. Least you'll have a roof over your heads and a bit of protection. If you put all your stuff around, you could make a sort of shelter. And you'd be nearby for when them lot come home again."

Reluctantly, we settled on it. What else could we do?

The two nights we spent there were a nightmare best forgotten. We arranged the furniture to block off the worst of the cold air and hung bedding and curtains around to give us some privacy, but it wasn't the best place for a family of six. I pretended to the children that it was a special adventure, a fun game, but they were only half convinced. Though it's nearly summer, the air was cold at night, but thankfully dry. Will disappeared off and came back with some bread. Whether he begged or stole for it, I didn't ask. We were too hungry to care.

In the daytime on Sunday, the children ran around the park happily, letting off steam and enjoying the sunshine. Meanwhile, courting couples passed by, taking the air and showing their feelings at our cheek in being there.

"How disgusting," I heard one woman say. "Making a filthy mess in the park! We should report it, Archie. It's not right."

"Yes," he replied. "I'll talk to a constable when I see one, get them moved on. They're just a load of tramps – awful!"

I worried all afternoon that the law was likely to arrive at any moment, but no one showed, thankfully.

On Monday, Mary and her family finally returned home, and Will begged her to let us stay for a few days. Though they don't get on too well since their mother passed, she relented and for the rest of the week we lived with them. It was mighty crowded, and I was glad when Will told me he had found us somewhere to live. Mary kindly gave him the first week's rent (partly, I think to get us out of the way), and a bit of food to tide us over. When I saw our new home, however, I nearly cried – a damp, smelly, filthy basement in Lambeth with open sewers, rats and broken windows. What have we come to?

It is so rough and cramped that we've had to leave some of our better furniture with Mary for safekeeping – some chairs that Will inherited from his mum and my wooden dresser. We'd never get it all in here.

Still, we have to make the best of it and work towards better things. At least we have somewhere for the baby to be born. It won't be long now.

Kate's Diary 25 June 1903

Dear little baby Bill was born on midsummers day, just as the sun was rising over the grimy rooftops of London. But oh – what a labour it was – so long and painful. I thought it would never end. Hours of pain went by and still he seemed reluctant to enter the world. At one point, I screamed and screamed that I wanted my mam, and begged Will to send for her. Reluctantly, he sent Ern to fetch her, whilst Fred looked after the other boys. There was a midwife and old Ethel from upstairs helping out, but I needed Mam most of all. It seemed like hours but in fact it was no time at all before she arrived, as loving and concerned for me as ever.

"Kate, my dear," she said, "You're doing really well, now just keep pushing and it'll all be grand."

With her encouragement and love, I managed the final push and Bill was delivered at last; a large, healthy boy. Will insisted on calling him after himself.

"A man needs a son to carry on his name," he told me, almost as if he was the lord of the manor. I don't mind, though, as long as I can shorten it to Bill.

I am so grateful to Mam. I don't know what would have happened without her. She looked worn out afterwards and I worry about her. She's not as strong as she used to be. Sadly, she has gone away again, dismissed by Will with barely a 'thank you'.

The children came to visit their new brother later, and Joey in particular, was fascinated. Of course, he's been the baby of the family until now. I'll have to make sure he's not left out, otherwise he might get jealous.

Little Billy is perfect; all pink cheeked and smiling, gurgling with pleasure whenever I come near. Such innocence and beauty – what a shame he has to grow up here.

Kate's Diary 3 July 1904

Went to my lady today to pick up the laundry and she remarked on my black eye. It was embarrassing. I had to lie and tell her I'd fallen over, but I'm sure she knows the truth really. I wish Will would be kinder, but these days he is cruel and brutal most of the time. It seems we only pull together in times of crisis.

I'm sick of feeling helpless and not being able to provide for my children properly. We exist on handouts and charity. I even had to go to the soup kitchens the other day. It was awful. It felt like begging. I was so ashamed, queueing up with all the rest, just in order to survive. Bread and dripping seem to be the staple diet for my poor children these days. I just hope they are happy and don't realise how desperate things are. Barrack Street in Cork was the same, I guess, but we had a happy family life; me, Pat, Mam and Da; so that made such a difference. Will can be harsh to the children at times. I noticed some fresh bruises on Billy the other day, but he's a year old now and starting to explore. Maybe he just bumped into something – I hope so. He is thriving, in spite of this place, thankfully, whereas I can feel the accursed damp seeping into me, more and more each day.

Kate's Diary 10 December 1904

Today, the letter arrived, which I've been dreading for ages. After all this time, the Stanhope Buildings Committee have found out where we are, and they want their money. I thought they wouldn't find us here, but somehow, they have and are threatening legal action. It's not only the three months' rent now but has interest and charges on top; a massive amount, which we can never hope to pay.

When Will saw the letter, he screwed it up into a ball and threw it away.

"Just let them try!" he cried. "They won't get far."

"But Will," I reasoned, "this is serious. They could send in the bailiffs or something."

"Forget it!" he told me. "It's just a bluff. Nothing to worry about."

I hope he's right, but I have my doubts.

Kate's Diary 23 February 1905

Another letter, this time from the courts, giving us one month to pay or face the consequences. Will swore when he read it and then told me he's going to borrow some money to put on a horse! I tried to talk him out of it.

"No, Will, that's stupid. Surely it'd be better to pay off the debt with it?"

"Now who's being stupid?" he roared. "If we borrowed that much from *them*, we'd be in even more trouble. Do you realise the interest they charge?"

"Anyway, this is a dead cert," he continued enthusiastically, "can't fail. I've had a tip off and it's great odds. We could make a killing, then we'd be able to pay off everything."

It's a bold idea, I admit, but I can't see it working meself. We'll see.

Joe's Recollections, April 1912

One day, I came in from school to find Mum sitting at the kitchen table, her head in her hands, tears streaming down her face. For a moment, I thought Father had hit her again, but he wasn't home at that time, so it couldn't be that.

"Mum," I said anxiously, "what's wrong?"

For answer, all she gave me was a crumpled-up newspaper. I looked at the headlines – '*Titanic sunk, great loss of life*'.

"What's the Titanic?" I asked, never having heard of it before.

Her voice sounded strange when she replied.

"A liner, Joey, supposed to be the biggest and best. They think there's 1500 people dead; so many from Ireland – it's terrible!"

Slowly, I got the details out of her, though initially, she was almost paralysed with grief.

"The last place they picked up from was Queenstown – Cork," she said, "my hometown! All those poor people crammed into steerage, not able to escape. I travelled like that coming over here to Liverpool. It's no way to treat human beings, you can hardly move or breathe down there. When I think of them drowning, trapped, desperate – it tears my heart to pieces. All they wanted was a better life in America and look what they got." She broke down again and I did my best to comfort her.

"Easy, Mum, you'll make yourself bad again," I warned her. "Let me get you a brew, you'll feel better."

I bustled around and fetched her some tea whilst she sat there, staring at the paper. At the time, I didn't know why she felt so strongly about her Irish origins and how she could get so upset about people she had never met, but I was young then and have learnt to think differently since.

As she perused the long lists of casualties, she gave a small cry of despair.

"Oh no, poor Bronagh, my cousin, her and her family all gone –oh no!"

I didn't even know she had any cousins left in Ireland and so tried to ask her about her family.

"She was one of my Uncle Frank and Aunty Mairead's children. They all lived with us for a while when times were hard. Bronagh was a bit younger than me, but a nice girl. We shared a room. It's so sad. Aunty Mairead will be distraught."

255

"Why do we never see or hear from them?" I asked.

"It's a long way, Joey, and your father ain't too keen to keep up much. I write occasionally but that's all. Uncle Frank's passed now, and I don't even know where all the family are anymore. Aunty Mairead's about the only one I'm in touch with. This will break her heart."

The days that followed only brought more sorrowful tales from the dreadful incident, and as I'm sure you will know, it has gone down in history as a great tragedy. Yet, I always remember my mum and her grief above all else. For once, Father was kind to her, I believe; a rare occasion, to be sure. I heard him giving words of comfort to her that night, as she cried in his arms, and for a brief moment, I almost felt I loved him.

Kate's Diary 31 March 1905 Newington

Today will stay in my memory forever for it's the day we entered the workhouse. I swore I'd never come here, but fate has decreed otherwise. My poor dear children – how they must feel. Will told me last night that without me working as well, we can't manage. And yet, it's his fault! I know I make him angry, but I don't deserve what he deals out. He can be a brute at times.

Perhaps I shouldn't have said anything when he came home drunk again the other night, but I was annoyed. He was so late that I was getting worried about him, but I needn't have concerned meself. He was just out drinking as usual. Supper was ruined and most of his wages had gone. I'm afraid I spoke my mind for once and told him what I thought of him.

"How could you, Will? You know we need this money. Couldn't you have just come home instead?"

"Don't tell me what to do, woman!" he growled and lashed out.

In his drunken rage, he never even realised how hard he hit me until he sobered up and saw my broken arm. Then he cried and pleaded for my forgiveness.

"Kate, darling. I'm sorry. I didn't mean to."

It's always the same and I always forgive him. I'm a soft-hearted fool who can't resist his tears. It's all backfired this time, though.

When the bailiffs came to take our furniture, I wanted to stop them, but I wasn't strong enough. They were harsh and insistent, and what's more, they had the law on their side. There was nothing I could do. If only Will didn't spend so much money on drink, then maybe we could pay off the debts. He claims it's all because of me.

"You're a terrible housekeeper," he cried. "I wouldn't even employ you as a servant!"

I do the best I can with what there is and I'm sure it can't be *all* my fault, can it?

Will went mad when he found out what they had taken away. He grabbed me by the throat, and I thought he was going to strangle me.

"You stupid woman! You should never have let them into the house."

I really did try not to, but they were so rough. I feel bad that young Joey had to see it all. Poor little lad – he's only four. I told him a pack of lies in order to cover up, but I know he was confused.

Now here we are, in Newington – that is, everyone except Will. I don't know if we will see him again. We didn't exactly part on the best of terms. Whilst we stay here, he is going to pack up our family home and move into single lodgings. He swears he will pay off our debts and then come and get us, but I'm not sure I believe him. He left the house early this morning without a word to me.

Today, I've begged and pleaded with the authorities here. I've been invaded by their personal questions and insulted by their remarks. The relieving officer – what a name for a man who does little to relieve anyone's misery – a stern, unfeeling man, who seems to despise us all – well, he subjected me to an interrogation which seemed go on for hours. Meanwhile, the children are crying and protesting at their new surroundings. Why have we come to this? How long must we stay here? I wish I knew.

Kate's Diary 24 April 1905

Why has Will not come to see us? He must know what we are going through, to be sure. How can he abandon us like this? Tomorrow all the children, except my sweet baby Bill, will be taken over to the Hanwell school, where they will stay until I can get them out of here to a new home. Tonight, they were all angry and hurt. I can't blame them – I feel the same. I know we have no money and no home at the moment, but surely Will should be doing more. At least he could have come to visit us. I thought he loved me. Is this how he shows it?

Kate's Diary 6 July 1905

Oh, it won't be long now, surely, till we can leave here. The doctor said the plaster on my arm can come off next week and that means I will be able to work again. The only thing that worries me is this dreadful cough that I can't get rid of. I get fair out of breath at times and I thought I saw some blood on my 'kerchief yesterday.

Today, Will finally appeared and although he didn't stay long, he talked about getting another house for us all. I was so excited at the thought of being with all the family again, that I forgave him for not coming to see us earlier. Apparently, he has been working very hard. He promises that he'll come back next week and fetch me home. I can't wait!

Kate's Diary 20 July 1905

What has happened to me? I feel so ill. My arm is better, but I can hardly breathe. The doctor here says I have 'consumption' and that I must rest and not work. I'm so disappointed because I really wanted to be free of this accursed place.

And where is Will? He hasn't come as he promised. Maybe they told him I was ill and needed to stay in the infirmary. Surely, he could have visited me even so, but perhaps they wouldn't let him. That must be it. I know he would have kept his promise if he could. Oh, I am so wretched. I just want to be well and go home.

Kate's Diary 8 August 1905

Been in the infirmary for over two weeks now and I don't seem to be getting any better. I feel so helpless just lying here in bed. Today, Will turned up again and was surprised, apparently, to find I was ill. I thought he must have already heard but it seems not.

"What are you doing here?" he asked. "I need you at home, why are you lazing about in here?" Then he laughed, trying to make a joke of it. "Anyway, you know what I mean, Kate. I miss you."

His eyes were soft, gazing at me pleadingly.

"Come home with me, Kate. I need you."

"I want to, Will," I told him, "but I need to get better first and then I can take care of you and the children properly."

"Damn it, Kate!" he said angrily. "All you ever think about is them kids! We can't afford to have them all at home. We ain't got the money!"

"But surely, Will," I said, "If you're working and paying off the debts now, then we can get another home for us all."

He looked embarrassed.

"Well, I'm sort of between jobs at the moment," he muttered. "Those bastards tried to do me out of the money they owed me, so I told them to stick their job."

"Oh, Will, really! What about the bailiffs? You know we need the money."

"Don't tell me what we need, woman!" he snapped. "I'm doing my best. You get yourself fit then you can work as well, and we can get a house again."

"Seems like that's all you need me for!" I retorted, "Just to work to keep you."

"That ain't fair!" he cried, eyes blazing. "You're my wife and should be with me. It's your place."

With an effort, he softened his approach and tried to win me over, but I've heard it all before.

"What I mean," he explained, "is that I want you to come home again. We can fetch the children later – very soon, I mean. You know how much I love you all."

My ears heard his words, but my heart didn't believe him. At that moment, my illness threatened to engulf me in its murky depths again, and I couldn't think straight anymore.

"I need to rest," I told him and turned my face to the wall, trying to pretend he wasn't there.

He left shortly afterwards, promising to visit soon, but it's a shallow promise.

And yet, I still love him. I wish I didn't. Once I am well enough, I feel that I will be forced to make a choice – either stay here with the children or leave and live with him again. It breaks my heart to think of the children being abandoned, but what use am I to them here, anyway? I rarely see most of them, and I can't even look after my little Billy properly at the moment. He has been taken, screaming and crying, to the nursery to be looked after for the time being. It was heart wrenching watching them carry him away. I can't go through that again.

Kate's Diary 5 October 1905

My illness has receded like the ebb of the tide, but as surely as the sea flows, I feel those waves are bound to return sooner or later. The cough I had is a great deal lessened but I feel so weak. At least I am able to care for my darling baby Billy again. He has just turned two years old now and is growing fast, hardly a baby anymore, in fact. Such a sweet child. When I hold him the purest love of all fills my heart.

I miss all the children so much – Ern with his ready laugh, Fred's quiet seriousness, Albert's sheer cheek and Joe's kind and caring nature. Occasionally, I see young Joey, but mostly they are all over at the school. It is hard for them to be separated from their parents and from each other, but at least they are getting a good education. The other day, I asked Joe how he was getting on, but he just muttered that he hates it. Still, children never enjoy school, it's true. They'd rather be out playing games.

Kate's Diary 1 November 1905

Will visited me today but I feel it may be the last time. We had a right barney about his proposals. He was all smiles to start with.

"Kate, darling, it's good to see you looking so much better." He kissed me on the lips but after all these months it felt strange.

"I got us some new lodgings," he continued. "It ain't much but it's big enough for two, and I'm working again now, so I can pay off that debt to Mr Parker."

"The money you borrowed for gambling, you mean!" I said. "That should have been paid off ages ago. And what about the rent arrears for Stanhope?"

"Like I said, Kate, I had a bit of trouble with the last job, but that's all in the past now. With you working as well, we can pay the rent, the bills and afford to live. Wouldn't it be great to be together again?" he asked persuasively. "You and me, just like old times."

"And the children," I reminded him. "I ain't going nowhere without them."

"But they're all at school now," he pointed out, "and I'm sure you wouldn't want to disturb their education, would you? It'd do more harm than good."

He had a fair point, which I considered for a moment or two.

"Well, at least we can take Billy home with us. He's not at school yet and he's far too little to be left here."

Will frowned. "Of course, my darling, but there just ain't enough room in the new place. It's only one bedroom and a kitchen. Wouldn't be fair on him. Where would he sleep?"

"In the same room as us," I suggested. "Lots of children sleep with their parents."

"But what about us?" Will persisted. "I mean, men have needs, Kate, and you wouldn't want him to see things he shouldn't, if you know what I mean." He grinned suggestively.

"*Your* needs? Oh, Will, really! Don't be so selfish." I cried. "I'm not leaving here without him!"

He came dangerously close to me and grabbed my arm roughly.

"You're my wife, Kate, and don't forget it! I have my rights."

"And you have your responsibilities too, Will, and that includes your children! Don't you care about them?"

"Of course, of course," he said, "but there just ain't the room."

"So, go and find somewhere where there is!" I flashed at him, getting really angry now.

"Don't get on your high horse, woman!" he exclaimed. "You ain't got no say in it. Don't you know that you're my property?"

Then came the ultimatum I've been dreading, "You come with me now or stay here for good, with your precious children! Don't think I'll be back in a hurry. I'll find me another woman to keep company with. Someone more amenable like."

"So, go then!" I cried. "I'd rather stay here than desert my children."

Will stormed out, swearing and cussing as he went, and I'm ashamed to admit, I collapsed in floods of tears.

Now, it's evening and I feel totally desperate. I've cuddled up close to Billy, in the hope that this will comfort me, but the fear that I will never get out of here terrifies me. Perhaps I could get a job and lodgings meself if I left here, but with a toddler in tow, how could I work? And if the other children were with me, it would be nigh impossible. Could I go to someone else for help, perhaps? Mam is so frail these days that I doubt she'd be able to look after the children for me if I was working, and I'm not sure I'd trust her to either. And Aunt Louisa barely speaks to us now, after Will treated her so badly that time. Then there's Elsie – she's a good friend but she has her own family. Have I the right to put more pressure on her? Anyway, I have my pride, not that it's ever done me much good. Oh, I don't know what to do. I think my marriage is over and it breaks my heart, but I must think of the children now.

Kate's Diary 12 August 1906

I don't know whether to be happy or sad after today. Elsie visited me unexpectedly and found me here in this miserable infirmary again, suffering yet another bout of the disease which hounds me.

"Kate!" she exclaimed, shocked. "You poor dear, you look so ill! I'm so sorry. I didn't know you were here until recently. I thought you were with your husband, but then I saw him last week with another woman on his arm. He was embarrassed when I asked after you, and he had to admit you were in here. If I'd known earlier, I'd have taken you away to stay with me. You must come with me now. You can't stay here."

"I have no choice," I wheezed. "I can't leave the children, especially not my little Billy. I'm not allowing them to take him into the nursery again. It upset him so much last time. Besides, I'm ill, Elsie. I need the doctor's help and I could never afford it, outside of here. Thank you so much, but I can't leave. I wish I could."

My tears flowed like bitter rain down my cheeks and Elsie comforted me whilst I cried uselessly.

"Oh, Kate, it's not fair. Will should be looking after you and the children; it's his responsibility. Instead, he's gallivanting around with some floozy."

"I think it's all over between us," I said and told her my pitiful story. Even so, I couldn't resist finding out all the details of 'the other woman' – what she looked like, what she wore, how she behaved, etc. I feel hurt and (in spite of myself) jealous. It galls me to think he could be like this. Does he have *no* feeling for me anymore? I haven't seen him in ages, but I still keep hoping that one day he will relent and bring us all home again.

Now Elsie has gone, and I am wishing that I'd left with her, but I can't leave here whilst Billy needs me. Maybe once he's at school then I can get a job and try and find a place for us to live. Last week, I saw Fred and Ern briefly, but they've changed. Their childhood innocence has gone and has been replaced by a new tough exterior. It was so difficult to know what to say to them anymore. I promised them that we would all be together again very soon, but they just stared at me, almost as if I was a stranger. They didn't believe me, and I don't blame them. I don't believe it myself.

Kate's Diary 27 February 1907

Last night, Will came to me and begged me to come home. He even went down on his knees to plead for forgiveness. There were genuine tears in his eyes, and I struggled to resist.

"I hear you've been seeing another woman," I accused, but he protested his innocence.

"Of course not, my darling. Where did you get that idea?"

"Elsie," I told him coldly. "She saw you."

"That was my sister helping out. Honestly, Kate. I know what I said before, but I was bluffing. I was just desperate to get you back. You know you're the only one for me, surely?" He took my hand gently as he said this, and I felt my defences crumbling.

I tried to stay strong. "Where have you been?" I demanded. "Why haven't you come to see us?"

"I was working hard to pay off the bills and get everything in order again, my darling," he replied. "It took up all my time doing that, but I was always thinking of you."

He promises he will change and says he misses me so much. He seems genuine and I want to believe him, but I can't bear the thought of leaving the children behind. Will pointed out that as Bill is going to school as well now, I won't be seeing them anyway, so it would be best to move out and get a home ready for them. He has a new job now, is earning more money, and all the old debts have been paid off. He also tells me that he has stopped drinking (though I'm not totally convinced). He swears that as soon as I am working again and the house is ready, then we can have the whole family back together. I really hope so. I've only seen them for such short times recently. At least they are getting a good education in Hanwell and they're properly fed. At the moment, I can't guarantee that we could do that for them at home.

I need to be positive and think of the future. I've been so ill since I've been in here and I feel so very weak. If I can just convalesce for a while, then I can recover my strength and start anew. I want our family back together more than anything. Will has convinced me that he still loves me and really wants things to be different this time. I have to give him another chance, for the sake of the children, if nothing else.

I have decided to leave here tomorrow morning. Will is going to collect me and take me to our new home, which I have to admit I'm really excited about. I'm not sure what I feel about him anymore but I'm going to take the opportunity to leave here and build a different future. Dear Fred will be joining us as well, as he is fourteen now, and Will has arranged for him to start work as a printer's assistant. I hope this will be a fresh start for all of us.

Kate's Diary 15 July 1907 Bear Street

At last, I have a job again, doing the washing for a local family. They are quite wealthy and wanted someone to do their laundry, whilst the poor 'maid of all work' has to do everything else. That reminds me of how it used to be for me long ago. I'm glad I don't have to do that anymore! I must say I pity poor Annie who works there. Still, I am so happy to be working again and I'm feeling so much stronger. I can't wait to get all the family back again. It won't be long now, surely.

Will certainly seems to have turned over a new leaf. He hasn't been drinking lately and there seems to be enough money to pay the bills. Even his temper appears to have improved at the moment and I pray it will continue. (I can't take too much knocking around these days after my illness).

Of course, the minute I came home, he wanted to resume 'conjugal relations' which felt strange after so long apart, but he has always been a man of strong passions and I have no right to deny him. He is my husband, after all.

Kate's Diary 1 June 1908

I keep asking Will whether I can bring the children home again and he keeps putting me off. *'There's not enough money'*, he says, *'Wait until April'*. Now that's come and gone, and he says, *'Wait until the summer'*. Next, it'll be, *'Wait until Christmas'*! Doesn't he want them? They *are* his, after all. I need to do something, but what?

Tonight, I pushed him a bit too far on this and he lost his temper properly for the first time since I came home again.

"Shut up, woman!" he snapped and lashed out with his fist, just like the bad old days (it's a good job Fred didn't see!).

I am so disappointed that this has happened. I really felt that this time we had a chance of a happy life together, but now I'm not so sure.

Kate's Diary 30 November 1908

Last night, I told Will I am leaving him unless he fetches the children home immediately. He tried every argument in the book to persuade me not to.

"They're getting a good education," he said. "It's in their best interest. Besides, think of the cost."

But I've had enough. I've been home meself for over a year now and I'm in good health, thank the Lord. I'm working and bringing in money, and Will is keeping a steady job down at last. The house is a fair size (though it ain't nothing fancy), and there's no reason that they shouldn't be with us.

"They need to be with their parents," I told him, and I was real angry this time.

"Ern is nearly 14 now and should be getting a job, and the others need to be at home, going to the local school."

Will didn't want to listen but this time I wouldn't back down.

"They're *my* children and I love them. Fred is missing his brothers as well. I can tell he's fierce lonely. He comes to talk to me a lot and often says how much he wishes they were here with him."

"Fred's a useless idiot!" exclaimed his father, "and you're not much better. If you didn't spend so much money on the housekeeping, then we'd be able to have them here. It's all your fault."

I suddenly saw red and had to speak out, no matter what the consequences were.

"That's it, Will. I'm going to pack my bags and go! I'll find somewhere to stay and then I'll get the children back meself. I'll tell them their heartless father doesn't want them anymore!"

I stormed out of the room and upstairs, where I got out an old canvas bag and started to pack my clothes. I was so angry I couldn't even cry, and if Will had decided to hit me there and then, I felt I really didn't care. My children are everything to me and that was the only thought in my head.

Will followed me and stood in the doorway, watching. Then to my surprise, he started pleading.

"Kate, darlin', don't go. I didn't mean it. Of course, we'll get them home again. I'll do it tomorrow, you'll see. Please!"

I looked up and saw tears rolling down his cheeks, but I've been caught out by this before, so I tried to stay strong and ignore them.

"I mean it," I told him. "They come home or I'll go – that's my final say on it."

Of course, he's convinced me now to stay and swears he'll do as I ask, but I'm not sure I really trust him. We'll see.

Kate's Diary 2 December 1908

Today we've been married twenty years and Will wanted to take me out to celebrate. However, I told him I wasn't going unless he went to the Hanwell School first and did all the paperwork to get the children transferred to our nearby Southwark School. Not only that, but I insisted that they must only be there as day pupils, not as boarders. It's feckin' daft

270

for them to be living away from home when they are so close by.

So, at last, it's been done, and they will all come home at the end of the school term on 17th December. I saw them today and was able to tell them the good news. Bill has changed so much; he's not a cuddly little baby anymore – he's five years old! Poor Joe has really had to be tough since moving up to the bigger boys section last year, and Albert and Ern are fair grown up as well. I wish I'd had more contact with them, I feel I don't know them very well at all. Let's hope things get better again now. I'm looking forward to Christmas this year, to be sure.

This evening, we went out to the music hall and had a grand time. We wined and dined, danced and sang, just like we used to in the old days. For a moment there, I felt young again and I loved Will as much as ever. He was charming and funny, and I remembered what I found attractive in him. If we could only recapture that more often.

Kate's Diary 17 December 1908

All the children are home at last and I planned a real celebration, but it's all gone wrong. Will is in a massive sulk and has gone to the alehouse again (I hope he doesn't get too drunk). The children look bewildered and lost. They don't even seem to know what to say to each other, let alone me. I suppose it's been a long time and they've forgotten what it's like to be a family. I bought them each a present, but I didn't really know what they liked unfortunately. Albert tossed the toy boat I'd got him on the floor in disgust, saying, "I'm too old to play with that now, Mum. Honestly!"

Ern went off to talk to Fred in their bedroom upstairs and I didn't see them for the rest of the night. Joe and Bill seemed happy to see me, thank goodness, but they were tired and confused. Joe cheered up a bit when I got him to help me in the kitchen, but Bill was tearful, on and off, all evening. They've all gone to bed now, but I feel wretched. I was so longing to see them all here again, and to have a chance to make up for their hardship, but I don't think I can. It's too late.

Kate's Diary 1 September 1909

Here I sit this evening, my cheek throbbing with pain and my lip bleeding. Will really let fly at poor Joe today, and I felt I had to defend him. I know Joe had been silly and careless, but he was only trying to help out around the house. It's true that Will loved those chairs because his Mum gave them to him, and he's had so little from her over the years. He's always been passed over in favour of his younger brother, James, who can do no wrong. Perhaps if Joe had owned up about it, instead of hiding it, Will might have forgiven him more easily. But I understand – he was frightened. I often feel the same way. Whenever something goes wrong, I feel meself shaking, just before I have to tell Will. I never know how he is going to react.

Thank goodness Fred and Ern came home just at that time. It could have been so much worse. They're good lads.

Will promised me he'd given up drinking when we came out of Newington, and for a while he had, but he's slipped right back again and nothing I can say will make him stop. I know that's where he is now, and I dread his return.

Joe's Recollections, 1913

Ern had always wanted to join the army, and so, as soon as he turned 18, he signed up. I'd heard him arguing with our father about it a few weeks earlier, so it was no surprise to me. Our mother was very ill by then and Father told Ern, in no uncertain terms, that he couldn't leave us just yet.

"We need you to help look after your mother," I heard him say. "You know how ill she is. It'll break her heart if you leave."

But Ern was young, headstrong and determined.

"I can't stay here," he argued. "You just want me to work and bring in money, but I have to make my own life. Besides, I won't be far away. I'll only be training at first and that's local. I know Mum wouldn't want me to put things on hold. She understands how much I want this. I've always said that this is what I want to do."

So, just after his 18th birthday in 1913, Ern enlisted with the Duke of Cornwall Light Infantry. When he came home that day and proudly told us, our father went mad at him.

"How dare you be so selfish? Don't you ever think about other people? Is this all the thanks we get for bringing you up? You're letting us down very badly."

"Look," said Ern reasonably, "the training won't start for a few months yet. I shan't tell Mum, if you like. We all know that the truth is that, sadly, she doesn't have very long left. I'll stay around for as long as necessary but then I'll be off. I can't stay here with you, Father. I have to do my own thing. I'm sorry."

Father snorted and stomped off. Somehow, we all kept the news from Mum, though I felt bad that she didn't know. However, a lot of the time now, she wasn't conscious or she was very confused. In the rare times when she was clearheaded, she was coughing so much she could hardly talk. Her beautiful hair was thin now and streaked with grey, and her once handsome features were lined with pain. She lay in bed, white faced and barely able to sit up. We took it in turns to sit with her, feed her and talk to her. Sometimes she wanted me to tell her all the old Irish legends again that she loved so well, and I did my best, though it was a feeble attempt. I kept encouraging her to get well, knowing in my heart that she wouldn't, but trying to be positive for her sake. The consumption had got such a hold on her now that she was just wasting away.

Kate's Diary 23 October 1909 Borough Market

I had to get away from the house for a while, so I'm sitting here in the public reading room, but I can't stop crying. I can see a couple of people staring at me. I hope they won't turn me out. It's all my fault, I know, but I couldn't help it.

On the way to the market this afternoon to get some fish for Will's dinner, I got distracted by a disturbance nearby. There was a protest march going on by the suffragettes, so I stopped to watch for a minute. I don't know much about their cause – I mean I know it's something about rights for women, but what is that? Will says women ain't entitled to anything like property or voting. When I tried to discuss it, he just laughed and said, "They wouldn't know what to do with it. They'd only lose it or something. You can't even keep hold of the pennies, can you, Kate?"

I couldn't say anything. I think I do quite well really, but there's certainly never enough money to go round. At least this new flat is a bit cheaper.

Anyway, that's all I did, just stopped to watch. I never got involved or nothing, but when I tried to get out of the crowd, it was almost impossible. The march went past so slowly, and when I finally got away, I was late for the market.

"There ain't no fish left, dearie," the stallholder told me. "Should have been here earlier, we had some lovely stuff. How about a nice bit of tripe instead?"

With a sinking feeling, I knew that I was in for trouble. Will always likes a bit of fish at this time of the week.

I took what I could get and tried to bluff my way out of it. I'm ashamed to say I lied and told Will that they had sold out early. He was angry but believed me to start with. Trouble is, young Albert had seen me, it seems, as he came back from school, and he piped up with, "I saw you at the march today, Mum. Did you join in?"

"March? What march?" thundered Will.

"It was those women protestors, Dad," Albert said, "waving those silly banners of theirs."

"Is that why you didn't get my fish?" Will stormed at me, his face as black as night.

I felt meself beginning to tremble with fear.

"Well, I was held up by all the people," I admitted. "I couldn't help it. I just watched for a little while."

"How dare you?" exploded Will. "And you lied to me as well! What a thoughtless, useless wife you are! It's just typical of you, isn't it, to put me bottom of your list of priorities. I always come last, don't I, after the children, your marches, your silly writing and all your other things? I don't matter, do I? I'm just not important to you, I suppose."

"That's not true!" I protested feebly. "Of course, you're important. You know I always try to get you all the things you want."

"No, no, don't give me that! I'm bottom of the list. I know the truth. You don't care about me. How selfish can you get! You're a liar and a cheat."

I saw Albert laughing to himself and Joe looking shocked. Will came closer to me, looking threatening, and continued his rant. His voice was getting high pitched and hysterical now, like he does when he gets really annoyed and I knew his fists could follow soon after. My tears were starting to fall as I tried again to apologise and also to defend meself, but it was useless. Will wouldn't listen to anything I said. On these occasions, he just shouts over the top of me and I can't get a word in edgeways. I just couldn't face anymore.

"I'm going out," I said, getting my coat.

"You stay here, woman," he said, grabbing my arm forcefully, but I wrenched it out of his grip and managed to leave the house. I don't know what to do now, but if I stay here for a while, he may have calmed down by the time I get home. The trouble is, nothing is ever resolved. He never apologises for his rages, he just forgets about it. He's always in the right. I suppose I just have to accept it. After all I did let him down, but it was accidental. I didn't mean to.

Kate's Diary 9 February 1910

I been following all the talk about votes for women recently. I daren't let Will know, but I think about it quite often. Why shouldn't we be able to have a say? It ain't right. Gets me fair riled up if I dwell on it too much, so I mustn't. Will wouldn't like it.

The government have thrown out the bill they were going to pass (just like the Irish Home Rule bill), and the women are really up in arms. It's got fierce violent lately, with windows smashed and people going on hunger strike in prison. Mind, I'm not sure that I can see the point of starving yerself – what's that going to achieve? And Da always told me that violence don't help – it only leads to more of the same. He was probably right. I mean, look at Ireland.

Oh well, what do I know anyway? Will always says I'm ignorant and don't understand nothing, but I can't help pondering all the same.

Kate's Diary 7 May 1910

The King died suddenly yesterday. It seems like only 5 minutes since he was crowned! Yet, if I think what's happened to us in that time – the ups and downs – well, I can see it's quite a while really. That's the strange thing about time – some things pass in the blink of an eye and others seem to last an age. You'd think everything would go at the same speed but somehow it doesn't. It's curious.

Kate's Diary 18 November 1910

Today I seen such dreadful scenes I never wish to see again! It fair frightened me. What Da said was true; marching only leads to violence, but it ain't right that it should. Surely peaceful protest is the best way to express your feelings.

I heard there was a big march of the suffragettes going on and I have to admit I was curious. In the afternoon, I had to go out to return some laundry to my usual lady, and I was on me way home when I came past the Houses of Parliament. There must have been hundreds of people there; women of all ages and classes and loads of police. I never seen so many coppers in one place before. There were huge crowds of bystanders around as well, watching, jeering and generally egging them on. I couldn't make out whose side they were on – the suffragettes or the police – but they were a rough lot and appeared to be mostly out to make trouble.

I saw the women approach parliament and try to start some speeches, but the police suddenly attacked en masse, like a huge wave breaking on the beach. I heard someone say that there were extra coppers drafted in, special like. Our own London Met bobbies are okay, but this lot were real nasty. I saw them beat women with their truncheons and carry them off screaming down side streets, where the crowd joined in abusing and insulting them. Worse still, some women were being molested. One copper near me grabbed a woman protestor by the breasts and lifted up her skirts for all to see. It was disgusting. I couldn't have helped her – I was too hemmed in by people – but I wanted to. I felt tears come into my eyes at the thought of her shame and embarrassment. Women were being battered and then thrown into the crowd. Some were dragged away to suffer what fate; I dread to think. There were women on the ground, bleeding and bruised. It was awful.

I tried to get out of the crowd, but it was fierce difficult. I fought my way bit by bit towards the outer edge and finally pulled out of it into a small side street. But here there were even more terrible things to witness.

In the street I'd entered, there were more police gathered around a well-dressed lady on an invalid tricycle. A small crowd had also assembled. It was obvious that the lady was one of the suffragettes, but being immobile, the coppers had managed to wheel her away from the rest. There was a fair old barney going on as she demanded to be taken back to the march, but the police just stood around, mocking and laughing at her.

"You ain't going nowhere, lady!" one shouted, and all of a sudden, they grabbed her invalid carriage and turned it over, leaving her sprawling on the ground. Then they kicked at her and laughed again.

"Try joining in now!" one teased. "See how you get on!"

The crowd seemed a bit shocked at this and one man shouted, "Leave her be, coppers! It ain't fair on a cripple."

One of the police turned and threatened him with a truncheon, so he backed off. I kept meself flattened against a wall in the shadows. It was a fair nasty moment, and I didn't want to go home with a shiner. Will would have wanted to know what I'd been up to.

The lady pleaded to be allowed up into her chair.

"Please. Can't you see I can't manage like this? For goodness sake, please put me back on my tricycle."

The crowd murmured its agreement. The police appeared to relent and two or three of them grabbed her bodily (and very roughly) and put her back on her tricycle again, which some of the others had righted.

"You needn't think you're joining in again, lady. We know you're one of the ring leaders. You ain't going nowhere."

With that, two of the officers proceeded to remove something from the wheels of her carriage, whilst another held her arms behind her back viciously, so that she couldn't do anything to stop them. The carriage was now wrecked. The police laughed loudly, pocketed the things they'd removed and moved off, leaving her stranded. The crowd also started to disperse.

"Please!" cried the lady. "Don't leave me here. How will I get home?"

By this time, the crowd had thinned considerably, and I felt brave enough to approach. A man tried to move the tricycle, but it was stuck fast.

"I dunno what to do, lady," he said to her. "Sorry."

I was one of the only women there and I came closer. I could see her dress was torn and her breasts half exposed, so I went up and offered her my shawl to cover up.

"Thank you," she said gratefully. "That's very kind."

I blushed. Being spoken to by a real lady is not something I'm used to.

"Can I take a message somewhere, ma'am?" I asked.

"Oh please," she said, relieved. "My name is Rosa May Billingshurst. Can you let my brother Henry know? I'll give you the address."

Some of the people left in the street promised to look after her until he arrived, so I sped off with a note to a grand house in Regents Park. I never saw her brother, but the butler assured me he would deliver the note immediately. It was a long way and I'm fair tired out now, but at least I feel I helped in some way.

Thankfully, Will hasn't found out this time, though he did ask why I wasn't wearing my shawl. I had to pretend I'd lost it. I hate having to lie, but he would go spare if he knew the truth.

Kate's Diary 19 November 1910

Today, Will caught me reading the newspaper when he came home. Supper was all ready. It weren't like I'd neglected nothing, so it weren't fair really. I think it's 'cause it was all about the suffrage protest yesterday and he didn't want me to see it.

"What you reading that for?" he demanded. "Ain't you s'posed to be in the kitchen? Get my dinner, woman. I'm hungry!"

With that, he tore the newspaper from my hands and crumpled it up into a heap.

"I was just reading about the protest yesterday," I pleaded, "and about how well the police did."

This pacified him a bit.

"Don't go sympathising with those old bags who neglect their families to go off making trouble," he commanded. "They're unnatural!"

"Yes, yes," I told him. "I know all that. I didn't mean nothing by looking."

"Well, don't look next time. I don't want you getting any stupid ideas in yer head!"

It's ironic, really, as reading that paper certainly wouldn't have given me any ideas. The article was highly disapproving of the women, condemning their actions and saying that they 'refused to be happy until they were arrested' (Daily Mirror). No mention was made of the police brutality. No one would have known of the explicitly sexual attacks, the outright violence and the manhandling, unless they had been there. The only picture which showed a woman on the ground claimed she had collapsed with exhaustion. That's a joke!

The police were praised for their endurance and forbearance, but I know this isn't a true picture. Though I'm sure there were faults on both sides, I know what I saw. No woman deserves to be subjected to such treatment. In fact – not just women – no *person* deserves to be molested or attacked just because of what they believe. It ain't right.

Anyway, after yesterday, I'm too scared to get involved in any of that again. I know I'm being a coward, but I'm going to keep well away from any marches from now on. It's not my nature though and I feel real uneasy in my heart. If I could, I'd be standing there with 'em all, but I'm not free to do what I wish. I just have to try and get by, day to day.

Kate's Diary 21 June 1911

Feel so ill. I can hardly breathe (I've not felt good all year so far, if I'm honest, but I've tried to keep going). Finally had to take to my bed yesterday, and Fred insisted on calling the doctor. Just another attack of consumption, like I had before in Newington, that's all, he said. Nothing to worry about.

It's the coronation tomorrow, but they'll have to get by without me this time. I told the family to go and watch if they want to. Fred said he's staying to look after me, though I said there's no need really, but he's always been there for me. He's turned into a decent young man and I'm so proud of him. Ern has volunteered to take Joe and Bill along, as Joe was too young to remember the last one and Bill wasn't born then. It should be a good day out for them. Not sure what Albert is doing; he doesn't seem to join in with much 'family' stuff – just like his father!

Kate's Diary 17 April 1912

I can hardly focus on writing this, for my grief at what has happened. Poor Bronagh and her family – all gone! This awful news about the Titanic has fair knocked me for six. After being so ill most of last year, I don't want to get sick again, but this has really brought me down.

Dear Joe – he tried his best to help but he doesn't understand my loyalty to Ireland and my family. I ain't seen any of 'em in years; even Mam is virtually a stranger these days, but still they are in my heart.

Will was surprisingly sympathetic yesterday but has forgotten all about it today. That's like him – things that upset other people don't bother him for long, if at all. That tiny crumb of comfort was welcome, even so.

Must just rest today and try to recover. The family needs me to be strong.

Kate's Diary 28 April 1913

Today, the doctor talked to me real serious like and told me I don't have very long left and I should get my 'affairs in order' (whatever that means). I guess I knew it already, but it was fierce hard to hear it said aloud and I cried a bit afterwards. Mind, this ain't the Irish way, so I told meself not to be so feckin daft (must be the Britishers rubbin' off on me). We Irish know what death's all about. My da always said we have to face it head on and take what's coming.

I remember my da's wake quite clearly, to be sure. It was a grand affair, in spite of our grief. I recall he died at half past three in the afternoon. I know that because Mam stopped our big mantel clock at that time, as is the custom, and it seemed to me as if the whole world had stopped.

Mam and I spent time with Aunty Mairead and some other local women, washing and preparing his body. Then we wrapped him in white linen, fastened with black ribbon and laid him in the coffin. He looked so fine and peaceful, his hair and beard all groomed and smart, just like he was about to go to church on Sunday. My heart still aches when I think of it. We placed candles around his body and pipes for people to smoke, to ward off the evil spirits. We followed all the Irish traditions, and for the next couple of days, the open coffin was left in our parlour, with people watching over him all the time, day and night. So many people came: drinking tea, eating sandwiches, telling funny stories, smoking, arguing, singing songs. We even played some games.

I know Will and the children would find this strange, shocking or even disrespectful. Death over here is such a sombre occasion and so depressing. In Ireland, we always try to make it a celebration and we believe the deceased should be part of it as well. They aren't left alone for a minute until they're finally buried. We were still sad, of course, but all this makes it easier to bear, somehow. I'd really like this kind of thing for meself. I don't want to be left alone in one of them undertakers' shops. So cold and lonely!

After about three days, I remember we had Da buried at the local cemetery, then it was back to O'Hanlon's pub for a right ol' knees up. What a great way to be remembered – it's what I want.

Kate's Diary 29 April 1913

Today I told Will what the doctor said. I couldn't face telling him afore as I knew he'd take it hard. I think he's in denial 'cos all he said was, "No, don't be silly. You'll be well again soon. You just have to keep trying."

I s'pose it's the British way – try and pretend it's not happening, but it's not my way. I've accepted it now. Anyway, Will was in a real grump afterwards and went round the house slamming doors and shouting at everyone. I know he loves me, but I wish he'd be a bit calmer. It don't help none, him getting all hepped up about it, but I guess he's always been that way.

Looking back over my life, I wonder what I have achieved. Have I done anything worthwhile? I never wrote my novel, never travelled. I didn't make it back to my beloved Ireland; but still – I suppose I've been a virtuous and loyal wife, in spite of the hardships. Finally, I can see clearly what kind of person Will truly is – a cruel bully who only wants to control people. Yet he can be charming enough when he likes; but it's all a front. Unfortunately, I was taken in by it, but my eyes are open now. Perhaps my life might have taken a very different course if I hadn't married him; but who knows? It ain't no good thinking, *"What if?"*

The thing I feel most proud of is my lovely children. Despite the troubles we've had, I've always tried to be a good mother to them. My love for them has never wavered. I thank the Lord they have survived all this. They are the true achievement of my life, my pride and joy, and if that's all there is, then that will be enough.

I just wish I had more time to watch them grow up. Fred and Ern are both fine young men now and are still set on joining the army. Will wants them to stay in the printing firm but it's not fair to stop them (for their sake, I hope we don't end up in a war again). The other lads are still finding their way as yet, but I have great hopes for them. I'd have loved to been around long enough to see them married and settled, but it seems it's not to be. My grandchildren will never know me, sadly.

My other great regret is never having written more. It was a silly idea, I s'pose. Still, I've kept my diary and hopefully someone will read it all someday. Unfortunately, I've not had the energy to write much lately.

At least I'll be reunited with my little lost babies, and I'll see my dear old da walking in the emerald meadows once again. Ireland's in me blood and always will be. I know my soul will fly there when it is free at last, hopefully to rest in eternal peace, God willing.

Joe's Recollections, 1913

At the beginning of May in 1913, there was a sudden deterioration in our mother's condition. Up until then she had always fought to get well, but now she seemed to lose the will to live. She appeared almost resigned to the inevitable and had a calm serenity about her, though her mind often wandered and her thoughts were confused. She stopped eating, in spite of our continued efforts to feed her. Fred, in particular, spent hours with her each evening, trying to tempt her with broth. Father took over at night, Bill by day and I took my turn in the afternoon. Sometimes, I would just sit and read to her. Albert stayed, for the most part, out of the way, as did Ern. They seemed convinced there was nothing that could be done and said they couldn't bear to see her like that. Despite this, I felt I must be there for her and try my best, at the very least.

One afternoon, I was there with her and she suddenly became very clear headed again.

"Joe," she whispered, "Fetch me a pen and paper. I must write some things down whilst I still can."

I was surprised by the request, as I'd rarely seen her write more than a shopping list before, but when I said this, she smiled weakly and confided in me.

"I've always kept a diary, Joe, though not every day, mind. I wanted so much to be a writer when I was young, but it wasn't to be, so I just kept writing for myself. One day, maybe you can read them."

"Where are all these diaries?" I asked.

"In that chest," she replied, pointing. "Your father knows where the key is, but don't let him see them. He'd only be upset."

"Why?" I asked.

"It's difficult to explain, Joe, but you'll understand one day, I hope."

I did as I was asked and then left her alone. It seemed she was anxious to have some space to herself. When I went back later, the pen and paper were lying by her side, the paper folded over so the contents could not be seen immediately. She was sleeping peacefully. That evening, whilst Fred was caring for her, she passed away quietly, never having woken up again.

The funeral was a cold, sad, bitter affair. Just a simple graveside ceremony, no fuss or bother, traditional and subdued. Her mother came and a couple of other women I'd never seen before. One was an elegant, well dressed young lady called Flossie, who placed a bunch of flowers by the grave, and the other, a much older lady, with somewhat tired looking grey hair, who sniffed plaintively into her hanky. The vicar said a few words, but he didn't really know Mum, so it was meaningless, just observing the formalities.

Father was in tears, so I guess he really did love her after all. Fred was too, but there was no mutual comfort between them. There was no wake. Afterwards, Fred and Ern went off to a local alehouse and Father locked himself in the front parlour with a bottle of whisky. I don't know where Albert disappeared off to. He'd seemed strangely unmoved by it all. Bill and I sat by the stove in the kitchen, silently crying and trying to take it all in. Our mother – gone! I thought that I had prepared myself for it, what with her having been ill for so long, but now suddenly it was final. There was no going back. I had even thought that it might be a relief after watching all her suffering, but no, it wasn't. The loss was incalculable – a gaping hole in our lives. The only parent we had now was Father and he was scarcely reliable.

As for the diaries, I never got to read them. Father was devastated by our mother's death and the only way he could cope was by removing every trace of her from the house, to prevent painful reminders. Most of her clothes were given away and her personal effects and papers were burnt. Fred argued bitterly with our father over this, wanting to keep her memory alive, but as always Father had his way. We came home from work one day, soon after the funeral, to find a huge bonfire going outside and everything gone. When I went into the bedroom the chest stood open and empty. The only thing we did get to read was her final letter to us all, which was written that last afternoon.

Kate's letter to the family 22 May 1913

My dear family,

I have to write this while I still can, for I fear I don't have very long left. Please don't be sad. I feel it is nearly time for me to join my dear old da in an Irish heaven somewhere. I still remember that day we sat amongst the shamrocks to eat our lunch on the way to Waterford. That's close enough to heaven for me.

I have loved you all so much – dear Will, who brought music into my life again and rescued me from boredom. And you, my wonderful children – Fred, Ern, Albert, Joe and Billy – life is too precious to waste, to be sure, so mind you make every moment count. Being your mother has given me the greatest pleasure of my life and I thank you all for it.

One day we shall all be together again. I only came here for the 'craic' anyway, as they say. Until then,

Slan is beannacht (goodbye and blessings).

Joe's Recollections, 1913

As for Ern, it wasn't long after the funeral that he started his army training. Initially, it was local, like he'd said it would be, but later he was transferred to his battalion of the DCLI and went off to Exeter. Before that, however, he had found himself a sweetheart, Betty Alderman, a young woman of ample size and charm. Her generous figure reflected her affectionate and outgoing nature. Everything about her was large, from her sense of humour to her buxom stature (at that point I hardly knew Betty, though I got to know her much better, later on). Ern found her refreshingly honest and fun, after the depression of our own family. Even so, he still wanted to join the army, so he reluctantly left her behind to pursue his training, in the hope that he would be posted closer to home again in the future. Little did he know that the country was on the brink of war.

Ern's letters back to the family were sporadic. Fred heard more often from him than we did. They'd been close and everyone could tell that he missed him. The arguments between Fred and our father became more frequent and stormier as Father tried desperately to get Fred to fit into his plans. He wanted him to stay at home, working in the printing firm and help bring in some money, but Fred resented this. I guessed we were in debt again, as money was so tight that food was very basic, and even essential items, like a new pair of shoes for young Bill, were not forthcoming. Sometimes, official looking men knocked loudly on the front door, demanding to see my father, but he always told us not to open it to them. I suppose he owed them money for something.

Now that Mum had gone, Bill had been ordered to leave school by Father, so that he could cook and keep house for the rest of us who were now trying to earn our keep. I was only 13 and should have been still at school as well, but now had to start work. Albert was working as a baker's assistant (though not doing very well by all accounts), and he managed to get me a job cleaning out the ovens in the bakery. It was hot, dirty work but brought in some much-needed cash.

Fred started spending most weekends away – we didn't know where. He was also out regularly in the evenings. When he did come in, he refused to tell any of us where he'd been and so we assumed the worst. Father would spend the time when he was out, berating him and calling him a 'no-good waster'.

"He's always out drinking," he claimed, "and then tired at work the next day. He'll lose his job if he carries on like this, then where will the family be? We need his wages. Doesn't he realise he's letting us all down?"

That was a bit like the pot calling the kettle black, I thought, as Father's drinking habit had, if anything, increased since our mother died. I know Father genuinely mourned for her, but he attempted to drown his sorrows with no thought for the rest of us, which, even now, I find hard to forgive.

I bet you're wondering what sort of person Fred was. Well, it's difficult to say for sure, as I didn't know him that well. After all, he was seven years older than me, and by the time I was old enough to take it all in, we were split up in the workhouse. However, I can say he was deep. Quiet, intense, moody perhaps, but there was a lot going on in his mind. It's just that he didn't share it with us younger boys. I think he and Ern were close, despite their completely different personalities. Ern was happy-go-lucky, optimistic and cheerful; maybe that was what Fred needed to counteract his seriousness. I don't know. I do know that our mother absolutely doted on Fred. She loved us all dearly, I'm sure, but I have to say, if truth be told, Fred was her favourite. She fussed constantly about what he ate, what his health was like and so on. Maybe it was because he was her first child, or maybe because she always had a sense that he wouldn't be around for long. Not that Fred had a delicate disposition. He was strong, lean and rarely ill. Mind, I know that he and Ern spent a while in the infirmary together when they were very young. I'm not sure why, but I guess that's when they really bonded as brothers.

Mum's fussing used to drive Fred to distraction at times, but it was obvious he loved her in spite of this. He was devastated when she passed away and kept himself apart to grieve alone. Things were never the same in the family after that.

Fred's Letters
To Pte EC Duffield, DCLI, Exeter
From London 15 June 1914

Dear Ern,

Cheers! How are you, old mate? I hear you're training hard and may be going abroad very soon. There's talk of war in the air, so I wish you well if you get caught up in it. As you probably know by now, me and the old man had a real bust up the other day and I've left. I'm lodging at the above address for a while but am off to summer camp with the Territorials shortly. That's part of the reason I left. As you know I've been training with them part-time for a few months now, but last week, we had notification of the summer camp in July. Dad saw the official letter arrive and demanded to know what was in it.

"I ain't about to tell you!" I told him. "It's my business."
(I knew he'd never let me go, so I thought it was best to keep

it quiet). But you know what he's like – always needs to know everything. He kept on and on at me, thought I'd got myself in trouble or something. I suppose I should have come clean about it, but the more he tried to find out, the more I didn't want to tell him. I know it was stupid really, but it was a matter of principle. Anyway, then he started saying I'd always been secretive just like our mother. He was quite drunk at the time and started calling her all kinds of names, saying it was all her fault I was like this. I couldn't stand to hear him slagging her off, so I told him if he didn't shut up, I'd thump him. He just laughed at me and that really wound me up. I felt like a coiled spring just waiting to explode, but I tried to hold it, honest I did. But then he had the audacity to tell me to run off and see Alice, my girl, for sympathy. He called her a 'cheap whore' and that was it, I'm afraid. I just sprang at him and we wrestled back and forth round the kitchen. It was funny really, now I come to think of it. Two grown men, fighting next to the pots and pans! I gave him a black eye, but he managed to get in a good kicking to my ribs. The bruises are still coming out now! At the end of it all, I pushed him hard away and he landed in the bins, rather dazed. I took the chance to rush up and collect my things. On the landing, I saw the younger lads, looking shocked and horrified, but I weren't about to hang around. I can still remember young Bill, though, calling after me as I left, which made me feel bad. I expect that's the last time I'll see any of them.

Very soon I'm off to summer camp and then who knows where. I know the Territorials are only a part-time force, but we can be relied upon to help out if needed. My dearest sweet Alice doesn't want us to be parted, but somehow, I need to do this. I really want to do my bit – well, you know what I mean. It just feels the right thing to do.

I can feel the shadow of war fast approaching and I can't imagine what will become of us all in the future. I have to admit to feeling a bit scared, but excited as well. Maybe it will be our greatest adventure.

Well, take care of yourself, mate. I'll write when I can. Chin up, as they say.

All the best

Fred

Joe's Recollections, 1914

I was 13 when Fred left home, and I still don't know exactly what happened that day. I was upstairs with Bill when we heard copious amounts of shouting and swearing going on, down below. Just then Albert came running in gleefully, saying, "Here lads, you'll never guess what. Father and Fred are having a right set to!"

Telling Bill to stay put, I crept down to the kitchen to have a look. As I got nearer, I heard Fred shouting, "Don't you dare speak about her like that. She's worth ten of you any time. Stop now or I'll fucking thump yer!"

"Yeah? You and whose army?" laughed our father. "Go off and hide yourself in the arms of your cheap whore. That's about your limit."

"What do you mean?" exclaimed Fred.

"You think I don't know you've been seeing that trollop down the market? What's her name – Alice?"

Fred cried out and then I heard crashing sounds as he and our father launched into a messy and unpleasant brawl. I retreated hastily and reported back to the others. The noises continued behind me, as the contents of the kitchen flew in all directions during the struggle. I remember thinking how Mum would have been so upset to see all her best china getting broken.

Albert seemed to think it was funny, telling us how Father had got all worked up about some letter or something.

"Fred's in trouble again, I reckon," he said. "Father'll teach him how to behave."

After ten minutes or more, there was a final loud crash, then silence. Shortly after, Fred ran upstairs to his room. He left the door open and we could hear frantic rummaging going on inside. We all came out to see what was happening, and a few minutes later, he reappeared with a bag and his coat. His face was flushed with emotion and coated with sweat.

"Fred," cried Bill, "don't go! Don't leave us, please!"

Fred just paused and looked at us for a moment quietly, then turned and hastily left the house. He never came back.

Fred's Letters

To Alice Parsons, Borough Market, London
From Summer Camp, 30 July 1914

My darling Alice,

I'm here at summer camp with the Territorials and wanted to write and tell you how much I'm missing you. You've made me so happy, my dearest, by saying that you will be my wife, that I can't wait to get home again! I was so looking forward to training camp but now everything has changed. The last couple of months have been the happiest ones of my life. When I lie in my bed at night, all I can see is your dear sweet face and those lovely blue eyes of yours that I could drown in. All I want is to hold you close and make you mine, but I'm glad we have chosen to wait until we are married before we fulfil our love. I know that you are pure and untouched, like a beautiful white rose.

I'm so glad to have got to know your family. They are so different to mine – warm and friendly. As you know I loved my mother Kate dearly and I can still remember her trying to protect us all. But she's gone now, and what with Ern away in the army, there's no one at home that I can turn to. My two youngest brothers, Joe and Bill, are nice lads and I wish I could stay in touch with them, but I have to avoid Father at all costs. If I see him again, I'll probably kill him! Albert's a sneak as well and I don't trust him one bit.

Those last few days before I came here remain bright in my memory. I look forward to being with you again very soon. Please don't worry about these rumours of war that are going around. Everyone says it won't really happen. Anyway, the duty of the Territorials is to defend the home front, so I won't be going away, even if the worst comes to the worst.

Only another week and I'll be back with you again! Until then, my darling, take care and know that I love you truly.

Yours,
Fred

Joe's Recollections, 1914

Fred walked out in about June 1914, I would say. I know it wasn't long afterwards that rumours of war started to drift around like wisps of smoke from the kindling of a new fire. Then someone murdered Archduke Ferdinand and his wife, and the flames started to spring into life. There was much talk on the streets and in the newspapers about the prospect of war. Opinions went back and forth a good deal – *no, we shouldn't; yes, we should* – it was all very confusing. I thought of Ern in the Duke of Cornwall Light Infantry and hoped that he would be all right.

In the meantime, things blew up in Ireland. There had long been fears of civil war breaking out over there, due to the struggle for Home Rule. This had rumbled on for some months now. It wouldn't have concerned me at all, except for the memory of my mother's background. She'd always said Ireland should be free and independent from Britain, but I didn't really know why she felt that way, never having lived there myself. All I know is that she would have been very upset by the incident which took place on the 26th July that year, when British soldiers fired on civilians in Dublin, suspecting them of gunrunning or something. Several people were killed and many more wounded. It was only the outbreak of the Great War, just days later, which prevented further trouble. The Irish Nation, as a whole, supported the British war effort, despite their grievances, and much credit should be given to them for this. My mother would have been proud. She always told me that Ireland was a fine country, and I know that she secretly longed to return there. She would reminisce about the beautiful southern coastline and the unspoilt landscape, so unlike our own overcrowded, grimy, poverty-stricken part of London. Yet, from what I hear, Barrack Street in Cork was really no better than Southwark, where we lived, but no one could ever get Mum to accept that and so we left her with her rose-tinted memories. Maybe it's always the way that when we look back at our past, we only see what we want to see, not necessarily how it really was.

Finally, the flames of war blazed into life. On the 3rd August 1914, Germany invaded Belgium and attacked France, and Britain issued an ultimatum – either withdraw or face war. That day was an uneasy one for all of us. I think we all knew we would be at war by the following day. People milled around outside Downing Street all day, but there was no news and eventually they went home. I worked until late at the bakers, then walked home through the eerily quiet streets, wondering what tomorrow would bring.

I found Bill tearful at home, worrying about the future. Father, as always, was scornful of his feelings.

"Grow up, you little rat," he ordered. "Stop snivelling, it won't do you no good."

Bill was only 11 years old and was very scared. I tried to comfort him but didn't feel much better about it myself.

"It won't affect us here, Bill," I told him. "It'll all happen in France, I reckon."

"As if you'd know!" sneered Father. "But anyway, I guess you're probably right. Britain's been at war before and it's never affected London."

"What about me, Father?" whined Albert. "I don't want to go and fight."

"They'll only use the army," Father reassured him. "You don't need to worry."

"What about Ern?" asked Bill. "Will he be sent abroad?"

"I expect so," replied Father, "but that's his own fault for signing up. I told him it was a bad idea, but he wouldn't listen."

The following day, everyone went to work as usual. I remember it was a Tuesday and it seemed so odd to be carrying on as normal at a time like this. But that evening, Bill, Albert and I went to join the crowds outside Buckingham Palace. I don't know why, but it seemed like the right thing to do. The sheer volume of people was enormous, but at 11pm, silence fell and as Big Ben chimed the hour, the announcement came through that war was declared. People started cheering and waving flags. Some were singing the national anthem, and everyone was calling for the king and queen to come out. This they duly did, and in spite of our worst misgivings a, spirit of wild patriotism and enthusiasm for war prevailed. After a few brief encouraging words, the royal family disappeared from view and the crowds began to disperse. We all felt buoyed up on an air of national pride and self-importance, which did not evaporate for several weeks. The next day, Lord Kitchener called for men to 'do their duty for the country' and thousands flocked to the recruiting offices to enlist. I went past the local one in Southwark that week and saw a queue stretching down the street. Loud rallying music was playing outside, and women were standing there, waving flags and encouraging their men to sign their lives away. Of course, no one realised what it would really be like. Everyone thought it would be '*all over by Christmas*'. I would have liked to have joined them, but I was far too young and quite small for my age, so wasn't likely to be able to fool anyone into thinking I was 18. Many did, however, and so Britain's youth was decimated by its own enthusiasm.

A couple of days after war was declared, we received a hastily written note form Ern, saying he was in good spirits and looking forward to a great adventure, whatever that might bring. His battalion were shipping out that week and would be in the very forefront of things. He sent his best wishes to us all and promised to write soon, however it turned out to be a very long time before we heard from him again. The letter ended, "I feel privileged to be able to do my duty for our glorious country. God Save the King! Cheers. Ern."

"Father," asked Bill anxiously, "you won't go off and sign up, will you?"

Father laughed derisively. "No fear!" he said. "You won't catch me fighting some stupid war. I'm too sensible, me. All these bright young men going off to be heroes – it's ridiculous. Ern's a fool!"

At that time, I was naïve enough to admire Ern for it and to want to join in myself, so I took the opposite view, wrongly, I suppose, as it turned out.

"At least he's doing what he thinks is right," I retorted. "*He's* not scared of being killed. You're just a coward, Father!"

The back of my father's hand caught me sharply across the face and it smarted.

"None of your cheek, my lad! Anyway, who do you think'll look after you lot if I'm away? Your good for nothing brother, Fred? Not likely! I hear he's off living it up with that cheap slut, Alice, who works down the market. He couldn't care less about us. If he did, he'd be here right now, seeing if we are okay."

The day after was a Saturday, and Bill and I went down to the station to watch the troops moving out. It was an

300

emotional yet strangely gay scene. Husbands and wives were saying tearful farewells, but the overall tone was cheerful. Flags waved, music played, flowers were thrown, songs were sung. It seemed the whole nation was swept up in the enthusiasm for war. Patriotic fervour had taken hold, and everyone was keen to participate in any way they could. Bill and I stood, waving and cheering with all the rest of the crowds, even though we didn't know anyone there. Ern's battalion were being shipped out from Ireland, so wouldn't be passing through our way. It didn't matter. We were just keen to encourage 'our boys' on their way to a fate unknown. The horrors that they would face were never suspected for a moment. We were foolishly convinced that there would be one glorious battle and that Britain would be victorious in a matter of weeks. How wrong we were.

Fred's Letters

To Alice Parsons, Borough Market, London
From St Albans, 5 August 1914

My dearest Alice,

This is a difficult letter to write. Have no fear, my darling, my heart still belongs to you, but war has intervened, I am sorry to say. Now that Germany has so aggressively invaded and attacked Belgium and France, our units have been mobilised. I know everyone thinks the Territorials are a bit of a joke (as Kitchener had the cheek to say, 'men playing at being soldiers'), but we can fight with the best of them. We've all been transferred here for intensive training prior to being engaged in the war.

Now please don't be cross with me, my darling, but I have volunteered to go overseas to fight. I know you will be upset but I feel I need to serve my king and country. It is my patriotic duty, and I can do it best with the rest of the men in France. The good thing is, we are now getting proper training before we go, so we will all be up to full battle readiness. Watch out Germany! Here we come!

There is a wonderful atmosphere here of camaraderie and loyalty. Everyone feels honour bound to do their bit. I feel this will be a great adventure and a chance for me to prove myself. I'm sure your brothers will be signing up as well, and you wouldn't want to be ashamed of me, would you?

We are staying in St Albans for a while and are billeted in a school at present, though what happens when the new term starts in September, I don't know. Everywhere you go in the town, the people cheer and welcome us, even though it is swamped by the troops. The public is right behind us, which is very encouraging.

Even so, I long to be with you again and hope we will get some leave before we embark for overseas. I had hoped to have been back home again by now, but it can't be helped. They say this war will all be over by Christmas, so hopefully we can get married early next year. I hope to make you proud of me before that, then you'll be able to tell our children all about it in years to come.

Will write again soon.

All my love,

Yours,
Fred

Fred's Letters

To Alice Parsons, Borough Market, London
From St Albans, 1 September 1914

Dearest Alice,

My darling – thank you for your last letter. I am so relieved and thankful that you understand my need to serve my country overseas. It will be hard on you, I know, but please try not to worry. I will be back home again in no time.

Last night, I had a strange dream. It seemed I was a child again, running along in a meadow with my dear mother. She was young and beautiful, her laughter like music floating in the air (in a lot of ways, sweetheart, you remind me of her. I can't say why exactly, maybe it's your lovely smile).

In my dream, I was so happy, and it was as if the bad times had never happened. But then the sky darkened, the winds howled, and I was torn away from her, screaming. I woke up in a cold sweat. My mate, Arthur, who sleeps in the next bunk, laughed at me and said I was whimpering in my sleep, but I guess I'm not alone in that. Many men here are tormented by fear of what is to come. Some have never been away from home before and have left their jobs and families behind in order to do their bit.

I'm sorry for my ramblings, my darling. Ignore me!

This week, I hear, we are moving out of the school, though the officers haven't said where we're going yet. When I know more, I'll let you know. Please keep writing; your letters mean so much to me.

As always, I send all my love to you.

Yours,
Fred

Fred's Letters

To Alice Parsons, Borough Market, London

From St Albans, 8 October 1914

My dearest Alice,

Two months have gone by since I arrived here, and we are still miles away from the front. I miss you like mad but wouldn't mind half so much, if it seemed worth it. Days of drills, gun training and army discipline go by and still we are not embarking for France. We have now had to move out of the school and are camped, would you believe, in tents in a local park! The officers are all very elderly, as the younger men are already at the war. They are a decent sort, I guess, but maybe a bit out of touch. They tell us camping in the fresh air will prepare us for what's to come. Maybe they're right. The weather is getting chilly now, quite autumnal. When I see the leaves falling down, I think of you and remember this time last year, when we met. How different things were then.

This week, we are learning how to dig trenches, which, apparently, are what the troops are using now. After the Battle of Mons, it has become clear to everyone that this war is not going to be over as easily and quickly as we all thought. The Germans' first attack was stalled by our brave Expeditionary Forces, but there is more to come, I fear (poor old Ern must have been in the thick of it all. I do hope he is okay).

People laugh at the Territorials and I've heard we often get used just for duties like supplies or communications, but this isn't fair. Our regiment (The London) is being trained hard into a real fighting force who'll truly give the Hun something to think about! The Kaiser will have cause to remember us! I'm proud to say I'm in the queen's battalion (God rest her soul) and will do my best to serve and protect our country, whilst I still have breath in my body. I just wish we could get started. The waiting is killing me.

I know you will be glad to know that I am safe and well at present, and I pray that you are bearing up. I love you as much as ever, my darling, and were it not for this dreadful war, would rather be in your arms than anywhere else. But I know that you understand that I must do this, both for my country and myself. I need to show that I am a brave and honourable man, who can stand up for what is right.

Believe me when I tell you that I am always thinking of you, dearest.

All my love,

Yours,
Fred

Joe's Recollections, Autumn 1914

Few people remember now that Britain was bombed in the First World War. Of course, it was eclipsed by events just over 20 years later, but it happened nonetheless.

But I'm getting ahead of myself. Where was I? Oh yes. In the weeks that followed the declaration, enthusiasm was high to start with, but then reality started to kick in. Prices of food rose and lists of casualties emerged, and the promised victory suddenly didn't seem so certain anymore. The initial euphoria evaporated like autumn mists on a sunny day. By the end of August, we'd heard that the British troops were having to retreat bit by bit from Mons, fighting bitterly all the way. The Times newspaper reported that there were 'terrible losses', and that the British Expeditionary Force now consisted of 'broken bits of many regiments'. I thought of Ern in the thick of it and said a silent prayer for him in the dark of the night. Bill avidly collected all the news clippings he could about it and compiled them into a scrap book. He kept asking me questions about the places mentioned – questions I couldn't answer. My knowledge of geography hadn't really been improved by my time at Hanwell School. Albert scoffed at Bill's interest.

"Stupid," he said. "What's the point? Makes no difference."

"But I want to know," insisted Bill. "I want to understand where Ern is."

"Who cares?" laughed Albert. "Probably living it up in some French brothel, I reckon!"

But Bill continued his scrapbook, I continued my prayers and the casualty lists continued to grow. Every day, I feared a telegram and hoped, instead, for a letter from Ern. Both failed to arrive, which brought equal measures of relief and disappointment, respectively.

September came and went, and now families were beginning to feel the pinch here at home. The Defence of the Realm Act, issued immediately the war started, had given new powers to the government, allowing higher taxes to be imposed in order to pay for the conflict. The cost of essentials like potatoes, milk and butter all doubled. Not only that, but Father told us that the landlord was putting up our rent.

"You'll all have to work harder and bring in more money," he ordered. "Joseph, you shouldn't be working for that 'Hun' anyway. Get yerself another job."

My employer, Mr Muller, was a German by birth, but had lived in Britain for many years. He was a kind and honest man and I liked him. I never really thought of him as an 'alien' and certainly not as the 'enemy'. Albert, who had worked there for a while, had moved on and was currently working in a different establishment. So, Mr Muller had given me the chance to learn more about the baking process, which I enjoyed. The Aliens Act had come into force in August that year and Mr Muller had to register his nationality, but it never occurred to me that this would be a problem. After all, hadn't he lived in London for over twenty years?

By October that year, things were beginning to look quite bleak. Big Ben was silenced, and the streetlights were dimmed; everyone was scared of the prospect of invasion. Imaginations ran riot and people thought they saw German spies around every corner. What's more, there were rumours of German atrocities taking place in Belgium. From what the newspapers said, it was only 'divine intervention' from the angels, or possibly St George (depending on which version you heard), which had rescued our troops at Mons. I can't say I really believed all this myself, but maybe my prayers for Ern were heard – who knows?

Now both sides were having to dig in for the winter. Trenches were being created and everyone could tell this was not going to be a 'short term' war. Anti-German feelings were running high.

One morning, I came into work as usual to find a commotion going on. Overnight, someone had thrown a brick through the front window of the bakery and there was broken glass everywhere. What's more, filthy words had been scrawled over the shop door. Mrs Muller, an English woman, was in tears and her husband was distraught.

"How can they do this?" he said. "England is my home. I've lived here for twenty years. I've already tried to join up, but they won't have me. What else can I do?"

I didn't know how to answer him.

All the employees, myself included, cleaned up the mess and tried to carry on as normal, but it was hard and not much got done that day. Orders were filled but domestic bread supplies were minimal. Customers came and went and were shocked to see the damage. We boarded up the window and tried to make the place secure, but everyone was shaken and nervous. What else could happen, I dreaded to think.

It was nearly Christmas and things weren't getting any better. There were fears that we could be invaded by Germany at any moment. People were panic buying, which was causing food shortages in the shops. One person who seemed surprisingly cheerful about it all was our father, who mysteriously seemed to have more money, all of a sudden. He went round whistling to himself happily, and had various visitors after dark, who he never introduced us to. I didn't really know what he was up to, but I had my suspicions that it probably wasn't legal. However, no one who had any sense ever questioned my father on his activities. They were likely to receive a sharp retort, at the very least.

On December 17th, we were all shocked to the core to hear about the shelling of Scarborough, Whitby and Hartlepool, the day before. The German Navy had fired from ships just off the coast, killing over 100 civilians, destroying properties and sending people fleeing for their lives. Most of all, however, this spread panic and fear amongst the whole country. Never before, had British civilians been targeted in wartime. It was beyond belief. Bill cried himself to sleep that night and I was so scared I couldn't stop shaking. Now no one was safe. The world had changed, and not for the better.

Fred's Letters

To Alice Parsons, Borough Market, London From St Albans, 18 Dec 1914

Dearest!

Good news! We have been given a few days leave for Christmas, so I am coming home. I will be arriving by the midday train on Christmas Eve and have five whole glorious days to spend with you. I hope your family will not mind having another mouth to feed at Christmas. I will, of course, add in my army pay to help out with costs.

Looking forward to being in your arms again.

All my love,

Yours,
Fred

Fred's Letters

To Alice Parsons, Borough Market, London
From St Albans, 9 Jan 1915

My darling Alice,

It was wonderful spending time with you and your family this Christmas. Please thank your dear mum and dad for their kind welcome. I am so looking forward to the day when they will become my family as well. The only hard part was leaving you all again.

I finally had a letter from Ern this week, which I was delighted about. Fortunately, he is safe and well at present. He says there have been several quiet periods on the Western Front since the trenches were created and that this has led to a 'live and let live' attitude amongst all sides. I've been reading in the newspapers this week about the Christmas truce and can hardly believe it. Surely, we are supposed to be enemies. Why would anyone want to sing songs and exchange gifts with the other side, even if it is Christmas? It seems very strange. Isn't this the same nation as the 'baby killers' of Scarborough? I can't understand it. Ern said at times everyone stops firing in order to allow for meals and rest periods, and that the Christmas truce was just a continuation of this. His unit played football on Christmas day apparently! Are we at war, or not?

Please don't get me wrong, my darling. Peace is very much to be welcomed, but surely it should be a lasting thing, not a temporary lull in hostilities? I can't imagine playing football with a man one day, then trying to shoot him the next. Maybe I would understand more if I were there. Perhaps I'm not really qualified to judge. All I know is I'm keen to fight and defend our country, whatever that takes. I wish we could just get on with it.

I wasn't with you at New Year, as you know, so I want to wish you and all your lovely family a very happy 1915. Let's hope this war ends very soon and then we can get married and start our new life together.

Loving you as much as ever.

Yours,

Fred

Fred's Letters
To Alice Parsons, Borough Market, London
From St Albans, 14 March 1915

My dearest Alice,

We are shortly going to be embarking for France, so this is my last letter for a while. I had hoped that this war would have been over by now, but things don't look so good for Britain anymore. It looks likely to last a fair while yet, what with both sides fully 'dug in' now. I am still keen to do my bit, but the news coming back from the Front is very worrying. The newspapers say we are making good progress, but the casualty lists are very high. I pray that Ern and your two brothers are all safe and well. I haven't heard anything recently and 'no news is good news', so they say. I can only hope this is true.

You don't need to worry about me, my darling. Our training has been very good, and we feel fully prepared to meet our German foe. Let them do their worst – just see what they'll get!

Thank goodness we had some leave. It was wonderful having a few days at Christmas with you and your family. My only regret is that my mother isn't here to see how happy you've made me. I wish you could have met her.

I have to say I worry about you all at home. There are rumours of more raids, like the one on Scarborough, so take care of yourself, won't you, dearest? If I ever had any doubts about wanting to fight, they have all gone now, after the tragic deaths of those civilians. It breaks my heart to think of that poor little child that was killed. The only thing I wonder about, is whether I will be able to kill a man. What will it be like to take a life, I ask myself. I know I shall not glory in it, even though it is the enemy. Life is too precious a thing to waste. Still, it is our duty to fight for what we hold dear and if that means killing, then I suppose it must be so. Don't mind me, my darling, I am just rambling.

I will write when I can, but I believe letters back from the front may be few and far between.

I love you and look forward to being home again very soon.

Yours,
Fred

Joe's Recollections, 1915

Albert was due to turn 18 in early 1915, but showed no sign of wanting to enlist. When I asked him about it, he just sneered at me.

"Why should I want to do a stupid thing like that? Ain't none of my business what the Germans do over there. Let 'em get on with it!"

"And what if we're invaded?" I asked him angrily. "What if we get bombs dropped on us, just like in the north?"

"They won't bomb London," Albert laughed derisively. "They're just warning shots. They don't need to attack us here. What would be the point?"

I could only hope he was right, but I had my doubts.

I came home from work one evening to find the house in a state of uproar. Father, for once, seemed really rattled. Bill was dashing around and there was no sign of Albert.

"What's going on?" I asked.

"Albert's been beaten up," exclaimed Bill, "and he's in hospital."

"Yes," confirmed Father. "Some idiots at his workplace accused him of being a coward just 'cos he is too sensible to join up. Then they beat him up, the no-good louts. Just wait till I get hold of 'em!"

The truth turned out to be slightly different. True, they did call him a coward, which was possibly unfair. I mean, Albert was lazy and selfish, but a coward? Well, I don't know. I did feel a bit ashamed of myself then, because hadn't I been doing much the same just a few weeks before? At that time, the recruiting drive was still going strong and men were being targeted by every means possible. The campaign was unrelenting, pulling on every emotion to get men to enlist. Posters such as, 'Daddy, what did *you* do in the Great War?' attempted to shame those who wouldn't take part. Not only that, but women were giving out white feathers to any young men they saw who weren't in uniform. The stories that came

313

out later showed us that this emotional blackmail was the undoing of many, for so few returned. However, we were naïve enough then to still believe in doing the 'right thing' for our country.

Rightly or wrongly, it was Albert who threw the first punch and pretty soon the argument developed into a full out brawl in the back room of the bakery where he worked. This time, however, Albert took on more than he could handle and ended up in St Saviour's Infirmary with two broken ribs. I almost felt sorry for him, but when I heard the names he called his fellow combatants, I could see he certainly hadn't learnt any lessons.

Father was all over him in the hospital, soothing and comforting him, which was quite sickening to see, especially as Father never had much time for me or Bill. If we weren't well, we just had to get on with it.

A few days later, Albert left hospital, but the doctor told him that he mustn't work for a whole month, in order to allow the ribs time to heal. Whenever he moved, he wheezed painfully and got very out of breath. He was looking forward to recuperating at home, but he had an unpleasant surprise coming. I came home from work that day to hear strong words and raised voices coming from the front room. Very unusually, Father and Albert were arguing.

"You can't spend a whole month at home, expecting us to look after you," Father said firmly. "We just can't afford to have you here without you bringing some money in."

"But Father," whined Albert, "I can't help it. You know I can't work at the moment."

"I know that," Father replied. "You'll have to go to Newington Workhouse. They'll feed you and look after you. We just can't. I'm sorry."

"No, not there!" pleaded Albert and I thought I saw tears in his eyes. "That dreadful place – no, not again!"

For once, I agreed with Albert. To expect him to go to the workhouse was too much.

"Father," I reasoned, "surely if we all tried to do a bit extra work and we cut back on a few things, we could manage, couldn't we?"

Father turned on me, glaring.

"You don't know what you're talking about, Joseph, so don't interfere! It'd be the same if any of us were ill. It's the only way."

"But Father, you don't know what it's like," moaned Albert. "It's awful and everyone is so unpleasant there. Please."

But Father wouldn't listen, and Albert was packed off the next day, much against his wishes. I can't say I missed him that much, but I pitied him, nonetheless.

Fred's Letters

To Alice Parsons, Borough Market, London From France, 30 March 1915

Dearest Alice,

I hope you are keeping well. I think about you often. Thank you for the parcel you sent me. The sweets, cake and cigarettes were much appreciated. Do you think you could please send me some boxes of matches next time?

We have been having a fine time of it here. The chaps are all in good spirits and we are making real progress against the 'Hun'. We all expect to be home again soon. There have also been some entertainers around, giving concerts and the like. Not as good as the music halls at home, but it whiles away the time.

I have made friends with a couple of the chaps – Charlie, who is also from our part of London, and Billy, who is a real country lad. We have some great laughs, I can tell you! But to be serious, they are all keen to do 'their bit' for king and country, just like me. This is the kind of thing that brings us all together and makes 'men' of us all.

I miss you, my dearest. Just thinking about you makes me long to see you again, but it won't be long now, I'm sure. Keep your spirits up.

I am yours,
Affectionately,
Fred

To Alice Parsons, Borough Market, London From France, 1 May 1915

OFFICIAL POSTCARD

Dear Alice,
 I am quite well.
 I have received your letter dated 5th April

Letter follows at first opportunity.

Signature only Frederick Duffield.
Date: 1 May 1915

Joe's Recollections, Early May 1915

Have you ever noticed that events that happen many miles away can sometimes affect you personally in totally unexpected ways? So, it was with the sinking of the Lusitania. I'm sure you've heard about it – it was a disaster, second only to the loss of the Titanic. Except that this was not just a tragic accident, but an act of war.

It was the 7th of May 1915, when a German U boat torpedoed the luxury liner, the Lusitania, as it passed by the south coast of Ireland. It sank in a matter of minutes, leading to a terrible loss of life. Over 1000 people died, all civilians, including many women and children. Bodies washed up onto the shores of Cobh, near Cork, for days afterwards. I thought of my mother's love of that particular place and felt sad that it should be a place of such grief. The newspapers were full of it the next day, painting Germany as the very devil himself. It didn't matter that the enemy had in fact sent out a warning about it beforehand, or that their country was being blockaded and starved out by our own ships. None of this was ever mentioned at the time.

It was indeed an awful tragedy and people could talk of nothing else. The individual stories of personal loss and suffering were heart-breaking. Little babies and children were swept away by the mighty waves, never to be seen again. Public anger was simmering, in particular against anything or anyone remotely connected with Germany. It would all come to a boiling point soon enough.

I went to work on Monday 12th May as normal, and although everyone was nervous at the bakery, there seemed no reason for alarm. That night, after I had gone home, however, things changed beyond all belief.

Anti-German rioting broke out, like a wildfire spreading through the boroughs of London. Angry crowds stormed through the streets, destroying property and terrorising innocent German civilians. Mr Muller and his business did not escape their attentions, sadly.

I turned up for work the next morning to see the bakery virtually destroyed and the other staff standing around, gazing at the devastation. Horrified, I asked Betsy, the woman who made the cakes, what had happened.

"It was awful," she told me. "The mob done chased our poor Mr Muller right into his house and then threw him out that there window!"

She pointed and we stared in disbelief.

"I live over yonder, as you know. Me and John both came out and tried to stop it but there was too many of 'em for us and they wouldn't listen. Then…" (and here she choked back a sob) "…then they ripped off most of his clothes and left him in the street. Half-naked, he was! His missus came out and tried to cover him up, but they turned on her too. Fair knocked around; they both were."

"Not only that," added Betsy's husband, John, "but then the swines passed all their furniture out the windows and the crowd took it all away. Every stick! There ain't nothin' left in the house or the bakery. Even the baking pans have gone and all the flour's spilt. It's a crying shame!"

We entered what was left of the bakery and it was quite true. Everything was either taken or destroyed. Windows were smashed, doors wrenched off their hinges and the place was in pieces. The bakery and the home above it were now no more.

The few policemen who were around at the time were so busy with similar incidents all over the city that little could be done to help. I eyed the destruction in shock. Though I fully sympathised with the loss of the Lusitania, I knew Mr Muller was a good man who didn't deserve this. What purpose did it serve to hurt people, just because they were of the same race that we were at war with?

Just then Mrs Muller came up to see all the employees who had gathered for work that day. She tearfully explained that there would be no more employment and apologised profusely.

"I'm so sorry," I muttered, "this is all wrong." My words were awkward and inadequate. She mumbled her thanks and left. I felt ashamed to be British at that moment, I can tell you.

The next day all male 'enemy aliens' were rounded up and interned. Mr Muller was sent to a camp on the Isle of Man for the rest of the war. His wife was not allowed to go with him. They were destined never to be together again. Although I didn't hear about it until later, I ran into Betsy again a couple of years after the war ended and she told me that Mr Muller had died shortly before they could be reunited, and Mrs Muller had ended her days in a home for the mentally confused.

Having lost my job, I tried again to sign up for the army, but the recruiting officer just looked at me, and said, "How old are you, son?"

"18," I lied.

"Pull the other one!" he said, laughing. "You're barely old enough to shave. Get outta here!"

So, I found work in a factory making parts for aircraft and at least I felt I was doing something for the war effort. But truth to tell, I still missed the bakery.

Fred's Letters

To Alice Parsons, Borough Market, London

From France, 20 May 1915

Private And Confidential

Dearest Alice,

Just a quick note to send this packet of letters to you. These are all the letters I've written since I've been here. I couldn't send them before because our mail is censored. Anything negative about the war gets removed by the authorities, but I kept writing anyway, just in case you should ever be able to read them. I'm giving these to my mate Charlie, who is being shipped out tomorrow (lost a leg, poor chap). He says he'll post them when he gets back to 'blighty', so I hope you'll get them. This is the truth about what is happening out here. I hope it won't shock you too much.

I love you and look forward to being reunited with you very soon.

All my fondest love.

Yours,
Fred

Fred's Letters
To Alice Parsons, Borough Market, London
From France, 27 March 1915

My dearest Alice,

I hope you are well and in good spirits. Here I am, somewhere in Northern France, but it's not exactly what I expected, I can tell you. I can hardly begin to properly describe what it's like over here, but I will try.

When we first arrived, we were put to work digging a new frontline trench. There must have been several hundred of us working all day on it. It was backbreaking work. Not only digging but trying to stop the earth collapsing in on us all the time. Using wooden frames and boards, we attempted to keep it all back, but there were frequent falls of soil. One man near us on the line got buried by a bad slip, but we dug him out again, double quick, thank goodness, before he suffocated. He was hysterical with fear by the time we got to him, poor chap. Last night, I had a nightmare about it. I dreamt everything was falling in on me and I couldn't escape. It was horrible. I was sweating when I woke up.

Anyway, then we also had to dig out places for stores, latrines, sleeping quarters and more, further back in the communication trenches. This is the only way we 'Tommys' can survive and be supplied with what we need. Food isn't too bad at the moment – stew and biscuits for supper and lots of hot, sweet tea. I've heard the men going into battle get an extra tot of rum beforehand, to give them some courage, I suppose. From what I've heard, they'll need it. I've seen men come back from the front; legs blown to pieces, arms hanging off, stomachs gaping with holes. It's terrifying to think I'll be out there amongst them myself, soon.

At the moment, I'm just on trench duty; digging, digging, digging all the time, fighting against the natural gravity of the earth. When the rain comes, which it does like a torrent at times, everything washes down and becomes a mud bath. Our feet are so soaked with water that they swell and become very painful. We can't escape the mud, but when the weather's dry, the dust is just as bad. It rises up in clouds and chokes us, filling our eyes, mouth and nose. Still, it's better than the poison gas, which I've heard is being used by both sides. What a barbaric and cowardly thing to do. It's not even good honest fighting. How can anyone be so inhuman?

I'm sorry to write these lines and frighten you, my dearest. I probably won't be able to send them anyway, which may be for the best, I guess. Still, I hope that one day you'll read them and understand.

My love always.

Yours,
Fred

Fred's Letters
To Alice Parsons, Borough Market, London
From France, 11 April 1915

My dearest Alice,

Today the sun is shining here, my darling and it reminds me of last summer, when we were walking out together. Do you remember that lovely afternoon we spent in the park, feeding the ducks? I was so nervous because I wanted to tell you how I felt, and I hoped you would feel the same. Thank heavens you did! It will always be one of my finest memories, though I hope we will make many new ones in the future once we are married. I can't believe it is the very same sun that warmed us that day, which is here now, looking down on this ruined landscape.

At the moment, I am safely behind the frontlines and in the far distance I can see the French farmland and cottages. But it is bleak and desolate here and even worse the nearer to the front you get. This week, I am on ration duty, collecting food and supplies from the stores to take up the communication trenches to the boys at the front. Sometimes we have been fired on and once I went through a terrible shell hole, full of broken and rotting bodies, swarming with flies. These were the first corpses I'd seen since I got here, and it was awful. I'm ashamed to say I was dreadfully sick. What a fool I must have seemed. I expect I will get used to it, eventually.

I can stand the sound of the firing because we were trained well in the Territorials, but even so, the suddenness and randomness can be terrifying. Men seem to meet their fate in the blink of an eye. It is tragic.

Day to day life back here is hard but okay. We rise early when not in battle, and repair trenches, check guns, replenish supplies, etc. Some are on sentry duty but everyone else tries to grab some 'shut eye' when they can. No one sleeps much at night because it the busiest, noisiest time. That's when patrols and raiders go out and often full-scale battles erupt. It's impossible to sleep with the sounds of gunfire and shelling, and the thought that men are dying out there. By contrast, daytime is often quiet and in fact very tedious.

Unfortunately, washing facilities and latrines are what you might call 'basic'. Most of the men smell disgusting, and my mate Charlie, who has been here a few months now, told me confidentially that he is covered in lice. This makes me feel disgusted, but I expect I will end up the same. There is only one tin full of water for every 40 men to wash in, so if you're unlucky enough to be at the back of the queue, you end up washing in a filthy 'soup' which could contain anything. I've given up shaving, I'm afraid. I know you prefer me clean shaven and I'm sorry. I promise I'll shave again when I get home, honest! There's just not enough water.

Many soldiers seem to go down with diseases. I don't know what, but they are terribly sick, vomiting and feverish. There are rats running around the dug outs so may be that has something to do with it.

However, it's not all doom and gloom. We do have some spare time at the moment and things can be quite jolly at times, in spite of the boredom. Billy got me into the football team here and this has helped keep me amused. Many men seem to enjoy this, and we have a tournament going on at the moment. There is talk of a concert party coming to visit as well. Of course, we still get some of the newspapers from home, plus the unit produces its own magazine. It's a bit of fun, but rather rude in places. You should see the cartoons (No, on second thoughts, it's probably best that you don't)!

We all sing songs, especially when we're working. It helps to keep the spirits up. The thing that helps the most of all is receiving letters from home, though I must say I've seen men sitting there crying whilst they read them. It makes us feel like human beings again, and part of a better, kinder world. Without that contact, we feel isolated in our own particular form of hell, so please never stop writing, my darling. I can't always reply, but you must know that I want to and am thinking of you always.

I love you.

Yours,
Fred

Fred's Letters
To Alice Parsons, Borough Market, London
From France, 30 April 1915

My dearest Alice,

I miss you so much. I keep thinking of your beautiful face, your soft skin, your deep blue eyes. When I get home, we will set a date for the wedding, I promise. Then I will settle down and work hard so that we can have a family. Maybe I'll even try and reconcile with my brothers, though I swear I'll never speak to my father again, after what he called you.

One of the things we have to do regularly is to get information about the enemy. We all take turns, and last night, me and Billy were selected. We go out in pairs, our faces blackened to prevent us being seen. The two of us crawled out on our stomachs into 'no man's land', that dreadful wasteland, full of blasted machinery, burnt trees and corpses. Occasionally, we came upon wounded men, stranded out there, and we did our best to get them safely back to our own side again. I attempted to help one young lad, but his whole stomach was blown to pieces and there was little could be done. I had to leave him where I found him, unfortunately, his dying groans following after me like wraiths.

The process of crawling forward, inch by inch, is a tortuously slow one; fear of discovery and death making you freeze completely at times. At one point, Billy and I were unable to move for a whole half an hour, due to nearby snipers. My nerves were shredded. I'm sure I heard others moving about in the area as well. Were they wild animals or birds in this desolate landscape, or Germans trying to find out about us in return? I'll never know but I breathed a sigh of relief when the rustling sounds moved off elsewhere.

We eventually reached the German lines and spent our time listening to their movements and operations, but it gained us little knowledge. I couldn't understand their language and could only report on approximate numbers and the structure of the trench, when I finally made it back.

On the way back, unfortunately, Billy sneezed; a sound which reverberated across the wilderness. All hell broke loose as the enemy suddenly realised someone was nearby. Shots were fired and before I knew it, Billy lay dead with a single gunshot wound to the head. I lay frozen still until all had been quiet again for some time. Silent tears ran down my face, I have to admit, out of pity for poor Billy. I remember him telling me proudly of his young wife and baby son, back in rural Norfolk. They will never see him again, and for what? We didn't even gain any information.

I couldn't leave him there in no man's land, so I half carried, half dragged his dead body back to our trench. If I go, I hope someone does the same for me. I don't want to be left out there to rot.

I'm sorry, my darling, this has probably horrified you now, but be strong. I'll be okay and on my way home in no time. Keep smiling.

I love you.
Yours, Fred

Fred's Letters
To Alice Parsons, Borough Market, London
From France, 19 May 1915

My dearest Alice,

I hope you are bearing up under all this strain. All that keeps me going here is the memory of you. I live my daily life in thoughts of home, trying not to think about this awful reality. Like all the rest of the men here, I am trying to pretend it is not really happening, but I fear that even so, it may be the end of me. I have a dreadful sense of foreboding, which I pray is misplaced. Always remember that I love you.

Last night was the worst night of my life. We were sent on a night raid and I don't think I will ever forget it. It was like a journey into the depths of Hades. I feel my soul (or whatever it is that we have) will carry the stains of it forever.

I told you about the reconnaissance mission we had to carry out the other night. Well, this was ten times worse. There were about thirty of us, I would guess, all with blacked out faces and wearing camouflage. We were ordered to remove all identifying marks or tags from ourselves and to carry knives, clubs and any other weapons we could manage. The aim was to attack and take prisoners.

We crawled out on our stomachs, snail like, across the dreaded no man's land, towards the enemy. It was so dark that I couldn't see what was in the area and bumped into several dead bodies, left rotting out there. The stench from one was so awful that I nearly retched and only the fear of being discovered managed to prevent me. Charlie was by my side, somewhere in the dark. I could hear him breathing but couldn't see a thing. It seemed like hours but eventually we got to the German trench and started to cut the barbed wire. My hands were shaking with fear so much that I could hardly hold the cutters. Then at a signal from the sergeant, we bounded over the top and down into the trench. Some of our men had carried ladders, which we used now. Our idea was to be as quiet as possible, surprise the enemy, wreak havoc and take a few prisoners. But no sooner had we entered than we came upon a group of German soldiers and found ourselves fighting for our lives. I've never wanted to kill anyone but there was no option. Their faces were contorted with rage, and the ferocity of their attack on us was startling. I slashed with my knife and watched as they went down. Our group quickly despatched them, though sadly two of our own men 'bought it' as well. There was no time to think, however, as we made our various ways off into their trench system in different directions. I ended up alone around a narrow corner and came face to face with another German soldier. It was clear he was very young, no more than 18, I would think, and also very frightened. I grabbed him and was about to attack but he put up no resistance and I could see he was trembling. I had no heart to kill a man in cold blood, so I decided to take him prisoner. I hauled him along by his shirt collar through the trench, the boy pleading with me in German, all the way.

"It's okay," I told him quietly. "You'll be our prisoner, you'll be safe."

Returning to where we had entered, our men regrouped with their spoils of goods and prisoners. Much damage had been done to the enemy trench by our side, and we started to climb out. I was one of the last to leave, bringing my young charge along with me. As I climbed out, however, our officer on the other side ordered, "Leave him, Private. We got enough now."

He pulled the lad from me and threw him back down into the trench, before I could object. Then to my horror, the same man turned, took out his gun and fired down at him. I heard the terrible gasp of the boy's dying breath.

"Can't leave no survivors," he muttered. "Now let's get out of here!"

I felt sick to my stomach, but it was too late to do anything now. The sound of gunfire had roused the whole trench to life and machine guns fired and shells exploded all around us. We stumbled, ran and crawled through no man's land to get away. I fell into a shell crater and found myself surrounded by dead bodies. I struggled desperately to find my way out and escape. Our own side was giving us covering fire now, and somehow, I made it back. But the party who had set out were eight men short when they returned. Two of the prisoners had also been killed on the way back. Many of our men had also been injured. Charlie had been badly hit by a shell which had damaged his leg beyond repair. He was screaming in pain. I tried to comfort him, but he could hardly take in that it was me. They took him off to the casualty clearing station, and he's still there now. I hope he makes it. He's a good chap.

This sorry episode has tormented me now for hours. Today, I've tried to rest, to sleep and forget, but I can't. The young soldier's scared face haunts me. What has happened to turn men who were once reasonable human beings into deliberate, cold blooded killers? I can understand killing in a battle, but this? It will stay with me forever.

My darling, I hope you won't think less of me when you read this. I don't know how I will ever get it out of my head.

In a few days' time, we are due to start a big offensive, I hear. The whole lot of us will be going 'over the top'. The officers say it will be a decisive battle and could bring this dreadful war to a close. I hope so. More than anything, I want to be home again with you. If I don't make it back, I want you to know that I loved you truly.

My love always.

Yours,
Fred

Joe's Recollections, End of May 1915

Albert returned from the workhouse towards the end of May 1915, I think. I know it was just before the war got rather too close for comfort. He bragged smugly about how he'd spent the whole time in the infirmary and managed to do as little work as possible.

"I gave the nurses a right run around," he laughed. "Told them I couldn't breathe proper every time they asked me to do anything!"

I despised him for this, but I suppose I can't really blame him. It's all about survival, after all, isn't it? What's more, I thought I detected a shadow on Albert's face that hadn't been there before, but I could have been wrong. I certainly hadn't missed him. Now that Albert was the oldest son at home, and as ever, Father's favourite, he took every chance to bully us younger boys. Bill got the worst of it, really, as he was the youngest, but I felt for him and always tried to protect him.

That first night back, Albert shoved Bill out of his usual chair at the table, saying, "Clear out of it, youngster. That's my seat now!"

"But you never sat there before," protested Bill.

"Well, I changed me mind and I want to now!" He pushed Bill out roughly and I made room for him next to me.

"Don't worry about it," I whispered to him. "It's just a whim."

Albert scowled at me across the table.

"You can shut up too," he snarled.

That was family life at that time – petty disagreements and unpleasant scenes over nothing in particular. Father was only interested in Albert, who he then found a place for in the printing firm where he worked. We were still not allowed to talk about our absent brother, Fred. His name was officially 'blacklisted' in our house. Father occasionally muttered swear words about him under his breath, but nothing more was to be said.

I told you about Scarborough, didn't I? Well, after that and a few other incidents around the ports of Britain, everyone was nervous about aerial attack. But we all knew the Kaiser was related to our own Royal family and wasn't likely to allow any bombings on London. After all, you don't attack your cousins, do you?

One night, I was deep in dreams of our lovely mother, running after her in a field of long grass, calling 'Mum, Mum', when suddenly my fantasy was interrupted by noise and confusion. I came to, suddenly, hearing unearthly sounds from outside. Bill was standing by the window, calling to me to come and see. Rubbing the sleep from my eyes, I went to look. The sky was alive with the light of fires all over London. I heard shouts and screams and the sound of explosions. Bill had tears streaming down his face and I tried to comfort him, but I felt shocked and numb. What was happening? Father and Albert appeared, still half asleep and as confused as the rest of us.

"The filthy Hun is bombing us!" shouted Father. "Come downstairs. Let's get under cover."

We crouched under a table downstairs for what seemed like hours, until the attack finally subsided. Witnesses afterwards described having seen a giant airship, very high up in the clouds, barely visible, except when the moon came out briefly. It was, we later learned, a German Zeppelin.

We finally emerged, stiff and cramped, into the slow sun rise of the new day. We were intact, but several houses to the east of us had been destroyed. Lives had been taken and people injured. London was a sadder, wiser place that morning, and nowhere felt safe anymore. Not that this stopped the sightseers going down to view what had happened. It seems human interest is piqued by other people's misfortunes and the crowds gathered. I went to work as normal, but Albert took the morning off and went there to stare, and I think, to gloat that we were okay and they were not. He told us all the news with glee that evening.

"There's been seven people killed," he told us whilst we were having supper. "A married couple and some children! Not only that, but the whisky warehouse got hit! The people won't stand for having the Hun in our midst at this time. They can clear off!"

"Too right," agreed Father. "They're a nuisance."

But I thought about the innocent civilians like Mr Muller and felt sorry for them in my heart.

"They reckon there'll be more attacks, Father," continued Albert, "so we'll have to be prepared."

"Some people are talking about sheltering in the underground stations if it happens again," said Bill. "Maybe we could do that."

"That's daft," Albert declared scornfully. "How would we get there in time? You're stupid, Bill, really. Just grow up!"

Poor Bill wasn't so daft after all, as it turned out. Many Londoners did indeed shelter quite successfully down there, including us on occasions. The only trouble was that we often didn't get much warning, so it depended where you were at the time. The attacks on London continued throughout the war and though few people remember it now, it was certainly a terrifying enough ordeal. It may have been a slight incident compared with the Blitz of 1939-45 but to those who lived through it, it was never to be forgotten. It was such a shock to be a target. Before this, war had been a distant overseas thing, and never on the home front. This brought us all into it together. Those of us who weren't actually in the trenches were fighting our own battles in our living rooms.

Fred's Letters

To Alice Parsons, Borough Market, London
From France, 24 May 1915

My dearest Alice,

Today at dusk we go 'over the top', my darling, and I feel that this may be my last letter. Forgive me.

If I do not return, please move on with your life and find another young man to take care of you. Do not worry that I will be angry. I only want you to be happy, and I am sorry to have caused you any pain.

Until we meet again, my love, in this life or the next.

I am yours always,

Fred

Joe's Recollections, June 1915

One day, a telegram arrived for my father, edged in black. I tried to see what it was, as his face looked emotional, but he was very secretive, telling me to, 'Get yer nose out!' when I asked about it. After he'd gone to work, however, I searched around and eventually found it, ripped up and tossed in a dustbin. Piecing it back together I read, 'Regret to inform you... Frederick Duffield... killed in action, 26th May 1915...'.

I was shocked to the core, not even having known Fred had enlisted. I couldn't decide whether to tackle my father about it and also, whether to tell my brothers. Tormented by the knowledge, however, my conscience would not let me rest. When Father came home, I stormed up to him, determined to have it out. Waving the remains of the telegram in the air, I demanded he explain himself.

"Why didn't you tell us, Father?" I asked. "Fred's dead, isn't he? Killed in action – a hero – not a waster like you said he was."

Just at that moment, young Bill came in and overheard it all. He turned pale.

"What?" he exclaimed.

"Clear off, you!" shouted my father at him, and I could tell he'd been drinking heavily again. "This is man's talk, not for the likes of you."

He picked up a nearby empty beer bottle and threw it at poor unsuspecting Bill, who fled from the room. The bottle smashed noisily on the floor.

"Now, you," cried my father, "so you've found out, have you? Well, that bastard's been dead to me for a long time, so it makes no difference. I don't want his name mentioned again in this house. You're not to talk about it, you hear me?"

With that, he came dangerously close to me, his eyes blazing with rage.

"No Father!" I declared, "It's not fair to Fred's memory." I felt myself shaking with fear. It was the first time I had ever stood up to him. "It's wrong."

Next thing I knew, I was picking myself up from the floor, where my father's punch had landed me. Blood dripped from my cheek and one eye was nearly closed. I felt dizzy and stunned.

"Now, see here," ordered my father, "any more talk of this and it'll be the end for you and your pathetic little brother. I'll turn you both out on the street!"

With that, he turned and walked off into another room, slamming the door behind him. I was sure I heard sobbing coming from there later, but the door was locked when I tried it, so I left well alone.

In spite of my father's warnings, I'm sure you may guess that I discussed it with my brothers. Young Bill was very upset by it. Although there was an age difference of nearly ten years between him and Fred, he'd always looked up to him. Albert, however, had a different attitude. After his recent spell in the workhouse, he had become cold and bitter. He laughed sardonically, saying, "Well that's what you get for trying to be a hero then!"

I believe I called him a hard-hearted bastard and stormed off. I'd never been close to Fred either, but he'd done his duty and didn't deserve to be spoken of like that. There wasn't much point in letting Ern know at that time. He was out in the thick of it himself and certainly didn't need any bad news to make things worse. I remember praying that he would be spared to return home safely to us.

A couple of months later, I was down at the local marketplace when I ran into Fred's sweetheart, Alice. I'd managed to avoid her the last time when I'd seen her, but today she saw me first, and called out "Joe!" as she ran over to me. She had long black hair, eyes the colour of cornflowers and a sweet, sensitive face. I knew I would make her cry and I dreaded it. She peered anxiously at me now.

"Joe," she said in a worried tone, "have you heard any news about Fred? I'm really worried – his letters have stopped."

"He wrote to you?" I asked, surprised.

"Yes, letters back from the front and from his training camp. They came every week, but they've suddenly stopped. Have you heard anything? Has he been wounded?"

I knew I had to tell her, but I could hardly bear to.

"Alice," I said, gently, "I'm sorry, but Fred's dead. Killed in action."

I watched as my words visibly hit her, one by one, as if she had been struck. She staggered and I grabbed her arm to steady her.

"I'm sorry," I repeated. "I know you were close."

"We were going to get married," she replied, tears in her bright blue eyes, like a cloud over the sun. "I begged him not to go, but he's always been keen on the army, first the Territorials and now the real thing."

"The Territorials?" I asked. "When did he join those?"

"A year or more ago," she told me. "Surely you knew? He was always going off on training days at the weekend and then last year he went to summer camp. That's when they told them all they'd be joining in the action for real, very soon."

"We never knew about that," I replied. "When he went off at the weekends, we thought he was going to the races or out drinking with his mates. And last summer was when he left home for good after that awful row with Father."

I realised then how little we actually knew of Fred. He was never the 'rake' everyone thought he was, quite the opposite, in fact. I found out later that Ern had known the truth all along, but he'd been away in the army himself, since before the war started, so I'd hardly spoken to him in ages.

Joe's Recollections, August 1915

Ern was discharged from the army in August 1915 but came home a different man. He was quieter, with a shadow over him that hadn't been there before. He'd suffered badly in the trenches from trench foot and frostbite, resulting in the loss of most of his toes. I had never realised before, just how much balance we get from those small appendages. Humble and unnoticeable, they yet keep the body upright and stable, just as the poorest workers keep the economy of a country going. Without the special built-up shoes provided by the army, Ern would have stumbled and tottered around.

His homecoming was hardly a hero's welcome. On the day he came home, I remember Father jeered at him for his wounds.

"You stupid idiot!" he cried. "You can't even be a hero properly. Call that an injury? It's pathetic!" With that, he walked out of the room, shaking his head derisively.

Ern sat down heavily in the front room, while I made him tea and tried to welcome him. All the while, I was wondering how to tell him about Fred. Of course, he hadn't heard, what with being away, first in action and then in hospital. I didn't know how to start, but then as always, Albert butted in with his usual lack of tact.

"Cheers, Ern, mate! Good to see yer. At least one of you made it home then."

Ern looked shocked.

"What do you mean? Where's Fred? Don't tell me – surely not…" His voice trailed off and he turned a ghastly shade of white.

Albert laughed. "Got what was coming to him, I reckon!"

Ern stood up and would have hit him if he could have moved fast enough, but Albert went out the room, still laughing and I was left to calm Ern down. Just then, young Bill came in and threw himself on Ern, enthusiastically hugging him.

"Ern – it's so great to have you home!" he declared, and Ern softened again.

We told him all we knew about Fred's unfortunate demise and asked him about his own experiences.

"I can't talk about it, lads," he told us, shaking his head sadly. "I'm not even sure I can take it all in myself yet. Nothing seems real anymore." His knuckles were clenched tightly as he held his teacup, as if by hanging onto it, he could hang onto his own sanity (I found out later, from Betty, that he had received several medals for valour and good conduct, but he never spoke about any of it to us).

It was only a matter of days before Ern moved out for good. He took lodgings near Betty and promptly resumed their courtship. When he left us, he was tense and drawn, his face rigid with the pain of having seen too much. At the time, I didn't really understand the effects that the horrors of war had had on Ern, until later I too witnessed events that will stay with me forever. Like him, I have spent the rest of my life trying to evade the memories.

Several months later, I saw him in the marketplace, looking relaxed and happy. Fortunately, Betty and her family had somehow worked a magic that we never could have and restored Ern to himself again. He was one of the lucky ones.

Joe's Recollections, 1916

The first time that I met the whole Alderman family was at Ern and Betty's wedding in January 1916. They were a lively, jolly bunch, so unlike our own family that I could see the attraction for Ern, and in fact, felt rather jealous. There were nine grown up children, most of whom were quite a bit older than me, except for the youngest daughter, Kathleen, who appeared to be disabled, for she had a hunched back. Not that this slowed her down in any way. She was just as spirited and vivacious as the rest of them. No one ever made anything of her disability, and consequently, it never worried her.

The main reason for this happy family appeared to be their parents, who had brought them up to be decent, hardworking and happy. The father had been a London policeman for many years but was now retired from the force. Together with his wife, Ellen, he ran a small draper's shop, where several of the sisters, including Kathleen, often worked. I heard some stories from Ern about his father-in-law having been involved in trying to subdue the suffragette riots, and I wondered if he had ever come across our mother. Kathleen later told me that he had seen much brutal treatment of the women there and felt appalled by it. He felt bad even to have been involved but he had to do his duty. Nevertheless, he tried to carry it out with respect and forbearing.

Some of the older sons were still fighting in the war, like Ern and Fred had, but although worried for their safety, the whole family just carried on regardless. I could only admire the genuine feeling they had for each other, which made them so strong as a unit. I wished my own family could have been more like them and took every opportunity to visit Ern and Betty from then on. There always seemed to be a party going on at their house, though the people attending varied each time. My only regret was that our mother never met them, for she would have loved all the fun.

Joe's Recollections, 1916

You wanted to know more about the war, didn't you? I'm sorry, I'm an old man now and tend to ramble a bit. Please bear with me.

I'm not sure exactly when conscription started but I think it must have been quite early in 1916. I remember because Albert came home from work in a foul mood one day, complaining bitterly about it.

"It's not fair!" he cried angrily. "I'm nearly nineteen and that makes me eligible for call up! Why should I go and fight their stupid battle? It's not my quarrel."

"What about the bombs on London?" I asked. "Don't you remember what happened last October? Children burned in their beds! People killed whilst enjoying themselves at the theatre!" (It's true. It was a terrible night – 71 dead and many injured) "What did they do to deserve that? Surely that makes it our quarrel?"

"Huh!" he snorted and went off to consult with our father about it. Between them, they put their heads together and came up with a plan. The following week, Albert took up work at the nearby munitions' factory, which I thought was a bit strange as he'd never wanted to before. His motto since he came out of the workhouse the year before (and truth to tell, even earlier that that) had been 'take it easy', and that's what he usually did. After his 'incident' at the bakery, he'd moved on to running errands at the printers where Father worked, but never anything too strenuous. An enthusiasm for hard work was not one of Albert's virtues. Therefore, this seemed somewhat out of character.

Maybe he has turned over a new leaf, I thought charitably, but the truth soon revealed itself.

I think it must have been about March that year when his call up papers arrived, but instead of being horrified he seemed oddly calm. It soon became clear that Albert's new job was a 'reserved occupation', and that, combined with his previous injury, which he declared made him 'medically unfit', managed to exempt him. Paperwork was completed and a tribunal attended but Albert did not have to join the war. He was issued with a 'certificate of exemption', which he proudly displayed at every opportunity.

"Of course, I would be only too happy to serve my country," I heard him tell someone, "but I just can't. My work is too valuable." What a hypocrite!

Of course, an increasing number of women were now working in the factories, in order to free up men to take part in the war, so really there was no need for Albert to be in a 'reserved occupation'. There were plenty of others willing to take his place.

In July 1915, there was even a Women's March down the Embankment designed to show enthusiasm for their 'Right to Serve'. It was a grey, drizzly day, but in spite of the weather, they walked proudly along, with banners held high. There must have been thousands of them, many dressed in red, white and blue, just asking for the chance to 'do their bit'. It was a Saturday and my day off, I remember, and whilst out and about in town, I saw, in the distance, a sea of people stretching as far as the eye could see. I could only admire them.

We'd all heard about the supposed shell shortage on the Western Front, and I often wondered if that's why Fred had died so soon, so it seemed a good idea for women to help out in producing more munitions. Mum would no doubt have been keen to take part as well, though I don't suppose Father would have let her. He liked her to work, well enough, but only at things that suited him.

Joe's Recollections, 1916

Mum had a lovely gentle Irish accent, soft and musical, and her laughter was like a bubbling silver stream. Unfortunately, it wasn't too good an idea to appear to be Irish in those days, and sadly Father stopped her from cooking her favourite Irish recipes like colcannon (which I loved), because he '*didn't want no more Irish nonsense*'.

Mum told me once that she'd lost a job because of her origins.

"Why?" I asked, confused.

She smiled softly. "They were scared," she said, "and they didn't understand that most Irish people just want a peaceful life. But to be sure, the struggle to get home rule has cost many lives on both sides and it's not over yet."

She paused, suddenly thoughtful. "My da always said it's wrong to fight and that talking is the best way, but I'm not sure that it's achieved much, so far."

Certainly, the talking had stopped by Easter 1916 when the Irish people rose up and declared a republic. Reprisals from the British side were swift and overwhelmingly brutal. By the end of that week, the centre of Dublin lay in ruins and over 450 Irish people had been killed. Many others were arrested and later executed. My mother would have been distraught.

Worse was to come, at least from Mum's point of view, when in 1920, Cork bore the brunt of British anger over the killing of a soldier. Cork City Centre was burned to the ground, and those brave souls who tried to stop the flames were shot and killed, with their firehoses still in their hands.

I'm glad Mum was not around to see it. She would have been devastated to see her beloved city so damaged and broken, the places she knew as a child no longer recognisable. A sad time for a great city.

But to go back to 1916. Life was no easier for Britain either, with the Battle of the Somme raging furiously and uselessly on for months and months. The enormous loss of life was shocking, and the casualty lists in the newspapers grew ever longer. There was scarcely a family untouched by it in some way. Ern perused the lists every day, Betty told me, and shook his head sadly as he recognised names of friends. People I knew at work wore black armbands and faces of grim suffering. Only Father and Albert seemed to go on blithely, day by day, unaffected by the nation's grief.

Joe's Recollections, 1917 onwards

Did I tell you how I got to know my wife? Well, if you remember after Ern and Betty got married, I spent a lot of time over at their place. It was so much more fun than our home, which was a gloomy and ill-tempered abode. Albert and Father were always at odds with me and Bill, and we could rarely do anything right. Once Bill started working as well, I didn't feel so responsible for him anymore and felt able to make my own way. Throughout 1917-18, therefore, I visited Ern's house regularly and got to know the whole family. Betty's youngest sister, Kathleen (known as Kath) was the same age as me. She was a lively, quirky person, full of vitality and humour, not afraid to speak her mind. At weekends, we all played card games, sang songs, enjoyed impromptu picnics, etc, in spite of the war and the air raids. On these occasions, Kath and I joked, teased, laughed, argued and irritated each other in equal measures. I have to admit I have a streak of my father's filthy temper in me, and at that time, I had a fair chip on my shoulder. This made me react badly to any perceived criticism, even though I always regretted it afterwards. Kath didn't take offence easily, however, and laughed it off. I gradually learnt to relax more and not to take things so seriously.

You could say that we grew into adults together and were more like brother and sister than anything else. I'd never had a sister, so I wasn't used to the ways of girls. It was both delightful and annoying to be with her, though I never thought anything of it at the time.

Joe's Recollections, 1917

As you can imagine, working in the aircraft factory was tiring and monotonous, not at all like the rewarding feeling of baking bread. The factory smelt of oil and soot, so unlike the delicious scent of new baked loaves which I'd known before. But it was work at least and brought home much needed money. It also gave me the feeling of doing something worthwhile. There were mostly youngsters, women and old men working there now, as men of service age had either signed up or been conscripted, as time went on. Despite the noise and the arduous nature of the job, it was a jolly enough crowd. Having a lot of women working there made me see just how capable and hardworking they were, and I began to understand why my mother had been so keen to stand up for women's rights. I got very friendly with some of them, in particular Mrs Glass and her friend Peggy Bolton, who lived near to us in Southwark. There was a whole bunch of us who lived around the same area and we often walked back together in the evenings. Some of us young lads would then head off to the pub, leaving the ladies at their doors, laughing and calling after us.

"Don't forget you gotta get up in the morning, lads!" they'd warn us. "Go easy on the booze!"

We would laugh, wave and head off cheerfully into the twilight. In fact, usually I didn't go to the pub. My father's drinking habits had put me off the idea of that. I either went over to Ern and Betty's, or straight home. With all the air raids we'd had recently, it wasn't always safe to be out at night, anyway. There was usually very little warning and all you could do was to try and shelter in the nearest underground station, if you had time to get there. At least in the Second World War we had air raid sirens. In the Great War, all we had were policemen riding around on bicycles, with signs saying, 'Take Cover'. Later on, there were some horns sounded and rockets fired, but if you weren't in the right place at the right moment, it was unlikely that you would have heard them. I heard a rumour since that the lack of warning was because the government didn't want the population to panic, but I don't know whether this was true or not. It seems a hard-hearted thing to do, if so.

There are a couple of incidents I remember vividly from that period. One Friday evening, early in the new year of 1917, sometime in January, as I recall, we were all walking home from the factory as usual, sticking together for safety in the dimly lit streets and watching out for another air raid. Suddenly, there was a massive explosion over to the east of us. I'd never seen such a fireball before – a mighty orange glow, spreading rapidly upwards and outwards. Though were some distance away, we were all knocked flat to the ground by the force of the blast and lay there, winded. The windows in every house nearby seemed to have been shattered into a thousand pieces, though thankfully, there was no more serious damage than that. Most of us had minor cuts and bruises and were very shaken up.

"Blimey!" exclaimed one of the lads. "What the heck was that?"

We could see a gigantic fire in the distance and heard people shouting and sirens sounding.

"I reckon it's the Germans – they've invaded us!" cried Mrs Glass. This was the general opinion of most of us and we were very scared. We hurried home to find our loved ones, though for me that was really only Bill. He came running out to meet me.

"Joe – thank goodness! I was worried. Do you think they've invaded or is it another bomb?"

I couldn't say, but we barricaded ourselves into the house that night, with Albert and Father, and gathered up what makeshift weapons we had – a rolling pin, a kitchen knife, a shovel and so on. What good these would have done in a real invasion, I dread to think, but I felt safer clutching them tightly and hiding behind the sofa. In the morning, after an anxious night, we heard the news that in fact, it was not the Germans at all, either by land, air or sea. What had happened was that the huge Silvertown Chemical Factory, in West Ham, had exploded. They had been producing TNT there for the war effort and a small fire broke out, and as anyone will tell you, TNT and fire don't mix well! Sadly, the explosion claimed 73 lives, injured 400 people and destroyed 900 homes. A further 70,000 properties were also damaged. We were lucky that we hadn't been closer to the blast or we could have been seriously hurt. Rumours continued to abound that it was all down to the Germans really, but the evidence was overwhelming that it was just a tragic accident. I thought to myself that at least the factory I worked in didn't produce any dangerous chemicals, and I was thankful for that.

Mrs Glass was a plump, kindly woman with three children, whose husband was serving out in the Middle East. Two of their children were grown up, a daughter, about twenty I reckon, who was courting one of the lads from our group, and a son, Stephen, who was away in the navy. The youngest daughter, Emily, was still at school and was looked after each evening, until their mother got home, by her older sister. She was always at the front door to meet her mother when we dropped her off. I liked the family; they were good-natured people. I'd known of them for a while, but not really spoken to them much until now. We ended up working quite close by in the factory and had a right laugh at times.

"Call me Emma, dearie," she told me. "We're all mates here now, after all."

I asked her what she thought about women working.

"Well," she replied thoughtfully, "it's a great thing to help the war effort and to keep our men folk's jobs going, but I'll be only too happy to get back to the housework again once this is all over and me old man comes home. I can see that those suffragettes had a good point, mind. I mean we deserve to be able to vote if we want to, but working in a factory? No, it's not for me."

She laughed cheerfully and told me how much she was hoping for her son to come home on leave.

"He must be due some leave soon," she said. "I worry so much about him being away at sea, what with all the submarines torpedoing our ships. If only he was safe back here again."

October 1917 was a wild and stormy month, with frequent gales and heavy rain. The evenings were drawing in rapidly and people were glad to get home at the end of the day. At the beginning of October, Emma Glass came into work positively bubbling with happiness.

"Guess what, Joe?" she said, "I've just heard that Stephen's coming home on leave for a whole week in October. It's only two weeks away. I can't wait!"

I was glad for her but wished privately to myself that I had been able to see Fred come back on leave. I knew that would never happen now. He would forever stay on the Western Front, along with the thousands of others who didn't make it home. But it seemed Mrs Glass was luckier, for Stephen arrived home safely on the 16th October. She was delighted, and every day that week regaled us with tales of his recent exploits on the high seas. She could hardly wait for Friday night, when she would be able to spend more time with him over the weekend. We left her that evening at her house in Calmington Road, waving cheerfully to us, young Emily beside her as usual. It was a cold and windy night, and I was glad to get home into the comparative warmth of our house. Father was never too generous with firewood but this evening the stove was lit, and it was almost cosy. Albert and Father were out drinking until late, but Bill and I sat there playing cards and chatting before heading to bed. In the middle of the night, however, as we were tucked up in our beds, we were woken up by a tremendous noise. It sounded like another air raid but this time, without any warning rockets. We jumped out of bed, grabbing warm coats and headed down to the cellar. On the way downstairs, I looked out of the window and saw the nearby skyline alive with the orange light of flames. A bomb had dropped in our neighbourhood, it seemed. I remember wondering where it was and feeling sorry for anyone caught up in it. We all huddled in the cold, damp cellar, bleary eyed and dazed with sleep.

"Someone's bought it, I reckon," remarked Albert, in his usual blunt manner. "I can see one of them Zeppelins up in the sky, look."

We peered up through the tiny cellar fanlight and saw a monstrous airship sailing through the sky off to the east. We heard further explosions as it went and saw flashes down below.

"It's very nearby!" cried Bill. "I hope everyone's okay."

"I have to admit, I thought we'd had it that time," Father said gruffly. "Bit too close for comfort, that one!"

We tried to sleep but it was difficult. I had an uneasy feeling that something dreadful had happened.

The next morning, the population of the local area emerged warily from cellars and underground stations to find out what had happened. Smoke still rose from the shattered ruins of three houses completely destroyed by a massive bomb. The entire corner of the road junction had gone. As we got closer, I could see where it was, and I was horrified.

"Calmington Road! Surely not?" I cried. "Let's hope everyone is safe."

But fate plays cruel tricks and Mrs Glass and her entire family had died, blasted out of existence along with two other families in the same road. The raid was silent, owing to the strong winds blowing and no one ever knew it was coming. They literally didn't know what hit them. Ironically, even Stephen, safely home from the war, was taken as well. Only the father would be left now, and he was far away. We stood there, staring with tears in our eyes. Strangely, I almost thought I heard Mrs Glass say, "Come on dearie, pull yerself together. It ain't so bad. At least we're all together."

But I could still see the little girl, Emily, in my mind's eye, as she was, just last night, grabbing her mother's hand and pulling her into the house.

"Come on, Mummy, tea's ready," she said.

I choked back sobs and turned away. Was it only yesterday we'd last seen them? How quickly things can change sometimes.

Going back to the factory on Monday was a subdued affair. No one spoke about it, but everyone was thinking about it, all the same. It was just too hard to deal with. Mrs G's friend, Peggy, worked silently with tears pouring down her face, and as for the walk home – well, we took a different route. No one said why. We just did it.

Time has passed now, and Calmington Road has completely disappeared. What remained of it was further damaged in the blitz of World War Two, so in the end they knocked it all down and put Burgess Park over the top of it.

Somehow, I feel that the ghosts of those shattered houses still haunt that cheerful green space, forever searching for salvation. I hope they find it.

Joe's Recollections, 1918

Everyone knows about the food rationing in World War Two, don't they, but did you realise we had it in the First World War as well? No? Well, we did, although it didn't start until 1918, it's true. Food had been getting scarcer as the war progressed. Cargo ships were being targeted by German submarines and many never made it here. Long queues for food outside shops became a regular sight, and people were often hungry. In our house, however, food seemed to appear mysteriously on the table, and we rarely went short. Father and Albert whispered in corners and refused to tell us the origins of our dinners, but we didn't complain. It was strange that we ate better in wartime than we had beforehand, but though I wondered about it at times, I was wise enough not to ask any questions. I have to say I feel a bit ashamed about that now, but there you go – we had to survive. Mind you, when rationing came in, we struggled along with the rest, though the odd unaccountable extra did sometimes still find its way to our table.

The local park was dug up and converted to allotments, and people started to 'grow their own'. Ern, Betty and their family had one of these and started to grow as much as they could. I helped out at times, especially if I knew Kath would be there. It just made it more fun when she was around. That's all.

We heard the war was going badly abroad and dreaded the prospect of defeat.

"What will happen if the Germans win?" Bill asked me one evening. "Will they take over the country?"

I wasn't sure. It certainly seemed like a strong possibility and we began to wonder how we would cope with that. *Maybe we would all be imprisoned, or under martial law?* It was a terrifying idea.

In August that year, I struggled to get to work when some of the women workers went on strike. A lot of them were employed on the buses and trains and were annoyed that they were getting much lower wages than the men. Unfortunately, I ended up losing a day's pay, because on one occasion, I just couldn't get there. I didn't mind too much, but Father went mad at me when I told him I couldn't give him quite so much money that week.

"Couldn't you have walked, you lazy idiot?" he cried. "We can't afford to be without that money. You're so selfish, aren't you?"

"It's a long way, Father," I tried to explain, which was true.

"Don't give me that! Those women are to blame, anyway. That's just typical of them – feeble workers, always wanting the same as men, when they can't even do the job properly."

"I think they do quite well, actually," I told him. "The buses are always on time and they work hard."

Father glared at me. "Don't go talking like that, Joseph! It's people like you who allowed them to get the vote! You should be ashamed of yourself."

It had only been just before this that some women over 30 had been granted limited voting rights at last.

"Well, if it wasn't for them in this war, we'd have no one to do the work at all," I replied. "They deserve it."

Father grabbed me roughly by the collar and threw me against the wall.

"We don't want none of that suffragette nonsense here!" he exclaimed. "I wouldn't have it with your mother, and I won't have it with you!"

He swept out of the room angrily and I heard him shouting at poor Bill in the kitchen, who was busy making dinner. I rubbed my bruised shoulders and took a deep breath. Tangling with Father was a bit like being caught in a hurricane. You never knew what state you'd be in when you finally emerged on the other side.

Joe's Recollections, Armistice day 1918

I was still working in the factory, but I longed for the day when I could join up and fight for king and country. However, the Armistice was announced in November 1918 and my hopes were dashed. I know it probably seems stupid to you, but no one was more disappointed than me that the war had ended. Don't get me wrong, I'm not a warmonger. I don't believe in killing for the sake of it, but at that time, I felt I needed to do my bit. Fred's death hung heavy on me and seeing Ern's limp from his poor maimed feet made me feel guilty and ashamed that I had not been able to help them.

On the day that peace was declared, I had intended to go to work and then head over to Ern and Betty's in the evening. As I went out that morning, however, it was obvious a great change was in the air. By 11am, everyone had heard the news and all work was abandoned for the day. We packed up and

354

headed outside. Church bells were ringing, horns and whistles blowing and people dancing in the streets. There was a party atmosphere everywhere. You have never seen so many crowds and so much joy and relief. Without any direction from anyone, London as a whole made its way to Buckingham Palace and called out to see the king and queen. I was swept along by their enthusiasm and sheer weight of numbers, even though I could not fully share their joy. By some miracle, I met up with Bill, and together, we stood outside the palace and watched as the royal family appeared on the balcony. The king said a few words and everyone cheered until they were hoarse. Then the whole crowd sang the national anthem and Rule Britannia. It was an amazing event.

Later, I made my way over to Ern's house, but I was in a black mood, angry at myself for being so young and useless. It seemed the whole country was celebrating, except for me. Kath opened the door, beaming with joy. There were colourful flags up everywhere and music sounding out from within. Betty, as usual, was preparing a huge meal for the Alderman family, who were rapidly gathering.

"Joe!" cried Kath, her eyes shining with happiness. "Isn't it wonderful? Come in and join us. We're having a party!"

I was in no mood to celebrate, but I joined them sulkily and spent the time moping in a corner. Later, Kath came up to me and said bluntly, "Look here, Joe – cheer up, for God's sake! What's wrong with you, anyway? Don't you know you look like a wet weekend?"

I scowled at her and retorted unpleasantly, "It's all right for you! You'll get all your brothers back. Fred will never come back, and I couldn't even do anything to help!"

I stormed out, my mind filled with anger and my eyes filled with tears. I got as far as the local park, before I realised that I was being followed.

"How can you be so stupid, Joe?" Kath cried, for it was her behind me. "We all feel bad for those who aren't coming back, but we've done all we can. We've tried to help out the war effort in our own ways. Don't you think we've suffered enough? Don't blame yourself because you're too young to fight. It's not your fault."

I sat down heavily on a nearby park bench and she joined me.

"Joe," she continued firmly, "You must stop this. You're not doing yourself any good."

Then she repeated gently, "It's not your fault," and she took my hand in hers. With that, I burst into wild tears and cried for ages on her shoulder. I suppose I'd never realised how bad I felt about it all. I did my best to explain it to Kath, and to my surprise, she didn't laugh, but listened, soothed and reassured me instead. Afterwards, we returned to the party and at last I was able to enjoy myself. It was then that I began to realise that the world had changed and that the nightmare was finally over.

From that day on, our relationship changed and deepened. Not that we were lovers, but instead of behaving like children, we now acted towards each other as mature, caring adults and became the closest of friends.

Joe's Recollections, 1919

You may well be wondering why, after falling in love, I went off to serve in the army. Well, there's a couple of reasons for that. For one thing, I'd already started the process a while before I realised that Kathleen was the one for me, although maybe I could have pulled out of it if I'd really wanted to. But here's the thing – I didn't want to, because, in my heart of hearts, I still felt that I needed to serve my country. All the time, during the war, I kept thinking my time would come, but I wasn't old enough. Conscription only applied to men over the age of 18 and I didn't get to that age until the last few months of the war. Even then I thought I might get called up as the draft went on until the middle of the following year, but no; I missed out. You might think this was a good thing, but I felt differently. Fred and Ern had done their duty and paid a high price. Albert had spent most of the time since he turned 18 trying to wriggle out of it, which he managed to do on the flimsiest of excuses, of having a reserved occupation and of being ill the year before. He looked as right as rain to me, but maybe I am being unfair. And after all, who am I to judge? The tales that had finally come back from the front were horrifying – men slaughtered in their hundreds or being sucked into seas of suffocating mud. They never found Fred's body. I guess he's still out there in no man's land, somewhere, with no stone or cross to mark the place. We all go back to the ground eventually, anyway, so I suppose it makes no difference.

I was determined to join the army, however, and on my 19th birthday, I went and enlisted to do seven years military service in India. I'd always wanted to travel and see the world and at least then I felt I could call myself a man. There would be some time before I would be sent away, and in the meantime, I had to attend a local training centre. My father told me I was a fool, and Albert, as always, agreed. Bill was worried he wouldn't see much of me for a long while and turned more to his friends at work. He'd spent most of Armistice Day celebrating with them anyway and was beginning to make his own way in the world now.

Another reason for joining up was my father. It was around this time that he took up with a local widow, again called Catherine, would you believe? She was a rather rough and loud-spoken cockney woman, full of raucous laughter and ripe language. I couldn't understand what Father saw in her myself, but I guess she cheered him up. He had little interest in anyone or anything else, and for once, Albert seemed a bit lost. Consequently, he took to either getting drunk or gambling. He never seemed to keep a job for long. I heard rumours that he was lazy and rude at work, and that he was getting a bit of a reputation.

Later, Father suddenly decided he was going to get married again. I couldn't stand seeing him with someone other than our mother and refused to have anything to do with it (Albert went to the wedding and was a witness I believe, but I couldn't face it). I was glad that I was well away from it all. Of course, shortly after signing up, I fell for my dear Kath. Bad timing, to say the least!

Joe's Recollections, 1918-20

You're asking me what happened to change friendship into love? Well, as 1918 turned into 1919, the war began to be a more distant, but still painful memory, and the country began to get its life back together. I left the aircraft factory and got work in a little bakery nearby. It was a relief to get away from the smell of oil and hot metal. All through that year, it seemed as if England gave a huge sigh of relief and slowly relaxed again. Soldiers gradually came home, many of them wounded or shellshocked – broken fragments of shattered men trying to fit into civilian life again. Strangely, people didn't seem to know what to say to them, so nothing was said. Jobs were reclaimed and women were (often abruptly) returned to their 'rightful' place in the home. But things had changed, and women had now begun to get the right to vote, though not all of them initially. I thought of my mother's supposed sympathies with the suffragettes and knew she would have been pleased.

Meanwhile, I spent much time over at Ern and Betty's house, most of it deep in conversation or debate with Kath, who also seemed to be a frequent visitor. We were like two sparks on a fire when we were together, dancing and clashing, joining and separating. I know I'm not a particularly easy person to get on with – far too prone to sense insult when there is none, and to react accordingly. Maybe it was my childhood which made me like this, or maybe that's just an excuse. I don't know. All I know is as I got older, I stood up to my father and Albert more and was quick to defend myself in any situation. The trouble is that, even now, I often speak without thinking.

Well, my dear Kath was just as bad. I think it was her disability which made her determined to stick up for herself and speak her mind whenever she saw fit. We had an interesting relationship, a mixture of healthy debate, shared interests, laughter and argument. Somehow, neither of us took offence at anything the other one said, or not for long at any rate.

However, a young man's fancy, as they say, turns to thoughts of love, and in the early summer that year, I started seeing a girl called Gladys, who worked in the shop next door to the bakery. She had mousy hair but a buxom figure and seemed experienced in the ways of the world. She was placid, easy going and keen to accompany me to the pictures and the like. In July 1919, we even watched the great military parade on Peace Day together.

The visits to Ern and Betty's became fewer as I got out and about more, but I still told Kath all about it on the occasions when I saw her. One day, I thought I saw her face change, however, when I recounted where I'd been with Gladys.

"Why do you have to go on about her all the time?" Kath flared up suddenly. "That's all I hear anymore. I don't know why you bother to come."

"But I like seeing you," I said, puzzled. "We're friends, aren't we? You know I always tell you everything."

I still planned to sign up for army service, so in September 1919 that's exactly what I did. I was overjoyed when they accepted me and went straight round to see Ern, Betty and of course Kath. Ern was pleased.

"Good on you, Joe. You'll enjoy the army. It's a great adventure for a young man, especially now that the war's over."

Kath seemed less than delighted for some reason, but wished me well, nonetheless.

"What's wrong?" I asked her later. "You don't seem very pleased for me."

"I am," she said hesitantly, "but seven years is a long time. I'll miss you, Joe."

"You'll soon find yourself a young man and settle down," I teased her. "Then you won't even think about me anymore."

I realised as I said this that this was actually the last thing that I wanted. The thought of her forgetting me was like a sharp knife in the heart, and for a brief moment, I regretted my decision.

"Yes, of course," she laughed. "In fact, I'm going out with John next Saturday. How's Gladys?"

Truth to tell, Gladys and I had decided things weren't really working out. The feeling was mutual; it seemed there was no passion, no chemistry, just a pleasant blandness, so we called it a day. I told Kath what had happened, and she expressed sympathy, eyeing me keenly at the same time.

As I left the house, I kept thinking about her going out with John and it disturbed me. I couldn't think why. After all, it didn't matter to me, did it? But that night I tossed and turned in bed, unable to rest. If only I'd been able to talk to Mum about it, maybe she could have shed some light.

The next few times I visited Ern and Betty, Kath wasn't there. She was out seeing John, it appeared, and I began to get anxious to see her again. The first commemoration of the armistice came around and I remembered how we were together the previous November, but still I didn't see her.

My army training started in January 1920. I was based locally and able to live at home for the time being. However, I knew I was due to leave for India in 9 months' time, and that if I was to see Kath again, it needed to be soon. Next time I saw Betty, I asked her where I could find her sister.

"It's just not the same without her," I said. "I miss her. Is she still seeing John?"

"I don't think so," Betty told me. "I don't think he could put up with her being so outspoken! Maybe you've still got a chance, Joe."

"What do you mean?" I demanded. "We're just friends."

Betty grinned widely. "Oh, get on with you! It's obvious you two belong together. You always have. Now get on down to the drapers' shop where she works and tell her so!"

I didn't argue. I knew exactly what she meant so I took off as fast as Cupid's arrow and arrived at the shop just a few minutes before closing time. The shop sold dress materials and sewing accessories, so I approached the counter somewhat hesitantly.

"Joe!" exclaimed Kath. "What are you doing in here? Do you want some material?"

"I've come to see you. You're never around these days."

"But what do you care?" she said. "You're off soon anyway. I've got my own life to lead."

"With John?" I asked.

"Oh, don't be silly! No, he's not the one."

"Is there someone else?" I said, dreading the reply.

She blushed.

"Well, if you don't know the answer to that, then you're more stupid than I thought!"

"Oh, Kath, really? I mean you know I care about you, surely?"

She looked straight into my eyes.

"But in what way, Joe – as a friend, a 'brother' or more?"

"Much more," I reassured her, "but I've only just realised it. You're right – I *am* stupid."

"The only thing is," she said, looking worried, "how will this affect our friendship? I mean, you know what I'm like. I speak my mind and I'm never going to change. It's just my way."

"I know," I said, "and I love you for it. I need that banter, that exchange of views. All I had with Gladys was just lukewarm water. You're the fire that I need."

We walked out the shop together at the end of that day and started a whole new chapter of our lives.

Joe's Recollections, 1920 onwards

Over the next few months, I hardly saw anyone at home. When I wasn't training then, I was mostly seeing Kath. On the rare times when I *was* at home, I would only see Bill, just in from work, or very occasionally, Albert mooching about like a lost dog. Father was always out seeing the new woman in his life, which was no great loss, as far as I was concerned, and Albert was a regular at the local pub.

My relationship with Kath developed in leaps and bounds, and I'd never been happier. The spectre of parting loomed large, but Kath understood my need to serve my country and never questioned it. A month before I left, I asked her to marry me, if she could bear the wait, and she agreed at once.

Bill, Kath, Ern and Betty all saw me off when I sailed for India. Father and Albert refused to come and had made their opinions very clear the night before.

"You're just being selfish doing this," Father said. "Not thinking of us at all."

"Sheer self-indulgence, I reckon," agreed Albert. "No family loyalty."

I turned to Bill, who was sad at my leaving, but supportive of my decision. He was the one person in the family whose opinion I valued.

"Bill, do you think so?"

He thought for a moment.

"No," he said, "I know why you need to do it. I don't blame you. It's for Fred and Ern. You must do what you feel is right."

I hugged him. "Thanks."

"Downright stupid!" my father snorted and stomped off. Albert followed.

I left the house with Bill very early the next morning and never saw either of them again. When I returned from India, I went straight to the Alderman's house and lodged with them. There was no going back for me.

I did feel emotional as I sailed away, seeing their faces getting smaller as the ship made its way out to sea, and I realised what my mother must have felt when she left Ireland, but I'd made my choice and had to live by it.

The seven years seemed an age, but, like all things, it passed in the end. Letters and occasional periods of home leave helped ease the pain of separation. Bill kept me up to date with all the family news. Whilst I was away, Father married Catherine South, but after just five years, she died suddenly. Bill left home, got a good job and a steady girlfriend. Albert was somewhat lost until our 'stepmum' died and then he moved back in with Father.

I did my duty in the army and saw some wonderful places and things, but I also saw things I'd rather not talk about, things I wish I'd never seen. I'm sorry but I can't tell you about that, it's best left alone. Finally, at the end of 1927, I came home and took up civilian life again. It was strange at first, but Kath helped me adjust. In spite of the long gap, nothing had changed between us, so we got married soon after. My mother would have been delighted for me, I know, and I was sad that she wasn't there to see it.

Bill also wed in 1930 and has been very happy, I'm pleased to say. As you know, his hobby is being a conjuror for children's parties (though what prompted that interest, I really don't know!). Father died in 1932, after a short illness, and after that Albert finally moved away, and I heard, found himself a wife rather late in life.

Strangely, just yesterday, out of the blue, I received a parcel from Albert. I haven't heard from him in years, as you know, but it seems he is very ill now and wants to make some kind of peace with me. In the parcel were all our mother's diaries that I thought had been consumed by the angry flames so long ago! Surprisingly, Father had secretly kept them. Not only that, but whilst I was away in India, Fred's sweetheart Alice came to see the family. She told them she was getting married and felt it was time to move on from all those bittersweet memories, so she gave them back all Fred's letters. Albert only discovered the letters and the diaries when Father died, and by that time, none of us were on speaking terms, so he kept them to himself.

I still miss my mother even now and wish I'd had more time with her. My greatest regret has always been that I never had the chance to find out about her earlier life and her family, so it is wonderful that I will now have this opportunity to listen to her heart. I can't wait to read the diaries and understand her better.

Kath and I spent many happy times with Ern, Betty and their family until dear old Betty died suddenly in her sixties. When Ern remarried so quickly, we could never understand it, but I guess he needed the company. As for poor Fred, well, there is no grave to visit, just his name on a wall somewhere, which seems little reward for the ultimate sacrifice. At least his letters will help keep his memory alive.

What an odd coincidence that I have been talking to you about it all, lately, and that here, at last, are the missing pieces of the puzzle. Finally, I will be able to hear their inner thoughts.

The spark that Kath and I had lasted the whole of our married life and I could never have asked for more. My father was right – there are no shamrocks here – but I found a world of love and happiness and that's enough for me.

The End

Note

Readers of my previous novel *The Glass Bulldog* may be interested to know that Kathleen and Betty Alderman are directly descended from Tom and Phyllis Finnimore, via their mother, Ellen.

Books and Articles

The Five – The Untold Lives of the Women Killed by Jack the Ripper by Halle Rubenhold, published Doubleday

Portrait of an Era – An Illustrated History of Britain 1900 – 1945 Readers Digest Publications

The Western Front by Rosemary Rees, Heneimann History

London in the First World War article by Jerry White, Cahiers Bruxellois – Brusselse